WING
COMMANDER

WING COMMANDER

RON KARREN

Quest Press
Franklin Park, New Jersey

Copyright © 1993, 1998 by Ron Karren

All rights reserved. This book may not be duplicated in any way without the express written consent of the publisher, except in the form of brief excerpts or quotations for the purposes of review. The information contained herein is for the personal use of the reader, and may not be incorporated in any commercial programs or other books, databases, or any kind of software without written consent of the publisher or author. Making copies of this book, or any portion of it, for any purpose other than your own, is a violation of United States copyright laws.

Published by:
Quest Press
P.O. Box 84
Franklin Park, NJ 08823-0084
732-940-1410 / FAX: 732-821-7720

Printed in the United States of America

ISBN: 0-9662083-0-7

Publisher's Cataloging-in-Publication
(Provided by Quality Books, Inc.)

Karren, Ron K.
    Wing commander / Ron Karren. -- 1st ed.
    p. cm.
    ISBN: 0-9662083-0-7

    1. Aviation--Fiction. 2. United States. Navy--Aviation--Fiction. 3. Persian Gulf War, 1991--Fiction. I. Title.

PS3561.E77W56 1998   813'.54
                                 QBI98-322

For my grandmother
Alice Garey
in heaven,
And for my mother
Hope
here on Earth....

13 December 1100

The flight deck of the USS *Excalibur* shimmered under the blazing Caribbean sun. The two F-14D fighters hooked onto the port side of the flight deck looked like a pair of quavering silver ghosts when viewed through the heat mirages. Up on Vulture's Row, high on the carrier's island superstructure, the off-duty observers, some of whom were nugget flyers, young pilots on their first cruise, shielded their eyes from the intense glare of the noonday sun. One of them spotted a familiar pair of figures in full flight gear and gave them the thumbs up sign that the taller of the two, a man in his early forties with close cropped sandy hair and a lean wiry body, returned.

Commander Anthony Zachary "Anzac" Edwards, the deputy air wing commander, thought he recognized the dark haired young man who had signalled him but it was hard to tell from where he stood on the flight deck. He could think of a better way to pass the sparse off-duty time the air wing had seen on this cruise than to spend it getting one's eardrums shot to hell while watching other folks going up into the blue. But he remembered what it was like to be fresh out of flight school and gung ho to test out your wings. He'd been there once, many moons ago, and smiled to himself as he and the commander of the carrier's air wing, the CAG, headed out to the Tomcats.

"Promise me you'll be gentle, CAG," Anzac admonished the woman whose thick auburn hair was short and efficiently styled to make the most of her angular face. The legs of her speed jeans made audible *kzangs* with each step she took and he smiled liking the way his best friend moved, the she-wolf on the prowl. Her flight gear obscured a physique that was the envy of all the iron pumpers on the boat and, as the two of them approached the F-14Ds, he added, "That JAFO in your back seat—"

"Relax, Anzac," Commander Xavier Perry McNeil, Jr., interrupted with a slight chuckle. "You'll live longer."

She was not only the boat's chief pilot but also the current number one flyer as judged by the carrier's Landing Signal Officer. So Perry McNeil decided this time she would personally see to it the Admiral's orders concerning the reporter, who was researching a book on Navy aviation, were executed. She had delegated most of the responsibility for keeping their civilian guest out of harm's way to her junior officers. When the request for a ride in the Super Tomcat came across her desk, she thought this was the one assignment she would take care of herself. After all, she would be forced to chew the ass off the hotshot pilot who thought he'd have fun and pull some high G maneuvers "accidentally" causing the reporter-playing-Radar Intercept Officer to experience a grey out or, even worse, black out completely. But, since this civilian was assigned to the carrier for the duration of the cruise and was, at least for this upcoming flight, under her authority Perry knew no one but the Admiral would say diddly squat to her if she was to "accidentally" do the same thing.

McNeil's face was permanently tanned and her green eyes crinkled at the corners from many years of high exposure to the unrelenting sun. When her gaze met Anzac's, he blanched slightly as he caught her wicked grin and heard her say, "I won't make him bleed...much."

Anzac took two seconds to realize he was getting his chain royally yanked and laughed shaking his head. He had been looking forward to this hop all morning. As much as he enjoyed flying as Perry's RIO, the chance to pit for someone who would be flying *against* her was a challenge he was more than willing to take on. It would have been even more fun if they borrowed a couple of Hornets and went head to head. He first got hooked up with Perry when she joined his F-18 squadron. However, the Eighteen was a single-seat aircraft. Unless they used the trainer version, it would not have been possible for them to give the reporter, Martin Wolff, a chance to experience the thrill of mock combat. Even so, he knew Wolff had specifically asked for a ride in the Tomcat and had been spending much of his spare time trying to learn the RIO's job. Anzac could understand the attraction. When the opportunity came for him to cross-train on the F-14, he had leaped on it like a cat on a rat. Much as he enjoyed flying the F-18, he had never regretted mastering the RIO's spot. He was pitting for one of the Navy's best pilots. What could be a better job than that?

He gave her a grin that was as devilish as hers and said, "You know I'm really going to enjoy getting the chance to shoot at you. Before this hop is over, Big Daddy is going to know all your little tricks and we are going to nail that tight little ass of yours to the wall."

"I see a turkey shoot is what y'all call a contest," she shot back letting her Georgia twang come through loud and clear. They walked around the plane checking for rips in the tires, leaks in the hydraulic lines or junk in the two giant intakes of the twin engines. As she executed her exterior checks of the Tomcat, Perry said, "Look, if you really want the chance to take me on, son, I'll cut this no load RIO loose and reschedule his little tour, draft someone who gets off on a little rock 'n roll and we'll go up and have ourselves a party."

"You're on," he replied sounding a little too ready to accept the chance to challenge his friend who was not only one of the few Navy aces still flying but also one of the most well respected one on one adversaries to teach at the Navy's Fighter Weapons School.

"You going to fly this bird or just sit around here admirin' her plumage?" inquired a friendly baritone from behind the two flyers.

The two turned simultaneously to face Commander Beau "Big Daddy" Beaumont, a strapping six-footer from the heart of Texas. He looked like he could jump into the ring with Hulk Hogan and come out smiling just as broadly as he was right now. "You ready to take our guest up for a white knuckle special?"

"Thanks, Big Daddy. The idea here is *not* to give that poor guy a heart attack. We're supposed to show him how a Tomcat can stand on its tail, not kill the poor sonovabitch!"

CAG McNeil and Big Daddy exchanged a knowing smile and Anzac, who instantly recognized the mischievous looks, threw up his hands in disgust. Whenever the CAG had one of the members of her unofficial flying circus, the Ghostriders, as her wingman, the fertilizer was destined to hit the rotating oscillator. All the Ghosts were two things that made them a cut above the other flyers on the ship: all had real combat experience and were not only kickass pilots but whiz-kid engineers as well. The running gag in the dirty shirt wardroom was that the Ghosts could scratch build themselves their own air wing if given access to enough parts and Crazy Glue.

Anzac suspected a game was afoot when Perry told him she'd be taking "Paper Boy," the call sign the Ghostriders had bestowed upon the journalist when he first came aboard, up with her. His suspicions weren't confirmed until he saw he'd be in the pit with Big Daddy as his driver. Perry and Beau were always a couple of cowboys whenever they went head-to-head during Aerial Combat Maneuvers. Both loved a good dogfight and had reputations for always doing the unexpected. That made them the team you'd least like to have as an adversary but the first one you'd sign up to gun for you if your side ever went to war. They were going to make Martin Wolff, the *Times* reporter who sat awaiting them in the

Tomcat's back seat confronted by the most high-tech gadgetry he'd ever seen in his entire flying life, sweat a little. But he also knew that CAG and Big Daddy were among a handful of pilots on the carrier with a perfectly clean safety record. Yeah, they liked to play the game hard and fast but they tended to play it by the rules.

"Look, this hop is being logged as a maintenance flight, so no one is going to be doing anything extreme," Perry said more to Anzac than Big Daddy. "It would be real hard for him to write something worthwhile about his ride in the Tomcat if he spent the bulk of it in dreamland."

"Well, if you can't take the Gs, stay out of the cockpit, I say," remarked Big Daddy. "You weren't around enough to hear this guy Wolff go on and on about his own "flyin' experience." Personally, I think he deserves to be shown what a *real* pilot can do!"

"And he will get that chance right now," she replied. They watched her make a last minute check of the ordnance attached to the hardpoints on the Tomcat's left wing. "And, if he isn't suitably humbled by our little air show, *then* he'll get a quick succinct definition of the term "G force"!"

Had Martin Wolff come up to the flight deck with Anzac, Big Daddy and the CAG, he probably would have regretted pushing so hard to get his ride in the Super Tomcat. He'd endured a lot of kidding from the pilots about buzzing around in an aircraft whose top speed was not much greater than the velocity achieved by the catapult during a shot. Although nothing he'd ever flown was as complex as a Tomcat, he wasn't as intimidated by the collection of keys, dials, gauges, scopes, handles, sticks, knobs, buttons, pedals, circuit breakers, hose connections, and warning signs as a nonpilot would have been if placed in his boots right now.

One of the RIOs who'd been prepping him for his debut flight leaned into the open canopy and reviewed with Martin one last time the essential procedures he'd have to follow once the engines were running on the flight deck. When Lieutenant Bob "Poindexter" Viel seemed satisfied Wolff had a handle on what was expected of him, he stated with a knowing grin, "Your test is going to be to see if you can work all that stuff while you're flying upside down. Or, better yet, during one of CAG's infamous turn and burns."

Wolff had heard about McNeil's aerial stunts from enough sources to know it wasn't just a lot of loose talk drummed up to scare him. She had to know her shit cold or none of the arrogant know-it-alls in her air wing would give her the attention and respect her position warranted. He'd been given access to more detailed information about Commander McNeil, such as the Bekaa Valley battle where she had earned her Medal Of Honor, but most of her past had been kept from his prying eyes. Her being a hero notwithstanding, she must have moved the same mountain as Mohammed before becoming the first woman ever to command an air wing, Wolff thought. He set up the systems in the aircraft under Poindexter's watchful eye. Even though women had finally been given the right to fight and die for their country, Wolff knew that Naval Aviation was still very much a man's game. All the women of the air wing he spoke to have made it plain that there were plenty of male chauvinists aboard the USS *Excalibur*.

That is, all but Commander McNeil. Not that she didn't experience any prejudice during her career. Wolff was certain she must have since all the other women did, but he had no idea how much resistance she faced because he never got the opportunity to ask her. She'd been so busy juggling her time between flying with the two F-14D squadrons, the two F/A-18A squadrons, the squadron flying the A-6F plus all the desk duty that went with a command that she'd barely had a chance to log a straight eight hours of sleep. Wolff felt he should count himself lucky that Perry McNeil made the time to take him up personally. He silently hoped she'd be in a talkative mood and willing to answer the list of questions he'd brought along just in case.

"Heard the Skipper's gonna have you park the boat for him when we hit Rio for Christmas liberty," Big said with a teasing grin.

Perry glanced away from the missile she was checking. When she saw the expression on his face, she realized he was going to have some fun at her expense. Her eyes were twinkling as she quipped, "Yeah. And guess who I'm going to hit up for change to feed the meter?"

Beaumont chuckled shaking his head. "You know, considerin' what you're like when you're behind the stick, I thought the Captain showed a lot of courage by letting you drive this thing down here. Personally, I think you did great. But, then again, it's kinda hard to screw up when your motoring around in the middle of the Atlantic Ocean. But this? The Old Man either has a whole lotta faith in you or he's lost his mind."

Perry shot him a mock glare but he knew she was waiting to return the jest. Anzac grinned. He had been on the bridge when Perry had been given a taste of what it would be like to sit in the

Captain's chair. Although he knew she felt more at home in the cockpit than on the bridge, she acquitted herself very well that day. Captain Graff could be as inscrutable as Fu Manchu and as parsimonious with compliments as Scrooge was with a dollar. But Anzac noticed a faint glimmer of approval crossing his face from time to time as Perry put into practice all the theoretical knowledge she had on executing the position of ship's captain.

"Have you read the documentation on anchoring yet?" Anzac asked.

Perry turned towards Anzac and saw instantly that he was serious. "I started it. God, it's more complicated than you'd think."

"Can't just toss the anchor over the side, huh, Perry?" Big teased.

"I could, if the other end of the rope was tied around your ankle!" she retorted.

Big laughed and motioned to Anzac to go with him. They had their preflight checks to do. Much as she enjoyed the rare opportunity to hang loose, she just plain didn't have the time. She was operating on a tight schedule. Before the flight she had completed an inspection tour of compartments assigned to the Air Wing. Captain Graff, the ship's skipper, led the tour. After her hop was done, she had to discuss the negative findings with those members of the Air Wing responsible for the zones the Captain had deemed unsatisfactory. Barring any emergencies, the rest of Perry's day was going to be spent on the ground, in her office, giving several junior officers very firm guidelines as to how they should do an inspection.

Wolff's attention was momentarily diverted by the sound of Commander McNeil climbing into the cockpit seat in front of him. He saw her strap in quickly and watched as the two members of flight deck crew leaned into the pit and pulled the long pins with red flags attached to the seat and ejection mechanism. Poindexter had explained to him during his training that the pins were there to keep something from going off accidentally, like the ejection seat rocket, while the plane was parked in the hanger or on the flight deck. Wolff activated the mechanisms that could be started before the engines were turned on and waited for the Commander to close the canopy.

"You all strapped in back there?" she asked over the hot mike.

"I'm so wired up I feel like I'm going in for a coronary bypass!" Wolff stated with a laugh.

"After this hop you might need one," cracked McNeil as the plastic bubble swung down over their heads and locked itself in place with an audible clunk.

Both of them snapped on their oxygen masks as the Commander started her engines. Wolff could hear her breathing quicken and wondered if flying excited her as much as it thrilled him. True, he didn't pilot anything nearly as impressive as the bird he was currently strapped into, but Martin always considered the time he spent flying some of his life's golden moments.

"Want me to talk you through your preflight checks or did 'Dexter and Anzac manage to effectively preach what they practice?" she asked.

"I think I can handle it," Wolff said as he executed the procedures he'd learned from the two RIOs, and had been practicing while awaiting her arrival. He was determined to do the job and do it right. He knew he was new at this game but if he did halfway decent and didn't give her cause for concern she might relax enough to be willing to grant him the interview he'd been wanting since the day he came aboard.

"They're breaking us down," McNeil informed him as she watched the Green Shirts detach the chains that had them hooked onto the port side of the flight deck. "Look, Paper Boy, if you're not sure of something, ask. I know both seats in this aircraft, so if you've got any problems..."

He said, "No, I'm fine back here, really," a little too quickly and realized it only after he'd spoken and hoped to God he didn't come off sounding cocky. He didn't want to give McNeil the wrong impression. He wanted her to accept him and, hopefully, like him.

The *Excalibur* had been at sea for a little over two months and, in that time, Wolff spent as much time observing as he did writing. And one person he had been keeping a close eye on during that time was Commander McNeil. Now he was finally going to get a chance to do more than exchange pleasantries with the Wing leader. He knew it was going to be hard gaining a rapport with her. And not because he was going to be questioning her while they were cruising at thirty thousand feet and she would be absorbed in the job of flying the plane. Wolff had made many attempts early on in the cruise to interview Perry but all of them had been politely rebuffed with the same excuse. True, her responsibilities did keep her days quite full but Wolff was savvy enough to realize when he was being given the brush-off. However, now that he had Commander McNeil all to himself, he was intent on finding out what lay beneath the gutsy jet jock face she always wore while on duty.

Wolff swiftly pushed back any last minute doubts he was having about his ability to handle the radar intercept officer's spot, and concentrated on the job at hand. He twisted the WCS (weapons control system) knob to standby and watched as the light beside it lit. Reaching left and back he flipped the liquid cooling switch to the AWG 9 position to keep the electronics cool and prevent them from burning out at a crucial moment. He twisted the Nav Mode pointer switch to the left of the radar scope onto Nav, turned the Identification of Friend or Foe knob to standby, and then turned the radio knobs to BOTH and ON.

"How's it goin' back there?" McNeil asked as a Yellow Shirt, playing traffic cop, directed the Tomcat toward the catapult. "We're getting ready to launch."

"The AWG 9 light's out and right now I'm giving the computer our current longitude and latitude," Wolff told her.

"Don't forget to check for popped circuit breakers," she reminded in a tone that sounded almost casual to him. He knew she was an old hand at all this but he liked hearing her talk to him like he was one of her regulars instead of Just Another Fucking Observer, or JAFO, as he was called in jest by many members of the air wing.

"Keep your head back against the head rest during the shot," McNeil advised. "You don't have to monitor anything during takeoff so you don't need to worry about having your eyes always on your instrument panel during the launch like I do. Once we get airborne, it'll be a different story. This is being logged as a maintenance flight but we're going to have a little fun up there. I hope you didn't eat a big breakfast because, unless you're immune to air sickness, there's a chance you may be getting a repeat performance of what the wardroom served at oh-eight-hundred."

"I never get sick," Wolff lied through his teeth.

"Well, then stand by to rock 'n roll!" came her cheerful response.

Wolff kept a keen eye on the flight deck crew that scurried around like bees around a blossom and tried to make mental notes of who did what in those crucial few seconds before they launched. All the apparently choreographed moves of the deck crew made him feel like he had orchestra seats to the Navy's version of the American Ballet Theatre.

He saw a Purple Shirt holding up a board showing the fighter's total takeoff weight and over the hot mike heard McNeil explain what was going on around them as she gave the man the thumbs up, "The strength of the cat shot is determined on the basis of our weight, the bulk of which is fuel. So it's essential that my numbers and those of the deck crew jibe."

"What are those Red Shirts doing?"

"Checking to make sure our missiles are ready to fire. And there's a Green Shirt under the plane checking our hookup into the catapult gear."

Wolff nodded. He'd been allowed on the flight deck during the launches of other Tomcats and had seen what went on under the jet. The launch bar went from the front nose gear to a big hook sticking up from the surface of the deck. Under the flight deck and out of sight was a steel wheeled trolley. When the fist of steam punched into the launching piston, this would haul the hook-shaped shuttle and the plane attached to it down the deck.

"Father, Son, Holy Spirit, Amen," Perry whispered softly as she swept the stick forward, back, left, and right so the Yellow Shirts outside the aircraft could see if the flight controls were working correctly and then pushed the left and right rudder pedals down with her feet. Her father had always used that abbreviated prayer as a check to make sure he wiped the controls clean in his F-16. Colonel McNeil was the one who introduced her to the wonders of flight. Not only did she carry on his name but she also picked up many of his habits, both good and bad. The good ones were what kept her alive in this dangerous business. The bad ones were the reason she'd been a two-time loser in the marriage game and was, at forty-four, not very likely to go for strike three.

"Looks like we're a go," she informed Wolff. "Got your harness locked?"

"All set," he replied.

Both Wolff and McNeil glanced at the light on the signal island to their right. It was green. They were go for launch. Wolff pressed his helmeted head against the side of the cockpit canopy so he could see past McNeil. The sea looked like it was only a few feet down the road and Wolff was beginning to get nervous. His mind flooded with all the things he'd been told could go wrong.

He knew he was in it for the duration when he saw the Commander salute the bow catapult officer, who was seated facing aft at his control console between the catapults, to signal their readiness for launch. The yellow-shirted launching officer scanned the length of the cat, rechecked the plane at full power, and pushed the fire button on the catapult releasing the torrent of pent-up steam against the huge piston under the flight deck.

Wolff gasped involuntarily as his head snapped back into the head rest. He felt his eyes flatten as if pressed back into his head by some unearthly invisible hand. He tried to look out of the cockpit but caught little more than a blur of ship grey and sea blue. He found himself paying an odd amount of attention to the rattle of steel wheels beneath him as he tried to keep the sequence of events surrounding his first launch straight in his mind. For the three second dash down the deck everything he saw, felt and heard ran together as one in his head. It was going to be real tough to describe *this*, Wolff mused as images of riding on Disney's Space Mountain somehow found their way up from the depths of his memory to haunt him.

"Good shot," McNeil said as she slapped a gear handle up with her left hand. She allowed the nose to rise to the optimum eight degrees and held it steady there while she trimmed and accelerated. At 200 knots she raised the flap handle and, with the flaps up, she lowered the nose of the accelerating fighter. She leveled when they hit the altitude she intended to be the hard deck for their upcoming ACMs—fifteen thousand feet.

"You okay back there, Paper Boy?" she asked.

"Just fine, Commander. This sure beats the hell out of Six Flags."

She laughed and, glancing back and left she spotted her wingman, Big Daddy. She remarked, "This is what two turkeys look like when they're flyin' casual."

Wolff looked to his left and saw the other jet flying several hundred feet away. From spending time with both the Ghostriders and the members of all the official squadrons on the *Excalibur* he'd learned enough Navalese to understand what she'd just noted to him. "Turkey" was their word for the F-14D Tomcat and "flying casual" meant flying in a loose formation. In the few short weeks he'd been living with the air wing he'd managed to pick up enough of their slang to blend in with the rest of the brown shoe crowd, even if his khakis didn't bear a rank insignia.

"Up for a game of bear hunt?" she asked as she eased the throttles aft a percent or so to give Big Daddy a power advantage, and then scanned her instruments. EGT, RPM, fuel flow, oil pressure, hydraulics, all were a go. No warning lights. They were ready to go for it.

"That depends. Are we going to play Ivan or are they?"

"Well, if they're it, they're Ivan. If we're on the hot seat, then you'll be playing Boris Badenov, I'm Natasha and our pals Big Daddy and Anzac will be doing a Rocky and Bullwinkle."

"I love it," Wolff said laughing. "I'm up for being Badenov. Can you do a Commie accent?"

"Vatever you vish, Keptin," she replied sounding a lot like Chekov from *Star Trek*. "Ve vill rid de skies of dese kepitalist fools."

Martin was beginning to get into the spirit of things and had relaxed enough to snap off one side of his oxygen mask and look around. The view of the world was a wonder from their perch in the sky. The seats were mounted high so that the pilot and RIO would have the maximum field of view when the jet was engaged in combat. Wolff wasn't used to being surrounded by so much window and it was a little unnerving at first. It felt like he was flying through space in a chair without anything keeping him aloft. He glanced down and from their height the carrier looked like a tiny grey speck with a white tail. The thin layer of clouds above were their neighbors now. It was a perfect day for a dogfight.

McNeil radioed Big Daddy and Anzac. "We're mean ol' uncle Ivan," she quipped. "After I give Paper Boy a little demo, I'll hit the Texaco, then we'll play."

"That's a Roger, CAG," Big Daddy responded. "One thing though, no hard deck for this one. Let's go at it like it's for real, okay?"

"You're on. But no heavy stuff."

"Roger that. We're going to get a little extra in the tanks so we'll be ready to go for broke when you get back. We'll be hanging around at the pumps, okay?"

"Roger, good buddy," she signed off and both of them heard Big Daddy's chuckle for a brief instant before the communication ended.

The other Tomcat banked a hard left and veered off leaving Commander McNeil and Wolff on their own.

"Okay, now that you've got my undivided attention, is there anything special you'd like to ask me before I get this bird honking?" she asked.

Just before launch Wolff had tucked his mini cassette recorder in the chest pocket of his flight suit and the note cards under his left thigh believing that to be the easiest and most accessible place to put them. The recorder he produced with the greatest of ease; but, as they say about the best laid plans of mice and men, it wound up taking a considerable bit of fumbling before he was able to produce the list he'd so carefully prepared during preflight. He heard her chuckling softly over the intercom and realized she must have heard his fidgeting around through their sensitive radio link. Of course his G-suit would pick that exact moment to decide it wanted to make a semi-permanent connection with his notecards, Wolff griped inwardly, but Murphy has a way of striking when his presence is least desired.

"Notes get stuck in your speed jeans?" she offered and, when he didn't come back with a quick reply, added, "We don't have time for a formal Q and A. Not if you want to see me strut this turkey's stuff."

"I got my questions," he responded a little breathlessly. "And the tape's running."

"Good, and I'll have some answers. That is, so long as you ask me about the activity of the moment."

Through his sinking feeling, he queried, "Like flying?"

"You mean there's something else we're doing at fifteen thousand feet?"

Wolff sighed. I guess all the personal stuff will have to wait 'til next time. Careful not to let on that she'd just shut down three-quarters of the material he had planned for their session, he said, "Well, I guess any other subject would seem vastly inappropriate. So, if we're going to talk flying, I've got two questions on the subject. Who first got you into the cockpit and what is the best plane you ever took a hop in."

"My number one bird? Are you serious?"

"Yes," he replied. "If you say your favorite is what we're in right now, then you'd get no argument from me. This is one helluva ride!"

"The Super Tomcat's got something special all right," she agreed. "But my numero uno is the one I cruised around in during my high school's summer vacations. I was part of a flying circus and we toured across the state doing air shows. Dogfighting for dollars, I used to call it. The money I earned helped put me through Georgia Tech. Anyway, I spent four years driving a perfect replica of the Red Baron's Fokker Dr-I triplane. Let me tell you, son, that was one righteous aircraft."

"A real tits machine." he concurred somewhat surprised by her choice.

"Yeah, even more so than the Crusader, and *that* has always been the club favorite when we get to waxin' nostalgic," Perry paused briefly to check her instruments before continuing, "As far as who got me into this business in the first place, it was my dad. He was an Air Force pilot, who flew anything they gave him the keys to. I grew up surround by jets and jocks, so I guess my windin' up here was sort of inevitable."

Wolff glanced down at his notes. Colonel Xavier P. McNeil, Senior, the Commander's father, was recently retired from the Air Force. He had enjoyed a long and very distinguished career. Perry's being named after him was unusual, but Martin wasn't going to ask her about it. He had a feeling that was one subject she had probably explained until she was blue in the face. As far as he was concerned, how she got her name wasn't as important as what she had accomplished over her twenty-plus years of flying for the Navy.

He had not anticipated her reluctance to discuss anything other than her aerial activities and consequently found he had to scramble to come up with a second inquiry. All his questions related to her pursuits on the ground and with how she had managed to earn herself the coveted spot of air wing commander. Wolff pondered for a moment whether or not to go on with his next question. It had to do with flying even though he had listed it under the heading of "personal data" on his notecard.

Nothing ventured, nothing gained, he thought as he inquired, "Why are you flying for the Navy instead of the Air Force?"

Perry's eyes widened slightly. The Colonel had asked, no, demanded, an answer to that same question on the day of her graduation from Georgia Tech. As she stood there clutching her diploma with her gown completely obscuring her Navy dress uniform from view, Colonel McNeil looked at her like she had driven a knife through his heart. Perry never wanted to hurt her father. He was all the family she had, since her mother died of cancer when she was twelve, and she knew how much he had wanted to have her flying his wing and sharing his life. She couldn't meet his eyes. She knew she wouldn't be able to keep the tears from coming if she faced him. "Pop, I love you but I can't *be* you. And I can't live my life in your shadow. I don't want to be Perry Junior, the Colonel's kid. I want to be *me*."

The Colonel just stared at her making no reply. He was stunned. He had no idea she felt this way. After all the time they had spent together talking of the future, for her to do this was like she'd slammed a door in his face. It was hard enough for him to understand her choosing Georgia Tech over the Air Force Academy but he had accepted her decision. She immediately entered the ROTC program and now, four years later, was leaving as her class's top Navy ROTC student. That small detail was like salt in a festering wound. The path Perry had chosen was to keep them estranged for nearly three years. It wasn't until she was about to embark on her first cruise that she and the Colonel made their peace.

"Commander?"

The inquiry made Perry jump slightly. It took only a split second before she realized the voice was coming over the ICS and not the radio. Wolff wanted an answer to a question she wasn't really up to answering just then. Instead of responding to his query, she decided to volunteer some information about something she felt more comfortable discussing. She knew during his first week or so with the *Excalibur's* air wing, Wolff had overheard many very off-color suggestions regarding her seemingly meteoric shot into the CAG office. She also knew he was perceptive enough to have noticed the sudden sharp decline in snide comments after she put her life and her Navy wings on the line pulling a nugget's fat out of the fire.

"Want me to tell you about Boomer? You know, the guy who almost cost me my commission?" she offered.

"Was he the reason you were put in hack two months ago?" Wolff asked. He remembered there were a few days early in the cruise where he didn't see very much of the Commander. The scuttlebutt about her whereabouts had been flying fast and furious. "The rumors were sailing four sheets to the wind for a while there. I tried to pry the story out of Commander Edwards, since I know he was up there with you guys and those Phantoms, but he wasn't too willing to talk."

"Well, it's hard to get someone to open up about the time they said, "Jesus!" and then almost met the man," she said, her usual tinge of wry humor coloring her tone of voice. "I know Boomer won't say jack. He's still pissed at himself for screwing up. Radar, on the other hand, might answer a question or two. He forgave me real damn quick for getting him dressed down by Big Daddy and the Admiral once he heard what grade he I gave him for his performance. Not only did he forgive me, but he's been bendin' Big Daddy's ear nonstop to get assigned to me as my RIO. Way the boy acts, it's like I invented the Navy, flyin' and the goddamn Tomcat!"

Wolff laughed openly. "Your first fan! You should be flattered."

"I'm a pilot, not a movie star," she stated, her distaste over the situation readily apparent. "Look, you media people might get off on this hero worship crap, but not me. It's tough enough to command the bunch of airborne egos I've got on this boat without having to worry about some star-struck kid hanging onto me like I'm the next best thing to God."

"Considering where you jet jocks spend all your time..."

Wolff never got to finish the sentence because, when she got an inkling of the opinion he was going to voice, she pulled up hard into a power climb. The force of five Gs suddenly connecting with Wolff's body swiftly silenced the civilian, who had not developed any tolerances to the stresses of combat flight. She could understand people finding what she did exciting and wishing they could join the party, but comparing fighter pukes like her to the Almighty was just going a little bit too far. She wasn't exactly the most fervent Catholic, something the ship's chaplain never failed to point out whenever the opportunity arose. But she was born and raised Irish Catholic and, although she hadn't been inside a church since her last marriage fell apart, she still respected her religion and intensely despised abject blasphemy.

"Shit!" she swore under her breath. I should have listened to Big Daddy. He warned me in preflight this guy was bound to piss me off. She sighed deeply and altered her course for the Texaco, the KA-6D tanker, where she knew Big Daddy and Anzac would be waiting. Big Daddy will laugh when he hears that I almost K.O.'d Wolff with a power climb, she mused with a naughty grin. Anzac on the other hand is bound to read me out for sure. It took a lot to make the even-keeled Anzac lose his cool. She knew he often wished she would follow his example and try to keep a reign on her Irish temper. After over two decades together, that was one example he provided that she *still* couldn't master. She promised 'Zac she would be good and take it easy on the guy but he *deserved it*! That short fuse of yours is going to cost you your job if you're not careful, she thought. One of these days...!

"That was...pretty intense," she heard Wolff say in a shaky voice.

"Glad you liked it," she replied casually knowing full well another move like that one probably would make him lose his lunch. "Would you like to see a negative G pushover or a turn and burn next?"

"Uh, actually, I'd like to hear about Boomer," he told her doing his best to sound as normal as possible. "If that's okay with you."

She remembered the tape recorder Wolff had activated when he began his interview and realized he probably still had it going. "Sure, fine, " she responded glancing at her gauges and, seeing she didn't need to rush to get to the tanker to refuel, she eased the Tomcat to cruising speed and began talking to him and the slowly spinning spools.

27 October 0400

The *Excalibur* was just ten days into the cruise when the Air Wing began performing blue water ops at night, which was the toughest and most risky assignment a pilot would ever draw during peacetime. For that reason, Perry was teaming her nugget drivers and RIOs with the more seasoned members of her squadrons, some of whom were pulled from the ranks of the Ghostriders, with the hopes the new guys would benefit from the wisdom of their senior partners.

McNeil herself was flying with a RIO fresh from a Jacksonville RAG who had been christened by his buddies with the utterly predictable tag of "Radar." She agreed it was unoriginal to say the least but, with the surname of O'Reilly, the boyish-looking carrot topped ensign was lucky he didn't wind up with something worse.

Flying dash two and covering her six was another new graduate, Lieutenant (junior grade) John "Boomer" Price. The kid had come out on top of his class and was full of both untapped potential and King Kong's ego. She liked the confidence he displayed when behind the stick, but found the unrelenting cockiness he was full of more irritating than fingernails scratching a chalkboard. He didn't give his squadron commander much cause for complaint but he often needed prodding to follow any orders she gave him. This annoyed her, especially since she knew he was being difficult only because she was a woman. Perry had come close to planting him into a bulkhead on those occasions when his slowness on the uptake got her Irish up. It was only Anzac's tempering presence that kept her from rearranging the anatomy of the young flyer blessed with both the rugged good looks of a Hollywood film star and the arrogance of a heavyweight champ.

They were flying in a tight formation over the Caribbean and would have been a sight to behold from the ground had the pair of F-14s not been engulfed in the inky blackness of the night. The *Excalibur's* mission was to act as an operational deterrent against the increasingly well armed, and bold as brass, South American drug lords had, so far, been well met. The swift moving Cigarette speedboats may have maneuverability on their side but can't carry the payload of a *Nimitz*-class carrier and DC-9s and Lear jets can only dream about outrunning a Tomcat on the prowl.

So far their patrol had been quiet. Nobody was flying except people who were supposed to be up there, like the Red eye express to Caracas they'd spotted shortly after becoming airborne. The scuttlebutt about black market bought F-4s, F-15s and French-made Mirages being used as air support to protect shipments crossing the Gulf got the flaps up on all the trigger-happy newbees dying to make aces of themselves. Although he always acted like he was a cut above the rest of the crowd, Boomer somehow found himself caught up in the fever.

They had been given clearance to engage any aircraft refusing to either identify themselves or obey instructions concerning course changes for landing at one of the several airfields the DEA had established with the cooperation of the Department of the Navy as points for search and seizure of suspicious planes. The Drug Interdiction Accord gave the military organizations of all the signatory nations a great deal of latitude, and this included the right to shoot down the aircraft of "suspected smugglers." The idea of blowing civilians out of the sky didn't sit too well with Perry McNeil but she was a soldier and would follow orders. The very thought of fighting someone who didn't know the first thing about ACMs seemed dishonorable to a seasoned veteran.

"Think we'll catch the sunrise?" she heard Anzac inquire, his voice giving away just how much he despised night landings in general and ones made with an inexperienced driver in particular.

"Sorry, we don't have enough gas to go chasing the sun," she responded casually trying to sound reassuring. "Hey, come on. Sky's clear, viz excellent and you've got the only wing nut besides me who's tagged the three wire on every night hop we've had since we left Norfolk."

"We've only been at sea ten days, CAG," O'Reilly reminded her over the intercom, the ICS.

"I know," she replied. "Anzac's gonna have an ulcer by the end of this cruise if he doesn't learn to ease up on the throttle a little."

Radar's grin was lost behind the oxygen mask but he had to work at keeping the amusement out of his voice as he reported, "I'm receiving the Hawkeye's data link. We've got three bogeys at one hundred and sixty miles, bearing zero two zero."

Perry eased right to that heading and adjusted the gain and brightness on the HSD, the Horizontal Situation Display, on the instrument panel in front of her knees. On the scope she could see a copy of the picture her RIO had on the Tactical Information Display in the rear cockpit and, as she had anticipated, there was the threat display.

"Looks like we've hooked ourselves a live one, huh, Radar?" she commented.

"The word is they're not responding to any hails and, if they make no deviations from their current heading, they'll be over the Everglades at about oh-six-hundred."

"Does this sound at all suspicious to you, Ensign?"

"Yes Ma'am," he responded eagerly. "Are we going to wave the big stick at them, CAG?"

"You betcha," she said as she issued the order to "Go Tactical" to Anzac and Boomer. This was their signal to use the squadron's assigned radio frequency, something their adversaries would not be able to monitor, and, after they came back with the "All Secure", she informed her partners of her intentions to pursue.

"They're going two eight zero at about four hundred knots, CAG," Anzac told her. "You and Boomer could slip onto their tail if you come right another twenty degrees and descend to twenty five thousand feet. If you do this nice and gentle, we'll have them right where we want them—*dead* in our sights."

"You got that, Boomer?"

"Roger," he said. "I'll follow your lead."

She peeled off with him neatly tucked under her wing. The two Tomcats quickly encountered their quarry: two F-4s escorting a DC-9 Skyblue. The DC-9 was painted sea green on the top and sky blue on the bottom, the camouflage pattern was designed to make the aircraft harder to detect from boats doing aerial lookouts and from planes doing searches for low flying aircraft. In the grey white glow cast by the three quarter moon, the Skyblue's 'flage pattern was barely visible. However, to the experienced eyes of Commander McNeil, who was familiar with the multitude of camouflage patterns used by both domestic and foreign military, the darker top and lighter bottom of the plane was all she needed to see to know what guise this bird was flying under. She doubted her novice partner noted the paint pattern in the dim light of the nighttime sky.

Boomer positioned himself behind the three nine line of the Skyblue and Perry had the flaming tail of the Phantom flying off the DC-9's right wing at her two o'clock. Although the three jets were behaving as though they were unaware of the presence of the two Tomcats, both pilots knew they were being watched and were probably spotted long before they made visual contact.

"These guys got a lot of guts," remarked Boomer. "Should we

find out what's on their minds?"

"I'll hail them, Lieutenant," she said. "Stay off the Rhino's tail. The stations look fully loaded and they could be packing rearward firing Sidewinders."

"Roger, CAG."

Perry got on the radio to the Skyblue and issued the formal address the members of every squadron were required to commit to memory, "This is Commander McNeil of the United States Navy. In accordance with the articles set forth in the Drug Interdiction Accord, you are hereby required to—"

Before she could order them to respond with their clearance code, the two Phantoms broke sharply out of the formation leaving the transport on its own. The RIOs in both Tomcats were carefully tracking the movements of the two F-4s. The two F-4s made a wide loop around and coming back hard to engage. Alarms screamed in Perry's cockpit and she instantly knew they were locked up. Perry dropped flares, knowing she was too close for her adversary to be using radar homers. Almost from instinct she performed a high-G wide angle corkscrew barely managing to evade the missile. She brought the Tomcat under control in time to reacquire her opponent.

"This shit's hard enough to do in daylight!" she heard Boomer complain as he angled in for an attack. "Figures these assholes would decide to be uncooperative!"

"Not everyone pulls over for the flashing red light in their rearview mirror, Boomer," she countered tersely. She closely pursued her F-4. She got him in her sights and fired short bursts from the Vulcan 20mm cannon mounted in the port side of the Tomcat's forward fuselage. As she was firing, she saw her opponent execute a deft turn and burn avoiding her cannon fire. "This guy's stupid to think the missile would do the job for him, but lucky enough to get out of the hole his stupidity dug for him," she remarked over the ICS to Radar, who only grunted in acknowledgement. "I'm switching back to missiles, he's out of range for guns."

"CAG, check six!" she heard Anzac warn. "Our man is running from us and gunning for you."

"I see him," Radar said looking back and left. "He's closing fast!"

The Phantom's canopy reflected the moonlight making it somewhat detectible, even though it was running dark: no anticollision lights, or illumination of any kind, to make it visible to ground control or other aircraft. These people are obviously up to no good, she thought. Why else would they go through such pains to try and hide, much less, have the balls to engage two of the hottest thirty million dollar killing machines ever invented.

Warning lights flashed and the intermittent tone of a threatened missile lock momentarily flustered Radar. He was trying real hard to stay calm and concentrate on the job of keeping his driver's backside covered. "That Phantom's closing fast, CAG!" he said as he flipped his gaze between his instruments and the cockpit window. "He's almost on us!"

"I know."

Radar saw the rogue F-4 was almost on them and realized that, instead of speeding up to evade, they were doing exactly the opposite. "CAG, what are you doing? We're slowing down!"

"It's all right. I'm drawing him in a bit closer."

"Closer? Are you nuts?" Radar cried a bit panicked.

"Trust me on this one, kid," she replied coolly confident. "I'm going to hit the brakes and he'll fly right by."

Radar saw the F-4 get dead on their six and almost wet himself when he heard the familiar high pitched tone warning them their adversary had missile lock on them. In the split second it took for the lock on to sound through the cockpit, Perry popped the boards, the speed brakes, and the Tomcat jumped up and back. This allowed the Phantom to come charging forward into perfect position for her to nail him. The two well-placed Sparrow missiles lanced through his starboard engine and port wing.

The F-4 exploded in a blaze of yellow and orange looking oddly like a misfired Fourth of July firework to the eyes of young O'Reilly. He sighed with relief and quickly put out of his mind the thoughts about how close he'd just come to buying the farm in precisely the same way. "Boomer's got the other guy on the run," Radar informed her and she smiled inwardly at the pride in his voice.

Perry knew Patrick O'Reilly and John Price were good friends and, from what she'd noted of the temperaments of the two young men, they were much like she and Anzac were at that age. One all gung-ho and the other the voice of reason and temperance. They had the makings of a good Tomcat team. "The DC-9 has altered course." she heard Radar say. "Looks like they're headed home."

"Any guesstimate as to where home might be?"

"Well, they probably have enough gas to get them to South America but whether they are destined for Brazil or Columbia is hard to say but my money'd be on Columbia. That was the hot spot last cruise, or so I've heard."

"We must have been hanging around the same people because I heard the same story," she concurred as she adjusted her course to intercept the DC-9.

Boomer had his hands full trying to get the Phantom in his sights to make the kill. The F-4 pilot was considerably more experienced than his pursuer, who was having a hard time anticipating which evasive maneuvers the Phantom would use in the situations given and compensating for them. Anzac was doing the best he could to suggest strategy but, although Boomer was a good technical pilot, he just hadn't developed the ability to read his enemy and use the weaknesses he saw against him. The truly great flyers were instinctive tacticians, but strategy was something that could be learned and, when mastered, make a good fighter pilot a better, more effective, one.

"Watch out, Boomer! You're in perfect position for that guy to pull a maverick on you," Anzac warned trying to keep the frustration out of his voice. He wasn't sure if Boomer knew what a "maverick" was by name but, since his hot-shot front seater saw *Top Gun* all the times it was playing in the ready room, he was fairly certain Boomer could figure out the maneuver his adversary might try to pull on him.

They were on the F-4's tail as it blasted across the nighttime sky and, from what Boomer could conclude based on the F-4's current trajectory, it looked to him like the Phantom was making a beeline for South America. "This guy is running, not fighting, Anzac," Boomer countered. "Maybe we should let him go and have the Hummer track him back to his base."

"Well, I don't know—"

"Shit!" Boomer swore as the F-4 popped up and its sleek outline disappeared against the nighttime sky. "Where'd he go? I can't see him!"

"Goddammit, Boomer, I knew it!" Anzac stated as he frantically searched both the sky and his instruments to get a clue as to where their adversary went. Seconds later lock on alerts screamed through the Tomcat and Anzac commanded, "Get out of here! Move! Now!"

"Where?"

"Anywhere! Just go!"

Boomer broke a hard right and descended five thousand feet.

Their swift action was just barely enough to save their asses. Another second longer and the missile the Phantom had fired would have split the Tomcat in two. Even so they were still in a bad situation because now *they* were the hunted instead of the hunter and their wingman, their back up, was nowhere in sight.

McNeil caught up to the DC-9 and noticed it had wing and engine damage suffered from the near miss with the rogue missile. She knew it would only be a matter of time before it ditched. She decided to follow it until Radar ascertained where Boomer and Anzac were slugging it out with the other F-4.

"CAG, we've got a problem," Radar began but was cut off when he heard Anzac's voice over the radio.

"Barnstormer, where are you?" Anzac demanded using the call sign he'd known Perry McNeil by since they met in Flight School.

"I crisped my bandit. Right now, I'm tracking the Skyblue. Need help?"

"Desperately! Get here, ASAP!"

"On my way." she signed off.

"I'm going to try and get us clear of this guy," Boomer said.

"You had plenty of opportunities to get him and you blew them all!" Anzac declared. "The driver in that F-4 is a helluva lot more experienced than you. So far he's managed to evade every one of your attacks. We'll cut an intercept line with the CAG." He barked the vector at him. "He can't dodge both of us at the same time. With CAG here, we're guaranteed to get the chance to make this clown take a swim."

"But we gotta get him before he gets us, 'Zac," Boomer said in a mixed voice of fear and determination. "Or we may not be here when the CAG arrives. Find him, fast!"

"Shit!" Anzac muttered under his breath. He tried to get a bearing on the Phantom while simultaneously checking with the team in the E-2 Hawkeye. If this kid gets me fried, I'm going to kick his ass from the Pearly Gates to Purgatory. He craned his neck to see behind the Tomcat's flaming tail and searched the skies above and below. The moonlight gave him some light but picking out that camouflaged jet against the almost starless sky was going to be rough.

"I don't see anything," Boomer said scanning the skies. "Think this time he bugged out?"

"I doubt it," Anzac replied in a cold tone that made the hair stand up on the back of Boomer's neck. "He's out there somewhere waiting for you to do something stupid."

Anzac's insinuation wasn't lost on the young lieutenant, who was still firmly resolved to keep himself and his bird in one piece. Boomer executed a neat classic Immelmann turn—a partial loop followed by a half-roll that gave the Tomcat some altitude while simultaneously reversing its direction of flight. He was backtracking in the hopes of finding the F-4 before the Phantom found him.

He didn't have to wait long. The Phantom's afterburners glowed like a comet against the nighttime sky as the jet blazed toward them cannons blazing. Boomer broke hard right pulling five Gs as he bat turned away from his pursuer. Both he and Anzac grunted, fighting the force of the Gs created by the maneuver. Boomer barrel rolled the huge fighter escaping the first salvo of deadly blasts. However, the F-4 had managed to stay with them and fired a second salvo that ripped across the F-14's starboard side lacing its engine and the twin fuel tanks. They began losing gas at a rapid rate.

Alarms went off inside the cockpit, as the starboard engine sputtered noisily for a few long seconds before losing power. "Engine one is down," Anzac stated his voice emotionless as he watched the indicator on the fuel gauge drop down at an alarming rate. "We're bleeding fuel like crazy, Boomer. Head back for the boat. Now!"

Boomer swiftly altered course and kicked in the afterburners though he knew somewhere in the back of his panic stricken brain that this would suck gas. Better to come in riding on fumes than not to come in at all, he thought as he moved to put as much distance between himself and the F-4 as possible.

Anzac saw the familiar pattern of a Tomcat's anticollision lights coming up hard and fast on their eight o'clock. Thank god, he said to himself, Perry will keep that Phantom off our ass. "CAG, we've been hit," he told her. "I'm not sure if we've got enough gas to make it back."

"If you're so damn low on fuel then why the hell are you guys going full throttle?" she chastised.

"Maybe because we'd like to keep from getting more holes in our ass!" Anzac declared hotly. "And, secondly, I'm not driving this goddamn bird, so don't give me any shit!"

"Boomer, slow down! The Phantom bugged out so your six is clear," she commanded as she maneuvered alongside them. "How low are you?"

"Six thousand pounds and dropping like a stone," Anzac said his anger abated somewhat but he still sounded very displeased with the current situation. "Christ! Please don't tell me we're gonna have to take a swim. The water's cold and it's too goddamn early in the morning!"

Perry noticed the other Tomcat had not altered its speed and said, "Boomer, ease down to three hundred knots. If you keep going at your present rate, you'll never make it! Radar just called you in as an emergency. Use the ACLS for this touchdown. I know you hate the damn machine as much as I do but you'll use it tonight and that's an order. You read me, mister?"

"Roger, CAG," he responded sounding like he actually intended to follow her orders immediately for a change.

"We're going to head in first. If you're leaking as badly as you say, your bird is going to foul the deck and we don't have enough gas to circle until they clean it. Boomer, just stay on my tail and follow me home."

When Perry's F-14 departed banking left and descending toward the inky blackness of the Gulf, Boomer's attention was focused completely on trying to keep his hands from shaking. Dodging cannon fire in a simulator had been a whole lot easier than doing it for real. He'd been the best dogfighter in his class but he'd been up there in the blue battling his classmates, who were all a bunch of rookies like himself, or the instructors. Maybe he wasn't the hottest thing to ever to strap into a F-14, he thought as he fought to regain his composure. Maybe he ought to get out of this business while he still had a whole skin.

"Boomer, we are way low on gas," he heard Anzac say over the ICS. "Let's land this turkey!"

Boomer looked around and down but couldn't see anything but darkness. He closed his eyes and tried not to think about what it would feel like to take a splash.

Although Perry had advised Boomer to use the Automatic Carrier Landing System, she disdained the use of the contraption that could land her plane on the boat all by itself. Half the adventure of being a carrier pilot was getting yourself back down safely on that deck with the three wire firmly snagged in your tailhook. All the automated gizmos they kept sticking into airplanes was making it less and less of a joy to fly. Ah, if they could only modify my old Fokker to endure the stresses of a cat shot and carry a full payload then I'd be in heaven!

The Landing Signal Officer's voice broke into her reverie. "Good lineup, Ghost Leader. Easy on the power. Call the ball."

Calling the ball was essential because it told the LSO that the pilot could see the light, or "ball", presented by the Fresnel Lens Optical Landing system located on the port side of the landing area. This device uses a yellow light arranged between two green reference, or datum, lights to give pilots a visual indication of their position in relation to the proper glide path. Perry knew if she kept the ball centered in the datum lights all the way down to the deck, she would catch the third of four arresting gear wires rigged across the flight deck.

"Tomcat ball, Three Point Five."

Down in Carrier Air Traffic Control Center, or CATCC, the last fuel state for Ghostdancer 00 was erased off the status board and "3.5" for thirty five hundred pounds of fuel left. This was noted next to where Perry's name should have been but where, instead, some wag had inscribed the phrase "Double Nuts." The CAG's bird got that nickname because of the identifying number it carried, usually 100 or 00, but the comedian probably wasn't thinking of that at all when he scribbled in the jest designed to poke fun at what their CAG's anatomy was lacking.

The humor wasn't lost on the skipper of the Tomcat squadron VF-69, the Renegades. Big Daddy Beaumont chuckled, when he noticed how Perry's flight had been listed on the board. He joined the air boss to watch the closed-circuit TV monitor that gave them a picture from a camera buried under the flight deck and aimed up the glide scope. The images they viewed were visible not only in the CATCC but in every ready room on the ship. Perry's landing would be graded by the LSO but her success or failure would be seen by many of the men in her command.

The hook was down and ready to grab that Number Three wire. Perry was only seconds from making her controlled crash onto the flight deck when she heard Anzac's voice announce over the radio, "We've got a real problem, 'Stormy. Boomer's just circling up here. I think that run in we had with the Phantom fucked up his head. We aren't going to make it back!"

Radar silently cursed himself for not seeing the problem Anzac just announced and telling the CAG before they reached the ship. He made a mental note to apologize for his oversight to her later in debriefing.

"Hang on, I'm coming!" she told Anzac and quickly pulled up

in time to prevent the hook from catching. She gunned the engines and blasted off again.

"Bolter, bolter, bolter!" she heard the LSO's voice announce as she went into her climb. "Shit, CAG, you had that turkey down cold! What the hell are you doing?"

"Going back for Boomer."

"You don't have the gas for this, 'Stormy." This time it was Big Daddy. "Somebody else can rescue that snot-nosed kid."

"He's my wingman and my responsibility!" she insisted. "I can't leave him."

"Get your candy ass back here now!"

Perry gasped. That last command came from the Admiral. Rear Admiral Oliver Wendell Jones, the commander of the *Excalibur's* battle group, was the only man on the boat whose authority no one questioned. At least, not if they valued their careers and their hides. He was the only one, other than God Almighty, whose wrath could make the veteran warrior quake in fear. She felt the hair on the back of her neck starting to rise because she knew from past cruises with Ollie that when his voice dropped into the bass ranges he was fighting mad.

"Oh, shit," she heard Radar say in a small voice over the ICS. "That was Admiral Jones!"

"Relax, his beef is with me, not you. You're just along for the ride, remember?"

"Goddammit, McNeil. Are you listening to me? You are to about face and land that plane!" Jones ordered, his vocal octaves unchanged. "If you're forced to ditch, you'd better start swimming north because when I get my hands on you—"

Perry snapped off the radio. "I don't know what it is, but I seem to have a bad effect on the Old Gentleman's blood pressure," she quipped to the junior officer in the pit. "Don't worry. When I bring this plane and Boomer's back, I'll be forgiven. Jonesy knows I'm the best, or else he wouldn't have pulled the strings needed to get me both on his ship and into the CAG chair."

"I hope you're right," Radar replied still uncertain and trying to resist the temptation to turn the radio back on. "But you really shouldn't have turned off the radio, CAG. Stuff like that shows up on the monitors in the CATCC."

"What shows, Lieutenant, is that the signal cut out, not how or why. I think you know what to do to make our loss of communications look like a malfunction. Just belay that order until we get Boomer safely back home, okay?"

"Jeezus, CAG, we could both wind up in hack for this, or worse!" Radar stated. Figures the first major conflict he gets to participate in, he's in the pit for a wildcard senior officer, who's determined to turn them into fish food or brass bait. And he couldn't figure out which was worse. "Are you really sure you can pull this one out, Commander?" he asked after a short pause while he made a mental note of how he intended to sabotage the radio. He hoped he was as good at being a sneak as the Commander seemed to be or else he'd have not only Big Daddy to answer to but the Admiral as well. And Radar was sure of one thing: he did not want to endure a disciplinary session with Admiral Jones and spend the rest of the cruise feeling like Hamburger Helper.

"Even if we had the chance of a nun in hell I'd still be out here, kid," she told him. "Find him on the scope?"

Radar didn't answer immediately. He was too surprised to find that they already had the correct bearing to intercept Boomer. This lady must be psychic! "He's dead ahead, CAG. Just keep going the way you're going."

She made contact within fifteen seconds of sighting the other Tomcat and easily slipped in alongside taking the lead in their two man formation. As she maneuvered into position she told Radar, "There's a sign back there. Use your grease pencil and write the frequency number I give you on it and stick it where Anzac can see it. Use your flashlight to get his attention. Understand?"

"Aye, aye," Radar said. After finding the sign that was blank on one side and had "Pull over asshole" printed in neat block letters on the other, he quickly complied with her order. He used the flashlight to catch Anzac's eye and, when he saw the other RIO was looking his way, he illuminated the sign as best he could. When he saw Anzac give the thumbs up sign in acknowledgement, Radar added, "You know, if the guys back in the CATCC figure out you're on this channel, then they'll know there's nothing wrong with the radio."

"That's a chance we'll have to take," she said and, when she caught the sign from Anzac, she queried in a coolly conversational tone, "You boys seen an aircraft carrier?"

"This is serious, 'Stormy. We've got less than twenty five hundred pounds and are counting down at warp speed here. Do something with Boomer! He's not talking!"

"Boomer, are you listening to me, son?" No answer. "Look, I know you can hear me. Relax, and do what I tell you." Still no reply. Perry felt the chill of fear to the marrow of her bones.

Boomer had frozen. That was the most dangerous thing that could happen to a fighter pilot short of combat. If she didn't break him out of it, both he and Anzac might not survive. There was no way she was going to lose both her best friend and most promising young pilot. Although her odds of getting through to him in time were fifty-fifty at best, Perry was intent on giving it her best shot. Her green eyes steely with resolve, Perry commanded sharply, "Listen up, sailor! I want you to stay on my wing and follow me in. Do you read me, mister?"

After a pause she heard two clicks of the mike in reply. A pilot's way of responding when he was too busy to speak, so she knew he had heard and understood her. Now all that remained was seeing to it he got back to the boat before his tanks bled dry. She banked, and made a lazy 180∞ turn, and sighed inwardly with relief when she saw Boomer was right with her.

"CAG, Boomer isn't the only one who's low on fuel," Radar told her. "We'll be lucky if we make it back ourselves."

"I know," she replied, her uneasiness about their situation not at all evident in her voice. "We'll be experiencing a tailwind for most of the ride back and I intend to make use of this bit of divine intervention. The Tomcat may not be able to ride the winds like a Sopwith Camel, but I think I can convince this bird to let nature help keep her wings up."

She saw Boomer starting to drift and said, "Stay with me, Boomer. You snag the three wire with that turkey and I'll let you fuck me silly."

Radar's mouth dropped in shock. "That-that was a joke...right?"

Perry laughed quietly. "Of course. But right now I'd promise that boy a night with every whore in Rio if I knew it would get him back safe. Hell, I'll beg, borrow or steal to keep my air wing alive and flying. That's just the way it is."

"God, Big Daddy wasn't fooling when he said you were a real piece of work."

Perry's only response was a soft chuckle.

The radarman informed Admiral Jones and Big Daddy that the two Tomcats were returning as he tracked CAG McNeil and Boomer on his scope.

"Still can't get the Double Nuts, Admiral," the communications officer stated. "Radio must have gone out. The LSO says that after the CAG traps the only bird we'll be waiting on is Renegade Two Oh Two."

Big Daddy shot a sideways glance at the Admiral. Jones stood right beside him fuming inwardly. He was angry with McNeil for disobeying his direct order but Big noticed there was also a furrow of worry on the brow of the peeved battle group leader. He knew Jones had a particular fondness for Perry, though the Admiral would never admit it to anyone, even himself. However, it was only on those rare occasions, like now, when she took off to do what she thought best, that Rear Admiral Oliver Wendell Jones really wanted to forget he had a vested interest in her career.

"She'll be okay," Big Daddy tried to sound reassuring. "She's made it home under worse circumstances."

"Every goddamn cruise it's always something," was all the Admiral said.

The LSO watched as the Double Oh slammed almost vertically onto the deck instead of gliding in at a slant and the tailhook just barely tagged the two wire. The landing was passable. The LSO had seen a lot worse in his day and was inclined to cut the CAG a break on the grade because she was forced to do it with only the minimal cues he could give her with the flares, the radio outage kept her from receiving the benefit of his verbal guidance. The deck crew quickly got the CAG's F-14 squared away so the way could be cleared for the last plane to come home—Renegade Two Oh Two.

Anzac heard the CCA (Carrier Controlled Approach) controller's voice over the radio, "Two Oh Two on line very slightly right, three-quarter mile, call the ball."

"Did you activate the ACLS, Boomer?" Anzac asked and, when he got no answer from the front seat, added, "Well, you can't collect the debt the CAG owes you if you're plastered all over the deck."

"The ACLS is on," he heard Boomer reply in a distant tone. Over the radio he stated in the same faraway voice, "Tomcat ball, Oh Point Five."

"Christ, those guys are riding on fumes," muttered Big Daddy.

"Crash team is on standby," the LSO told the team in the CATCC. "And we're all set to take a dive for the net if this kid screws up." The safety net was a horizontal nylon fence surrounding three sides of the LSO platform and was there to protect the deck crew if the plane missed going down the center line and headed in their direction instead.

"Attitude, Two Oh Two. Loosen it up a bit," the LSO said as he carefully tracked the movements of the approaching F-14. He could see the anticollision lights on the wings bobbing up and down and commanded, "Keep it level, Two Oh Two." The wings steadied as the undulating whine of the Tomcat's engine was heard in the CATCC via the LSO's radio link to the control center.

In the faint light on the flight deck the huge, angular F-14 appeared with elevators flapping and nose headed straight down the center line. The jet slammed into the deck, its engine burning at full military power, and trapped successfully, its tailhook snagging the preferred number three wire.

As he felt the arresting gear slow the plane, Boomer mechanically slapped the throttles to idle, flipped the external light master switch off, and raised the flap handle. The Tomcat jerked to a halt and rolled backwards. Boomer pushed the button to raise the hook, then applied the brakes. The F-14 stopped with another jolt and then ceased all movement.

"Shit, that was too close," Anzac said. He heard the engines cut out, not because Boomer turned them off but because there was no more gas for them to burn. "Pop the top, Boomer. I want out!"

Boomer complied and opened the canopy. Anzac unstrapped himself and climbed out as the deck crew began swarming all over the shot up fighter to assess the extent of the damage. He cast an eye around the deck and quickly locked on to where the Double Nuts had been guided to park. He saw Perry and young O'Reilly climb out while a group of Blue Shirts proceeded to chock and chain the F-14 to the deck. He managed to catch her eye and she quickly crossed the tarmac to meet him.

"I heard some chatter about your radio being out. When did that happen?" he asked. He found himself forced to practically jog to keep up with her as she made her way over to Boomer's plane.

"Radio kicked out after we boltered and headed back for you."

"But—"

"I know," she interrupted stopping to face him. "As far as you're concerned, I used sign language to guide Boomer back." Quickly she added before Anzac had the chance to voice any protests, "Don't argue, just nod."

He stood there totally perplexed as she resumed her trek to the blasted F-14. She was up the ladder and peering over Boomer's shoulder by the time he decided that making sense of her instructions wasn't worth the effort. He would just obey. It was a hell of a lot easier.

Boomer was fumbling with the buckles on his harness when Perry poked her head into the cockpit. She reached in and undid the latch saying, "You're damn lucky you had *me* as your wingman, mister. Ah doubt anyone else would have risked their necks and their commissions to save your sorry ass."

Boomer dared to meet her glowering green eyes and barely managed to whisper, "Thanks, Commander."

"Get your butt to sickbay. If you get the green light from Bones, report to your squadron leader. And, after Big Daddy gets done chewing on you, if he leaves any meat on those bones, you're *mine.*"

Boomer didn't know what had him shaking the most right then: almost getting waxed by an F-4 or the prospect of being turned into lunch meat by both the Skipper of the Renegades and Commander McNeil.

A hand tugging at the leg of her G-suit caught Perry by surprise and she looked down to see Yeoman First Class Tim "Trudy" Truesdale standing at the foot of the ladder. The young man with the fresh scrubbed boy-next-door good looks was her aide and the concern she saw in his oversized brown eyes was also evident in his voice. "Commander, the Admiral said you were to get out of your flight gear and into his office ASAP. He also wants you to bring Ensign O'Reilly."

"How did he sound when he asked you to tell me this?"

Truesdale knew she was trying to glean Ollie's mood from the tone of the order and said, "He's pretty P.O.'d, but I think he might be persuaded to forgive you in light of your success."

"Yeah, ah will only be in hack instead of in the brig," she quipped shooting Truesdale a wry grin. She turned back to Boomer, her expression sober again, and warned, "You better pray the Old Gentleman is in a generous mood tonight because the more he laces it into me, the more ah am going to be inclined to take it out on *you.* Now, fall out!"

She climbed down the ladder swiftly and paused long enough to be certain Boomer was going to follow her order right away. The second she saw him deplane and start across the flight deck toward the castle, Perry turned to her aide saying, "Make sure O'Reilly is apprised of this situation. He's still by the Double Oh making post flight checks and listing our gripes with the bird."

"Yes Ma'am."

Perry sensed a familiar presence at her elbow and turned to face Anzac. "Here are the keys to the kingdom." He looked puzzled again as she put a handful of keys on a Mustang key ring in his hand. "You're the deputy CAG, remember?"

"Yes, but—"

"You'll need to get into my office, my files, maybe even my quarters, who knows? You're my pit man, 'Zac, I'm counting on you to cover for me."

"You really think Jonesy is going to nail you to the boards for this?" When Perry didn't respond, he muttered, "Shit."

"It might not be that bad, Ma'am," Truesdale offered hopefully.

"Trudy, did anyone tell you what went down?" Perry asked.

"Are you serious? It was all over the wardroom how you blew off the Admiral and headed off on full afterburners after Boomer. By now the news probably reached the boys in the boiler room."

Perry rolled her eyes heavenward with a "why me, Lord" look. "Great," she sighed. Her gaze rested on Anzac, who looked as though he knew exactly what she was thinking, and he shook his head ready to protest. She cut him off saying, "You knew damn well when you became first runner up in this contest that, if anything happened to me, you'd be wearing the thorny command crown. I wouldn't have recommended you for the deputy spot if I didn't think you had what it took to sit in the CAG chair."

"I know that, Perry," he replied staring at the keys in his hand. "Covering your ass I can do with my eyes closed. I've been doing it for so long I can't remember *not* doing it. But I'm not out to steal your thunder. I don't *want* to be the CAG."

"What you want isn't relevant. If anything happens to me, the ball's in your court, like it or not." she told him.

"I know that, too. But, if I had my way, all I would do would be to get up there and fly, plain and simple," he replied wistfully. He reached over and brushed a stray wisp of hair out of her eyes adding, "And the only person I'd ever want to fly with just happens to be the most awesome driver in the Navy. You."

She gave Anzac a wan smile. He very rarely let anyone see his sentimental side and she was touched by his words and the love she knew was behind them. Perry allowed her closest friend to put his arm around her shoulders. Anzac gave her a tight squeeze and nuzzled her neck, tickling her and making her laugh despite her anxiety about the upcoming meeting with the Admiral.

"Relax, Stormy," he admonished lightly. "You'll live longer."

Captain Graff glanced down at the thick folder sitting atop the Admiral's desk. It was McNeil's file. The very slim one beneath it was O'Reilly's. He had read her jacket from cover to cover. She was a Rubik's cube, a real puzzlement. It was clear from the success rate of her squadron during the War that she knew the importance of discipline and teamwork. But, there were several incidents where she seemed to forget that she wasn't operating as an independent unit. Jones had noted in her file that those incidents were a result of Perry's acting out of a combination of selflessness and the need to prove herself. He sighed. The only thing that came easy to Perry was the flying. The rest of it had been a struggle from the get-go. For every one officer she had in her court pulling for her, there had been five others who didn't think a woman had any business driving a fighter or leading men into combat.

Jones seemed to sense what he was thinking when he commented, "She's worth the effort, Vince."

Graff nodded. He didn't know her very well but, from what he had read and observed, he was very much inclined to agree with the Admiral. Perry was bright and very hardworking, a combination that had proved winning for many other up-and-coming Navy officers. After her heroic wartime efforts, she should have made captain but didn't. Half the reason was that her CAG had been one of those "five other officers" that disliked the idea of having a woman squadron commander and, consequently, gave her a bad performance rating. The other half of the reason was Perry's own fault; In her effort to prove she could run her squadron effectively, she bent the rules from time to time to keep her team's birds flying and maintain their high mission success rate.

Perry's need to prove that she belonged where she was worried Graff. Her constant quest for acceptance hadn't caused her to really step in it yet. *He* could deal quite well with the changing times. But he noticed she had been giving 110% when she served on his bridge and, under his watchful eye, performed the duties of ship's Captain. Her deputy had been there as an observer. Anzac's presence helped her to keep her composure, as she did her best to fill a pair of shoes she obviously felt were two sizes too big. Graff knew she had a very good technical grasp of the job but also noted she was behaving as though someone had placed a huge spotlight on her. Had she been able to relax, Graff believed she might have been able to see the enjoyable side of commanding a carrier.

"She's a fine officer," Graff said. "But what we think is meaningless. *She's* got to get past this need to show everyone she belongs where she is. When she first joined up, things were different. I know there are still some folks out there who don't think women belong on a fighting ship, but *I'm* not one of those people. But I haven't been able to convince her of that fact."

"She'll figure it out in due time," Jones told him. He picked up her folder and, finding the entry he desired, showed it to Graff. It was her performance rating from her wartime cruise. "You read this?" Graff nodded. "I was on that ship. I saw what she did. True, Perry always was a bit of a maverick, bending the rules on an as needed basis, but she *did not* deserve this. Bellamy was out to nail her from day one. And I am not about to let him destroy with one pen stroke what I had been working on for almost ten years."

Graff didn't need to be told what strings the Admiral pulled to get Perry aboard as Wing Leader. He also didn't need to be told why Jones had picked the strong-willed flyer as his protégé. He got an inkling of what made her special the day she spent with him on the bridge. He knew there would be many more days like that one. Jones wanted Graff to groom her for what could be her next shipboard posting and the Captain was more than willing to comply with the request. Perhaps over time she'll relax enough to discover the up side to a shipbound position, Graff mused. Landbound jobs will be all the Navy will have to give her once her flying days are over.

His mind back on the reason he was in Jones's office, Graff asked, "What are you going to do to her, Oliver?"

"The usual," was all the Admiral said.

As Perry stood awaiting the command to enter the Admiral's office, she tried to calm the air wing of butterflies that were doing an alpha strike in her stomach by using the relaxation and centering techniques that were central to the mastery of Tai Chi. Her deep controlled breathing and meditative stance would look to the unschooled eye like she was merely taking a respite from the burdens of command instead of steeling herself for the verbal keelhauling she was no doubt going to receive.

Ensign O'Reilly stood at her side worrying a loose thread on his squadron ball cap. He needed to be covered to salute the admiral and aboard ship ball caps were *de rigueur*, everyone wore them. He burned the thread with a match, and discreetly patted out the flame, and put the cap on over his curly hair. He noticed the Commander was wearing a cap with Casper riding a Sidewinder, the logo of the Ghostriders, on it. To him a ball cap on someone whose uniform displayed four rows of ribbons and several major awards, including the Distinguished Flying Cross, just didn't look, well, right.

The skipper of the Renegades came walking down the corridor and approached the pair waiting outside the Admiral's office. He took a few thoughtful drags off the remnants of his well chewed cigar. He cast an appraising eye over the duo and couldn't help noticing how attractive Perry McNeil looked in her khakis. The overstarched slacks hid her legs, which he'd seen enough to know were as hard and muscular as the rest of her body, but the fitted short sleeved shirt kept nothing from view. Perry had disdained a tee shirt because of the heat so the cotton fabric of her uniform clung to her like a second skin. Her body was as sleek and hard as the machines she flew in. There wasn't an ounce of fat on her, and she still had the same angular lines and fine definition that got her trophies galore in the body building circuit during her youth. In Beau Beaumont's educated opinion, Perry McNeil was definitely one helluva shit-hot bird.

Radar fidgeted under Big Daddy's intense gaze and the skipper commented, "Son, in my eyes, a junior officer who doesn't get himself put in hack at least once in his career just ain't drawing any water."

"Yeah, well, if some of us take on any more water we're going to be kissing Davey Jones's ass," Perry stated flatly.

"That's one thing I always liked about you, McNeil. Your unflagging optimism."

Big Daddy's sarcasm wasn't lost on Perry, who countered, "Are you going to stand there and tell me I've got nothing to worry about? Because, if you were, I'd say you were a goddamn liar and I'd be right."

"Look, I'm not going to blow sunshine up your ass, Stormy. You fucked up and you know it. Case closed. But Ollie isn't going to ship you Stateside with your tail between your legs. You just saved the lives of two of my men and saved the taxpayers over thirty million dollars. Where I'm standin', those are mitigating circumstances that could keep you your career. Yeah, you'll feel like you just survived being sucked through an A-7's intake, but this won't be the first time you've been beat on by the brass."

Perry noticed Radar giving them both a curious look out of the corner of his eye and she just grinned. "Yeah, well, you know me," she quipped eyes twinkling. "Nothing but trouble."

"Only too well," he replied stubbing out his cigar under the heel of his size thirteen brown shoes. "There are times when I wondered how I put up with you all these years, Xavier Perry

McNeil. You've gotten me into so many scrapes..." He let the thought trail off for a moment before continuing in a different vein, "You've really got to cool it, Stormy. Don't screw up the one good thing you've got going for you."

She pulled off her cap and ran her fingers through her damp hair. She knew exactly what he meant by that last comment. The Wing Command was the one bright spot in her life right now. Her second divorce had become final just days before she shipped out. Her daughter Katherine, the product of her failed first union, had been visiting her when her lawyer presented her with the official papers declaring her a free agent once more. She had also stayed around after that so she could see Perry off at the air station. Saying goodbye to Kate had been hard. But being kicked off the boat and sent home because she screwed up would be harder still....

"McNeil! O'Reilly! Get in here!"

Perry jumped at the sound of Captain Graff's stern summoning and quickly put on her cap. Big Daddy opened the door for her and she entered the office followed closely by Ensign O'Reilly. The two officers snapped the Admiral a crisp salute, which he returned, and stood at attention. Standing behind and to the right of Admiral Jones was Captain Vincent Graff, the skipper of the *Excalibur*. Commander Big Daddy Beaumont took his place on the Captain's right. O'Reilly looked nervous but Perry's face was devoid of emotion. It soon became readily apparent to the Ensign that it was McNeil, not him, the Admiral intended to turn into his late night snack.

Admiral Jones cast a hard look at Perry and crooked a finger at her. She followed the silent command and took her place to his left. Protocol was all that was keeping her from getting her due right then, for a senior officer was never reprimanded in front of their subordinates no matter how serious the offense. She knew she was going head first into the meat grinder the minute Jones was done saying his piece to O'Reilly.

"Don't think that being in the back seat gets you completely off the hook, mister," Jones began, his voice back to its usual rich baritone. "A RIO is fifty percent of the deal, Ensign. There's an old Tomcatter saying that a driver is only as good as his RIO, and it's true. Take it from someone who's been there. Now son, the only thing saving your hide is the fact that you are a junior officer and had no choice but to follow whatever orders your driver gave you." He shot a disparaging look at Perry, who suddenly found the bulkhead really intriguing to look upon, and then returned to face

O'Reilly. His expression hardening and the tone of his voice dropping an octave. "but, if I find out your little radio problem was caused by something other than equipment failure, I'll have you out on the flight deck on your hands and knees, scrubbing it down with a toothbrush. Understand?"

"Yessir!" O'Reilly said hoping his guilty conscience didn't show on his face. He had heard enough about Admiral Oliver Jones to know the man truly would have him out there washing the deck if he found out the radio was sabotaged.

"I'll let Commander Beaumont decide your punishment, Ensign. That's his job. You are dismissed."

Beaumont caught the young man's eye and growled, "Your butt in my office. Now!"

"Yessir!" Radar saluted the four officers, spun on his heel, and left in silence. Perry sighed as she watched him go and felt a little sorry for dragging him along on her little escapade.

"I'd be more concerned about my own ass if I were you, McNeil," Jones snapped. Perry flushed slightly at having been caught giving Radar a sympathetic look. "Because it's in a pretty big sling."

Sensing the finger in the dike was not going to keep out the flood any longer, Big Daddy Beaumont made his graceful exit saying, "I've got a hop to take and a junior officer to chew on so, gentlemen, if you will excuse me..."

Perry, along with the other two senior officers, returned Beaumont's farewell salute and she cringed slightly when she heard the door snick closed behind him.

"That was a very noble thing you did up there, Commander," Jones started approaching her. He did not stop until he was only a few inches away. "What you *should* have done was land your plane! That Tomcat isn't yours, it's the taxpayers! You work for them, remember?" He pulled off his ball cap revealing a shiny ebony bald head and tossed the cap with the *Excalibur* logo on it onto the desk. "You see this?" he queried hotly indicating his hairless pate to her with a stubby forefinger. "I had a full head of hair before I met you. You've made a healthy career out of being a pain in the ass, McNeil. Do I have to stand here and list all the shit you've pulled and got away with because somebody, God only knows who, in Higher Authority, thought you were worth a damn?"

Perry found herself staring ahead with no expression and felt as comfortable as a nude in church, during Midnight Mass.

"Yeah, you're all contrite now that it's time to face the music. I wish I knew what your problem was. When you bother to do what you're supposed to, you're a damn fine officer and the men respect you. But every cruise you go off and do something half cocked that gets you this close—" he held his thumb and forefinger an inch away from each other "—to getting your butt tossed in the brig. You keep this shit up and you won't be flying for the Federal government, you'll be flying for Federal Express!"

Perry winced.

Suddenly, seemingly rendered speechless, the Admiral stood with his back to her trying to find the right words. After what felt like an eternity to Perry, he spun around to face her saying, "You've been CAG, what, two weeks? Two weeks! You were in a real big hurry to screw up your big chance, weren't you? You're the first woman ever to sit in the CAG chair, McNeil. I thought, maybe incorrectly, that you'd start thinking more like an officer instead of a jet jock if you were given something more important to do than just tear up the skies at Mach 2. If you were a nugget on their first cruise like your pitman O'Reilly this sort of thing could be written off as impetuousness or inexperience. But for Chrissakes, you've been around for two decades and fought in one helluva battle where you really showed your colors as both a flyer *and* a commander. Is it too much to ask to see a bit more of the hero who took the day at Bekaa Valley instead of her ego driven twin sister?"

Perry sensed that she was expected to reply and said quietly, "No, sir."

"You're damn lucky you were able to pull off that little rescue operation of yours, Commander. Because, if you had failed, and wound up splashing two airplanes, your ass would've been in the brig so quick it would've taken your body a few minutes to catch up to the fact it was missing!"

Perry chewed her bottom lip obviously aware that he was leading up to the *piéce de résistance*.

"For the next seventy-two hours, my dear," and he said the words "my dear" in a clipped scissorlike tone of voice, "you are in hack. Unofficially. To write you up at this stage of your career would sink your little ship for good. But I'm warning you, you ever, *ever* blow me off like that again and you will be *out*, is that clear?"

"Yessir."

"Good. Now get out of here before I forget that I ever actually *liked* you."

Perry saluted and departed feeling like she'd just been shrink wrapped.

She returned to the O-3 level and the solace of her office where she found Anzac there waiting for her. When she walked in, he was sitting on the edge of her desk looking over a maintenance report. He looked up from the papers expectantly. "Well?"

"I'm in hack."

"I kinda figured as much. How long do you need me to run the show?"

"Three days."

Anzac let his breath out as a low whistle. "Ow," he said rising and he gave her the once over remarking, "It could have been worse. You still have some ass left."

"Cute, 'Zac," she muttered collapsing into her chair. "I seem to have a god given gift for letting my ego write checks my body can't cash. If I screw up again, I'll wind up flying one of these—" she wagged the pen she was holding in her hand "—for sure."

"Well, as far as I'm concerned, you didn't do anything wrong. You saved my bacon, Perry. And there are three people sitting Stateside who are real glad you did."

Perry smiled up at him and, seeing the twinkle returning to her eyes, Anzac rolled up the report he'd been reading and teasingly clunked her over the head with it.

13 December 1230

"That's quite a story, Commander," Wolff said as he put a new tape into the recorder. "I hope I got it all."

"I hope so, too, mister. Because I'm not in the habit of repeatin' myself," she stated as she wheeled towards the KA-6D tanker, the Texaco. "Have the boys in the Wing been cooperating with you?"

"Yes, for the most part. I've gotten some pretty interesting stories." Some of them were about the Commander's exploits, both on and off the job, but he wasn't about to tell *her* that. She didn't need to be reminded about her wartime acts of heroism. He also doubted she would want to hear about what she did during the liberty parties where alcohol and emotions both often flowed a little too freely.

"Oh? Anything y'all care to tell?" she prompted. "Like a good 'how I spent my liberty tale'?"

"Sorry, Commander. I was asked to keep what I was told confidential."

"Oh, well, I guess if I want to hear those stories, I'm going to have to buy your book," she quipped, her grin hidden beneath the mask. "Well, I'm glad you're a newshound that knows how to keep his big mouth shut. First one I've ever met with *that* talent."

Wolff had heard about her bad experiences with the press. He knew she had been hounded quite a bit after she came back Stateside. She was the War's first female air ace and everyone wanted to get her story. From what he saw and read, Wolff quickly noted that no one was able to do more than just scratch at the surface. It had not been easy but Perry managed to maintain her privacy despite all the attempts made to make her life a dish for public consumption. Since privacy was important to her, he was going to do his best to respect her wishes. But he was still intent upon getting an insight into her for the sake of his readers. He was aware she earned her command based on both her professional skills as well as her seemingly innate ability to lead. That much he had gleaned from his research. Yet, what no one managed to see was what made Perry unique. He was going to find out what that special something was but, at the same time, he did not want to come off as just another nosy newshound out to get a piece of her. It was going to be a challenge to get what he needed without annoying the Commander.

"Look, anything you don't want made public I'll keep to myself," he reassured her. "Like how you tried to put me into a coma with a ferocious power climb."

"I thought you were a pilot," she said pointedly. "A few Gs shouldn't bother you."

"I've taken enough razzing from you hot shots about my flying," Wolff stated annoyed. "It's getting a little old."

"If you can't take the heat, you never should have stepped into the oven," McNeil informed him. She watched the tanker unroll a long black hose and headed for the end of it marked by the basket. A round plug-in spot that looked like the feathered end of a shuttlecock. She pulled out the switch that slid the probe out of the right side of the F-14's nose section like a horizontal periscope. She carefully closed the distance between the Texaco and her Tomcat. Perry wasn't at all bothered by the fact the two aircraft looked as though they were almost touching, and was concentrating on making that precisely timed midair collision of probe and basket.

The probe speared the basket with a resounding clunk and Perry got on the radio saying, "Fill 'er up, boys. This turkey's hungry today."

Wolff heard chuckles from the tanker crew and one of them cracked, "Want us to check under the hood, CAG?"

"Nah," she replied going along with the joke. "Next time."

Wolff was thankful for the midair pitstop. It meant he could enjoy a few more minutes zooming around in the Super Tomcat. Though he would feel a lot more relaxed once that big airplane got off their laps. The break also gave him a chance to regroup his thoughts and recover from the rolled up newspaper on the nose slap he'd just gotten from the CAG. It was true he had talked a bit too much about flying but it was hard *not* to when he spent so much of his time surrounded by pilots. He loved flying as much as they did. It was the only thing he had in common with them. He sighed. He would have to get back on her good side if he wanted to get her to consent to a more lengthy interview later.

It wasn't very long before he heard McNeil telling the tanker crew she was gassed up and ready to go. The F-14 slowed to break the lock on the long hose and they stayed by the KA-6D until Perry saw the hose had been reeled in completely. Wolff knew she was following procedures, she was required to inspect the exterior of the plane after fueling to make sure everything was in order and the hose had retracted completely. Once Perry was satisfied all was in order, she ascended a bit and gave the Texaco team the thumbs up before heading off to find Big Daddy and Anzac.

Perry and Martin Wolff scanned the sky for their quarry, the F-14 sporting Yosemite Sam in full flight gear with his six shooters blazing on its vertical tailfin, the squadron markings of the Renegades. They spotted their adversaries below them and Perry descended gracefully slipping into a tight formation with Big Daddy. He maneuvered into positioned as the lead plane in their two man pattern.

"You finished givin' our guest the grand tour?" Big Daddy asked unable to keep the hint of mockery out of his voice.

"Yes, we're ready to kill you now," she replied. "Prepare to defend yourselves from the pride of Mother Russia, Imperialist dog!"

Big Daddy laughed. "All right, you little Commie chippie, let's see what you've got."

The Renegade F-14 peeled off and made a dive for the Gulf with Perry in hot pursuit. Martin felt himself growing dizzy as the two planes wove in and out, spiraling downward. Each trying to gain the advantage over the other for a good clean shot. When he saw the water coming up hard and fast, Martin gasped fearing for a split second they were going to take a splash. Perry pulled up at the last minute and kept on Big Daddy's tail. He sped along skimming the wave tops just barely keeping the sapphire colored seawater from being sucked up his F-14's intakes.

"We're awfully low, aren't we?" Wolff stated. He watched the choppy seas zoom by so fast his eyes perceived the whitecaps as white streaks staining the deep blue of the Gulf.

"This is what we call getting down and dirty," she told him. "One miscalculation and we'll be taking a bath for sure. But, don't worry, I know what I'm doing."

"I sure hope so," he said trying to keep the anxiety out of his voice.

"You been keeping an eye on that radar scope?" she asked.

"Yeah, but we're too close to use missiles. If we did and this was the real thing, we'd either be caught in the blast and buy it, too. That, or the bloody thing wouldn't have time to arm itself and we'd be shit outta luck."

"That's true, but I'm going to back off a bit and give you a chance to use that equipment you've been tryin' so hard to master. If you can hit a tricky sonovabitch like Big Daddy, then you can be sure you've got what it takes to sit in the pit."

"I'm game," Wolff said. "Go for it, Commander."

Perry eased up and allowed Big Daddy to get ahead of her and into missile range. Martin, meanwhile, thumbed the tiny wheel on the radar stick and zeroed in the missiles on the green water bug of light skating across the scope. As long as he kept the radar focused on his target, Wolff knew the radar-directed Sparrow missile would follow those radar beams right into the target and blow it out of the sky. Wolff felt like he was playing one of those computer arcade games, the graphics on the scope looked like what would appear on a monitor and the stick he toggled was not too different from a gamer's joystick. All he had to do was thumb the wheel, jiggle the stick, punch some buttons and fire. But, unlike in the arcade, if you miscalculated and your enemy got away, you couldn't just put in another quarter and start over.

Wolff was having a hard time getting a lock on Big Daddy, who was very creative with his evasive maneuvers. He pulled up into a hard seven G vertical climb which Perry followed with less severity. She didn't want to risk having Wolff black out. Perry felt like her hands were tied during the mock combat. Normally she'd pull out all the stops and do the hard climb, get on Big's six and nail him but good. Having to worry about the G forces her tactics would put on Wolff kept her from getting in tight and on the mark with her usual deadly ease.

"God, he's good," Wolff remarked as he struggled to get a lock on the dodging Tomcat.

"That's why he's still alive and flying," Perry stated. "He was my wingman during the Second International Bekaa Valley Turkey Shoot. That was the hairiest furball ever to hit the skies in twenty years. Nothing like it was ever seen since 'Nam."

"Yeah, the Israelis were grateful for the American assist. They were none too pleased when the word got out that one of our boys who aced themselves was a girl. Of course they denied it had anything to do with being sexist. They were just "concerned" about what the enemy would have done to you had you been captured. It was a lucky break your fried Turkey managed to hold out until you were over the Med and could bail out within a short hop of the carrier."

"The old One One Four did right by me that day," Perry said wistfully. "Managed to send seven MiGs into the sand before one lucky towel head nailed me. It was a cannon hit that, at first, looked like nothing. But slowly, one by one, we started losing essential things, like an engine, hydraulics, and so on. When I first got hit, I thought I was more wounded than the plane. You see, some of the blast penetrated into the cockpit and I took shrapnel in the knee and side. Hurt like hell. I don't know how those clowns in the movies with a dozen bullets in them keep running around and shooting like they just got scratched. Let me tell you, I was lucky I was able to keep my bird in the air. It was nothing more than sheer stubbornness keeping me flying that day. No way I was going to let a bunch of guys who wear dishrags on their heads whip my ass."

"That was the fight that got you the Medal of Honor?"

"Yes, and a few other commendations besides. Made the month and a half I spent in that hospital in Naples almost worth it. Almost. Walking with all those stitches was no picnic and there was a brief while there where it looked like my flyin' days were over. But somebody Up There must like me because, as y'all can see, I'm still airborne. And I'm ready to rock with the best of 'em."

"I guess that's how you got this job," Wolff observed. "Once the civilian papers got a hold on this and ran with it, the Navy had to make the most of all this positive publicity and get themselves even more air time. So they gave their first female war hero her own command. I know you're not into all the media hype but you have to admit it did serve a useful purpose."

"What? You mean it got me the CAG chair? Look, even if Bekaa hadn't been splashed all over the front page of every paper in Christendom, I would've gotten this job eventually. You paper boys just managed to get those old sea turtles to haul shell and give me my air wing on my first cruise after Bekaa Valley instead of, say, my second or third. Don't think I'm not grateful because I am, believe me. It's just that all the publicity made it impossible for me to go on any more cruises in the Med. This isn't something I decided. The boys from Intelligence made the recommendation to Sixth Fleet that I not be assigned to their ships; I might not survive the hitch."

"Assassins?"

"So they say. As you can see, being a hero does have its definite down side."

"Yeah, guess so. But there is one positive thing all this guts and glory stuff did for your reputation."

"What's that?"

"No one will ever accuse you of having used the horizontal method of career advancement."

Usually a comment like that would have angered Perry but, this time, she just laughed. She had managed to keep Big Daddy within range while she and Wolff talked, and was in too keyed up by the thrill of the mock combat to find any japes the reporter threw her way annoying enough to garner some retribution. She kicked in the afterburners and closed in for the kill.

"Hey, we're getting too close to use the missiles," Wolff stated when he saw them closing in fast on the tail of the other Tomcat.

"If you see a shot, take it now," she advised. "Party time is almost over. I've got to kill this clown and get us back to the boat by sixteen hundred. We've got about another ten minutes."

"Shit!" Wolff griped not realizing they'd been up already for almost two hours and not wanting his hop to end. He quickly manipulated the wheel on the radar stick and soon had the pin dot of light fixed on the "enemy" plane on the scope. The monotone of a successful missile lock filled the cockpit and Wolff said, "Fox One."

"Hey, *I'm* supposed to say that!" Perry growled. "The RIO just lines 'em up. I'm the one who takes them down! I thought my boys taught you the right way to play this game."

"I know the driver is supposed to do the shooting," Wolff agreed. "But, the RIO can light the Phoenix and Sparrows himself. So, technically, he can log some of his own rock and roll time."

"You're really getting into this, aren't you?" Perry observed not at all surprised.

"Hell, yes!" he concurred, then asked half in jest and half serious, "Do you think it's too late for me to enlist?"

Perry's only response was a long groan.

Anzac waved to Perry and Wolff as Big Daddy took lead once again, and their two man formation headed back to the *Excalibur*. Wolff returned the wave and said to him over the radio, "You guys look pretty good for somebody that just got vaped."

"You got a lucky shot," Big Daddy stated.

"No, he's just an ace pupil," Anzac defended. "Taught that boy everything I know."

"That must've been a *real* short class."

Perry's soft laughter filled everyone's ears for a second. "We've got a new recruit. Got any room in your squadron for someone who has a good command of the English language and isn't half bad on the stick?"

"I could use a junior officer who can manage to do his reports right the first time," Big Daddy told her. "Sign that boy up now before you land and he changes his mind!"

"I would but I left all the paperwork in my office!"

"Damn!" he breathed. "Got to get 'em while they're hot, CAG. I mean, you can't beat this job, Paper Boy. The Navy's really good to us jocks. They give us a thirty million dollar airplane to tear up the skies in, a three billion dollar boat to land it on, a crew to keep that bird gassed up and battle ready, and, to top it off, they pay you! Now, what could be better than that?"

Wolff laughed. There was one universal thing he noted during his hitch with the Air Wing: as tough as life on the boat got, the flying made it all worthwhile. "The only bad hop is the one you don't come back from," was the one quote that seemed to sum it up best for him. What surprised him was that it wasn't one of the many cocky drivers who said it but a rather mellow country boy RIO who showed him how to handle an F-14's back seat. Anzac caught him off guard with that declaration and Wolff soon found out that the CAG's right hand, and best friend, too, was another one who was full of surprises.

The two Tomcats zoomed over the carrier from stem to bow high enough not to endanger anyone. It was low enough though to rattle the windows in Pri-Fly and make Captain Vincent Lucarelli, the Air Boss, lose the Coke he was drinking to the front of his shirt.

"Son of a bitch!" he swore as he shook the foaming liquid off his hands. "Shit! Second time this week!"

His number two, often called the Mini Boss, merely stood by and tried his best to stifle a laugh.

13 December 1300

After having her split second of fun buzzing the boat, Perry turned hard left into the break at 400 miles an hour and made an ascent to 800 feet. She had been at less than half that elevation when she'd made her high speed pass and she knew she'd need some altitude going into her landing sequence. She veered around to a course that would keep her parallel to the carrier on her downwind leg and swept the Tomcat's wing's forward. As she dropped speed she lowered the landing gear, slates and flaps and started her descent. Wolff watched as they made another left turn about two miles astern of the *Excalibur*, crossing her wake at what looked like a 90 degree angle, and aimed for that white stripe going down the center of the carrier's canted flight deck. They were only seconds, and less than a mile, from the deck when he heard Perry announce over the radio, "Double Oh Tomcat. Ball. Four point five."

Perry kept the ball lined up with the green beams of lights as she guided her bird in for its controlled crash on the deck. Wolff looked out the left side of the plane and saw the lights. He couldn't tell from where he sat how well they were aligned for their landing. What he could see was the flat rectangle of black steel coming up at them hard and fast. He wondered how Perry managed to see, much less snag, the third of those four threads that lay stretched across the deck. Oof! They hit the deck with a bang and a screech and Wolff shot forward like a rocket but was held into his seat by the shoulder harness. The screams of metal meeting metal echoed through the cockpit as the tailhook on the F-14 snagged the three wire. The jet rolled forward a few dozen feet in a controlled skid before rolling more slowly backwards allowing the arresting wire to fall out of the tailhook. They were back and the thrill was over for now. Wolff sincerely hoped he could wrangle another hop in the Super Tomcat. That trip had been the biggest thrill he ever had in his thirty six years as a denizen of planet Earth.

Perry parked the Double Oh and popped the canopy open. Both she and Wolff simultaneously unbuckled, yanked off their oxygen masks, raised their visors, and climbed out into the tropical heat wave that seared the flight deck. The shimmering heat made mirages appear wherever they looked on the ship. She pulled off her helmet and wiped her wet hair back with her black gloved hand. Wolff sighed as he removed his helmet and he gave her a big dopey grin.

"That was awesome," he said feeling like he did when he was ten and had just completed his first-time-ever ride on the Cyclone at Coney Island. "Where do I go to sign up to join this man's shit-hot Navy?"

She cracked up saying, "You wouldn't be so ready to jump on the boat if you saw what was waiting for me in my "In" basket."

"If I were on this cruise for real, I'd be a J.O. I wouldn't have your workload or your responsibilities, Commander."

"There are days when I'd give my ribbons to be an ensign again," she said. As she watched the Blue shirts finish chocking and chaining her Tomcat to the deck, she accepted a clipboard with a post flight check list on it from a crewman. While she filled out the form noting any gripes the Double Nuts had that would need tending, Perry commented, "Shakespeare had it real right when he said "Uneasy lies the head that wears the crown." A lot of the guys may think being the CAG is great, but they'd change their tune right quick after a day in these boots."

"I'm sure they would," Wolff agreed. "Even if it was just because their feet were killing them."

It only took split second for her to catch the gag and she broke up. "You've been spending too much time with Anzac. He would've come up with a line like that."

"Maybe, but I didn't need his influence to get my mind bent this way. I was like this before coming aboard."

Still grinning, Perry pulled her shades out of the shoulder pocket of her flight suit and slipped them on. The sun was brutal. Perry guesstimated the temperature on the flight deck was probably coasting around the 100° mark. The humidity made breathing the air, that felt like it was made of pea soup, almost impossible. The day had looked like it was going to be a steamer when she'd launched but she was shocked by how conditions had changed in the two hours she'd been away. The deck crew all looked like they'd taken a dunk in the Gulf. In the short time she'd been standing by the Double Oh filling out her maintenance report, Perry, too, felt herself becoming drenched in sweat.

Wolff unzipped his G-suit and opened the flight suit beneath it as well. He was wearing nothing under the flight suit. She tried not to notice the fact Wolff was very well put together for a guy who spent the bulk of his time on his butt in front of a computer terminal. He wasn't exactly what *she* would call handsome. He lacked the craggy, battle worn exterior so many of the senior officers in her command had, that she found very attractive. Martin's altar boy good looks reminded her of her first husband, Crazy Kyle Mcloughlin. Both men had the smiles of "Golden Age" screen stars, and eyes to sigh for. But, unlike the Crazy man, Martin Wolff didn't stand eye to eye with her but was a good half a head taller. He was also built long and lean whereas her ex had the body of a pit bull and, when he was a fighter jock, the beast's killer instincts as well.

Perry wasn't in the habit of mentally undressing the males in her command but it had been a *long* time since she'd enjoyed the company of a man between her sheets. Martin Wolff was one of the few men aboard who didn't violate her personal ROE, Rules of Engagement. She didn't outrank him, since he had been given the protocol rank of commander for the duration of the cruise so, technically, they were equals even though he didn't have the authority to tell anyone to do anything. Second, like the civilian contractors attached to the Air Wing who helped keep their planes flying, Wolff was not military and not a threat to her career should she ever decide to play around with him.

But, as things stood now, he had an ice cube's chance in Hell of getting *that* close to her....

"I"m hitting the showers," she told him. "I'll catch you around the campus."

He was about to let her go when out of the corner of his eye he saw coming over the horizon what looked like three jets in tight formation approaching the carrier. The distance and the heat mirage combined to make their shapes indecipherable and their contrails were long hazy white clouds. But there was something about them that convinced Wolff those planes just didn't belong there.

"I think we've got some uninvited guests," he told her and she followed his gaze to the port side of the ship where she saw in the distance the three jets bearing down on them.

Captain Lucarelli saw the trio of planes closing in and grabbed his binoculars for a closer look. As the head of the *Excalibur's* Air Department, Lucarelli was in charge of the carrier's fight operations and knew what should and should not be airborne. The trio of jets closing in were *not* theirs, of that he was dead certain and, not sure of the intruders intentions, Lucarelli hit the claxon summoning General Quarters. He got on the horn to both the flight deck and the ready room of the Renegades to announce the launching of the Alert Fives, two fighters kept armed, crewed and fueled at all times and ready to fly within five minutes. The second he got off the line, Lucarelli, who was well versed enough in international aircraft designs to make an instant recognition of most anything currently flying, took another look at what was headed their way and declared dumfounded, "Shit! That thing looks like a MiG 29 that had an Art Deco nightmare! It's *not* ours and I don't think it's theirs either!"

"That's impossible!" his assistant stated. "How could anybody get *this* close without the Hummer, the boys in the CIC or us spotting them?"

"Damned if I know," Lucarelli said more frightened than anything else. If they were expecting company, he would've been told. If they were hostiles, the boys down in the CIC *should* have picked up the problem long before he made visual contact and given the call to arms. No such order came from below. He grabbed the phone ringing up the chief radar officer in the ship's Combat Information Center and growled, "Are you all asleep down there? What is the range on those three aircraft?"

"What?" came a perplexed reply. "What three aircraft, Boss?"

"The three that look like...oh, shit!"

The three jets had gone supersonic in the few seconds Lucarelli had been on the line to the CIC and they buzzed the *Excalibur* at slightly over Mach 1. They came in so low the extreme vibrations shattered all the windows on the island. It was like they had gotten hit by a tornado, for the windows imploded with such explosive intensity that the safety glass split into a combination of bullets and knives. Shards of glass went flying in every direction. Lucarelli's glass enclosed domain in Pri-Fly became a sea of flying see-through daggers and clear pebble-sized balls and no one in the room escaped being struck by either the knifelike slivers or the crystalline bullets. A few members of the Boss's crew were downed by larger fragments that protruded from their bodies like bloody pie wedges.

The Boss himself got hit and hit badly. He had been facing the three sided window when they burst and was struck full force by the blast that sent him flying back hard against his chair. He was sliced from his head to just above his knees from the flying fragments but the worst of his injuries were caused by the two foot plate of sheared glass that was imbedded in his abdomen. Blood dripped down his face from the cuts on his head and cheeks and

Lucarelli was amazed to find himself still clutching the phone.

Biting back his pain, he said weakly into the receiver, "Oh, God, we've been hit. Medic…"

The claxon summoning General Quarters startled Wolff, who suddenly realized he couldn't remember where he had been told to go or what to do during an alert. The flight deck was organized pandemonium as the deck crew raced to get the two F-14s designated as the Alert Birds airborne. He recognized one of the two alert teams straight off; Boomer and Radar were saddled up in the lead jet being hooked up for the cat shot. He tried to see who'd pulled wing duty for the emergency hop but never got the chance because Perry was dragging him by his flight suit's harness toward the island.

"Off the deck! Now! Move!" she ordered pulling him with a strength that surprised him. "Go to your quarters and stay there!"

"And miss all the action?" he queried breaking free of her grasp but continuing toward the island under his own volition.

"If you think having your ass blown off is exciting, you're not gung-ho, you're fuckin' nuts!" she declared still physically urging him on toward the safety of the carrier's interior. "Now, get inside!"

The sky exploding with the familiar thunder of supersonic flight made Perry gasp. Her brain suddenly jumped into tactical mode and she knew what the aggressors intended to do.

"Hit the deck!" she screamed hoping her voice would carry over the Alert Bird's engines roaring. She grabbed Wolff by the harness of his G-suit shoving him face down into the non-skid and letting him lie there breathing in the burned rubber odor of the deck surface. She threw herself on top of him to keep him safe in case the shit started flying.

The three jets rocketed over them, the roar of their engines deafening to Perry and Wolff, who were not wearing the protective headgear that all the crew on the deck did. Perry looked up in time to see the bellies of the trio as they passed overhead and she was surprised by how their midnight colored hulls reflected the light. They sparkled like black diamonds sending glints and glimmers of rainbowed light shooting all around them like technicolor fireworks. She wasn't sure if the effect was caused by something the bogeys dropped on them or if it was how the material the aircrafts were made of reflected and refracted the intense tropical sun.

Perry heard first and saw second what the concussion, caused by the supersonic pass, had done to the island. She averted her face in the nick of time to avoid having it struck full force by the shower of glass that rained down onto the flight deck fouling the starboard section of the runway. A sharp pain lancing through the back of her head, and needle-like prickling sensations around her ear and neck, made her wince. She knew she'd been cut by the fallout from above. Her pain was as swiftly forgotten as it was incurred when the Tomcat that had been revving up on the bow catapult captured her full attention. It was shot skyward the moment the intruders were no longer immediately overhead. Perry watched as it made a swift ascent and veered off in pursuit of the fast-moving trio. The second F-14 was shot seconds later from the waist catapult and it, too, pursued the three unmarked jets.

She rose carefully to her feet. Slivers of glass ranging from the size of dust particles to hand sized slivers rained off her flight suit. She tried to avoid having any of them fall on Martin Wolff, who slowly turned over onto his side and sat up rubbing his head. He'd always though the flight deck was just a major highway transplanted into the middle of the ocean, but found after meeting it face to face that it was actually made of solid steel covered with a grooved rubber-like material. No wonder his introduction to it hurt so much; He might as well been slammed into a corrugated bulkhead.

"Jeezus, I think my ears have died and my head's gone to mush," he muttered. He looked up at Perry, whose eyes were scanning the skies where the intruders had flown and her people had followed. His mouth dropped in shock at the sight of blood covering the left side of her head. "Commander, you're bleeding!"

"Yeah, I know, it's okay," she responded absently not bothering to meet his gaze. "You better get inside. This deck has to be purged fast. We weren't the only ones flyin' today. I've got some boys still up there who want to come home."

She looked a mess but she didn't appear to be bothered by her injuries so it was hard for him to tell if she had just scratches or something to be worried about. Sighing, Martin pulled himself to his feet glad he still had on the fireproof gloves he'd been required to wear during his hop in the Super Tomcat. Glass slivers as sharp as razor blades were everywhere and he shook off the few bits that hit him in the spots Perry's physical barricade didn't cover while trying to get a bearing on what just happened. He looked up and saw the empty window casings surrounding the bridge and Pri-Fly and his eyes widened in surprise.

"What a mess!" he stated softly squinting hard to see past the sun's intense glare. "I hope the guys up there are okay."

Perry looked up and saw the disaster. "Oh my God," she breathed. She said a quick silent prayer for the Captain and his XO, Mr. PiÒo to be unhurt. If they were both out of commission, as next senior officer, she would have to step in and take command of the ship. "I'm going to the bridge. You get to your quarters and stay there, understand?"

She was off and running before Martin had a chance to reply or argue.

Inside the situation was chaotic. The Marines stationed aboard the *Excalibur* were manning the carrier's guns and taking up defensive postures inside the shattered tower. Perry disdained the elevator in favor of the stairs; It was always faster for her. It was a long climb to Pri-Fly and the bridge but, unlike many others in her command, she could do the trek two steps at a time and stride into the Boss's domain looking like she'd done nothing more than walk across the room. But, traffic using the stairwell was just as heavy as that using the elevator. She had to cling close to the wall to get up past the corpsmen who were running up at full speed carrying medical supplies, litters and emergency shielding to temporarily replace the ruined windows.

As she took advantage of a break in the traffic flow, her mind was racing ahead, preparing for the worst, and not on where her feet were going. She missed a step during her two at a time climb. Perry fell and fell hard smacking the side of her head smartly against the bulkhead. Colorful lights danced before her eyes for a few moments and she lay there staring dazedly up at the stairs.

"Corpsman, get over here!" she heard a familiar voice command and she tried to focus in on the face. Someone was gently helping her into a sitting position on the step. "Are you all right?"

Through the haziness she caught Wolff's concerned gaze and tried to force the cobwebs to clear. One of the many corpsmen called in to handle the casualties answered Wolff's summons and took the reporter's place by the Commander's side. He held her by the arm and forced her to stand still long enough for him to inspect her wounded head. When he brought out a penlight to check her eyes for signs of a concussion or worse, she turned away and tried to stand.

"You'd better get to sickbay, Commander," he advised keeping her seated. Wolff helped him detain her so he could finish his examination. He knew he really shouldn't let her run off but he was also aware he lacked the authority to order her to go to the hospital, which was where he thought she belonged. "You're going to need some stitches to close that gash on the back of your head."

"I'll go after I see the Captain," she said as her vision cleared. Her eyes once again were full of their usual steely determination. "Patch me up so I can have some time up there."

He quickly applied a pressure dressing to hold closed the long cut that still oozed blood even though the bandage held its cleanly sliced edges together. The moment he was satisfied she wasn't going to be bleeding her life away, he said, "That bandage isn't for long-term, Commander. Get down to sickbay as soon as you can."

Perry nodded and rose saying sternly to Wolff, "Don't follow me. You'll only be in the way."

"But—"

Perry interrupted him stating hurriedly, "You want to see the Wing in action? Fine. Go to the CIC and observe. Just don't get underfoot. Understand?"

She was again bounding up the stairs taking them two at a time long before he had the chance to acknowledge her instructions.

Perry hit the bridge looking both concerned and a little out of breath. The carrier's executive officer, Captain Jesus Pilo, stopped her at the entrance. He knew exactly why she was there but was peeved because he thought she should've checked their status via the phone lines and not come there in person. His dark eyes flashed through the lenses of his wire-rimmed bifocals and he stated sharply, "What the hell are *you* doing up here when we've got two Alert Fives in the air?"

"How's the Captain?"

"He'll live. Now, get your butt to the CIC and make sure we get those bastards!"

Perry took a quick glance past PiÒo and saw the ship's Chief Medical Officer tending to the Captain. The skipper was lying on a stretcher and talking quietly to his staff people while the doctor worked on his slashed body. She could see he had a particularly nasty cut on the side of his face and his expression looked pained. He caught her concerned gaze and smiled weakly at her motioning to her to leave, since he had heard what his exec had commanded.

Biting her lip anxiously, Perry spun on her heel and left.

For once Wolff didn't mind following the Commander's orders. He was glad he had dogged her trail even though she had initially commanded him to go to his quarters. He knew she was just concerned for his safety but his place was in the thick of it. He was assigned to cover the Air Wing. Now that there was a real emergency for them to handle, Wolff was determined to be there in the thick of it. Relating how they coped with their current situation would make great copy for his book.

He managed to slip unnoticed through the passageways and silently entered the CIC. As per the McNeil's wishes, he stayed in the background careful not to disturb anyone, especially Commander Beaumont, who, unfortunately, was one of those few people in the Air Wing not delighted to have the press along for the cruise.

Beaumont, who was watching the Alert Birds on the ship's radar, talked to them through a headset he wore over his thinning sandy hair. He could see his two Tomcats on the screen but what they were following did not appear at all though, according to his two pilots, they were within visual range of the three bogeys. Stealth technology was not Big Daddy Beaumont's field of expertise. What he did know of it made him convinced that, whoever was responsible for sending those three birds to buzz the boat, their opponent had access to some pretty state of the art equipment.

"Can't get a lock on these gomers," Wolff heard Boomer state, the frustration evident in his voice. "As far as our equipment is concerned, we're up here fighting ghosts!"

"You'll have to get in tight and do it with your eyes and judgement, kid," Beaumont told him. "If you've got to, get on his ass and nail him with the guns."

"Roger," came the uncertain reply.

Wolff slunk further into the shadows when he saw McNeil enter the room and take the headset proffered by the communications officer. She took a fast look at the radar screen and assessed the situation in a heartbeat. "That's how the bastards got in without being seen. They're stealth fighters."

"That explains how they beat the radar our eyes in the skies carry. How come no one we had flying or down here in the CIC saw them coming? We had enough eyes on the sky today that *somebody* in the battle group should have spotted 'em!"

"Not so. They can see us and avoid us, which is why no one saw them until we *saw* them," she told him quickly before refocusing her attention back on to the pursuit and asking, "Boomer, how far are you from those gomers?"

"In missile range, CAG. But we're closing."

"Good. See if you can nail him with a Sidewinder. If they've got something going to beat the heat, then you'll have no choice but to gun him down at point blank range. I know that'll be tricky, but we gotta get these guys!"

"Roger. Will do," Boomer stated and sighed.

He knew to guarantee beating the flares his enemy would probably drop to elude the Sidewinder, he would have to get in tighter than the barest minimum safety distance for a missile shot, then make his attack, and, hopefully, break away before the missile connected. If he timed it incorrectly, then, he, too, could wind up getting fried should he make contact with the fireball his enemy would become provided he was able to score a direct hit on the black jet's engines. If the missile failed, then he would resort to the guns. The young flier knew he wasn't an old fashioned down and dirty dogfighter like the CAG but, if the situation demanded it, then he was ready to give it his best shot.

Radar was well aware of what his friend intended to do to make his strike successful. "I've got a bad feeling about this," was all the young RIO said.

13 December 1330

"The Alert Fifteen birds are standing by," came the word from Pri-Fly. Perry recognized the voice. It was Commander Gastineau, the assistant Primary Air Controller, or mini Boss. He sounded a bit frazzled. Considering what had just happened, Perry was thankful Gastineau managed to escape being creamed and was together enough to keep the flight deck operational.

"Get 'em flying," Perry said. "We got two nuggets up there, so we've got balls. Now, what's needed are some brains. Who's driving the eighteens?"

"Sparky and Anzac."

Her deputy wasn't on the schedule to man the Alert Birds. She got on line to the Hornet standing by on the bow catapult and asked, " 'Zac, what are you doing?"

"Waiting for the green light," he replied sounding very happy to be where he was. "Last minute substitution, CAG. It's okay. I cleared it with the skipper. Besides, you've been on me to keep up my hours on the Hornet. Something about me getting lazy and spoiled by constantly being chauffeured around the skies by you. So, here I am. Doing my own goddamn flyin'!"

"Just be careful, will you? It's not like I can get another deputy at the drop of a hat. I need you in one piece," she told him sounding more like a concerned parent than a commanding officer. Her tone drew a few curious glances from the CIC officers but Big Daddy cast an understanding eye on her.

Perry smiled when Anzac got the green light for launch. For a fleeting instant, a loud raucous war whoop filled her ears and the ears of everyone else in the room who had a headset on. She knew 'Zac only did that during a cat shot when he was behind the stick because, in his words, it "intensified the sensation" of the steam driven dash down the deck. He enjoyed flying just as much as she did, but Perry was worried because he was behind in his hours on the Hornet. He was due to requalify to even be able to do hops off the carrier in the F-18 in the first place. Anzac was a fine pilot but she knew from her personal experience if you haven't been driving a particular jet for a while, it takes a little time to get back into the groove.

The skipper of the VFA-36, the Killer Bees, snagged herself a headset and joined Perry and Big Daddy by the radarman's station. Commander Tamar "Gypsy" Lindsay looked as though she'd just been roused from her bunk and cast a bleary-eyed glance at the scope. "Damn! Don't tell me we lost those gomers!"

"No, we've still got them," Perry said. "They just don't show on the radar."

"Killer Three-Oh-Five and Three-Ten are going supersonic. We'll intercept in fifteen seconds," Anzac informed the three tacticians hovering by the radar station.

"Roger, Three-Oh-Five," Perry acknowledged. She sighed deeply and cast a sideways glance at the slim black woman. "Cats have dragged in things looking better than you, Gypsy. What happened?"

"Night Ops," was her tired response. "My biorhythms are so screwed up it's not funny. I don't know how you can go from day to night and back again like a pendulum and not feel it."

"It's easy when you never sleep," Big Daddy said almost accusingly.

"I sleep," Perry said giving him a dirty look. "Not very much or very often, but I *do* sleep."

"What's Anzac doing up there?" Tamar asked. "Godot was supposed to be on that bird."

"He said he—shit!" Perry fumed and inwardly growled at Anzac, who she intended to gnaw on seriously the moment he got back to the boat. "Sonofabitch lied to me!" she told Tamar, who ran her fingers through her close cropped Afro before putting on the headset, and the Hornet squadron skipper rolled her eyes in disgust.

"If that boy thinks he's getting away with this shit, he's got another thing coming," Tamar stated. "Goddamn hot dog. Probably thinks he's got you in his pocket and you'll smooth the way with me."

"Fat chance," Perry assured her. "It's into the Cuisinart with that boy when he gets home."

Anzac, with Sparky on his wing, took the HOTAS, the hands-on throttle and stick, integrated aircraft controls and weapons systems, and shoved his bird into Zone 5 full afterburner. Within minutes the duo caught up with the two Tomcats. Once they were in visual range, they eased back on the throttle and quickly moved in to a cover spot. In the distance ahead were the three bandits, still flying as a unit. As he and his wingman took their place as the back-up team, he saw the two F-14Ds moving in to engage the unidentified aircraft.

The second the F-14Ds closed in, the trio of fighters split. The lead plane climbed and his two wingmen veered off one to the left and the other right forcing their attackers to separate and choose opponents for a one on one battle. This is becoming a furball, thought Anzac as he heard Boomer announce he was taking the leader. His wingman was going after the bogey who'd peeled off to the right.

"I'll catch this guy," Anzac announced his intent to follow the remaining bogey over the tactical frequency. He made a deft wingover initiating his pursuit.

"And I'll skin him and grill him," japed Sparky as he followed close behind Anzac who had the lead Hornet.

Perry peered over the shoulder of the radarman and watched the four planes as they danced around the scope. Anyone unaware of their situation would think her boys were out there chasing phantoms, she mused. Nothing could be farther from the truth. She worried her lower lip while pondering strategy. All they could do would be to nail them with the heat seekers or guns; nothing radar driven would work against these gomers.

"You've got to splash at least one of these guys," Perry told all the Alert Birds. "We've got to find out what they're made of and whose birds they are!"

"We're workin' on it, CAG," Marc "Eggroll" Wu, the pilot of the second Alert Five Tomcat, told her. "We've got some talent here. This guy I'm on is one sly fox. Thinks I'm afraid of the water. Watch me make him take a bath!"

"Watch your altitude, Eggroll! *You* might wind up getting wet if you're not careful! Don't go below seventy-five feet, no matter what that gomer does."

"Aye, aye."

"Boomer, you go any higher, son, and you'll be in orbit!" Big Daddy scolded.

"My bird isn't the only one that's got a ceiling, sir," the young flyer responded. "He thinks he can scare me off. Well, he's wrong! Two more seconds and he's going to get the hot flash of a lifetime!"

"Two more seconds and you could find yourself reaching for the loud handle! Descend now!" Perry ordered.

"He just passed over sixty-five thousand feet," a crewman monitoring the combat told her. "He'll break up if he keeps going on this high G power climb."

"Boomer, you stupid—"

The sound of an explosion interrupted her and she held her breath. She hoped the daring nugget hadn't pushed that Tomcat past the breaking point. Suddenly, she

heard a familiar voice proclaim proudly, "Yiii-haaa! Two down and three more to go 'til acedom!"

"Get your ass to Angel's thirteen now, Boomer!" Perry fumed, annoyed by his disobedience but inwardly pleased he managed to crisp the bandit. Down at thirteen thousand feet he would be able to maneuver in and intercept the second bogey. In a calmer voice she continued, "Your job's not over yet. Eggroll's in a knife fight with his bogey and they are ascending as we speak." She gave him his wingman's location and asked, "Think anything survived the shot?"

"I didn't see a chute," Boomer told her. "As far as the jet itself goes, I don't know. Whatever fragments there are will be spread over a really wide berth. Recovering anything useful may be tough."

"It's worth a shot. Give me the coordinates. We'll get a helo out there to scan the area."

"Roger. Will do."

He radioed the requested information on the kill and they were quickly forwarded to the helicopter, which had gone airborne shortly after the Alert Fifteen birds took wing. Perry always made sure there was an Alert search and rescue helo flying, just in case something went wrong. She knew from experience it was always better to play it safe. Now, instead of fishing downed aviators out of the sea, the Davey Jones, the name by which the members of the HS-14 helicopter squadron were known, would be scanning for debris in the waning light of day. Perry knew it would be like looking for a needle in a haystack but they had to try. They needed to find something, anything to give them a clue as to what they were up against.

Anzac sighed deeply and checked his airspeed. Their adversary went supersonic and he and Sparky had to follow suit to keep on his tail. Their opponent was no novice and managed quite handily to stay either just out of range of their guns. He would jink and unload flares keeping him out of harm's way whenever Anzac or Sparky thought they had him dead in their sights for a missile shot. The two Hornet pilots were beginning to get a little frustrated. Things seemed to be going from bad to worse when they saw their pursuit of the ebony jet was leading them towards a squall line.

The billowing cumulus layer looked like a mountain of grey-black cotton, and there were flashes sparked at various points along the weather front. With nothing more than visuals to go on, Anzac knew they could easily lose their quarry in the clouds. We'll have to nail him now, thought Anzac. The minute we lose visuals, it's all over.

"'Zac, this is embarrassing," griped Sparky. "This guy is making us look like a couple of amateurs. Once we hit that front, this gomer's a goner for sure."

"I know," Anzac agreed. "I think it's time to get radical. I don't know what he's expecting, but I doubt having us crawling up his tailpipe is tops on his list. Time for maximum warp, Sparky. Time for a Blonde Death strike."

"Roger that, 'Zac."

Simultaneously, Anzac and Sparky split out of combat formation and into a parallel side by side pattern while accelerating to Mach 2. They had worked out several attack strategies in their years of flying together. The maximum thrust, converge and kill pattern they called "Blonde Death" because both of them were fair-haired. Their Hornets also dished out one helluva nasty sting. It had been proven to work quite well in the past. The two fighters made their move and were in range to deal out their killing blow just as they hit the clouds. Both Sparky and Anzac fired their missiles as the mist washed over them obscuring visibility nearly completely. They hoped the fighter didn't jink again and, once more, elude their best offensive maneuver.

They waited to hear the explosion. Seeing anything through the dense cover would be difficult at best, but there was nothing but silence. After a brief pause of flying through the rain with nothing except the thundering of Mother Nature and their aircraft to listen to, Sparky said quietly, "We've done all we could, 'Zac. Let's go home."

"Must be a goddamn conspiracy!" Eggroll Wu told Boomer via Tactical, the Renegade's particular radio frequency, as he lost his bogey to the tropical storm. "Guy must've known I had him dead to rights when he ducked into that cloud! I'm never going to ace myself at the rate I'm going."

"Relax, Egg. Just because I've been real lucky—"

"Boomer, that's the biggest understatement of the millennia!" Wu interrupted as he performed a deft wingover and started his landing descent. "You did a complete about face, kiddo. Folks were real worried about you for a while there. I don't know what the CAG and the Skipper said to you but, whatever it was, you heard that pop as your head came outta your ass."

"The Skipper had me for dinner," Boomer told him sounding none too pleased by the memory of that event. He sighed, adding, "And then the CAG munched on what was left for dessert."

"Snap, crackle, pop," joked Wu and he laughed when he heard Boomer groan.

Changing the subject quickly, Boomer asked, "Where do you think those gomers came from?"

"Beats the hell out of me," his wingman replied. "We're within range of a few islands, including Cuba."

"You think those birds are Cuban?"

"I don't know. I know they used to get their hardware from the Soviet Union, but Castro had never rated anything better than the Flogger or the Fishbed. I'm sure they've got other stuff, but nothing of *this* caliber."

"Yeah, well, I can't see how any of the little two-bit banana republics could be behind something like this," Boomer stated. "Shit, *we* don't even have stuff that can beat *all* our instruments. This project reeks of major money and the kind of cutting edge technology only a handful of countries have. They're not ours. If those aren't Russians, then whose—"

"I think you'd better keep your speculations to yourself, Boomer," Wu broke in. "Or, at least, don't go expounding them to everyone in the wardroom."

"I don't intend to," Boomer assured him. "The only person who'd care to know what I think, or is in a position to act on any likely leads, is the CAG. She's the only one I'd tell. That is, if she'll give me the chance."

"After the stunt you pulled last week? You'll be lucky if she gives you the time of day," stated Wu, who had been around to witness the practical joke Boomer had played on Perry.

"It wasn't easy rigging that raft to inflate the second she opened her office door," Boomer said with a chuckle. "And convincing Radar to be the one to snap the Polaroid of her face when she saw that sucker filling the room was even tougher. She wouldn't have known I did it if Radar had ejected before that raft had the chance to trap him in the room. Poor guy was stuck taking the initial heat for my gag."

"Good thing the CAG's got a sense of humor," Wu said. "And,

you'd better be careful. She might be plotting something really evil to even the score."

Boomer cracked up. "I sure hope so. I'm looking forward to seeing what sort of revenge she has in mind for me."

Radar sighed. Practical jokes kept things from getting too tense. Especially when there was a long gap in time between liberty ports. But pulling a gag on a senior officer was risky business. If it backfired, it could do major damage to your career or, if the person was really angry, it could do major damage to your body as well.

Over the ICS, Radar said, "Boomer, you have to admit, the raft gag was *not* one of your better ideas. When she found out it was you, the CAG almost introduced you to a bulkhead. One would think you'd learned your lesson."

"I did," Boomer insisted. "I learned I've got to be a whole lot more inventive."

"I don't know who's more hazardous to my health," Radar moaned. "Those strange jets or you."

13 December 1500

Perry McNeil stood in the thick of the crowd on the LSO platform and adjusted her headset's lip mike while she watched Renegade Two Oh Two glide in to a perfect three wire trap. The LSO for the VF-69 turned to her remarking, "He keeps going at this rate, that kid'll be number one before this cruise is over."

Perry smiled. "If I let him live that long," she quipped back.

The LSO laughed. After his shaky start, Boomer's 180° turnaround in both his performance as a pilot and attitude towards the CAG surprised everyone. Especially Perry, who had visions of spending her entire cruise trying to pound some sense into his thick skull. After she verbally boxed his ears for his aerial misdeeds, Boomer caught her a little off-guard by apologizing to her for his poor attitude. He felt lousy for having behaved so badly towards the one person on the ship who cared enough about him to risk their neck to save his ass. He did not leave her office until he was sure he had made his peace with her.

It wasn't long after that fateful night that Boomer began to gain a reputation for something else besides skillful aerodynamics. He got off on pulling shenanigans that really pushed the envelope. Boomer got away with a few stunts, that would've put anyone else in the squadron in hack, simply because someone higher up on the totem pole than the subject of the joke thought the gag amusing enough to insist it not earn the young flyer a reprimand. He'd even been bold enough to try and put one over on the CAG, who had always been one to enjoy a good jest. Not liking to be one upped, especially be a junior officer, it was rumored around the Air Wing that Perry had been carefully plotting her revenge.

But, whatever was in that devious mind had no doubt been shoved onto the back burner. The time for off-duty pranks was over. The *Excalibur* battle group was locked and loaded and ready for anything. The air wing would be flying round the clock until the order came through for them to stand down. The Renegade's LSO looked on while his colleague, the LSO for the VFA-36, the Killer Bees, took center stage to guide in the two returning Hornets.

Even with her sunglasses on Perry had to squint to see the F-18 coming in from the west. The storm front that had enabled their enemy to elude them was coming in from the northeast. The waning light of day was soon to be totally enveloped in the blackness of the swiftly moving thunderheads.

"Bad day for a bear hunt, huh, 'Zac," Perry remarked.

"That's if they were even bears," came his disgruntled reply. "Not all MiG drivers are Ivans, CAG, and I'm not so sure those things even *are* MiGs."

"True," she agreed. "But, even so, José would have to sell a jungle full of bananas and sugar to be able to afford even one of those birds."

"True, but a couple of drifts of snow and ice could net him all three no sweat."

Perry made no reply. The thought those three planes could belong to some very well heeled drug smugglers occurred to her long before Anzac's hint. It seemed so unlikely, since the Soviets were as anti-drug as their Western counterparts, but not impossible. She doubted Moscow would allow any of their planes to get into the hands of the cartels, no matter how many rubles they were offered. Even so, with no leads of any value to go on, Perry had to consider even the most far-fetched ideas until something more concrete to work with became available.

The Killer Bees LSO's talker called out, "Three Oh Three, all down, clear deck. Clear deck!"

Perry listened as the voice of the CCA controller. He was watching the approach in profile and in plain view on his radar scope, as his words were heard by not only her but the Air Boss, the LSO, as well as most importantly, it was heard by the man behind the stick of the incoming Hornet. "Three Oh Three on line very slightly left, three-quarter-mile, call the ball."

She smiled slightly when she heard Anzac announce, "Three Oh Three, Ball, four point four." So far he had everything under control.

The LSO saw the Hornet coming in. He could hear the thunder of its engines as they easily drowned out Mother Nature's own rumblings and watched for the trap. It looked good almost until the plane was down, but Anzac was coming in too sharply and was waved off at the last moment. The Hornet's wheels touched the deck for a split second before thundering off back toward the clouds. She heard Anzac cursing under his breath over the radio.

"Attitude, 'Zac," Perry said, the word choice appropriate because it encompassed both what he was doing wrong with the plane as well as within himself. "Loosen up a bit, okay? We all know you're out of practice but we'll discuss *that* after you land."

Sparky's F-18 was next to approach but was hard to see because he had forgotten to activate the anticollision lights. "Three One One, check external lights on please,"
the LSO said.
Suddenly the red and green wingtip lights appeared. "Sorry, guys," Sparky said a little embarrassed at having forgotten something so basic.
"Okay, Three One One. All down, clear deck. Clear deck!"
The CCA controller was back on line again calling Sparky's approach. Perry was only half listening to the familiar chatter while she scanned the clouds for her Deputy's plane, circling to make another approach. The grey plane would've been invisible against the angry sky if not for the red and green antismash lights. She hoped he'd trap on his next attempt. If he boltered again, he'd be flying in the incoming storm and having to trap on a wet and possibly even slick deck.
"Come on, 'Zac. Get that bee back to the hive," she said quietly to herself as she turned in time to see Sparky's bird glide in for a passable four-wire landing.

Anzac's F-18 bounced erratically in the turbulence kicked up by the tropical storm. Rain pummeled against the canopy and windscreen but was quickly swept away because of his speed. He knew that once he decelerated to approach velocity he would have to be concerned about seeing through the rain. He toggled the bleed air switch to make sure, when he slowed to landing speed, the air would keep his screen clear. He cursed under his breath when he saw it wasn't working. He checked the circuit breaker. It was in and seemed okay, so the problem lay elsewhere. No bleed air meant landing would be a royal pain in the ass, even with the ACLS to aid him.
The ACLS! He quickly activated it and sighed with relief when he saw it was functioning. "Three Oh Three is on the glide path, on centerline" the LSO informed him.
"The bleed air isn't working," Anzac said. "If the ACLS kicks out, I'm going to be in deep shit."
"Relax, Three Oh Three. Everything is on track."
Anzac pulled off his mask and wiped his sweaty face with his free hand. His other one was busy, its fingertips lightly on top of the throttles. Feeling their reactions as they moved in response to the commands sent to them by the ship's computer. With the ACLS coupled to the Hornet's autopilot, the F-18's computer would

instruct the plane's autopilot where the plane was in relation to the glidescope and centerline. The autopilot could fly the bird down all the way to the deck.

He looked at the crosshairs display on the ADI in front of him and saw he was exactly on speed. The angle-of-attack needle was frozen in the three-o'clock position. He was coming down in the first calm pocket he'd found in the storm and he hoped it would last until he was safely down on the deck.

A blinding flash of lightning startled him, and he felt the Hornet bounce violently in response to both being struck by nature's fury. Anzac blinked his eyes trying to get rid of the spots clouding his vision, and he gasped in panic. The crosshairs from the ADI were gone and the autopilot had dropped off line. He tried to restore the connection but it was to no avail: the lightning had fried something in the system and now he was forced to land the plane himself.

"Oh, shit!" he swore to himself. Over the radio he said in as calm a voice as he could muster under the circumstances, "I've been hit by lightning. The ACLS is gone and I can't see a goddamn thing!"

Through the sheet of water Perry saw Anzac's Hornet approaching. He was high and fast and, without the bleed air to clear his windscreen, he was literally flying blind. His wings were level but his attitude was bad; If he didn't pick it up he would slam nose first onto the deck possibly destroying the plane and part of the deck in the process.

"Anzac, get the nose up!" she ordered. "And cut your speed. You're too fast."

She watched for a few anxious moments worrying her lip as she waited for him to execute her command. His angle of attack improved, and it looked like he was decelerating, but he was still coming in too high. When he connected with the deck, he slammed down almost vertically putting the entire weight and force of his landing on the rear landing gears. The right wheel buckled under the strain and collapsed just as the arresting hook tagged the third wire. The gears below deck sprang into action performing their job of absorbing the millions of foot pounds of kinetic energy. Sparks flew from the right wing as it skidded along the deck for the few brief seconds it took the arresting gear to stop the movement of the Hornet. When the bird finally came to rest, it looked almost forlorn. It lay there soggy and bent over to the right resting on its scraped up wing.

The silver suited fire and rescue crew were the first to get to the damaged jet. They swiftly sprayed the right wing with foam as a precautionary measure and the red shirted damage control team were hot on their heels. One of the rescue workers quickly extricated Anzac from the cockpit. Once he assured them he was okay, they waved off the medical team that was standing by just in case. Anzac yanked off his helmet allowing the rain to bath clean his perspiration stained face and headed over to the castle.

He saw Perry standing there with arms akimbo and a look of pure murder in her eyes. She had left the LSO platform the moment she saw the damage control crew had secured the jet and it was apparent Anzac was okay. There was no one near the island and that was all Perry needed to insure she had the freedom to speak her mind the moment her Number Two made it over to where she stood waiting.

He sauntered over to her and said in his best good ol' country boy drawl, "Any landing you can walk away from—"

He never saw the backhanded smack that landed him rump first on the deck, but the pain shooting from his jaw told him he'd been hit and hit hard. "You fool," she began in glacial tones. "There are times I'm convinced you don't have the smarts to load a gnat up to max gross weight. Did you really think you could pull this shit off?"

Anzac stared up at her dumfounded. She'd flattened him before but he'd always seen it coming. This time she caught him completely by surprise, and it took him a long moment before he realized why she was so pissed off. "Well, I thought those nuggets in the Alert Fives could use some seasoned backup, Perry. Sparky and I used to fly together all the time last cruise. I didn't think Gypsy would mind—"

"You're right, you didn't think!" she interrupted speaking in a hushed tone, her anger at him still readily apparent though she addressed him *sotto voce*. "You had no business taking that aircraft without Tamar's okay. On top of that, you're out of practice on that bird. But that isn't why I'm seeing red, mister. I can handle gung ho just fine, thank you very much. But what I *won't* put up with is being lied to. *That's* why your butt's on that deck. And why your ass would be in hack if I didn't need you so goddamn much."

He slowly got to his feet licking away the blood oozing from the corner of his mouth. "Sorry, Perry," he said quietly. "It won't happen again."

"Sure as hell better not if you value your life," she fumed.

The door opened and a couple of crewmen, who'd been summoned from below to help work on the downed Hornet, came out on deck. They looked a bit surprised to find her glowering and Anzac looking like he'd had the stuffing knocked out of him. They didn't get the chance to look long. Perry, her eyes still flashing and anger unabated, turned on them like a cornered viper, "Don't just stand there gawking! Get that bird off the deck *now*! Move!"

Startled into mobility, the pair swiftly departed to attend to their assigned task leaving the Air Wing Commander and her deputy standing alone together on the deck in the steady downpour. Perry yanked off the cranial and sighed deeply. The cold rain drumming on her head stung in places but, for the most part, it felt good. It worked quite well to cool her emotions as it cooled off her overheated body.

The moment she felt calm enough to speak to him, without sounding as though she was about to separate his head from his neck, she said, "God, 'Zac, your timing really sucks, you know that?"

He shrugged. "Yeah, but it sure felt great to be in the driver's seat. It was almost worth it." She shot him a hard look. "I did say *almost*," he qualified quickly. Her expression softened somewhat and he continued, "Look, I know Gypsy probably thinks you'll let me get away with this because we're buddies. I understand you'll have to do *something* to me to make sure she won't go off thinkin' the CAG plays favorites."

"Damn right I'm going to do something," she stated her eyes stony again. "But I'm not the only one who's going to be getting a piece of you, mister. After your debriefing, you have a date with the Old Gentleman and the Skipper, so I suggest you get yourself looking sharp ASAP."

Anzac rolled his eyes and sighed. He had not done much during his Navy career to garner a dressing down. He had, however, tagged along on enough of Perry's youthful escapades to have gotten a bit tanned by the heat she'd fired up. Now it was *his* turn to feel the flames. But, any punishment he was to receive for his misdeed would come from his CO—Perry. And, considering his actions had resulted in one bird being downed during an alert, he knew he was destined to become an integral part of the flight deck for this fuck up.

"Since you're so hot to get back into the cockpit, you're going to be doing a lot of flying," she informed him. "You are going to requalify on the Hornet and fly as a part of Tamar's squadron until she's had her fill of you."

"But what about—"

"Oh, you'll still be taking hops with me. After Tamar and I are finished with you, you'll either be the best Hornet driver and Tomcatter RIO on the boat or you'll be wishing you were! Maybe, *maybe*, after all this is said and done we'll forgive you for acting like you just rolled in with the latest bunch of boys from the RAG."

Anzac groaned. Not that he minded all the flying he was bound to be doing. But he was certain that Perry expected him to keep up with all his ground duties as well. The only free time he could expect until Gypsy and Perry were satisfied he'd done his penance would be what he needed to eat and sleep. This was not going to be an enjoyable sentence. He had a feeling he would wind up wishing he had been put in hack by the time all this was over. It would've been a lot less painful.

"Tamar's going to kill me for trashing her bird," Anzac said. "And it wasn't my fault! I lost the ACLS to the storm, and you know manual landing is nearly next to impossible without the bleed air working. I couldn't see jack!"

"Of course you realize she's going to point out the small fact that you had no business being in that plane in the first place," Perry told him.

"I know," he agreed. "But could you do me a teeny tiny favor and back up verbally everything that's going to be in my report? I don't feel like having my head handed to me for smashing a malfunctioning jet."

She caught the pleading look in those puppy dog eyes and sighed. Perry hated to admit it but every time he'd look at her that way she found herself unable to say no. Anzac managed to wheedle more favors out of her than either of her two husbands. There were times she was convinced this man was a demon in human form. He seemed to have a knack for bringing out both the best and worst in her and on days like this. Again she found herself asking the same question her daughter had asked her on numerous occasions. How come she never tried to hook this fish when she had the chance? Because one of us would be in Leavenworth pounding rocks for life, that's why, she reminded herself. She grabbed his left shoulder harness in her free hand and led him by it into the castle. He allowed himself to be dragged like a mischievous schoolboy on his way to the principal's office and shrugged sheepishly when he caught a few crewmen casting curious eyes in his direction.

Once inside out of the rain she released him saying, "Get out of that wet gear and to your debriefing. I'll track down Gypsy and convince her sparing your life would be a good idea under the circumstances. A couple of her boys were observing up in Pri-Fly when the fertilizer hit the fan and they've been grounded for the next seventy-two hours."

"Was anyone killed in that attack?"

"No one bought it, but thirty-five people were wounded, eleven of them seriously. Both Captain Graff and the Boss took major damage. They're still cleaning up in the bridge and Pri-Fly. It's a mess. I've got to get to the Flag office by sixteen-thirty for an emergency meeting with the Old Gentleman and what senior staff are up and about. The Skipper and Jonesy will be expecting you about a half hour earlier, kapish?" He nodded and Perry paused by the steps. Not certain why she suddenly lacked the energy to make her usual dash upstairs, Perry shook her head baffled and pressed the up button on the elevator instead. She sighed, rubbing her eyes and continued, "At twenty-hundred there's an Air Wing meeting in the hangar deck. It's everyone and I'm holding it down there because it's officially unofficial, if you know what I mean."

"Gotcha," he nodded comprehendingly and, noticing the bandage wrapped around her head was bloodsoaked, asked, "What happened to you, Stormy?"

She gave him a half-hearted smile saying, "I was on deck when those birds hit and got cut by some flying glass. Corpsman patched me up so I'll live."

"That dressing needs changing. You should get to sickbay."

"I know," she replied. "I'll go after I take care of business." He was about to give her an argument when the elevator door opened and both of them had to step aside to let its three occupants exit. She stepped inside saying in as cheerful a tone as she could muster, "Don't worry about me, I'm fine. And, if you run into Tamar before I do, just remember one thing."

"What's that?"

"How to duck!"

Anzac was still laughing even after the elevator swallowed her up.

13 December 1930

Wolff watched the *Excalibur's* senior staffers as they filed out of the Flag office to resume their duties. A few of them acknowledged his presence, including Anzac who said a quick hello as he passed by. The majority filed past him silently, the grim set to their jaws telling him more than any words they would've said could. He glanced into the room and saw the Admiral, Mr. PiÒo, Perry, Major Vasquez, and Colonel Serric "the Grim" Grimmig. The Colonel was in command of the Marine detachment aboard the *Excalibur* and Vasquez was his executive officer. They all were still inside engaged in conversation. She looked like a drowned rat that just lost one round to an alley cat. Her soaked flight gear hung on her like a wet plastic bag, and she had rolled up the jumpsuit's long sleeves baring her forearms. He noticed she was wearing her pilot's watch with the face on the inside of her wrist. When he looked up at her face, he saw her eyes were glowing like the twin turbines on an F-14 and her voice was as resolute as her expression.

"We got caught with our pants down, Ollie, plain and simple," Wolff heard her say the minute the five of them were left on their own. "This stinks like week old fish."

Wolff noticed the door had been left ajar. The official meeting was over. The quintet who were still left behind were probably just wrapping up some business unrelated to their current crisis, thought Wolff. He was going to wait until the Wing Leader came out. He was hoping she could tell him what was going on.

"G-2 is sending a specialist on stealth technology out here tonight. He should arrive on the COD at about twenty-three-hundred, along with some engineers from Grumman and McDonnell-Douglas. The word is we might, and I emphasize *might*, be able to modify our instruments to pick up these gomers. I wouldn't bet my stars and bars on it," Admiral Jones told her sounding none too pleased with the situation. Wolff knew the man was a Vietnam vet, a participant in Operation Desert Storm, and had also been in on the fun in Lebanon. But being an experienced warrior didn't always mean one liked to make war.

The reporter caught a glimpse of the tactical display set up on the table when he peeked into the room. On the map their position in relation to the islands that could serve as home bases for the mysterious trio of jets had been noted. He saw PiÒo indicating other likely sources because of the *Excalibur's* proximity to the northern tip of South America. They were still discussing the attack. It seemed he was going to get an inkling as to what was happening without having to hit up Commander McNeil.

"Intelligence says there are no carriers in the Gulf but us, so those birds had to be from a land base," he heard PiÒo say. "And we've got to find out where they came from and fast. We only got buzzed this time. Next time they could come back with a full payload."

"I intend to make sure there is no "next time"," Jones stated flatly. "Five miles in every direction around this ship is to be so full of planes a fly can't get through without being seen. The wing is going to be airborne twenty-fours hours a day, seven days a week until we nab these bandits."

"Every bird I have that can fly, will fly," Perry assured him. "And, if those gomers are fool enough to try and attack this ship, mah boys will nail 'em to the wall!"

"Just like at Bekaa Valley, eh, Perry?" he remarked casting a wry grin her way and she returned the expression. He could tell she was keyed up, ready and raring to go by her voice. Perry's Southern drawl only reared its head whenever her emotions got the better of her. He added almost accusingly, "You're enjoying this, aren't you?"

"No, sir," she stated defensively. "I'm just ready to accept the challenge is all." But it was obvious to Jones that she did enjoy it. Perry thrived on the intensity of a combat mission.

Jones wasn't so sure he liked her gung ho attitude, but this wasn't the first time he'd seen her this way. He had been the Captain of the USS *George Washington* when she fought over Bekaa Valley as the skipper of the VF-13, the Grim Reapers. Before that he had been the ship's CAG, on their last cruise together prior to the war. Perry had a reputation aboard the carrier for being both the gutsiest person in the air and the most tactical-minded of the squadron leaders on the boat. Her performance in the battle proved that women in the service had what it took to do the job. Although by the time the action in Lebanon occurred, there were a few women flyers and officers serving on carriers, Perry kicked open wide a door that had been only left ajar. After Bekaa Valley, instead of there being only a handful of females serving as pilots, NFOs, and in support posts on the boat, the ratio dropped to a more respectable ten to one in favor of the boys. The gals still had a way to climb to catch up but the hill ahead of them was a whole lot less steep.

Perry spun around a chair and straddled it, her forearms resting on its back and her eyes still on the map on the table. Indicating the general area they currently occupied with a casual gesture, she asked, "Where do you think those guys came from?"

"Off the record?"

She nodded.

"I think they're Cuban," he told her. "Though I know we don't have the intelligence to back up my hypothesis just yet. They're the only ones in this part of the world who have access to the technology and know the right people, if you get my meaning."

"You could be right. After all, they do have the airfields and the military support structures needed to handle something like this," she concurred, her eyes not leaving the map. "But, I'm not convinced. After all, we did run into some F-4s during this cruise that were suspected to belong to the Medellin drug cartel. If they have the clout to get their paws on some Rhino's, who's to say they're not hiding something even more nasty up their sleeves?"

"True, but black market F-4s are hard enough to come by," Colonel Grimmig pointed out. "Buying stealth via that route? I'm not sure it's possible."

She inclined her head slightly as she pondered his words for a moment. "It's not *impossible*, though. I wouldn't rule out the cartels as a source. After all, our being here in the Gulf is putting the squeeze on their operations."

Grimmig nodded in agreement. As the five of them discussed likely suspects, Wolff leaned back against the bulkhead pondering what he had overheard. Stealth in the hands of the cartels was a scary thought. The same technology in the hands of the Cubans wasn't much better, although Wolff found it rather hard to believe the tiny island nation was about to become the mouse that roared. He had done enough research before embarking on this assignment to know they were up against something completely unexpected. He also knew from doing his homework that a well-planned air assault could take out a carrier. But that didn't answer the question that gnawed at him most. Who was after them? And why?

He heard Jones's deep basso laugh. Peeking into the room he saw the Admiral give Perry's shoulder a friendly shove as he said, "Get out of here. You have a meeting to get to."

She looked up at him puzzled for a moment, then smiled. "It was supposed to be unofficial. Just something to let the guys know what's flyin'."

"They know what's flyin'," Jones countered. "What they want to know is how to keep it from landing on them."

Perry grinned. "Too true," she agreed rising. She hesitated by the chair for a moment. Her eyes looked unfocused and she didn't look as though she was feeling very well. Grimmig caught her by putting a steadying hand under her arm. For a split second, Wolff thought he saw something other than friendly concern in the Colonel's dark eyes. Perry waved him off politely and rubbed her eyes with her fingertips.

"Are you all right?" Jones asked sounding a little apprehensive.

"I'm fine," she replied flashing her usual impish grin. "I'm just a little tired. I think I'll snag myself a cup of joe before I go downstairs."

"I think you should let Bones take a peek at you," the Admiral told her. "You look like hell. We're going to have a long night tonight and I need you to be up to it. Get your butt to sickbay and then get some rest before you drop."

"Is that an order, sir?" she inquired eyes twinkling.

He caught the look he'd seen a hundred times and chuckled shaking his head. "Pain in my ass, McNeil, that's what you are," he japed good-naturedly. She smiled back at him knowing he wasn't saying it completely in fun. She'd always been a bit of a handful. She was never content to just do the job. She had to be aware of anything and everything that could impact on her or the people she was responsible for. Perry's desire to know all she could about Naval aviation was the impetus that enabled her to cross-train at first on the F-14D and then later on the A-6F. This quest for knowledge also extended to carrier operations as well. Half the time Jones paid her a visit while she was off-duty, he caught her with her nose in a report or a technical manual. Perry was die-hard Navy and loved the seafaring life almost as much as she loved flying. This was one thing they shared in common and was one of the reasons he liked her. The other was that any cruise he went on with Perry McNeil always turned out to be anything but dull. His expression sobered as he added, "I mean it, Perry. Take care of *yourself* for once."

Perry sighed. "Yeah, well, after the meeting I'll turn the reigns over to 'Zac, let Bones do his thing, shower, and log a few Zs before the COD arrives. You know I want to be there to see what we'll be getting in the way of expert assistance."

"I'll see you on deck at twenty-two-thirty, Commander. Dress blues."

She nodded. "I'll be there."

He caught her by the arm before she was out the door saying, "Make that meeting a quick one, Commander. I know you're not feeling any pain now, but once that adrenaline rush wears off, you are going to be hurting."

"No kidding. I've been through this sort of thing before. Remember?" she replied her eyes sparkling with their usual impish glint. He knew what she was referring to and smiled slightly, more in response to her devilish look rather than the words she had just spoken. As she headed to the door, she added, "Like I always tell Anzac: relax, you'll live longer."

He chuckled quietly. "You really are too much, Perry." Giving her a stern almost fatherly look he added, "I meant what I said. Take care of your business then make sure you get yourself looked at. I'll catch you around the campus later."

"Aye, aye, sir," she gave him a salute that was more a friendly wave of farewell than the proper protocol gesture. He just rolled his eyes heavenward looking as though he both, wondered why he put up with her and, knew the answer to that very same question.

Perry nearly collided with Martin Wolff when she stepped into the hallway and gave the reporter a hard look. "How long have *you* been standing out here?" she asked suspiciously.

"I just got here," he lied quickly.

"You're full of shit, mister," she stated eyes flashing. "Out with it. Just what do you know that you shouldn't."

"Nothing!" he insisted. "I just came up here to see you. To find out what's going on and who those jets belonged to."

"We don't have the answer to that just yet," she told him. He looked unconvinced. She quickly warned, "Don't you dare go off speculatin' about who's to blame. Because if I hear any odd talk 'round my air wing about this, I will personally tie you to a catapult and shoot you off the deck. You read me, mister?"

"Loud and clear," he replied trying not to let on he was a little worried she might actually make good on her threat. Getting on her bad side was not something Martin had ever wanted to do. He'd heard the life expectancy of anyone she was majorly pissed at was extremely short. Not in the physical sense, but she had made life unpleasant for several of her subordinates. They had thought, incorrectly, that she would be a pushover because she was a woman. Some were still groaning about the extra duty they pulled due to their misjudgment, and word had spread quickly. Perry McNeil did not put up with crap from anybody, her friends included. Not even Anzac, her closest companion, had been allowed the freedom to bend the rules as he saw fit.

"Good," she said her voice still firm but her Southern drawl was less apparent. "You can sit in on my Wing meetin' provided you keep your ears open and your mouth shut. I know there's going to be enough loose talk floatin' around the boat without you addin' to it."

"Relax, Commander. I'm not going to start any unfounded rumors," he stated defensively. "I deal in reality, not fiction."

Perry was treating him as though he were some unruly schoolboy and he didn't like it. He also didn't like the fact he was just a little bit scared of her. What he liked even less was that he was finding fear to be a very potent aphrodisiac. Being turned on by somebody who could kill you with their bare hands was frightening, but exciting in a weird and twisted sort of way. He knew she had to be tough to get as far as she did, but she didn't have to be that way around him. However, he knew he'd have to set her straight or else wind up spending the rest of the cruise with her acting towards him as though her were one of her junior officers. Other than the Navy types who outranked her, Wolff was the one person who regulations wouldn't prevent from pinning the ears back on this Irish wolfhound. He just hoped he would live to tell the tale.

"Look, *Commander*, you have your job to do and I have mine," he told her. "If your Wing goes into battle, I'll be standing behind home plate doing the play by play and keeping score. I have the authorization to cover *all* the Wing's operations including combat, be it simulated or real. You're stuck with me for the duration, so you'd better get used to it."

That got her Irish up. "Look, mister, I'm not stuck with you," she came back sharply, her Southern roots in full evidence. "My Air Wing, maybe, but not *me*. I don't have to put up with you. I'll put your butt on the next COD if you give me cause to. I don't care who you slept with in Washington to pull this assignment. They don't have the authority to keep you here if it can be proven that you've been abusin' your authority by stickin' your nose where it don't belong. Like tactical sessions that *are not* for public consumption. And, believe me, if I catch you listenin' in on any more closed door meetin's, I *will* have you removed."

"If you want a fight, Perry, I'll give you one you won't ever forget," he countered his blue eyes hard as diamonds. "I may not do it for a living, but I'm quite capable of playing the part of a warrior if needed. After all, you can't survive on the streets of New York without learning how to take care of yourself."

Perry snorted and failed to hold back her laughter. "Y'all better watch out, Paper Boy, or I might just take you up on your challenge."

"You're laughing pretty hard when you don't know the joke."

"Oh? How about a date in the gym for the best two out of three falls on the mat."

He relaxed and cracked a smile deep with dimples. "You're on."

She laughed. "You're gonna regret this."

"So may you."

When their eyes met, they both chuckled quietly. "Walk me to the Renegades ready room," she ordered more than requested. Suddenly not minding her bossiness, he shrugged and silently complied with her command.

13 December 2010

Perry entered the ready room where an audience of senior officers and petty officers awaited her. Martin Wolff stayed in the doorway and watched as all rose to attention. Perry was quick to command them to relax and took her place behind the lectern at the front of the room. He stood by listening as she informed them of the impending visit from G-2 and ordered them to conduct safety reviews for their teams. After she outlined what she expected of them, she fielded questions.

A hand shot up toward the back and Perry acknowledged the young crew chief in overalls. He was one of the maintenance crew chiefs, in charge of keeping the Intruders working. He stated, "Some things aren't going to get done at all, Commander, unless Grumman can come up with those parts we ordered. I've got two birds that could be flying if I had the couplings and hoses I requisitioned."

Grumbles of assent rippled through the group. Perry got the impression this was not an isolated incident but a problem all her maintenance people had with their civilian contractors. "Are the other suppliers bein' slow to deliver?" she asked, and many heads nodded. "Shit," she swore under her breath then added aloud, "Look, I'll see what I can do to speed things up." She offered a few suggestions as to what they could do to help get things moving then cautioned, "meanwhile, make sure your people don't resort to cannibalism to keep my birds airborne. I know the temptation is always there when things get desperate but do the best you can. Borrowing from Peter to pay Paul never works in the long run, so don't get started down that dead end street, okay? And I want my skippers to tell their jocks not to even *think* of asking the crew chiefs to get that one little itty bitty part from a downed bird to fix their bird." She paused when she noticed a few hand-caught-in-the-cookie-jar looks on the faces of a few of her execs and skippers and added, "I'm not pointing any fingers here, but I know the boys do it. It'll be up to you to see that they stop. Understand?"

The leaders of the flying teams nodded and she heard a few murmured "Yes, Ma'ams." Satisfied, Perry concluded rising, "Look, when I find out exactly who and what we're up against, I'll let you know. Until then, you'll have to be pep leader, parent, slave driver, whatever it takes to keep your team together and on the job. Like I always say, let's be careful up there, awright?" Smiles lit up the few faces, who had heard her use that tag line before to end her speeches. Perry smiled back adding, "If you can spare the time, I'd like you all to join your crews in the hanger deck. I'm going to be dropping a few pearls of wisdom on them—" she paused as a few chuckles from her friends filled the room "—and Chief Gabriel will be there, too. That is all."

Once they were officially dismissed, the assembled group began filing out. It became apparent to Wolff that most of them were going to be joining them in the hanger for the CAG's State of the Wing Address. Close on Perry's swiftly moving heels, the reporter followed her through the maze of hallways to their next stop on her talking tour.

Anzac was standing by the elevator door when it opened revealing Perry McNeil and Martin Wolff. She was still clad in her damp flight gear. Perry led the way onto the hangar deck and Anzac announced, "Attention on deck," as she entered the vast expanse. The hangar bay held a dozen aircraft and, at that moment, a few hundred men and women as well.

"As you were," she called loudly enough for the natural acoustics, inherent in a room almost an acre large, to allow her voice to be heard by everyone. She was so accustomed to everyone snapping to attention when she entered a room that she usually gave the "as you were" command before she was two steps inside.

There were many smiles and a few nervous greetings from members of the flight deck crew as she walked past. Martin saw first hand something he'd been hearing since he came aboard; Perry was well-liked by both officers and enlisted men. Although she was a tough taskmaster, she never asked any more of her crew than she asked of herself. Which, as Martin Wolff had discovered during his research on the air wing, was quite a lot.

She paused by an A-6F that had a young man in his late twenties straddled with one leg in the Intruder's cockpit and the other on the top step of the ladder. He was playing a guitar and two women, one who stood two steps up the ladder and the other at its base, were keeping harmony with him while he sang:

>*When the jet sits before us like a rocket wrapped in steel,*
>*Then no words in any language can express the way you feel,*
>*Mingled joy and hope and terror as we're starting on our*

way,
And we suddenly considered that it just might help to pray.

So we pray to great green Mother Earth and the grim old gods of space,
The gods of flame and metal whom we've summoned to this place,
All you gods of flight and physics, now, you've got us in your care,
We hope that you will listen to a jet rider's prayer.

First we'll pray to Vulcan, ugly god of forge and flame,
And also wise Minerva now, we glorify your name,
We hope that you will hear us and please find it in your hearts,
To please help these lowest bidders who've constructed all the parts.

Next we'll pray to Mercury, who'll help us in our need,
Not only as the patron god of health and flight and speed,
We hope that he will aid us as we're starting on our trip,
As the god of thieves and liars, like the ones who built this ship.

"Hello Filk," she greeted at the break between verses. "Entertaining the troops again?"

"Just bein' the warmup," he replied grinning. "While everyone's waitin' for the main event."

"Mind if the "main event" joins in for a verse or two?"

"Be an honor, Ma'am."

She smiled at the BN who stepped down from the ladder to allow Perry to take her spot. It was Tyger, Filk's BN and fellow songster. She joined Peanut, a petite blonde who just barely met the Navy's minimum height requirement for pilots, at the ladder's base. Filk and the two women were attached to the VA-49, Sentinels, the wing's A-6F squadron and the one squadron having the most female members. Perry didn't know Peanut that well but she did know Tyger, who served as her BN when she flew with the Intruder squadron. Perry also knew the unit's exec, a free spirit with the innocuous call sign of Bambi, and her BN, another fun-lover tagged Thumper. That dynamic duo had pulled wing duty on a number of occasions.

The gathered company watched with growing curiosity as Perry climbed the ladder to join Filk. She leaned against the side of the cockpit and smiled at the dark haired pilot saying, "Music, Maestro, please!"

Together, her alto and his tenor blended to create a distinctive harmony as they finished the Sentinel's favorite tune:

> *As we make it up into the sky, the night's a starry black,*
> *We'll have time to praise old Mother Earth and hope she wants us back,*
> *And tell all the other deities who've helped us on our way,*
> *That it's nice to visit heaven but we didn't want to stay.*
>
> *Now we're headed back from battle, back from where the air was thick,*
> *With no jet fuel and the glide path of a highly polished brick,*
> *With naught but sheets of steel between our hides and holy hell,*
> *Better pray to Hell's own Pluto that you hit the deck real well.*
>
> *Now we're back on deck again, the sky's a lovely blue,*
> *All you deities we didn't name, you know we love you too,*
> *We hope that you're not angry and you'll keep us in your care,*
> *We may need your help the next time we're cat shotted in the air.*

The song drew a round of applause from the assembled company, many of whom were singing along toward the end. Filk and Perry exchanged a high five and she climbed down the ladder. A few of the flyers gave her the thumbs up as she passed by them on her way to the jury rigged platform set up against the fire wall. It was nothing more than a sheet of metal supported by a half dozen steel drums but it would enable her to be seen by everyone. Perry and Anzac clamored up and 'Zac gave Martin a hand in getting aboard. Martin kept a discreet distance away from the two Wing leaders as he surreptitiously slipped a tape into his tiny recorder and activated it.

"Good evening." She scanned the crowd doing a quick headcount. She turned to Anzac saying, "This is everyone except for the guys flyin' and the crew currently manning the deck, right?"

Anzac nodded. "This is being taped, so the guys on duty now can hear it all later. Your big TV spot and you come on camera looking like something dredged up by an anchor."

"Gee, thanks, 'Zac. I really needed to hear that right now," she said, her sarcasm not lost on her deputy. He only grinned. "While you were making yourself pretty, I was busy tryin' to figure a way out of this mess."

"I gather you intend to enlighten everyone as to what we're up against."

"Not exactly," she confessed glancing away from him and out into the crowd. "As you know, lots of ideas were tossed around but we don't have the intelligence reports to back up anyone's pet theories, including the Admiral's. Hopefully, we'll have something concrete before the night is out. Meanwhile, these folks have to know we're going to be in for some rough seas ahead."

Anzac knew what she meant by that and sighed. The deck would be jumping round the clock and no one was going to get much in the way of a break. "How long?" he asked softly.

"However long it takes to find out who and what we're up against. Until then, we'll be up and flyin'."

"Any clue as to who's responsible?"

"Well..." her voice trailed off when she spotted Poindexter edging his way through the crowd. The look of urgency on his face piqued her curiosity and she met him by the edge of the platform. Kneeling so they could talk face to face, she inquired, "What's the story?"

"Two things, CAG. Helo crew picked up the driver of the bird Boomer nailed," he told her. "He's still out cold but the Doc thinks he'll be okay. The other thing is when they found the pilot, the Jolly Rogers also found some fragments from the jet. One of our spooks who's up on aeronautics is giving the bits a look-see. I managed to get a peek at the stuff myself. It's pretty weird. Here, look for yourself."

He pulled a small four-inch almost square piece of obsidian material from his pants pocket and passed it over to her. Perry gave it a cursory inspection: it was obviously some kind of plastic but the way it glittered in the light told her it had a crystalline substance as one of its components. "How did you manage to get this without anyone noticing?" she asked.

He grinned, eyes twinkling mischievously. "You're not the only one who can be sneaky, Ma'am."

She smiled for a fleeting moment at his impish expression and shook her head. She sobered quickly saying, "Bad move, Robert. This stuff must be classified. Your butt will wind up in the brig if you don't put this interesting tidbit back where you found it before someone discovers it's missing."

"I will, don't worry," he promised. Poindexter knew she meant business when he heard her call him by his name instead of his call sign. "I just thought you'd want a sneak preview, that's all."

"Now I've had it, so get this back where it belongs. Also, pass the word around to the other Ghosts that I'll want to see them all in my office after the wing meeting."

"No sweat, Commander. Catch you later."

He blended back into the crowd and she returned to Anzac's side. "What did 'Dexter show you?" he asked.

"A bit of that bird Boomer hit," she said and his eyes widened a bit in surprise. "Don't say it, I know. He should not have snitched a piece but the G-2 crew won't arrive for a couple of hours yet. 'Dexter knows we've got some brain trusts on this ship. He probably thought they'd be able to figure out what we're up against. I just hope he came to me first. If anyone else saw that fragment..." The sound of restlessness behind her made Perry turn back to face the crowd. She glanced at her deputy adding quickly, "After this, all the Ghosts will be meeting in my office. With all the nuggets I got saddled with, I'm really going to need all of my best people to bring those kids up to speed."

Anzac nodded and she took a deep breath to focus her thoughts before saying, "Sorry about the delay." The moment the room was silent, she continued, "As you already know, we had some uninvited guests drop by today. Intelligence is still working on making a positive identification but, whoever they are, they will not get a second chance to buzz this boat. The wing is going to be up and flying round the clock until the order is given for us to stand down. This is going to be rough for everyone, but the people who'll feel it the worst will be the maintenance team and the deck crew. Without you, dumb jocks like me don't get airborne."

Titters.

"I don't know how long this situation is going to last. The reason I got everyone together instead of just having your skippers tell you what's what is because I expect us all to work together, enlisted and officers alike. The biggest danger we face isn't the enemy, but ourselves. If things go on, we're all going to be exhausted, short-tempered and likely to make mistakes. And I don't need to tell you that a mistake on the deck or in the air, or a wrong part put in an aircraft, can all result in somebody buying it. I don't want to see anybody dying because they were too tired to do the job right. Or too proud to ask for help."

Murmurs rippled through the crowd. The reaction to her statement seemed mixed but Perry sensed she'd struck a chord and continued, "Everyone in here is an adult and is quite capable of judging how they feel. We're all going to be pushing ourselves, that's expected. However, there's a fine line between doing it hard and fast and overdoing it. It's when the line is crossed that problems arise. Take it from somebody who's made a profession out of going over the edge."

Chuckles were heard from spots here and there and Perry knew the source was her fellow flyers. Many of them have seen her burning the candle at both ends. After advising the more experienced members of her Air Wing to keep an eye on the first-timers, she introduced the ship's Master Chief. Master Chief PO George "Gabby" Gabriel was the one man on the *Excalibur* who knew what lay in the hearts and minds of the sailors.

Chief Gabriel approached the makeshift platform and scanned around for a way up. Vaulting up onto the five foot high stage was out of the question for the somewhat "overfed" Gabby, and he cast a questioning eye up at Anzac and Perry. "What? No step boxes?" he asked.

"We got up here," Perry told him, eyes full of mischief.

"I'm too old to jump around like a rabbit," he stated. "That's all well and good for you kids. Have some respect for us old Navy men and get me a proper way up there."

She chuckled. "You're not old, Gabby."

"Older than you, Commander. And we all know you ain't no spring chicken."

Anzac chuckled and Perry gave him a dirty look which only made him laugh harder. "Okay, funny boy," she said to Anzac, who stifled his enjoyment of the jest quickly. When his eyes met hers, he saw she wasn't really as annoyed as she sounded. "Don't just stand there giggling. Help the Chief up."

"Yes, Ma'am."

It took a few awkward moments for Anzac, and the two maintenance crew chiefs he drafted, to find something suitable for Chief Gabriel to use to climb aboard the platform. Wolff found the process amusing. He also noticed he wasn't the only one who was laughing to himself. Perry's eyes were twinkling and she was trying hard not to crack a smile.

When the Chief joined Perry and Wolff on the platform, he said, "You know no one's afraid of a little hard work, Commander.

What's got everyone's feathers ruffled is not knowin' who we're fightin'."

"If I knew, I'd tell you," she stated.

"I know that," he assured her in an aw-shucks tone of voice. "We all know that. And nobody's gonna slack off because they don't know who the gomer is that got the drop on us. It's just a little easier to fight an enemy that's got a name and a face, if you know what I mean."

Perry nodded. The New Moon War, the sobriquet by which the battle in Lebanon was known, had held no mystery as to who they were fighting and why. Many of the senior officers and several upper ranking petty officers on the *Excalibur* had been assigned to carriers stationed in the Med and the Persian Gulf when the fighting broke out. Most had even been around when the first steps toward American military involvement in the region were taken back in the summer of 1990 with the invasion of Kuwait by Iraq. The situation in that part of the world was still tense but the affairs in the Persian Gulf were always fairly cut and dried; the one they were in the midst of in the Gulf of Mexico was not so pleasantly straightforward.

Perry turned to face the assembly and in a voice loud enough to carry but still tinged with just a bit of her typical humor, "I think the Chief has a few wise words he'd like to share with you, so hang in there boys and girls. Chief?" Gabby gave her a smile, liking the rather off the cuff introduction she gave for him, and Perry added, "I've got another meeting to get to. I'll have to catch your State of the Boat address later on TV. Sorry, Gabby."

He nodded understanding. The ship not only picked up international television via satellite hookup, but had its own station where they produced their own programs. The Chief had his own show, *Good Morning, Excalibur*, which was broadcasted on all the stations at 0600 every day. Shipboard programs that held information vital to everyone always took preference over the mindless jumble they picked up off the satellite. When it was shown later that night, the Wing meeting would also pre-empt all the civilian programming. No one was going to miss hearing the CAG and the Chief because a good rerun of *MASH* was on opposite them.

"Catch you around the campus, Commander," he said to her using the favorite farewell expression aboard the *Excalibur*. Anzac and Martin Wolff followed Perry. Suddenly feeling like a sinking ship, the Chief asked, "All of you have to go to this meeting?"

"It's Ghostrider business," Anzac explained. "And we invited the press. Sorry, Chief. Next time we'll leave Paper Boy with you so you can have your gems put in print, okay?"

The Chief sighed. The Ghostriders were a minute part of his audience. Unfortunately, those few members were culled primarily from the senior members of the air wing. Perry's fighting elite were no doubt gathering for a brainstorming session. Her little unofficial squadron was only a mystery to the uninitiated. Which meant the majority of enlisted personnel were unaware of the Ghosts. For that matter, many of the flyers were also in the dark. The Chief had had the pleasure of sitting in on a Ghostrider gathering and found it very informative, as well as fun. The Ghosts were the best of the best and, although he would've liked to have had her hear his address to the troops, he knew the Ghost Leader had to be present for the strategy and tactics session that was about to take place.

13 December 2120

Yeoman Truesdale shot Perry a puzzled look as she entered the CAG office. Both her office and the outer office, where her yeoman sat, were a sea of faces. Some very well known to her and others newer but none of them strangers. She sighed. Not everyone present wore her flying circus's identifying logo on their flight suits or ball caps and she was mildly annoyed. It had been stated the meeting was for Ghostriders only; It was *not* open to friends of the Corps, like many of their other functions usually were.

"Ghostrider meeting?" Truesdale inquired unsurely as he eyed the group occupying his small office.

"Supposed to be," she told him. She noticed Boomer and Radar were amongst the group. When her eyes met Boomer's, he grinned. "What are you doing here, mister?" she asked him.

"Applying for membership," he responded still smiling.

"It takes a lot more than fancy flyin' to get yourself inducted into *this* club," she told him. "You really think you have what it takes to be a Ghostrider?"

"Damn straight," he stated not breaking eye contact.

"That's pretty arrogant, considering the company you're keeping here," she stated coldly, then, cracking a broad grin and adding in a completely different tone of voice, "I like that in a pilot. You can stick around, so long as you don't do anything to piss me off. Got that?"

"No problem, Commander."

Radar chuckled to himself when he saw the Commander roll her eyes heavenward with a why-me-Lord look on her face. He knew it wouldn't be long before his driver did something to annoy the Commander and both of them got tossed out on their ears. But while he waited for the inevitable, he was going to enjoy being a part of this gathering of the greatest.

Perry signalled to Anzac, who was perched on the edge of her desk, saying, "Let's move this into the Grim Reaper ready room. The skipper was Anzac's XO after he took over for me during the war. I know he won't mind us borrowing the space."

"You heard the lady," Anzac told the group in the office with him. "Fall out, team."

Martin Wolff walked two steps behind Perry as she led the way to Warrior country. "Just how many people do you have in your company anyway?" he asked.

"Officially, there's only nine, including myself. Counting the Ghost groupies, then the number bounces up to roughly thirteen. But, as you saw, there were more than a baker's dozen crowding my office just now."

"I noticed," he concurred. "What gives?"

"'Zac's done some recruiting again," she said, not sounding very pleased. "And, because of that fact, a couple more wanna-bees have descended upon us."

"Boomer and Radar?"

"Kid's got a pair of brass ones, considering how he started off this little holiday at sea," she remarked not caring that the subject of her conversation was within earshot. Wolff chuckled. "True, but he's been on one hell of a streak."

"Yeah, but where I come from, a Smith and Wesson still beats four aces. He may have the cards, but *I'm* the one holding the gun. It's my decision whether he's accepted or not. And, as it stands now, I'm going to wait and see how long his luck holds out."

Beneath all that tough talk Wolff sensed there was just a spark of admiration for the young man and what he'd accomplished in so short a span of time. In a quiet voice so no one would hear but her he said, "Kid's got it, doesn't he?"

Perry smiled and, when she managed to catch Wolff's gaze, she nodded in assent. "Don't you dare tell him I said that," she ordered and Wolff's only response was a slight laugh.

"My lips are sealed," he promised as he followed her into the Grim Reaper ready room.

A few members of the squadron were in the ready room sitting in the overstuffed leather chairs that bore the squadron logo, a tomcat wearing a bandolier and leaning against a sickle, emblazoned on their headrests. They were reading their mail or reviewing paperwork. The two TV sets, fixed to the uppermost corners of either side of the blackboard at the foremost part of the room, were tuned in to the flight deck. Behind the center blackboard was hidden a large screen projection set which Wolff knew was used for reviewing mission tapes or for TACTS sessions. He glanced up at one of the corner monitors in time to see an Intruder make a successful trap. The Reapers present took one look at the crowd descending upon them and at Perry, who was standing behind the lectern at the front of the room, and didn't need to be asked to leave. They saw Perry and a few familiar faces wearing Ghostrider caps and knew what was on the agenda. They quietly departed leaving their former skipper alone with her troops.

A striking blonde approached Perry and offered her a Coke, which she accepted with a tired smile. "Thanks, Jugs," she said as she pulled off the top and downed a healthy portion in a few swift swallows.

"Are you okay?" Jugs inquired not failing to notice Perry's wounded head. "You look beat."

"Just the crazy hours catching up with me, I guess."

Wolff tried not to stare at the statuesque beauty talking to Perry but he found he just couldn't take his eyes off her. He'd caught glimpses of her in his travels around the *Excalibur,* but he'd never gotten within touching distance of her. Jugs deserved her call sign, though some of the other women aboard thought it was both tasteless and sexist. Her feminine pulchritude was even more exaggerated when she stood beside the well muscled, but flat chested, Air Wing Commander. The baggy olive drab jumpsuit Jugs had on didn't hide what the men of the Wing called a "spectacular superstructure." He could fully understand why the romantic liaisons of this particular lady were the hottest topic for discussion in the wardroom; However, it seemed the guys doing the speculation were the ones least likely to capture Jugs's heart or anything else for that matter.

Jugs caught Wolff looking and remarked, "It hasn't been *that* long a cruise, sailor."

Wolff felt his face flush and he quickly withdrew before he found himself catching barbs for daring to gawk at the Wing's resident beauty. He found a seat in the first row and sat next to Lt. Don "Sparky" Sparkman, who'd flown with Anzac as the second man in the Alert Fifteen team. Sparky wasn't wearing any Ghostdancer insignias on his jumpsuit. But it was obvious from the reactions of the people in the room that, not only did he belong there, but his presence was more than welcome.

Sparky gave the reporter a friendly grin remarking, "If you've got any designs on Jugs, then take a number. There's a *long* line of guys ahead of you waitin' to try their luck with her."

"All I did was *look*, for Chrissake! Come on, I'm only human."

"Ain't we all?"

Wolff laughed slightly at the younger man's comment. He had spent some time with Sparky in the past and liked the man's easy-going nature. Off-duty, Sparky was a lot of fun. With Christmas liberty close at hand, Wolff was looking forward to joining Sparky's admin for the fun in Rio. The Lieutenant had explained to him an admin resembled a fraternity house party. All the members kicked in to get a large suite destined to become the "house" for the duration of the liberty stop. And, like a frat house, the living room section would be converted into festival central and the bedrooms would undoubtedly be housing far more people than the hotel suspects or charges for. Wolff liked the idea of having a chance to act like a college boy again. He had agreed to kick in his share whenever the time came to pay up and Wolff was ready to celebrate the first liberty of the cruise with the boys of Air Wing 21.

Sparky's smile didn't fade as he turned to acknowledge Poindexter and a young woman. Her blue coveralls were inscribed with the insignia of the engineering section and she sat in the seat next to him. Wolff wondered what one of the "snipes," the name by which the engineers were known on the boat, was doing there. Part of the reason became obvious when the reporter caught the affectionate look 'Dexter had fixed on her. A RIO and an engineer made an interesting couple, Wolff thought. And a very unlikely one considering how much contact the members of the Air Wing had with those who toiled away below decks.

As Perry noticed Poindexter and a woman in blue, she came over to them and asked, "Who's our guest, 'Dexter?"

"Ensign Alanna Pearl from engineering," he told her. "She went to Steven's Tech, my alma mater. She's a Chem E, Commander, and did some metallurgical work as part of her work-study program. You know that fragment I snitched for you? Well, it had a brother and I, well, I took the liberty of giving it to Alanna to analyze for me."

"You *what*?" Perry stated more than asked her eyes widening in shock. She sighed heavily, realizing it was too late. She cast a taut glance on the dark eyed ensign. Her attention quickly focused back onto Poindexter and she inquired, "Did you share your find with anyone else, mister?"

"No, just Alanna."

"And you, Ensign?"

"No one, Commander. And I was alone when I did my research," Alanna reassured Perry in a voice clear and confident, and not at all in keeping with the timid mouse-like expression she wore. "We don't have all the right equipment here to do a real thorough workup but I can tell you this much. The piece I looked at was probably from the hull of the aircraft. It had a tri-layered structure. The outermost coating is Teflon. The middle a honeycomb-like web made of something similar to the substance used for making the bubble plastic used for packaging. The innermost layer is the thickest and is a very weird polymer of some sort. It's got a crystalline component, probably silicone, but the rest of it has been blended in so thoroughly as to be almost unrecognizable. I'm sure with the right equipment a more accurate breakdown could be made but this isn't the sort of thing we're asked to do on a daily basis."

"I know," Perry replied. The girl did good work, even though she should never have gotten within ten knots of those fragments. "You didn't see anything, do anything or know anything, understand?" she commanded Pearl and the girl nodded comprehendingly. "Good. Sit down."

Alanna did as she was told leaving Poindexter and Perry alone together. She led him to the right hand corner beneath the TV screen and, in a quiet voice that still managed to convey her displeasure with the situation, said, "You put *all* those bits back where you found them and you had better hope nobody catches you. Because if they do, your butt is going to be fried and *I'm* bound to catch some heat because *you supposedly work for me*! If you get snagged, this little bit of over zealousness on your part could cost you your Navy career. And, what's worse is, *I'm* going to be the one to have to launch that torpedo should you fail to put back what you never should have taken!"

Poindexter couldn't meet her stormy gaze and found his shiny shoetops easier to look at than her blazing green eyes. "Sorry, Commander."

"Not as sorry as you'd be if you got caught," she scolded. "Get moving, mister. You can find out what went on here from your engineer friend later."

He dared to look up at her. "Would you really get into trouble because of me?"

"Not exactly but I'd be forced to listen to comments about not bein' able to keep a reign on my troops. That kind of crap I can certainly live without. I know you acted independently but, when Higher Authority gets a gander at that patch you're wearin' so proudly on your shoulder, there will no doubt be some questions tossed my way as to why you chose to do what you did in the first place."

"I was only trying to help," he said in a small voice.

"I know that," she replied in tone that was an odd mixture of understanding and anger. She looked him square in the eye and stated, "I know it isn't goin' to be easy for you to give that stuff back but I have faith in you. I don't think you'll have any problems. You're a slippery little eel, 'Dexter. This should be just a swim downstream for you."

He rolled his eyes and groaned. Stealing it was easy, the stuff had been right out there under his nose and within easy reach. Now he was not only going to have to find out where the fragments were being kept, but also get into that place to mix his piece in with all the rest. Not an easy task by any means. But not only was his Navy career on the line but also his reputation with his fellow Ghostriders. The resident fox had to get away with putting the chicken back into the henhouse without being spotted by Farmer Brown. To accomplish this little feat, he was going to have to call in a few markers. Well, there were some favors coming his way that were long overdue...

"Time to go," she said showing him the door.

"Thanks," he muttered as he reassured himself the fragments were still in the left hand pocket of his flight suit. He perked up a bit adding, "Bekaa Valley is going to look like a stroll down Main Street compared to *this*."

"No *true* Ghostrider would balk at a chance to challenge his ingenuity, 'Dexter."

"Yeah, but we also like to bitch and moan about havin' to do things we'd rather not," he came back with his usual good-natured grin lighting up his boyish face. "That's an old tradition, established by one of our more illustrious members."

Perry chuckled shaking her head. "True, but I've been *trying* to refrain," she replied smiling up at him. "Not that I haven't had cause, mind you. It just doesn't go with the territory I'm coverin' right now."

"Kinda makes you wish you were still with the Grim Reapers, huh?"

"Hell, no!" she declared. "I may not have the luxury of complainin' about the tasks the Navy, in its infinite wisdom, sets out for me to accomplish, but that's a freedom I'm more than happy to relinquish. This job has its downside, but I wouldn't trade it for anything. Except to trade up, if you get my meanin'."

"Yeah. I hope I'm still around when you get to sit behind the stick of one of these birdfarms. The line to sign up to sail with you is bound to be a long one. You're the coolest CO I've ever had. Most of the guys I've had to work for were in the past were so anal retentive that the gang down in the MEJO bunkroom used to take bets on how many times a cruise they took a shit."

Perry broke up. She knew the type well. She'd had to work for more than one tight ass in her day and found it amusing to find her experience was far from unique. Through her laughter she said, "God, 'Dexter, sometimes you're worse than Anzac. And that boy is one tough act to follow."

Poindexter smiled saying as he departed, "I'd still be happy to sail with you anytime, CAG."

Perry returned the smile and sighed. She would love to command a carrier but she knew the day for that was a long way away. Even though the rules had changed, the Navy still had its share of MCPs, Male Chauvinist Pigs. They were mostly the older officers who'd been in the service for years and weren't too willing to adjust to the changing times. It had only been a score of years since women were allowed to serve on the mightiest warships of the U.S. Fleet—the aircraft carriers. When one pondered how long America had a Navy, that time span was a drop in the bucket. The next generation are accepting the women they work and fight beside, thought Perry as she scanned the few young faces in the room. They'll be the ones who will remove the old fashioned attitudes. Unfortunately I'll probably be retired by the time any of the up-and-comers possess the clout needed to make changes, Perry mused with a wan smile.

Without 'Dexter around to keep her company, Alanna felt a little not sure about staying in this room full of flyers. The other Ghosts, who had been milling about, found seats. Perry took her place behind the lectern and signalled for quiet. Her expression and voice were all calm determination as she said, "As you already know, we're flying 'round the clock and making a web around this battle group so tight a fly won't be able to get through without being spotted. Flying defense is something every one of us has done before and done under more tenuous circumstances. The reason I called you all here is to ask for a bit above and beyond the call."

There were murmurs throughout the room and, the moment it quieted, she continued, "What I mean by that is I don't want the skies to be full of nuggets new to this game. I want somebody experienced, either one of you or one of your equally seasoned squadron mates, to be up there keeping an eye on things. There's just so much I and my skippers can do while we're here on the boat. And since it's physically impossible for all the skippers and XOs to keep hopping up with their teams, we've got to make realistic plans to keep ourselves covered. I know our little group here has no official position on the *Excalibur* but you people do. You are all known for being the best at what you do and your opinions hold water. Use whatever influence you have to make sure our team is running the best defense the game has ever seen."

"It's not going to be easy keeping our asses covered against an enemy our instruments don't pick up on, Commander," Sparky pointed out. "And it's physically impossible to keep enough birds airborne to rely on what our eyes tell us. There's got to be *some* way to track these gomers. To see them coming *before* it's too late."

"We've got some experts from G-2 coming in on the COD tonight," she told him. "I hope, they'll have some ideas we can use to protect ourselves. In the meantime, we're going to be fighting the way your great-granddaddies did: sharp eyes, keen instincts and a whole lotta luck."

Her statement brought a few quiet murmurs from the younger team members, many of whom were more accustomed to relying on the technical marvels built into their high priced killing machines as opposed to using the natural means God gave them to do the job. The warriors of Perry's generation, like Big Daddy, had performed enough seat of the pants flying not to be scared off by the idea of butting heads with someone you had to see to sink. Still, after how they'd been caught looking that afternoon, even the veterans in the room were wearing expressions of concern.

"We don't know when, or even if, those gomers will be coming back for seconds," Perry continued. "But we have to be ready in case they do. Today they just took out our windows. Next time they could be aiming for *us*."

"Any of those fools takes a shot at me and they'll be drinkin' Gulf," Boomer stated firmly, from his place in the rear of the room. "I already splashed one bandit. Another one or two-"

"Boomer," Perry interrupted sharply. "Save it for the wardroom."

Her reprimand brought out a few nervous titters from the other flyers and Boomer shrugged, slightly embarrassed but still full of cocky enthusiasm. Perry noticed Radar didn't look too thrilled with his driver. The RIO was much more modest about his abilities and didn't like it much when Boomer ran off at the mouth. She smiled slightly to herself. Those two were so much like she and Anzac were as youngsters that she experienced a mild case of *déjà vu*. It wasn't only that the behavior was so familiar but also remembering being *that* young and full of herself.

Perry caught Anzac's wry grin and her smile widened. "I know, *I know*," she said to him and he chuckled softly. She turned away from him and focused her attention back on to the assembly saying, "Look, we all have our work cut out for us, so let's get cracking. Any questions or problems, my door'll be open as usual. But, Anzac's going to be running the show tonight, so please see him *first*. That is all." As the group began to disperse, Perry sighed and said to Anzac, "'Dexter told me the Jollys picked up the driver—"

"I know," Anzac interrupted. "When he wakes up, the boys from Intelligence will be talking to him. Hopefully we'll find out who these guys are and why they decided to pay us this unexpected call."

Perry nodded in assent and rubbed the weariness out of her eyes. "I've got to greet what's coming in on the COD at twenty-three-hundred. And Jonsey expects me to be all spit an' polish for this, too."

"He also wanted you to get yourself to sickbay and have Bones look at your head," Anzac reminded her. She looked all washed out, pale, and exhausted but, as usual, was fighting against her body's need for rest. "Perry, I think you'd better listen to Jones on this one. You look like you're about to fall on your face."

"I'll go, don't worry," she promised sounding like a child trying to silence a nagging parent.

Anzac sighed. He knew she would go and see the doctor eventually. She was just procrastinating because she feared her injuries would get her grounded and that was the last thing she wanted to have happen to her during an alert. He could understand how she felt. But she was also experienced enough to understand the risks of flying when you weren't operating at one-hundred-percent.

Out of the corner of her eye she saw Boomer was about to leave the room. "Lieutenant!" she called and he turned to face her. She motioned to him to approach her and he complied with her unspoken command. He was trying hard to look unconcerned but was not succeeding. "Wait for me in my office," she ordered.

"Yes, Commander."

He spun on his heel and left.

Wolff managed to catch Perry's eye and, before he could speak to her, she told him, "Your photos came back from our lab and they somehow made it into my mailbox instead of yours. Trudy is holding them for you. I'm sorry I didn't mention it before we shifted the Ghost gathering down here but I don't need to tell you I had more important things on my mind."

"I understand," he replied.

He followed her as she led the way back to her office. He spotted Boomer and Radar waiting outside her door. Perry gave the Rio a slight smile in greeting before indicating to Boomer to come with her. The young flyer obeyed and, as he stepped through the door behind her, asked, "What's on your mind, Commander?"

"Quite a few things," she replied not meeting his eyes. "What pertains to you I'll discuss *in my office*."

Boomer sighed and knew better than to press the issue. Wolff had the feeling she was probably going to dress him down for his behavior in the meeting and, although he personally liked the young man's cockiness, he sensed that Perry did not. There was a fine line between being self confident and being full of yourself and it no doubt about it Boomer has crossed that line in the eyes of the Commander.

Yeoman Truesdale looked up alertly at the sound of the door opening and greeted Perry with a smile.

"Anything new on the intelligence board?" Perry asked him.

"No, Commander. There hasn't been any sign of those jets and satellite photos of likely airfields so far have proven inconclusive."

"Damn. Keep me posted," she said and he nodded. She scanned the tiny outer office asking, "Where are Wolff's photos?"

Seemingly from out of nowhere Truesdale pulled the thick manila folder and gave it to her saying, "Right here, Ma'am."

"Thanks."

She handed it over to Wolff, who lost no time in opening it up to inspect the contents, and then motioned to Boomer to follow her into her office. Wolff stayed outside with Truesdale, who peered over his shoulder at the photos the reporter was carefully inspecting. The Yeoman seemed oblivious to the tone of the conversation going on in the next room, but Wolff had to force himself not to listen. Perry wasn't being very vocal about taking Boomer to task for his arrogance but the bulkheads weren't designed to be soundproof and her normal commanding tone carried easily. That was why she didn't use a bullhorn to address the troops during the Wing meeting and why if she did anything other than carry on a casual conversation in her office it would be heard by anyone waiting with Yeoman Truesdale.

Wolff noticed the young man checking out his work and asked, "How would you describe your job? It looks to me like you do a lot more than keep the Commander's paperwork flowing."

He smiled. "Well, there are some days when I feel like the guy in the circus who you see following the elephants with the shovel and pail. Other times, I'm a combination of secretary, spy, and security officer. And then there are those occasions when I'm on a marathon chasing the Commander all over the boat keeping her apprised on what's going on. And days when I'm acting like her old man, the Colonel, and kicking her in the butt to remind her to take care of herself and do basic stuff like eat and sleep. So, as you can see, there's a lot more to what I do than meets the eye."

"She listens to you when you get on her case about eating and stuff like that?"

"After a five minute B and M session, yes."

"B and M?"

"Oh, that's Ghostese for bitchin' and moanin'. It's what they do next best after flying. I'm surprised you haven't picked up on that by now."

Wolff shrugged. "I guess I haven't spent enough time in Ghostrider country." He looked quizzically at the young man and asked, "You're with the Ghosts?"

"Me? No, that's a flyboy club. I'm just very perceptive and, as the Ghost Leader's yeoman, I get to go to meetings now and then. You know, if the Ghosts ever all went up together, it would look like a twenty-first century version of Richthofen's flying circus. All those different airplanes flying in formation together. Those guys could pull off an Alpha Strike that nobody would ever forget."

Wolff was about to comment on that observation when he saw Boomer coming out of Perry's office. He looked like a whipped dog walking with its tail between its legs. The pilot barely acknowledged the presence of Wolff and Truesdale as he left and Martin Wolff felt a little sorry for the spirited young flyer. He'd come a long way and was currently the hottest nugget on the boat. Wolff had to admit the young man was a bit full of himself sometimes but so were a lot of the other jocks. There were times when it looked like she was ragging on him for things the other guys did all the time and she ignored. He was also beginning to wonder why the Commander let Boomer keep his wings if he honestly was such a colossal pain in the ass. But, he had been in the news business long enough to know not to make judgments based on appearances alone.

Perry came out of her office carrying a few flat blue velvet boxes of various sizes and shapes. She noticed Wolff was still there and asked, "Your pictures turn out okay?"

"Yeah, they look great. Want to take a look? I've got a few of you in here."

"Maybe later," she replied frowning slightly, her attention obviously focused elsewhere. She focused her gaze on Truesdale saying, "Anzac is running the show until the COD arrives. I've got to get my act together before that bird arrives. If anyone can't live without speaking to me, I'll be in my quarters."

"Yes, Commander. Don't forget to go to sickbay first. Admiral's orders," Truesdale reminded her sounding more mother hen than yeoman. "Also try to get few Zs. You look tired."

"All right," she assured him and he smiled, looking like a proud father.

"If our spies turn up any news, I'll buzz you. Okay?"

"Yes. And I want you to get on the horn to those guys who built our birds and tell them to get off their duffs and send us the parts we need. Also, bug the hell out of any of their reps on board, that you come across, to do their share. We can't run an Air Wing if our planes are going to be stuck in the hanger because they're missing a couple of screws."

"Yes, Ma'am."

Perry sighed when her eyes rested on the empty coffeepot sitting on top of the file cabinet behind Truesdale's desk. She was desperate for a cup of good strong coffee so she could keep her eyes open long enough to shower off the detritus of the day and get herself looking like an Air Wing Commander. Well, the wardroom wasn't that far out of her way and she'd still manage to catch an hour of nap time before the COD arrived. She had no idea why she was so exhausted. It had been a tense afternoon but she'd experienced far worse and she was beginning to wonder why she felt as lousy as she did.

Forcing her eyes to stay open and focused Perry asked the reporter, "Care to join me for a quick cup of joe?"

"Well..."

"I'll look at your pix in the wardroom. They'll keep me conscious until the coffee kicks in."

"Maybe you should skip the coffee and do what your yeoman told you to instead. You do look beat, Commander."

"I intend to get some rest," she told him leading the way into the corridor, "As soon as I get Bones to patch up my head, I'm going to strip, shower and collapse into my bunk for a while. Besides, I've put so much coffee into this body over the past three decades that I'd need a whole lot more than one cup in my system to be kept awake for longer than a few extra minutes."

They walked together in silence for a few moments before Wolff asked, "Mind if I ask you some quick questions while we're walking?"

She nodded.

"What's your secret, professor? How did you turn Boomer from a schlepp to a star?" When she didn't make an immediate response, Wolff added, "I know you're tough on many of the new flyers. I just picked him out because it seems he's the one who spends the most time in the principal's office."

Perry cracked a smile. "Too true. You see, he could be more than just some hot shot tearing up the skies at Mach two if he'd adjust his attitude a bit. Enthusiasm and confidence have their place. He's been going a bit over the line lately and needs to have his big feet stepped on to know he's gone too far. If he doesn't shape up now, he'll be stuck wearing railroad tracks for the rest of his Navy life. Take it from someone who's been there," she said. Wolff knew exactly what she meant. The Commander was once trooping around in the boots Boomer now wore, and he sensed she saw much of herself in the young pilot. "But I had Jonsey and Lt. Commander Mcloughlin to kick me in the right direction and look where I wound up. The same thing could happen to Boomer if he gets the benefit of a caring boot in his backside."

Wolff chuckled. "Well, I knew there was a good reason you kept him flying even though he seemed to be such a thorn in your side."

She smiled slightly quickly catching herself before a kneeknocker tripped her up and sent her sprawling. She paused to catch her breath remarking, "I must be more tired than I thought."

Wolff caught her arm asking, "Are you all right?"

She turned to face him and stared at him slightly dumfounded. His face disappeared into a blur and she squinted hard trying to get her eyes to focus. But they refused to obey her mind's orders. She heard Wolff talking to her again but his words sounded as though he was conversing to her from under water. Desperately attempting to get control over her failing senses, Perry tried to shake the fuzziness away but her efforts were in vain. She felt Wolff's strong hand latch onto her other arm just as the room disappeared into blackness.

14 December 0110

Voices and the shuffling of feet on metal flooring were the first clues Perry got telling her she wasn't going to find herself lying flat on her back in her bunk. The second was the smell of antiseptic mixed with alcohol that made her nose twitch. She opened her eyes and sighed heavily. The tiny surgery room did its best to comfortably hold the flight surgeon, Captain Jacob "Bones" Melman, the corpsman assisting him, and Admiral Jones. They had not noticed she had awakened and was currently taking stock of the situation.

The light over her bed was the only illumination but, because of the room's size, it was more than sufficient to see by. Perry tried to sit up and promptly sank back into the pillow. Her sudden movement made the room swim and go black for a few seconds. Her head throbbed violently and she thought she was going to vomit, but the nausea faded quickly when she laid back and allowed her senses to return to normal. Her head was still pounding when she attempted a second time to sit up but, this time, she moved with slow deliberation. She succeeded in getting herself upright without suffering from the vertigo that had dashed her earlier attempt and she proceeded to lower the bedrail on the right side of her bed.

As she was about to climb out of bed, Captain Melman sharply stated more than asked, "Just where the hell do you think you're going?"

"There a COD coming in at twenty-three-hundred—"

"Forget it," Jones commanded as Melman forced her back into the bed and snapped up the siderail with an audible clang. "That bird's been and gone. Commander Edwards covered for you." He saw the look of surprise on her face and, when she met his firm gaze, he added, "You are damn lucky, you know that? If you'd blacked out while airborne instead of on this ship, God only knows what would've happened."

"What's wrong with me?"

"Haven't got a clue, do you?" Melman accused, his tone indicating he saw this one coming from a mile off. "Figures. I'll give you a hint. What hurts?"

She looked at him puzzled for a long moment before replying,

"My head's killing me, but other than that—"

"I just put twenty-two stitches into that head of yours, Commander," the doctor interrupted. Her shocked expression told him far more than any words could. "I see you had no idea how badly sliced up you got by that flyin' glass. You really are a piece of work, Commander."

"I hardly felt a thing out there," she said still finding it hard to believe even though the pain told her the doctor was telling her the truth. Absently, she added, "Twenty-two stitches..."

"That cut on your head isn't the only thing wrong with you," Melman went on. "You have a concussion. Between the blood loss and that fall you took earlier today, it's a wonder you stayed on your feet as long as you did." He sighed shaking his head. "I think the only reason no one brought you down here sooner was you ordered them *not* to. Good thing Mr. Wolff caught you before you went face down into the deck. Otherwise, you'd probably be nursing a busted nose or jaw or both right now."

A wry smile crossed her face. "Nice catch," she quipped to herself. She looked up at the doctor and asked, "When are you going to let me out?"

"Let you out?" Melman repeated looking like he was ready to hand her her head.

"Yes, I feel fine."

"Fine?" Melman's voice reflected just a tinge of resentment. "You let me make that determination, Commander."

"Then make it already!" Perry's green eyes flashed fire.

"It has been made, to an extent," the doctor stated his tone still hard. "You're grounded, Perry. Until you're certified fit, you're not getting within a hundred yards of anything that flies."

Perry gasped. She could tell by the firm set to the Captain's jaw that he was dead serious about keeping her away from the one thing she loved above all others. "Grounded! You can't—"

"I can and I did," Melman told her. "Right now, you're a hazard, Commander. Maybe after a week—"

"A week? Those gomers could come back *tomorrow*! You can't do this to me! Not now!"

"Look, *Commander*, I'll give you a choice. I yield to your wishes and let you out of here and you don't fly 'til next week. Or you stay here in bed for the next three days, get nothing but rest, and, possibly, heal enough to get your wings back by Friday."

Perry pondered the alternatives for a moment before suggesting a compromise. "How about this? I do the bedrest deal, but someplace more comfortable, like my bunk."

"The only way you'd stay in your bunk would be if someone chained you to it," Jones broke in knowingly. "Stay here in sickbay and let Bones take care of you."

"I hate hospitals," she moaned. "Please?"

Melman and Admiral exchanged a look before the doctor responded, "You can recuperate in your quarters. But you'll have a corpsman with you round the clock to make sure you stay in your bed."

"Fine. Now, when will you give me my walkin' papers so I can get out of this place?"

"If I said right now, what would you do?"

"Jump for joy," she cracked, her remark garnering her a disapproving look from the Admiral. Still grinning impishly she added in a more serious tone, "I have to check in with 'Zac to see what our status is and what the latest intelligence reports have to say. You know I have to officially hand the reigns over to him. It'll be up to him to tell the squadron skippers what happened. After I'm sure he's got it all under control, I *promise* the only thing I'll inspect for the next three days will be the insides of my eyelids."

Melman thought about her reply for a long moment. He sighed saying, "I've already done all I can for you. I'm giving you some antibiotics to help keep any infections from setting in. I can also give you some pills for your pain but, knowing how you feel about narcotics, I know that would be a waste of time. You'd never take them voluntarily. I really should keep you here, because, even with my man with you, you'll still find a way to keep your fingers in the pie. But the Admiral wants me to get you on your feet ASAP. So, if you've got any sense, you'll follow my orders, stay in bed, and give your body a chance to heal."

"Bones, when you cut me loose, I'll be good and do whatever you tell me to do," she said in a compliant tone as she pressed the switch raising the head of the bed into a sitting position.

Perry was caught completely off guard when she heard Melman snap, "Bullshit!"

"But—"

"I know I never had you in my care before, McNeil, but I did bother to read your file. You sneaked out of sickbay to go on an air strike with your squadron during the New Moon War. Considerin' you were up there with a fever that had you talking out of your head half the time, it was a wonder you survived. It was also by the grace of God you weren't grounded for good for pulling a stunt like that, or else Bekaa Valley never would've happened." She was looking decidedly uncomfortable while the doctor related her past sins. "I know grounding one of you flyboys is like sticking a knife through your heart but sometimes its done for your own damn good. And remember *you* are grounded, Commander," Melman said in a tone that was all business. "I don't care what happens. You are to do no flyin' for the next seventy-two hours."

"What if they come back?" she countered. "Have you any idea—"

"Look, Commander, I *know* what's going on. I had to patch together all those people who got sliced up earlier today," he cut in with equal intensity. "Things could blow up or it could all be over when you're reinstated to full flight status. But there's no way I'm allowing you to get into a jet when there's even the slightest possibility you'll lose consciousness up there. All those fancy maneuvers you do have been known to make normal, healthy people black out. Never mind what they'd do to someone with a concussion who's lost a pint of blood and who already passed out once while on the ground."

"I won't go flyin', I promise. But there's a lot more to my job than that. You have to let—"

"Enough!" the Admiral boomed. "You are out of the fight for now, McNeil. Case closed. You will stay in your quarters, take whatever medication Bones gives you, and you will rest. If you dare to leave your quarters to go anyplace other than the head, you'll be doing your recuperating from a bed in the brig. Is that clear?"

She paused thoughtfully before replying, "Yes, sir, I'll stay in my quarters. But I don't need a corpsman to take care of me. If the government trusts me with the lives of over a thousand people, and nearly a billion dollars worth of hardware, the least you could do is trust me to follow your instructions."

"You burned the last flight surgeon you promised to listen to," he reminded her. "Sorry, Commander, but you have to earn my trust. I have a first class corpsman assigned to you and his job will be to make sure you follow my orders to the letter."

Perry made no comment but it was obvious from her expression that she would have wanted the situation to have been handled differently.

"If that's not to your liking," Melman stated, "then you are more than welcome to stay *right here.*"

"No, thank you," she said quickly. Perry sighed resigned to the fact she was not going to win this one. "Now, can I have my clothes? I can't exactly go back to my quarters wearing something so short my butt hangs out of it."

"You can if you have a robe over it."

She turned noticing for the first time the corpsman holding the familiar terry cloth garment. As she pulled back the covers and climbed out of the bed, Perry clutched closed the gown. She realized the ties up around her chest had fallen open revealing a lot more than just some cleavage to the appraising eyes of the three men. The doctor and corpsman looked as though they hadn't seen a thing; Jones, on the other hand, had politely averted his eyes. Though the corpsman was surprised to see the Commander sported a rather colorful tattoo, he maintained his professional demeanor. "Don't just stand there like a hat rack! Be useful and help me with my robe!"

Obviously accustomed to dealing with grouchy patients, the corpsman was completely unruffled as he silently complied with her request. He then accepted the three vials of pills from the doctor and stood by her side while Melman administered the first dose to the Commander. She didn't look at all pleased with her situation in general and the good doctor in particular. He stood by and listened as Melman outlined both his duties for the next three days and things to watch for in the way of complications. After he was confident the corpsman was ready to do the job, Melman gave Perry her release orders.

Wolff, who had been waiting just outside the door, saw the Commander leave sickbay looking like all the wind had been sucked out of her sails. If he'd ever entertained thoughts of what it would be like to break Perry's fighting spirit, Wolff got the chance to see what the outcome would be without being the one to do the deed. It depressed him to see her this way. He liked her feistiness. It was not going to be a pleasant three days if she was going to be spending her period of forced rest looking like the horse that had been asked to plow one field too many.

He followed her and the corpsman to her quarters, and went inside after her because the door had been left open. The room was claustrophobic by civilian standards but, compared to what Wolff had seen so far on the carrier, the CAG's quarters were a luxury suite. Bed, desk, chair, lamp and a narrow closet with a set of drawers. On the desk was a computer terminal with a color monitor, a clock radio, and a phone. A photo of Perry and a lovely young woman with flowing red hair posing next to a classic red Mustang stood beside the phone, and Wolff picked it up to take a closer look.

"My daughter," Perry told him as she drew down the covers on her bed.

"She's pretty," Wolff observed as he put the picture back on her desk. "She's in high school?"

"College. Sophomore year."

"Like the car. Yours or hers?"

"Mine," she said. "You like classic cars?"

"I don't know much about them but, yes, I like them. What year is yours?"

"Sixty-four. The engine had to be rebuilt a couple of times but the body is all original parts."

"I like the plates. Let's everyone know a real driver is behind the wheel."

She laughed lightly appreciating the little in-joke. As she stood looking at her old photos, her thoughts drifted back to the happenings the day she shipped out. Katherine, who she'd always called Kate, was very mature for her eighteen years. She had just begun her second year at the University of Virginia. The semester was approaching the midway point when the day came for the *Excalibur* battle group to depart. The squadrons her mom would be flying with to the carrier were departing from Oceana Naval Air Station, which was a short hop by car from the Virginia Beach townhouse Perry got in her settlement. Now Kate was going to do what she had done so many times in the past. She was saying farewell to her mom at the air station and watching as Perry zoomed off, with the rest of the members of the two Tomcat squadrons, the VF-69, Renegades, and the VF-13, Grim Reapers.

Although she had plenty of opportunities to learn, Kate McLoughlin never got bitten by the flying bug that at times seemed to have infected both her parents to the point of incapacitation. It was a combination of their love for the life of a Naval aviator and their pigheaded competitiveness that broke up the McNeil-McLoughlin Tomcat tag team. "Crazy" Kyle McLoughlin was a true jet jock. All yucks and rude jokes on the ground, but in the air he cut the raw meat when he had to. Perry admired the almost nonchalant ease with which he handled his bird. Flying as his wingman was still one of the only two good things she could recall ever doing with Crazy Kyle.

The second was having Kate. Kate was a great kid, even if she disdained flying. Perry never begrudged her the choice to remain landbound. She knew the girl had her reasons, chief of which was spending the bulk of her early years listening to her parents fight about who could do what better. When it got so bad they had to split, Perry got custody and Kate lived with her grandparents on their farm in Chagrin Falls, Georgia whenever Perry was at sea. That, in the eyes of Kate's father and the Commonwealth of Virginia, turned out to be more time than was thought proper. Perry wound up losing custody to Kyle and his new bride. When she tried to contest, she found out her ex had a top notch job with American Airlines, and, could provide what the courts called "a stable home environment." She lost Kate because the courts preferred to see her living with an airline captain instead of with a squadron commander, who spent two-thirds of the year away from home.

Kyle, however, didn't screw her totally. He had enough of a heart to make sure Perry had unlimited visitation. That was the only thing he could do to be fair because of her crazy schedule. Kate had had the luxury of being flown, at the Navy's expense, to visit Perry at many exotic ports of call where the sailors were let loose for liberty. Perry had made friends in high places during her career, and was owed many favors. When the time came for her to call in her markers, her usual form of repayment came in the form of roundtrip airfare for Kate to wherever in the world the fleet dropped anchor for a much needed rest. By the time she went to college, Kate had been to a good chunk of Southeast Asia and some Mediterranean countries as well. Being a Navy brat had its advantages but Perry knew Kate would have preferred having a mom who had a normal nine to five job and who could make a decent meal. Not that she ever heard Kate complain, but she could tell by the look in her daughter's soft hazel eyes every time they said goodbye at the hangar that she wished her life had been different.

The day Perry shipped out, her daughter had joined her for the ride out to Oceana NAS. Kate cranked up the volume on the car radio so the song "Wild One" could be heard over the sound of the wind and other cars they were passing at high speed. Perry had the fuzz buster on and, as usual, was driving her 1964 candy apple red Mustang the same way she flew her jets: pipes lit and burning, going full throttle, and leaving nothing but a long dust trail behind. The lively upbeat music fit Kate's mood. She leaned back in the soft leather bucket seat and took in the sensation of the Indian summer sun beating on her face. The wind whipped her wavy crimson hair out behind her like a crackling flame. Kate absently pushed the oversized sunglasses up on the bridge of her small upturned nose with her forefinger, and smiled slightly when she caught her mother looking her way.

Perry's eyes were completely hidden behind her mirrored aviator shades, but Kate knew, whenever her mom had that "full of the devil" smile on her face, her eyes were twinkling. Unlike her stepmother Shari, who was beautiful to look at but was about as exciting to be with as a loaf of Wonder bread, Perry was full of ginger. Kate thought Perry's lively personality more than made up for the fact that she was no beauty queen. Although they didn't always see eye to eye on everything, Kate would rather spend a day butting heads with her mom than go to the mall with the forever preening Shari. Kate glanced at the speedometer. Her eyes widened, and she bit her lip anxiously, when she saw the needle wavering around eighty.

"Mom, slow down!" she cried.

"Why?" Perry asked seemingly oblivious to the fact that they were leaving everyone else on the Virginia Beach-Norfolk Expressway in a cloud of dust.

"You're doing eighty!"

"I know. Relax. If there's any danger, that four hundred dollar toy on my dash will let me know. Until the alarm sounds, you might as well sit back and enjoy what you landlocked souls consider warp speed."

Kate sighed. Her mom always got a little speed freaky whenever she was getting close to launch time. Her father described the addiction to the intensity of combat flying many fighter pilots had as the "need for speed." He said some people actually suffered withdrawal whenever they were grounded for long periods of time. Her mom had been, according to her dad, a depressed and miserable soul to live with the whole time she was pregnant because she couldn't fly. She had even gotten violent occasionally, the worst bout resulting in the loss of almost every piece of crockery they owned. Although Kyle knew Perry had a fiery temper, he had no idea the grounding would do such a severe number on her head. Life settled down to normal the day she was allowed back into the cockpit. To hear her father tell it, Kate had no brothers or sisters because he feared, if he made Perry pregnant again, she would lose it even worse and wind up tossing him around instead of the china.

Looking down at the flat plainly wrapped package she had leaning up against the door by her feet, Kate said, "Dad gave me something to give to you. He said it was for your office."

"Why didn't you give it to me before? All my stuff's probably on the boat by now. The only thing that can fit in the Turkey's cockpit is me."

"This'll fit. Dad said so."

"What is it?"

"Want me to open it?"

"Sure."

Kate ripped off the paper to reveal a varnished maplewood plaque upon which was printed in fluorescent orange block letters, "Because I'm the CAG, that's why!" Perry turned away from the road for a split second to glance at the sign Kate held up by its sides. "I love it!" she declared her broad smile making deep dimples in her cheeks. "That's going to go over real big with the boys in the air wing."

"Dad thought you'd like it," Kate said simply as she put the sign back on the floor. "He also said you'd be getting a jet all your own. Is that true?"

"I always had wings of my own," Perry stated. "What your father probably meant was, as air wing commander, I'd have a bird specially designated as the official CAG machine. Unlike my old Tomcat, it won't bear the insignia of my old squadron, the Grim Reapers. However, it won't fly everybody's colors either, like the CAG bird usually does. My baby is going to fly the colors of the Ghostriders, my unofficial squadron."

"How can you have a squadron of all kinds of different planes? I thought they all had to be the same."

"I said it was unofficial," Perry pointed out. "The Ghosts are all good friends of mine, as well as being some of the best drivers, RIOs and BNs flying. If we were all to take wing together, our formation would remind people of Baron Von Richthofen's flying circus. When I got this command, and was given the opportunity to hand pick the fighter and attack squadrons I wanted for Carrier Air Wing Twenty One, I did my damnedest to get together all the squadrons I have ever flown with or for, so there will be a lot of folks on this cruise who'll know me or know *of* me. Which, as you can imagine, is going to make things interesting."

Kate changed the subject by asking, "Is the *Excalibur* battle group stopping anywhere exciting for liberty?"

Perry smiled, knowing full well what Kate was really asking. "We should be spending Christmas in Rio, if we don't encounter a situation that keeps us at sea. If everything stays calm, expect to find some tickets and a hotel reservation in your mailbox by exam week."

"Rio is beautiful," Kate recalled with a wistful smile. "I haven't been there since I was nine. Now I'm old enough to appreciate it and maybe wrangle an invite to one of those infamous liberty parties."

"No way!" Perry said shaking her head. "An eighteen year old girl left to her own devices with a bunch of airedales who, by that time, will have been without regular female companionship for over two months? Forget it!"

"Oh mom, come on! Those guys can't be any worse than the frat rats at Virginia. Besides, they'd be scared to do anything besides look and lust if you were there too."

"Damn right they'd be scared! Anybody who laid a hand on you would find himself flying without benefit of aircraft."

Kate laughed. Having a mom who was a black belt in Tiger-style kung fu and damn good at Tai Chi had its advantages. As long as the Commander was with her, Kate felt she could walk fearlessly into the valley of shadows, fearing no evil because Perry McNeil was the baddest bitch this side of the Atlantic. Kate had seen her mother in action, because the dojos Perry was attached to frequently ran demos and competitions. But she had only heard about Perry using her considerable skills for real from her father and Anzac, Perry's best friend and RIO. The first time Perry was ever put in hack was for a bar fight she got into while in liberty in the Philippines. With a little help from her squadron mates, Perry managed to trash a small sailor's bar in Cubi Point, taking out a few of the Marines who had started it all as well. No one remembers exactly what was said to rile Perry, but word about the incident travelled faster than a brush fire in a dry spell. After that incident everyone in PacFleet knew that she not only had a mean temper but a mean right hook as well.

The guard at the gate to the Oceana base snapped Perry a crisp salute before waving her through. She tooled the Mustang to Ops and parked where she saw a few other cars and their owners standing. She smiled at a woman with the two small children, who stood by a Chevy Caprice wagon's open back door, and the other woman waved excitedly back.

"Barnstormer!" she met Perry as she got out of the car and gave her a hug. "Anzac's checking over your wings. Oh, my god, I can't believe it! You're the CAG! And everyone thought it was such a big deal when the carriers first went coed and women were allowed to do everything the guys could do. This is definitely a film at eleven super scoop!"

Anzac's wife Caroline had to be the perkiest person Perry had ever laid eyes on. She was more cute than beautiful with short naturally curly blond hair surrounding a fresh scrubbed girl-next-door kind of pretty face. Her two children, a boy and a girl who were two years apart in age and very like their mother in temperament, joined Caroline. Tony Junior, the eldest of the two, showed off his Ertle F-14D replica by holding it in his chubby fist and zooming it around. His sister Beth looked on, obviously not impressed with the toy version of what her daddy flew around in. She sat quietly hugging her Cabbage Patch doll that had been dressed up in a nifty replica of the flight gear pilots wore when airborne.

"Hi, Mrs. Edwards," Kate said as she joined her mother and Caroline.

"My god, Katie! You look great!" Caroline gushed. "I swear you look so much like Crazy Kyle it's frightening. Your father was the wildest thing flying, you know that? It was a sad day for the Navy when he turned in his wings."

"Dad still flies," Kate reminded her.

"A 747? Darling, that isn't flying, that's taxying a bunch of people in the air. What this lady," she said putting her arm around Perry's waist, "and my man do, now *that's* flying!"

Perry returned the affectionate gesture of her best friend's wife saying, "I've got to suit up. We're going to have to leave soon."

"Wait! I have something for you."

Perry leaned against the side of the car and arched an eyebrow speculatively while she watched Caroline rummage through the organized chaos of her station wagon's back seat. After a long moment she pulled out a large Pembroke Mall shopping bag and, from inside it, withdrew a black leather bomber jacket. Hand painted on the back was the starburst logo of Carrier Air Wing 21 and, where each of the stars should have been, were the patches of all the squadrons in her command. On the shoulders were the patches of the different ships in the battle group and on the left breast was the patch for their upcoming cruise. Embroidered in a finely scripted hand beneath the cruise patch where she would have expected to see her call sign was the acronym CAG.

Perry took the jacket from Carolyn saying, "It's gorgeous! Thank you so much!"

"Put it on," encouraged Kate.

Perry removed her battle worn brown leather bomber jacket that displayed cruise and squadron patches accumulated from over two decades of Naval service and handed it to Kate. She slipped on the new jacket and luxuriated in its buttery softness. "It feels wonderful. How does it look?"

"Looks good from where I'm standing."

The good old country boy drawl sounded very familiar and Perry turned to see Anzac. He, too, was wearing a jacket identical to hers in all but one respect–his had "Deputy CAG" monogrammed beneath the cruise patch. He was holding a clipboard with the preflight check list on it and he cast her an expectant look.

"I know," she said, not waiting for him to tell her the blatantly obvious. "We've got a boat to catch."

"You guys want to see the plane?" Anzac asked his kids moreso than Kate or Caroline. His two offspring were up and at his side so fast they left little contrails of their own.

"How'd you manage this one?"

"I bribed security. I told them if they let me take my kids to see the Double Nuts, they could have a night of steamy passion with the *Excalibur's* CAG."

"And they went for it?"

"Once I told them you were a girl, sure!" he told her. His expression suddenly full of mischief, he added, "Let's face it, Barny, it's not only your temper that's hot."

"If I'm so hot, how come you never made a pass at me?"

He stopped dead in his tracks and turned to face her. She could tell by the glint in his eye he was holding back a very good retort. "Look, just like you have your own set of rules of engagement, I have mine. The number one being never screw anybody who can beat the shit out of you."

Her eyes twinkled. "Good rule."

"Are you two quite finished?" Caroline interrupted not liking their topic of conversation. "For god sakes, Tony. Your kids are here!"

Anzac put his arm around Caroline's shoulder saying in his usual good-natured way, "Relax, darlin', they gotta learn about this stuff sometime."

"There's no talkin' sense to you when you're this close to fly time," she stated in a tone that reflected just how used she was to seeing this behavior. She scooped up her daughter, took their son by the hand, and led them off toward the fence, on the other side of which, the jet sat waiting saying, "Let's go take a closer look at

Daddy's new toy."

"You really should keep a lid on it around your kids, Anzac," Perry admonished when Caroline was out of earshot. "You don't want them to become a pair of randy sailors now, do you?"

He laughed. "Never happen. I'm not home enough to provide that, much needed, bad influence. They have to learn it to copy it." He turned to Kate and continued, "Now, look at Katie here. She's nothing like you and you've been known to yuck it up with the best of them. See my point? My kids will turn out fine. Your kid sure as hell did."

Kate smiled when her eyes met Anzac's and she closed the distance between them saying, "One thing I will never understand is why the two of you never married when you had the chance."

"I'll tell you why," Anzac said not giving Perry the opportunity to answer. "What was it like growing up with a couple of jet jocks for parents?" Kate didn't answer, but he could see from her expression that she would have said it was no picnic. "That's why, Kate. The intensity of what we do makes it rough for two jocks to get *that* close to one another. Perry and Crazy Kyle get along much better now than they ever did while they were hitched. I know Shari isn't too tickled about the situation, she'd like things better if Perry and Kyle never said boo to each other, but, although their marriage didn't work out, they're still friends."

"You mean you weren't even a *little* bit tempted?" Kate asked expectantly.

"What? To try and see if I could succeed where Kyle failed? No, because I'm no fool. Caroline is the perfect girl for me. The only part of the Navy she wants to know from is the PX and the paychecks. She tolerates me when I get that weirdness from being too long between hops and really enjoys our get togethers during liberty. Our kids are getting to be real well travelled, but, I don't need to tell you all about that now, do I?"

Kate looked him square in the eye and asked boldly, "You mean you never ever tried to make it with my mom?"

He cracked up. Not because the idea of making love to Perry was funny, but because he was surprised Kate would have the guts to ask such a question. Then again, the girl was Perry's daughter and old Barnstormer never was one to beat around the bush. "Look, Katie, your mom is my best friend and, in my educated opinion, the best Tomcat driver in the Navy. That's all there is to it. We are *just friends.*"

Perry looked up at him. "It never, ever crossed that little pea brain of yours?" Anzac shook his head. "Son, you are so full of shit, they could use you to fertilize all of Governor County and still have some left over for the folks in Fayetville."

Anzac hid his face with his hand and turned away. Both Kate and Perry rounded on him unmercifully. They were not about to let him get away until he admitted he had been at least tempted to sleep with Perry. "Okay! Okay! I give up!" he said after he had endured all of the teasing he could stomach. "I've been secretly lusting after Perry for the past twenty years, and every night I dream about pinning her naked to the bulkhead and ravishing her until she faints from exhaustion. Are you satisfied now?"

Both Perry and her daughter were hysterical laughing and Anzac, too, was in stitches. It felt good to release some of the nervous energy the two flyers always seemed to have just before taking off to join the carrier. When Perry calmed down enough to speak coherently, she wiped the tears of merriment from her eyes with her hand saying, "We *really* have to get moving, Anzac."

He nodded in agreement but said nothing because he was afraid he would just start laughing all over again. He was following her back to Ops, where she was going to get her lift authorization, submit her flight plans, and do all the other preflight paperwork when Kate caught him by the arm. Proffering Perry's old jacket, said, "Give this to my mom."

"Hey, CAG," he called and Perry stopped and spun on her heel to face him. She looked a little surprised and he smiled at her saying, "You better get used to it. No one's going to be calling you 'Stormy or Barny on this cruise."

Perry chuckled softly. "I know, but after twenty years of answering to Barnstormer and the derivations thereof, it's going to take a little getting used to. What's the hold up?"

"You forgot your jacket. And the plaque," Kate said.

"The jacket is yours, Kate. Enjoy it. We'll find a place in the back seat for the plaque," Perry said while reaching into her trouser pocket for her wallet. She pulled out the billfold and handed Kate the laminated registration card and insurance paper for the Mustang as well as a set of keys. "Here," she said handing the paperwork over to her daughter who eyed it unsurely. "I want you to take care of the Chek Six for me until I come home. The insurance is paid up for the whole year, so you won't have that to worry about. Just make sure she gets plenty of exercise and high test in her belly and she'll be content. The Chek is a classic, so be good to her. It's not like I can just pick another one off the lot if she goes."

Kate stared at the keys dumfounded. The only thing Perry loved more than her flying machines was that thirty-something year old restored classic Mustang. She had owned it for as long as Kate could remember. The car had its original white leather tuck and roll upholstery seats and was the ragtop version of the car, which made it even more of a special item. Not too many convertibles were still on the road these days. For Perry to give her that old favorite jacket was one thing; To be given the keys to her second baby was another.

"Mom, I can't—" she started to say but stopped short when she saw Perry's expression. Her mom was beaming at her, the pride in her eyes was something Kate had only seen on a few rare occasions such as the day of her high school graduation. On that day she got her award as a National Merit Scholar and also found out she had won a full scholarship to the University of Virginia. She had no idea what she'd done to make Perry so proud of her this time and cast a puzzled look at her mom.

"I promised you a car when you graduated high school, remember?" Perry said. Before Kate had a chance to object, she continued, "I'm not giving the Chekker to you, you're just going to babysit while I'm away. However, you are going to have wheels of your own. Don't think I forgot, I didn't. It's just that I had no idea you were going to graduate from high school when you were sixteen. It's a wonder where you got all them smarts from with two wing nuts for parents. One of us must have had a brainy ancestor and you got his genes."

"Oh, mom, stop!" Kate cried embarrassed. "You and Dad are two of the smartest people I know. I mean, how dumb could you be and graduate fourth in your class from Georgia Tech?"

"That was many moons ago when the qualifications were a lot less stringent. You see, back then it was real hard to concentrate on your books with all the racket those Tyrannosaurus Rexes made whenever they beat up on them Stegosauruses."

"Yeah, and those Pterodactyls were really noisy in the morning, weren't they?" Anzac put in obviously enjoying the odd bend the conversation was taking.

Kate found her sides starting to hurt again as she again was overcome with laughter. Her mom always had a way of making their farewells less painful by finding a way to bring humor to the event. Perry could make Kate laugh all by herself but put her with Anzac and there was no way anybody was going to keep a straight face for long. Kate loved Uncle 'Zac, that was what she used to call him when she was little, because he was around so much it was like he was a member of the family. Crazy Kyle always liked his aw-shucks country boy style. He noticed, early on, the salutary effect Anzac had on Perry. She had a tendency to want to go through life at Mach 2 with her hair on fire. Anzac, on the other hand, moved at a less fevered pace and was quite adept at slowing her down. Kate would have been very happy to have had him as her stepfather. She knew her dad had done his best to drop subtle hints here and there about how good they were together, hoping they'd both take the hint. But, though things didn't work out that way, she was content he that he stayed a part of their lives.

Perry glanced at the inside of her wrist and bit her lip when she saw the time. "It's almost sixteen hundred," she told Anzac. "We are *late*."

He quickly went over to the jet and gathered his wife and two children to say his farewells, leaving Kate and Perry alone to do the same thing. Kate sighed. This was the worst part about being a Navy brat, the waiting while your parent was out to sea. The current cruise was for nine months, two months longer than Perry's last peacetime one had been. But their first liberty stop was scheduled for over the Christmas break, so Kate would get to see her mom again in less than three months. Kate preferred the times her mother had drawn shore duty, like the year she spent at Miramar as a Top Gun instructor, but she knew Perry favored the arduous life of a carrier pilot and the challenges shipboard duty had to offer.

Perry helped Kate into the bomber jacket. It swam on the slender teenager who, while almost as tall as her mother, lacked Perry's hard won upper body development. Kate didn't seem to mind being dwarfed by her new piece of clothing and quickly folded up the cuffs to a comfortable length. She adjusted her sunglasses and posed in as military a posture as she could muster and asked, "How do I look?"

"Like a cover girl for *Vogue*," Perry responded with a cheek dimpling grin.

"I was hoping you'd say I looked like you."

"You don't want to look like me," Perry said quietly as she turned up the edges of the shearling collar on Kate's jacket. "You're going to be a doctor, not a fighter jock. If you want to copy somebody, copy Shari. I know, she's got the intelligence of a tuna and that fish's sense of rugged individuality—" Kate's giggle made Perry pause and the two women shared a laugh at Shari's expense. "Look, what I'm trying to say is that your stepmom is basically a very cool lady, even if she doesn't know a Rockeye from a

Sidewinder. She knows how to mix in polite society. She's country club and boardroom, I'm sailor's bars and wardroom."

Kate looked at Perry crestfallen. "You're always putting yourself down!" she said defensively. "So what if Shari was a debutante and a member of the DAR. She's never *done* anything with her life. You have! I could spend a whole day listing all the things you've accomplished. It would take me five minutes to do the same for Shari."

"I may have done a lot over the years, but I'm not proud of all of it. You have a point but so do I. Life should be more than knowing where to shop." Perry saw Kate's expression brighten and continued, "Look, kiddo, I just want you to have a nice *normal* life and be happy. I'm glad you've got ambition, that's the McNeil side coming through. Just remember there's a lot more to life than a career, no matter how exciting that career might be."

"You're the last person who should be telling me this," Kate stated.

"No, I'm the *only* person who can tell you because I don't want you to make the same mistakes I did. I don't want you to wake up one fine day and find yourself old and alone because the job always stood between you and everybody else in your life, including your husband and your kid."

"You could retire. Dad did."

"Not now, I can't. I'm in so deep I'm practically in China," Perry's eyes twinkled a bit though her expression remained somber. "There are many people in Second Fleet who think that someday I could become the first female Captain of a carrier. Personally, that's one accomplishment I would like under my belt before I hand in my paperwork. I know it's a long way off. Which is good in a sense because there's no way I would accept the position as long as I was able to fly. But it *could* happen. So long as there's a chance, I'm in it for the duration."

"Captain McNeil does have a nice ring to it," Kate agreed smiling. "I hope you get your boat, Mom, I really do. It's just that when you're gone for so long…"

Perry embraced her daughter, who hugged her so tight Perry felt like Kate was saying goodbye to her for the last time. Both fought back their tears. Nine months was too long, even with the fairly frequent liberty stops. Their assignment was an important one: enforcing the Drug Interdiction Accord was a priority for the current Administration. She knew the President was being pressured by Congress to show the need for the multibillion dollar defense budget. Using the military to give the South American drug cartels a swift Sunday punch would hopefully garner the public support the President needed to keep the American big stick waving during peacetime.

But, understanding the need for a tough assignment didn't make the bitter pill any more easy to swallow. Perry sighed deeply before slowly releasing Kate. Her eyes were glistening from tears yet unformed and she said, "Take care of yourself. Thank the Crazy man for the gift."

"I love you, Mom."

Perry's only response was to hold Kate again and kiss her freckled cheek.

Wolff noticed Perry's absent expression and inquired, "Are you okay, Commander?"

"Oh, I'm fine. Just a little sleepy." she replied.

It sounded to him like her normal spunkiness was returning and, inwardly pleased to hear the liveliness back in her voice, he turned to face her. His eyes widened when he saw her pull a rather skimpy black satin gown from under her pillow and tuck it into a drawer. "If you want to change into your nightgown, I'll step outside—"

"No need," she interrupted an amused look glinting in her eyes. "I don't always sleep in nightgowns."

"Just what do you wear to bed?"

Her eyes were full of mischief as she answered, "As little as possible."

He took a step towards her and dared to brush aside a stray wisp of hair, his hand gently caressing her cheek. She didn't respond to his touch and he quickly saw why. Her eyes were slightly glazed due to the effects of the medication and she was a bit unsteady on her feet. He could smell the faint odor of antiseptic from the solution they had used to wash clean her wounds and get all the blood out of her hair. The bandage wrapped around her head looked like a gauze circlet and gave the Wing Leader in the flowing robe an almost medieval appearance.

She smiled slightly at him saying, "Thanks for everything."

"Glad I could help. If you need anything—"

"Not now."

"Are you sure?"

"Yes, quite sure. I'm tired and the corpsman will be more than able to handle what little I'll be needing tonight. But, thanks, anyway."

Perry went over to her desk, picked up the phone and dialed an extension. After a few rings a familiar yet tired voice said, "Edwards here."

"'Zac, it's me."

"Where are you calling from? Sickbay?"

"My quarters. You've got the helm for now. I should be back by Friday, God willing."

"It ain't God who's gotta be willin'," Anzac replied wryly.

Perry rolled her eyes. "Tell me about it." She sighed adding, "Keep me posted. I know the Wing's in good hands but, you know me. I won't sleep unless I've got your assurance that all's well."

"No problem. Take care of yourself. We'll talk tomorrow or sooner if anything happens."

"Right."

She rang off and untied her robe as she walked over to her bed. She shed it seconds before slipping between the sheets and the flimsy cotton of the gown she wore beneath it hid little of her physical attributes. Perry had a great body, even if it was a little war torn. She had scars on her left leg and side from shrapnel she'd taken when her F-14 was shot down during the Bekaa Valley battle. The ones on her leg were very unsightly and were the reason she called in several markers to get special dispensation to wear only the pants version of her various Navy uniforms. However, the scars on her side weren't too bad and did nothing to detract from the beauty of a body that spoke loudly of the years of work that went into molding it into its current state of being.

Wolff liked the athletic type but Perry McNeil was beyond that. She was a body builder, plain and simple. He thought she had a better physique than he did and he was in pretty good shape. He wished his abdomen was that firm, flat and nicely delineated. She had the body of a woman half her age and owed much of her stamina to the fact that she was in such good condition. She had an iron will to go with that woman of steel body and it was that combination that made her so alluring to the men of the air wing. It was also what he liked about her and he wondered for a fleeting instant what it would be like to spend the night with her.

Seeing almost every cut and curve of her hard muscular body stirred him physically. But, what had him really intrigued was a bit of colorful body art he glimpsed as she was settling into the bed. Perry had a beautifully executed tattoo of an Oriental tiger prowling on her left breast. He wondered what had possessed her to get a tattoo, since he knew officers, as a rule, didn't wear them.

He stared at her for a long moment. If the corpsman wasn't parked there on the CAG's desk chair with his eagle eye holding him under careful scrutiny, Wolff knew he would have been sorely tempted to spend more time with Perry. He'd like to get to know her better. He had heard a few stories from the boys in the Air Wing about her exploits during the war and those guys had managed to pique his curiosity. They only knew of a fraction of what she had accomplished and he had barely scratched the surface during their brief in-flight interview. There was so much he wanted to ask her. But he knew he would have to get on a better footing with Perry before she would open up to him about her past.

Perry lay on her back in bed, her green eyes like glazed glass from the effects of the painkillers. Most of lean muscular body was hidden beneath the covers. She lay stretched out on her bunk looking like a tigress basking in the warmth of the noonday sun. Wolff gave her a smile, as he covered the one bared leg with the edge of the blanket, and her only response was a tired-eyed glance. Although he wanted to spend time with Perry while she was recovering, he knew he had a lot of his own work to do. It was going to take some time for him to assemble all the data accumulated over the past twelve hours so it would make sense to his readers.

He approached the corpsman asking, "Can I give you a hand? Like bringing the Commander her meals, perhaps?"

The corpsman thought it over for a moment before responding, "I guess that'll be okay." He wondered for a fleeting instant what Wolff was up to. He handed him Perry's mealcard saying, "You'll need this. Don't get her anything that's greasy or heavy."

Wolff nodded comprehendingly and pocketed the card.

Perry turned over onto her right side and propped her weary head up on her hand. The pills she'd taken in sickbay were acting like a fifth of good Irish whiskey and made her feel like she was floating on a bed of cottony clouds. It was an odd sensation and one she had not experienced since she was hospitalized in Naples while recovering from her New Moon War injuries. Wolff heard her stirring and turned to face her. She noticed his concerned almost paternal expression and smiled tiredly up at him.

"Are you staying or going?" she asked her speech slightly slurred and her eyes heavy-lidded.

"Going," he replied. "It's late and you need your rest. I'll come back tomorrow to bring you breakfast."

She sighed heavily and let the blankets envelope her as she

sunk into a drug induced slumber.

Perry was out cold and he sighed quietly shaking his head. She probably wouldn't remember getting wounded when she gets up tomorrow morning. She is bound to awaken psyched to go back to work only to find a corpsman who was ready, willing and able to act on his orders to prevent her from getting anywhere near the CAG office. Wolff smiled to himself, as he waved farewell to the corpsman and silently left the room. That corpsman was going to have his work cut out for him. From what he had seen of Commander Perry McNeil, Wolff knew keeping her from doing her job would be like trying to keep a bear away from a honey tree. He had a feeling the next few days were going to prove entertaining....

14 December 0845

Poindexter was about to knock on the door to the conference room, when the threads of a conversation from within caught his attention. He didn't recognize any of the voices but the topic they were discussing was very familiar to the Lieutenant. The G-2 team were talking about the incident that got them brought aboard the *Excalibur*. But, that wasn't the reason why 'Dexter had paused to listen. It was *how* they were handling the subject that intrigued him.

"...this'll be the perfect opportunity for you to field test the variant on your Night Eyes system," a male voice said. "We'll find out if those birds are capable of eluding highly sensitive IR."

A chuckle. Then another man, his voice hinting of his Parisian origins, replied, "Yes, but, remember, my system was originally designed for search and rescue, for finding people, not planes. I'm not certain the modification will work."

A woman interjected, "It worked in the lab."

"*This* is not a lab," the Frenchman reminded her.

"Maybe so, but the guys at NAVAIR won't put your latest gizmo into that new plane of theirs until it's shown to work under real-life conditions," the first speaker said as he approached the door. Poindexter knew NAVAIR was Naval Air Systems Command, the procurement arm of naval aviation. He had read in his latest issue of *The Hook*, a carrier aviation journal, that funding was approved to get the Advanced Tactical Aircraft program back on line. "Hey, look. If it work, it works," the man said not sounding very worried. It was obvious he had great confidence in the Frenchman's abilities. "If not, then it's back to the ol' drawing board."

The door opened. Poindexter was alert enough to appear as though he had just arrived there. The lab-coated gentleman gave the Lieutenant a cursory glance as he walked past. Poindexter gazed into the room. He saw they had converted it into a makeshift lab. The group, four men, including the one who had just departed, and two women, was led by a tall well built man with eyes like January at the North Pole. The frosty-eyed man looked more like the leader of a hit squad than a scientist. When his gaze met Poindexter's, the young lieutenant felt the chill right to his bones.

"Come here, mister," the icy-eyed man commanded in a tone

reflecting he was quite accustomed to have his orders followed without question. Poindexter recognized the voice. He was the Frenchman.

Poindexter obeyed finding it hard to hold that glacial stare for longer than a few seconds at a time. The RIO had been sent by Anzac to pick up a report containing the analysis of the fragments the helo team had recovered. The deputy CAG had ordered him to do this errand for two reasons: Yeoman Truesdale was already up to his eyeballs in work and couldn't be spared and 'Dexter had been the first person Anzac had come across who happened to be free at the time.

The man toyed with one of the odd-shaped fragments while he scrutinized Poindexter. After a seemingly endless moment, the scientist asked, "What can I do for you, Lieutenant?"

"I was sent to pick up your report."

"I see..."

He stopped fingering the piece of obsidian material and tossed it lightly onto the table. One of his female assistants handed him a letter sized package bound shut with security tape and he accepted it smiling slightly at the young woman. "I was expecting a yeoman," the man stated eyeing Poindexter suspiciously.

"The Commander's yeoman was busy, so I got drafted."

"The Commander..."

Poindexter thought he saw a trace of something besides glacier in those blue eyes for just a fleeting instant. But it had been so quick he couldn't be sure. In any event, he sensed that this man might know Commander McNeil but 'Dexter couldn't ascertain this for certain. He couldn't read a hint of emotion in the man's inscrutable face.

"Yes sir, Commander McNeil," he added just to make sure Dr. Ice Eyes was indeed thinking of Perry. Poindexter caught what he thought was a glimmer of recognition in those cold orbs.

Poindexter quickly realized he had seen something that could be counted as emotion when he heard the scientist reply, "Tell Perry we should have something more detailed for her by this evening. Also, ask her to stop by here. That is, if she can manage to extricate herself from the cockpit for longer than five minutes."

The RIO found himself smiling despite how uncomfortable this man made him feel. It seems he did know the Commander after all. "Yes sir, I'll give her the message."

"Where is she?"

"Now? Probably asleep, but I'm not sure, sir. You see, she got hurt when those gomers hit us. Commander Edwards is in charge. If you need him, you can call the CAG office or the CIC. Or he could be flying patrol. I'm supposed to be taking a hop myself within the hour."

"You're a pilot?"

"No, sir. I'm an NFO, a RIO. I'm—"

"I know," the man interrupted. "You're a backseater in an F-fourteen. I've spent enough time around you flyers to understand your jargon." That statement surprised Poindexter. He met the man's eyes as the scientist continued in the same conversational tone, "Well, tell Perry I hope she gets better soon. Give my message to Commander Edwards and be sure you tell him before you go chasing clouds. Understood?"

"Yes sir."

"That'll be all, Lieutenant."

For a civilian, this man sure sounded all Navy brass, thought Poindexter as he spun on his heel and left. At least he'd caught himself in time to keep from saluting Dr. Freneau. The man had never introduced himself and, if 'Dexter's keen eyes hadn't caught a fleeting glimpse of the man's ID badge, he still would have no idea who the G-2 team leader was. Well, who he was only mattered in that he had to tell the Commander who had sent her the get well soon wish. He also had to tell her what he had heard Dr. Freneau and his team saying about the new IR system. The Wing Leader would be very interested in hearing about G-2's plans to use the *Excalibur* as the field test site for their latest piece of hardware. He glanced down at the report. He knew he should bring it straight to Anzac, since he was in charge while Perry was ill, but he also knew Perry would want to see it, too.

Well, her quarters were on the way to the CAG office, Poindexter rationalized. He tucked the report under his arm and walked down the hallway absent-mindedly humming one of Alanna's favorite songs.

14 December 0920

Anzac stared at the radar screen watching the multitude of blips as each one executed its own little dance around the screen. If they were to get jumped now, there would be one helluva furball, he sighed. Anzac, along with two squadron XOs and Big Daddy, were keeping tabs on all the birds soaring around the carrier. Since they had begun mobilizing the Wing, they had encountered nothing out of the ordinary, but it had only been half a day. Anzac knew from experience it was way too soon to tell which way the wind was blowing.

The deputy CAG wouldn't say it aloud to anyone but he was secretly wishing he could trade places with Perry. Not that he couldn't handle the responsibilities and headaches of a command. He could, no problem. It was just that he couldn't fly as good on the ground as he could in the air. Viewing the air through a CIC radar screen, and planning strategy based on that data, was tough. Perry could manage this handily in her sleep, but he had to make a conscious effort to accomplish anything resembling the sort of deviousness that made her infamous.

"Did the boys from G-2 sound like they might be able to give us a hand?" Big Daddy asked when he saw Anzac momentarily pull himself away to take a drink from his cup of lukewarm coffee.

Anzac shrugged. "I spoke to them just a little while ago. I now have an idea of what those jets are made of, but no clues as to whose they are. And, with no ID to go on, all we can do is keep the skies covered and wait. *Dr. Freneau* said he'd call the minute they had anything more substantial to offer."

"Freneau?" Big Daddy repeated, knowing the name and the man and disliking both intently. "*He's* on the boat? Does Perry know?"

"No, not yet."

"Are you going to tell her, or just wait until they bump into each other? Because, if you wait and the Perry's packing her H & K at the time of their meetin', we'll have one dead stealth expert and a CAG pounding rocks at Leavenworth."

"Look, she's over Leigh. The divorce became final before we shipped out," Anzac reassured him. Then adding with a wry grin, "Besides, Perry doesn't carry her sidearm around on the ship unless battle stations have been called and, right now, we're only on Full Alert. I guess it's lucky for him that she will only be packing her nine millimeter punch when we're flyin'."

Big Daddy shook his head. "You'd still better tell her. Because, if you don't, *I will*."

The sound of someone tapping on her door woke Perry with a start. She ignored the throbbing in her head as she switched on the small lamp at her bedside and looked at her watch. It was almost eleven-thirty which meant she'd been out for almost ten hours. She hadn't slept that much, all at once, since they'd shipped out. As she rubbed the sleep out of her eyes, the corpsman, who had spent the evening reading a Tom Clancy novel, dog-eared the page and went to get the door. Perry quickly threw on her robe and was tying it closed just as the door swung open to admit her visitor.

It was Poindexter and he gave her a warm smile. "I have some mail for you, Commander," he said handing her the manila envelope.

"Thank you, 'Dexter," she said. "It appears you handled that little assignment I gave you yesterday."

He grinned, his expression pure cocky confidence. "Just a walk in the park."

She rolled her eyes, knowing full well he must've pulled one of his usual foxy maneuvers to have succeeded in returning those fragments undetected. "Out," she commanded, her tone more jesting than serious. "I'll see you in a couple of days."

"Okay," he replied. He paused for a moment adding, "I heard the G-2 people talkin'. They're going to be testing a new IR system. They think it might help us spot those jets."

Perry raised an eyebrow speculatively. "Let's hope they're right." He nodded slightly in agreement. She gave him a knowing eye and said, "Look, if you happen to hear anything else of interest, let me know."

The resident sly fox returned the expression. "You got it. Want me to get you anything? A book, a magazine, a hacksaw baked into a cake?"

Perry laughed lightly waving him out the door. He gave her hand a squeeze in farewell before departing. She was about to tear into the envelope when another knock at the door made her turn. She opened it to reveal Martin Wolff. He was carrying a tray with something on it that she thought resembled breakfast, but couldn't be sure. The yellow glop on the plate could be either eggs or hot cereal. But the steaming black liquid in her old Grim Reapers mug was definitely coffee.

"Hi," he said smiling at her. "Thought you might like some food."

"I would, but I guess that stuff will have to do," she cracked as she backed away from the door to let him in.

Wolff chuckled to himself as he set the tray down on her desk. Perry joined him. She opened her top desk drawer, put the envelope inside, locked it shut, and put the keys into her robe pocket. Wolff watched as she went to her closet and pulled out a bath towel and a toiletry bag. Perry turned back to face him asking, "Can you stick around for a few minutes? I'm going to jump into a quick shower and get myself back to life."

He nodded.

"Fine," she replied. She took a long drink of the coffee. "Good. You didn't put anything in it."

"Your yeoman told me you took it black."

"Did he tell you anything else?"

"No, he didn't. But I could call your office and ask for the latest."

"*I'll* do that," she said as she headed for the phone. She draped the towel over her shoulder, picked up the receiver and dialed the extension. She got Trudy after the second ring. "Anything newsworthy happen last night?"

"Got the latest reconnaissance photos for you, Commander," he stated. "Want them now?"

"Yes. Stop by in about fifteen minutes. I'm hitting the showers."

"Aye, aye," he replied and rang off.

The corpsman stopped her before she could disappear out the door. "Time for your medication, Commander," he said proffering a couple of pills in a small plastic cup.

Perry scrunched up her nose in distaste but washed the drugs down with a couple of gulps of orange juice. "May I be excused now?" she asked sounding like a grammar school student asking her teacher for permission to leave the classroom.

He stepped aside to allow her to depart, but was no more than two steps behind her all the way to the officer's washroom. He stood outside the door and kept a careful watch on all who entered while he waited for Perry.

Wolff let out a tired sigh as he collapsed into her desk chair. Sleep had managed to elude him for most of the night. The adrenaline rush stirred by the prior day's activities kept his engines going full throttle and he had spent all those hours behind his word processor hard at work. The effects were just now beginning to wear off and Wolff felt his rump dragging a bit.

He scanned the room. Perry hadn't personalized her space very much. Her office had far more character than her quarters and he got the impression that she didn't bother to fix up the place because she spent so little of her time there. His eyes again came to rest on the photo of Perry and her daughter. He noticed their familial resemblance was not so much a physical one as one of manner of expression. The two women had the same intensity in their green eyes and the same wry smiles. But, Perry was all cocky jet jock as she posed next to her wheels, wearing her patch covered leather bomber jacket over her khakis, while her daughter resembled a *Vogue* model. She looked willowy and graceful in a pretty floral print dress.

A yawn overtook him and he stretched his tired muscles. The urge to sleep was very strong and he decided it wouldn't hurt to succumb to it for a few minutes. He rested his head on his arms, which were folded on the desk before him and dozed.

The sound of someone knocking lightly, then unlocking the door after a small pause, startled Wolff. His eyes snapped open as Truesdale entered the cabin. The yeoman stood there looking a little harried as he quickly scanned the room.

"The Commander still in the shower?" he asked.

Wolff nodded. He noticed Truesdale clutching a manila envelope marked "Confidential" and some other papers and asked, "You want to leave that?"

Truesdale pricked up his ears for a second to make sure no one was coming before he replied, "Yes. But I'm going to have to hide it. The Commander isn't supposed to be working so I kind of have to be sneaky about it."

Wolff grinned. "Don't worry. My lips are sealed," he said conspiratorially.

Truesdale smiled back and approached Perry's desk. He unlocked the top desk drawer, secreted the envelope between some papers and then locked the drawer shut. "Ask the Commander to call her office when she gets back, okay?"

"Sure."

He gave the reporter a sly wink before disappearing out the door.

When Truesdale left Perry's cabin, he almost bumped into Colonel Grimmig, who was just about to knock on Perry's door. He was glad he didn't collide into this wall of a man—it would have hurt. Grimmig looked sharp in his work khakis and sported as many racks of ribbons as Perry did. He was the commander of the Marine forces aboard the *Excalibur* and put in the same long hours Perry did. The yeoman heard he and Perry had become good friends when they served together aboard the *George Washington* during the War. She had always spoke of him with a fondness that she reserved only for those close to her. Truesdale noticed the Colonel was carrying a soft looking package in a plain brown wrapper and asked, "A little something from home?"

He smiled. "Not quite, Trudy," he said. "Is Perry up?"

"She's taking a shower. She should be back soon."

Grimmig nodded saying, "I'll wait inside and surprise her."

Truesdale smiled knowingly and, catching the Colonel before he entered the room, said quickly, "Mr. Wolff is in there, sir."

Grimmig raised an eyebrow. "Oh? Why?"

"I'm not sure. Probably wants to interview the Commander. You know, for his book. Until now she's been too busy to give him any time."

Grimmig nodded. That was certainly true enough. He hadn't been able to spend much time with Perry either. But, he knew it wasn't just the job keeping them apart. She had made it plain at the beginning of the cruise that she was going to need some time alone. The ink was barely dry on her divorce papers and the whole breakup had been hell for her. He wasn't sure if she was ready to have him back in her life but he wouldn't know how she felt until he tried.

He entered the cabin and gave the sleepy eyed reporter a smile. Wolff rose to meet him and they shook hands cordially. "Hi, Colonel Grimmig, I don't think we ever really got to meet," Wolff said trying his best to hide how tired he was. "I'm Martin Wolff."

"I know who you are," Grimmig replied. "I've seen you around. When are you going to talk to *my* boys? Now, you want to talk to some *real* pilots, hit up a few of my Harrier drivers."

Wolff grinned. "I already have. Too bad that bird is a single seater. I'd love a ride in the jump jet."

The phone in the room buzzed and the Colonel answered it. "Grimmig here."

Wolff could just make out the voice on the other end. It was Anzac and, no doubt, he was calling to check up on Perry. He was unable to make out exactly what was being said but, judging from the expression on the Colonel's face, the call was a personal rather than a professional one.

"I'll tell Perry—" he stopped short as he saw Perry enter the room followed closely by the corpsman. "She's back," he told Anzac. To Perry, he said smiling, "It's 'Zac, Perry. He's calling to make sure you're still alive."

Perry smiled warmly at Grimmig as she took the phone from him. "'Zac, I'm still here, don't worry. When you get some time, stop by and visit. It'll be a lonely three days if none of my friends come by…"

She let the thought trail off for effect and this was not lost on her deputy. He knew it wasn't strictly social calls she was after. "I'll be by later," he replied. "With some new reccy photos for you."

"Great," she said still smiling and trying to sound as casual as possible. She knew the corpsman was watching her and she had to keep it light in order not to arouse suspicion. "I'll see you then."

She hung up and turned to face Wolff and Grimmig. The Colonel handed her the package saying, "A little something from an old friend."

She beamed. It was obvious to Wolff, from her expression, that the Colonel was far more than just an "old friend" to Perry. He knew she was only recently divorced. When had she managed to find the time to hook up with the distinguished looking Marine, Wolff wondered as he watched their nonverbal interaction.

He suddenly remembered Truesdale's message and said, "Commander, your yeoman asked me to have you to call him when you got back."

Perry nodded. "Thanks," she said as she placed her toiletry bag, and Grimmig's present, on her desk and dialed her office extension. Truesdale picked up and she said, "What's up?"

"We're going to be getting a lot of great reconnaissance photos from now on," he told her. "I gave the latest to Commander Edwards. He put together a sampling of the more interesting stuff for you to look over. I locked them in your top desk drawer. The satellites are keyed directly over this area. They'll be taking pictures round the clock until the spooks tell them to stop."

"Excellent," she replied.

"I'll try and sneak you some more goodies," he said. "It's going to be tough with Old Hawkeye watching you every second."

"Tell me about it," she agreed.

"I'll stop by later, Ma'am," he promised and rang off.

Perry looked like the cat who just swallowed the canary as she hung up the receiver. Her expression was lost on the corpsman and

Wolff. But Grimmig, who knew her far better than they did, caught the naughty look. The Colonel gave her a knowing eye and she grinned. Glancing back at the gift, she asked, "Should I open your present now?"

He smiled, his eyes glinting mischievously, and replied, "Only if no one here embarrasses easily."

She chuckled softly. "I'll wait, then."

Wolff didn't need to be an expert at reading body language to know that, right now, he was definitely an unwanted third wheel. He cleared his throat meaningfully saying, "I've got to get back to work. I'll stop by later, Commander."

Perry's gaze shifted onto him for a second as she said to his retreating back, "All right. Later then."

The corpsman, who also sensed there was something going on between the Colonel and the Commander, said, "If you need anything, Commander, just holler. I'll be by the door."

Perry nodded slightly as she replied, "Fine."

The corpsman grabbed a chair, stepped outside, and parked himself in the chair next to the door. As he kept watch over Perry from the outside, he resumed reading his Tom Clancy novel. He had been warned by Dr. Melman that the Commander was a workaholic. It was believed she would do her utmost to stay on top of what's happening in the Air Wing. She was also not above recruiting her friends to help her in her efforts. Keeping abreast of what was going on was all right; running the show from her quarters was right out. His challenge would be to make sure she did only the former and not the latter. But, considering all the friends she had, he knew it was going to be hard for him to tell who was visiting out of sympathy and who was only coming there to help her keep her hand in. From what he had seen so far, all her calls had been strictly of a very personal nature....

The only way Perry was going to get a chance to do any work would be to sneak it in under the nose of her ever vigilant corpsman. She knew she had been given a direct order to rest. But she also knew she couldn't relax unless she was sure her Air Wing was being well taken care of. She had faith in Anzac's abilities to handle things while she was recuperating, but it was hard for her to just plop everything in his lap and forget it. She *had* to keep poking her nose in from time to time to reassure herself that everything was, indeed, going well.

She sighed deeply, as a wave of exhaustion suddenly passed over her, and smiled tiredly up at Grimmig. He gave her a hug and

Perry wrapped her arms around his narrow waist. "Want me to tuck you in?" he asked.

She snuggled against his chest. "Sorry, it just hit me suddenly."

"It's all right. You're supposed to be resting, remember?"

She gave him a squeeze. She had missed him *so* much. They had not seen each other since the War and, back then, they had been as close as a man and a woman could get short of physical affection. "Promise me you'll come by and see me again?"

He nodded and gave the tip of her upturned nose a little kiss. "I promise."

She slipped off her robe and climbed into bed, letting him snuggle the covers around her as though she were a little girl being tucked in by her father. He snapped off her light saying, "Pleasant dreams, 'Stormy. I'll catch you later."

Perry was still smiling contentedly even after sleep overtook her.

14 December 1410

Perry stretched leisurely and sat up. The short nap had given the medication a chance to work and, now that the throbbing in her head was almost completely gone, she was ready to get some work done. She noticed there had been a shift change while she slept. The new corpsman, a muscular black man in his early twenties, cast an assessing eye on her.

"Need something, Commander?" he inquired, his voice a rich baritone.

"Uh, well, a cup of black coffee would be nice," she replied. She got out of bed adjusting her oversized nightshirt to cover her shoulder and the colorful tattoo.

He closed the magazine he had been reading, left it on the corner of her desk and departed saying, "Mr. Wolff will be bringing you your lunch. Try to eat *something*, Commander."

Perry nodded and he closed the door with a barely audible snick. As fast as lightning, Perry McNeil was behind her terminal. She quickly pulled up on her screen what the radarman in the CIC had on his and saw the skies around the carrier looked very well covered. Aircraft circled at varying altitudes and distances from the ship in search of their elusive quarry. She grabbed the phone and dialed the CIC extension. It was at first answered by a technician, who quickly switched the line over to Anzac.

"Looks like you've got everything covered," she told him.

"No news is good news, I guess," he replied. "Got any suggestions?"

Perry pondered the screen for a long moment. "Yeah. Talk Bones into giving me back my wings."

Anzac chuckled softly. "Sorry, no can do. Anyway, it'll only be for a couple more days. If it would make you feel better, you could always slip down here—"

"I wish. Ollie threatened to toss me in the brig if I dared to go anyplace other than the head while I'm recuperatin'," she interrupted. "Anyway, I'm on-line over here, and, since we've got the phone, we can consult. Not that it looks like you need any help."

"Things could change."

"And when they do, call. I'll be here."

"Did you get a chance to look at the reccy photos Truesdale brought you?"

"No, not yet. Give me a coupla minutes," she replied. She quickly unlocked and opened her top desk drawer knowing full well that was where her crafty yeoman hid the work she was not supposed to be doing. There were two envelopes inside. She tore into the one containing the photos and removed the batch of pictures in one lump. As she went through them one by one, she recognized the layouts as being military airfields. The close up shots showed MiGs of various types in use. They were shots of Cuba's air arsenal, which she was able to tell by the markings on the jets, but not one of the planes in the photos looked anything like the ones they were seeking.

"Well?"

"Damn," she breathed as she examined one of the better closeups. "They've got Fishbeds and Floggers aplenty, but not the birds we're lookin' for. Anything new come in?"

"Yes, but nothing in the latest batch matches what I chased. So far, we've got a zero batting average."

"Maybe the Cy Young winner will get off the mound this afternoon..." she let the thought trail off and she smiled when she heard him chuckle softly. She put aside the photos and tore open the other envelope. It contained the preliminary report from G-2. As she scanned the paperwork, she paused to read a detailed account of the new IR system, code named Night Eyes. She didn't get very far into it.

"'Stormy? Are you there?"

The phone! "Sorry, 'Zac. 'Dexter dropped by and brought me G-2's preliminary report."

"He was *supposed* to fetch that for *me*," Anzac said meaningfully.

Perry sighed. "Maybe no one told him I'm officially out of the picture."

Anzac made no response to that. He said, "I'll have Trudy stop by to pick up that paperwork. I'll see you later tonight. Sooner if there is a major breakthrough."

"Fine," she replied her eyes again on the report on her lap. As she perused the paperwork, a thought stuck her. "'Zac?"

"What?"

"Hear anything about that pilot we picked up?"

"Only that he hasn't awakened yet. I'll keep you posted"

"Right...Later."

She hung up, leaving Anzac feeling rather pleased with himself. Perry rarely dished out compliments but her leaving it all in his hands, without so much as one word of advice, told him more than a dozen kudos would have. Duty alone told him she should be apprised of any status change, that he knew only too well. Even thought the findings of G-2 were important, 'Dexter should *not* have brought her that report. Especially when Anzac had requested it in the first place. When time allowed, Anzac intended to gnaw on 'Dexter for his misdeed. Meanwhile, he would give Perry some time to check out G-2's findings. She needed to know what was going on because the Wing was her responsibility. Though she had made it clear in her unspoken words she knew he could handle running the show in her absence, Anzac knew Perry would not be able to relax unless she felt assured she was keeping on top of things.

Anzac put the receiver into the cradle with a sigh. I guess telling her about having her ex-husband on board is going to have to wait, he thought glumly. And I hope they *don't* run into each other. Considering the circumstances under which Leigh and Perry parted company, an unexpected meeting between the two of them could result in more fireworks than a Macy's Fourth of July show.

He had been there to witness the event that led to Perry and Leigh Freneau's rather messy divorce. It happened the day Perry returned home from Naples. She'd been recuperating from wounds she'd received during the Bekaa Valley battle for nearly a month in a Naval hospital. She had flown back to the States on the same day the hospital released her. Perry's leg was still taped up and she needed a cane to get around but, other than that, she seemed back to normal. She was her usual wry and witty self when Anzac and Caroline picked her up at Washington National.

Perry met them by the crowded arrival gate and let Anzac relieve her of her overstuffed duffle bag—her one and only piece of luggage. Caroline noticed, by the loose fit of Perry's whites, that her friend had lost weight. She also noticed the Commander was sporting a whole new rack of ribbons. With her husband's expertise on identifying Naval honors cluing her in, Caroline quickly learned what new awards Perry had garnered on top of the major one she already knew about. Perry had received the Medal of Honor for her actions in the Bekaa Valley battle. Caroline had read in the newspaper that Perry was the second woman in history ever to have received that prestigious award. Anzac was given the Silver Star for his efforts, and became a bit of a celebrity back home after his face was plastered on the front page of their local paper. At first it had been kind of fun being recognized, and stopped in stores by kids and old ladies who treated him like he was a movie star. But, after a while, the novelty wore off and he wanted to return to living his life in obscurity. He was glad things were beginning to go back to normal; There was no way Perry would have had the patience to deal with all those people wanting to get close to a bona fide war hero.

The long days spent in the hospital seemed a lifetime away to the Grim Reaper's skipper, who smiled slightly as she walked toward Anzac's car. Somehow she managed to walk with her usual cocky swagger, even though encumbered by a cane and an injured leg. She would soon be home with the husband she hadn't seen since she shipped out close to a year ago. This was the only time Perry could remember looking forward to obeying a doctor's order to get a lot of bed rest.

Caroline drove because she knew Anzac wanted to spend the ride to Virginia Beach catching up on things with Perry. Since he'd been lucky and received only minor injuries, he had been sent home after only a week in the Naples hospital. He owed his life to Perry. It was her skill behind the stick that kept them both airborne until they were over the Med and within range of a relatively easy sea rescue. He had had no idea how badly wounded she had been until he found her after they bailed out. She was a bloody mess, lying unconscious in the one-man raft surrounded by a pool of dye. He had no idea how she'd managed to get herself into the life raft and mark the water before blacking out, but apparently Perry had a cat's own instincts for survival.

Anzac was on medical leave even though he'd recovered from his injuries weeks ago. He wasn't due to return to active duty until the end of the month. He was glad he was still off because, otherwise, he wouldn't have been around to welcome home his best friend. They sat in the back seat together, chatting and joking about old times, while Caroline tried with a titan's might to concentrate on the road. It was a long ride, not that the airport was far from Perry's home, which it wasn't, but Anzac's wife forgot how tough it was to drive and laugh at the same time. Perry could always break her up relating the lighter aspects of carrier life but this time she had hospital stories to tell as well.

As Caroline pulled into the driveway of the grey tri-story beachfront townhome, Perry fell silent. The garage door was open, and her husband's black Peugeot was parked inside. He was supposed to be in Alexandria on business, which was why she'd asked Anzac to give her a ride home. Something wasn't right, but she said nothing as she climbed out and let Caroline help her up the steps to her front door. Anzac brought up the rear with her duffle bag.

Perry's home looked like a page out of *House and Garden*. White carpet, stark white walls, and white furniture with splashes of color only in accent pieces like pillows, pottery and paintings. Caroline knew it had been done by a professional decorator at Leigh Freneau's expense and insistence. Perry didn't know a thing about homemaking and was away so much Leigh saw fit to do things to meet his standards for comfort and aesthetics. It was a little stark for Caroline's tastes but, then again, with two small children, there was no way any home she had would ever look anything but lived in.

"Want me to make you some tea, Perry?" Caroline offered as Anzac plopped the bag down next to the stairs.

Perry shook her head. "No. No, thank you. I'm going to go upstairs."

She went to grab her bag but Anzac beat her to it. "You walk, I'll carry," he said as he watched her hop the stairs, keeping the weight off her bad leg by using the railing as a support.

Perry used her cane once she reached the second level and made her way across the plush carpet to her bedroom. She paused by the door when she heard the strains of a Mozart sonata playing and a woman's laughter. At first Perry thought it was the television but, when she heard her husband's voice conversing quietly with the lady, she quickly realized that her homecoming was definitely *not* expected. A dozen emotions coursed through her but the ruler of them all was cold fury. Fury over having her trust betrayed and knowing that, while she'd been at war on the other side of the world, her husband Leigh had found someone else to keep the fires burning at home.

If her leg hadn't been injured, Perry would have kicked the door in. She had to content herself with bursting in unannounced armed only with her wooden cane and a Gaelic temper. Leigh was in their bed with a dark haired girl who looked barely of age to enough to vote, let alone have an affair with a man old enough to be her father. The girl screamed in terror and pulled the covers up around herself as though they would give her some protection. Leigh merely stared at his wife dumfounded. It was obvious to Perry from his expression that he had not been expecting her to be coming home this early.

"You sonovabitch!" she growled as she took a swing at him with the cane. Leigh ducked in time and managed to avoid having his head split open. She tried again, but he dodged the second shot by making a dive over the body of the terrified girl and landing hands and feet on the floor like a cat.

Anzac could see where this was heading and knew if he didn't do something fast Perry was going to be guilty of a double homicide. He entered and grabbed Perry arm saying, "Stop this!"

She roughly broke free of Anzac snapping, "Butt out!" As Perry was making her breakaway from Anzac, Leigh got up from the floor and made a mad dash for the master bathroom. Perry tried to cut him off, but Anzac's interference had given Leigh enough of a lead on her to keep himself from getting beaned. With Leigh hidden behind a locked door, the only one left around for Perry to vent her rage on was the unfortunate object of Leigh's affections.

"Please don't..." the girl begged eyes wide in terror. She looked so pathetic cowering beneath the satin sheets that Perry found it hard to believe her husband was actually attracted to this "thing."

Anzac was about to intervene on the girl's behalf but stopped when he saw Perry slowly lower the cane. He sighed with relief. She had come so close to a date with the rockpile at Leavenworth it wasn't funny. Anzac backed off and said nothing. Perry gathered up the girl's clothing and threw them at her commanding, "You got five minutes to get dressed and get out."

The girl didn't need to be told twice. She scooped up her things and fled into the hallway. She ran into the second bath and locked shut the door behind her.

Perry went to the door of the master bathroom. Her breathing was ragged, as she fought hard to hold back her tears, and in a choked voice said, "The only reason you're still alive, you piece of shit, is because Anzac was here. He saved your cheatin' ass." Anzac saw her green eyes go dark, and sighed softly. Leigh was going to wish she had managed to knock him unconscious after this night was over. "You can't hide in there forever. You are going to have to come out and face me and tell me why I had to come home from the war to find you in bed with someone young enough to be your daughter!"

Leigh had no answer for her, and Perry turned away from the door to meet Anzac's concerned gaze. "Don't worry, 'Zac, I'm not going to beat him into next week. Not that the bastard doesn't deserve it. I'm stuck on a boat on the other side of the world laying my ass on the line every day. Living like a goddamn nun for almost a year, and what do I come home to? This? Whoever said "War is hell" sure knew what they were talkin' about!"

"You want to come home with us?" Anzac offered.

"No, I'll try to work things out here," she said no longer hiding how painful her leg was. There no longer was anyone for her to be strong for or to look good for. She collapsed onto her bed with an audible sigh.

"If you need me—"

"I know," she interrupted with a wan smile.

He sat beside her and held her close for a long moment. That was the only time Anzac could recall that he had ever seen Perry cry. She shed many a tear while struggling to keep their damaged Tomcat airborne but she was in agony then and never truly cried. Her voice had barely quavered when he heard her speaking to him over the ICS. No, Perry had always been good at keeping almost all her emotions in check. The only one she couldn't seem to master was her Irish temper but, since so many fliers in their squadron lived in fear of her wrath, it was just as well she couldn't hack that one.

Leigh had been the one to move out leaving Perry to recuperate alone in their beachfront home, with only the rushing of the waves for company. She could have had Anzac, Caroline, and even her daughter or first husband Kyle over. She had turned them all down saying she needed the time to herself. Perry knew, from experience, that the Navy provided many useful services for people in her circumstances and she availed herself of them. She periodically visited a counselor to help her keep her head straight while she was going through the divorce proceedings. It was long and messy because Leigh wanted her to have nothing, on the grounds she hadn't been around enough to merit any kind of settlement. Fortunately, she had made enough friends in her Naval career to be owed some major favors. This resulted in her getting a lawyer who made sure she was well compensated for having to go through the agony of her homecoming.

The townhouse was beautiful, but it was never really home to Perry. She was only happy when she was at sea, but the property was very valuable. It was for that reason she was glad she got title to it as part of the settlement. She got assigned to Oceana NAS with the understanding she'd get another post at sea when she was no longer forced to juggle her time between the Navy and the court of the Commonwealth of Virginia. While she was biding her time at Oceana, Anzac, as her XO, was sent back to the *George Washington* to be the skipper of the Grim Reapers. The hardest part of the wait was Tomcatting without her best friend in the back seat.

Less than six months into her time at Oceana, the war ended and a year after that she got the orders giving her command of the *Excalibur's* air wing. The past year and a half had been a nightmare but the Navy had seen fit to reward her pain by giving her her dream shot. A nine month deployment aboard the hottest nuclear carrier in the fleet was going to be fun enough but, to top it off, she was going to sea as the CAG. She pulled a few strings and got to pick and choose the squadrons that would be a part of Air Wing 21. She also managed to get Anzac aboard as her deputy. When she got the papers declaring her free of Leigh the day before she shipped out, Perry was ready to dive back in to life head first.

Anzac noticed she was back to her old self when he saw her at Oceana, the day their squadrons were due to fly out to meet the carrier. Things went on like nothing ever happened and she never mentioned Leigh, not even in passing. It was like that part of her life just didn't occur. He knew this was her way of putting the past behind her and he never questioned her about it. Still, with Leigh on the *Excalibur* as their advisor on stealth technology, Perry was going to be forced to face that rather painful period in her life. It was not going to be easy for her to keep things purely professional while dealing with Leigh. Anzac silently hoped his warning her might have some mollifying effect on the tensions this situation was bound to cause.

A light tapping at the door made Perry jump. She turned saying, "Who is it?"

"Martin Wolff. I got your lunch, Commander."

Perry quickly opened the door to admit him. He gave her a smile, which she politely returned, and took the tray over to her desk. He stood looking for an unfilled spot to put it on when Perry said, "Let me move this for you."

She gathered up all the photos and anything else that looked like work, shoved it together into a pile, and stuck it into her top desk drawer. It was in the nick of time, too. The corpsman must have been two steps behind Wolff. He walked in just as Wolff was placing the tray down on her desk blotter.

"Your coffee, Commander," the corpsman said placing the steaming liquid within easy reach.

Perry gave him her best smile. "Thank you."

Wolff noticed the images on the computer screen. "New video game?" he inquired.

"Uh, yeah," she lied as she quickly switched off the monitor. The connection was still there. She could always put it on later. Perry caught Wolff's one-eyed conspiratorial wink and grinned. She decided to play this one out. "Had to do something to keep my mind occupied while I was waiting for lunch."

"Your yeoman said he will be stopping by later with your mail from home," the corpsman informed her.

"Great," she replied as she took a healthy bite of the tuna melt. It was pretty good and she quickly consumed the sandwich. While she ate, Wolff stood quietly by her desk studying her with an appraising eye. When she realized she was being scrutinized, Perry looked up at him quizzically. "What?"

"Nothing. I was just…"

He let the thought trail off because he was beginning to see her in a completely different light. She eased back into the swivel chair crossing her legs which, because of the silkiness of her nightshirt's fabric, made the gown slide. One leg was bared, as it rested on the top of her knee, almost up to her hip. Martin tried not to stare but Perry McNeil had great legs, even if one of them had suffered a bit because of a camel jockey's lucky shot.

She caught him looking and grinned. "There's still plenty of cold water left in the showers," she remarked.

"You mean you left some?" he retorted.

Perry chuckled slightly. It seems Paper Boy is beginning to learn how to play the game, she mused. She turned away glancing at the darkened screen saying, "I know you wanted to talk last night but I was too doped up to do anything but sleep."

"I know. I saw."

She looked up at him. She remembered that Wolff had been the one who took her to sickbay when she collapsed. He had also stuck around and waited patiently while she was being cared for by Melman. He had walked with her back to her room and had visited for a while. Since she had been injured, he had stuck to her like glue and treated her like she was his oldest and dearest friend. He had been nothing but nice to her from the start and, although he did get on her nerves sometimes, he didn't really ask for all the shit she had heaped on him. She wanted to apologize for having been such a bitch but she wanted to do it right.

When he leaned over to get a better look at what she had on the screen, Perry tilted the monitor up a bit so he could see the display. She was tapped into the CIC radar station and was watching the patrols. Perry picked up a potato chip and began to toy with it lightly. "Look, I'm really grateful for everything you've done," she said looking in his direction but not quite able to meet his eyes. "I probably didn't get a chance to tell you that last night."

"You did, believe me," he said simply and she met his gentle gaze. She has nice eyes, he thought. Full of untapped mischief.

She smiled slightly adding, "Look, I'm glad you want to help take care of me, but you've got your work—"

"Nothing that can't wait," he interrupted. "Besides, I've volunteered myself to be the bearer of bad food."

She grinned. "If you want to order us some good food, Domino's delivers."

"Out *here*?"

Her eyes twinkled impishly. "Why not? We'll stick Jonsey with the bill!"

He laughed. He liked her sense of humor, some of which was evident in the way the CAG office was decorated. He liked the sign that was hanging from the wall behind her desk loudly proclaiming "Because I'm the CAG, that's why!" and the little figurines on top of her filing cabinet, some in vulgar poses with wise-ass sayings printed on their bases. The rest of the office was serious business and told of the Wing's accomplishments or her own. It was Perry's second domain, the first being the cockpit of the Double Nuts and whatever sky she was flying through. It was where she liked to go whenever she needed a place to think.

He said, "I'm sorry breakfast was such a washout. At least this stuff's okay. I'll stop by later. And I'll do my best to scare up something you'll like for dinner."

She smiled slightly, when he gave her shoulder a friendly squeeze before turning to leave the room, and said to his retreating back, "Thanks. Catch you later."

As the door snicked shut, Perry sighed. She switched on the screen and tilted it so it faced her directly. She toyed idly with the mouse, so it looked like she playing a video game as she watched her Air Wing in action. Wolff was okay company and his visits helped to break up the monotony of her enforced rest. But, it was thoughts of someone, who had been her shoulder to lean on all War long, that she longed to see. She hoped Grim's schedule would allow him another chance to visit. Seeing him again brought back memories. Good memories, for the only happy times she had during the War were the times they shared. As sat there swiveling slightly in her chair, the CAG stared at the door wondering when Grimmig would be walking through it....

14 December 1715

Anzac tapped lightly on Perry's door just in case she was resting and smiled slightly when she opened it to admit him. He glanced around the room for the corpsman and saw he was busy putting fresh linens on Perry's bed. His back was to her and her desk, which was a good thing; What Perry had on her desk and up on her computer looked a great deal like Wing business.

"How are you feeling?" he asked.

"Fine," she replied. "I spent the day catching up on my letter-writing." She sat behind her desk with her gaze fixed on the computer screen. He joined her by her desk and peered over her shoulder at the monitor. She was keeping tabs on the Air Wing and he smiled to himself. He knew if she had to, Perry could get a mindless video game up on that screen in less than a heartbeat. His old friend was *really skillful* at being sneaky.

She caught his expression and gave him a playful nudge. He nudged back. He noticed she was wearing a pair of drawstring sweatpants and a T-back Annapolis tank top that clung to her like a second skin. His smile widened a bit as he enjoyed the view. She grinned back even though she knew he was giving her the once over twice.

"'Zac, did Trudy ever catch up to you about—"

"Yeah, Perry, I handled it," he reassured her. He gave her a knowing smile adding, "I not as good as you are at making JO's tremble in their boots, but I think I managed to put enough fear of God into those kids. I'm sure they won't make the same mistakes. The next time the Skipper sees fit to check the Air Wing's compartments, he's not going to find so much as a speck of dust!"

Perry smiled. "Good." She took the manila envelope from his hand saying, "Are these the latest intelligence reports?" He nodded. "Great. Our spooks come up with anything good?"

"Well, nothing on that guy we picked up. He's still out of it. But we know where those birds *didn't* come from," he told her. "The boys from intelligence think it could be Cuba but they also were saying that those jets could have just been flying over Cuba and then on to their real home base. The Cubans don't have anything to detect stealth of this caliber and anyone savvy enough to build those jets probably knows what the Cubans are lacking. They'd be more than willing to take advantage of their shortcomings. But, just to be sure, the Soviets were asked and, of course, they denied that they gave Castro any new and improved toys to play with. They also deny that they're testing anything in this hemisphere. I'm inclined to believe them, even if the boys in Washington have their doubts."

Perry settled in behind her desk to read the reports and look at the latest photos. "You know the Russians still get off on a good game of king of the hill. *Glasnost* be hanged. They want to be the number one superpower, even if they don't publically admit it. And they still like to see just how far they can stick their hands into the cookie jar before we give them a slap. Our boys are constantly chasing their boys out of our airspace."

"And their boys chase ours out of theirs," Anzac put in.

"And so the game goes on, it's only the rules that have changed."

Anzac smiled slightly as Perry pulled out the old stack of photos and added them to the new ones. There were a few shots of what appeared to be an aerospace industrial plant that made Learjet clones and small private planes. Perry surmised that facility could easily be geared up to turn out military aircraft but the photos she was looking at didn't do much to back up her conjecture.

Holding up the photo of the aircraft factory Perry said, "Back in the early 1990s, Gorbachev reduced the amount of military assistance Russia was willing to give Cuba because Castro derided Gorbachev for abandoning Communism in favor of an open-market system. This forced the Cubans to start fending for themselves , which, I guess, is why they've been concentrating on building up their industry."

"True, but they would have to sell a lot of spare parts to afford a squadron of stealth fighters. And that's assuming the Russians would be willing to sell them something with first strike capabilities. As it stands now, those birds that nailed us are far and away above what Castro's boys could have gotten their paws on with barely a decade of semi-autonomy under their belts. Hell, they're better than the stuff *we've* got and you know our stealth is no slouch."

"Yeah. My old man used to sing the praises of flyin' in something no one could see every time I was within earshot. The Colonel still hasn't forgiven me for joining the Navy instead of the Air Force. But how can you tell your old man that, much as you'd love to have him for your CO, you don't want to spend your whole life living in his shadow? You don't want to constantly have your flying abilities compared to his? I had to go someplace where I could be seen as an independent unit and judged accordingly. And, considerin' Colonel McNeil's rep with the 45th Tactical Fighter Wing, the Air Force was definitely not the place for me."

Her deputy gave her a knowing smile saying, "Yeah, and am I glad you did go Navy. God only knows who I would've gotten to cruise the skies with if you hadn't come along."

Perry grinned. Her expression sobered quickly as the photo in her hand again captured her full attention. "They could have built those MiGs. They must have the capabilities because they've been able to keep their MiGs up and flying. You know how much maintenance goes into keeping a fighting jet combat ready. They've got to have the parts and, if you got the parts, you've usually got the smarts to know how to put them together."

Anzac sighed thoughtfully. Their intelligence showed Castro did have a pretty sizable and up to date military operation going, but there wasn't any hard evidence to show he had stealth fighters. He had MiGs, mostly 29s and 31s but with a few 21s and 23s tossed in almost as an afterthought. There were some helos in the photos as well as shots of the landlubber army types but Anzac was more interested in the Cuban air force. Not only because they were the only ones who could attack them, but also because it was in the area of aviation that Castro's military buildup since his days of kinship with Mother Russia, was the most apparent.

"Those folks in Eastern Europe must be eating a lot of bananas and oranges and eating tons of sweets to pay for all those MiGs," commented Anzac. "All this hardware costs *mucho pesos*."

Perry put aside the photos showing farmland remarking, "No kidding. They have increased their exports. They *had* to in order to survive without Russia's financial support." She pulled the one that piqued her curiosity and showed it to Anzac. It was from too high up for the airfield to be identified clearly but the cylindrical black object being offloaded next to the hanger was recognizable to the two seasoned veterans. It appeared to be drop tank. "Does that look like a fuel tank to you?"

Anzac took the photo from her hand saying, "Yes, kind of. Hard to tell for sure because it's too far away. But it's the right shape. Color's on the money, too."

Perry eyed the photo. "Can't tell where that was taken, though."

"I know."

A light knock on the door caught her attention and she turned in time to see the corpsman enter the room. He had her mail and a glass of juice. The mail was all personal, not so much as an interoffice memo in the lot. The juice was a fruit concoction that was too sweet for Perry's taste but she was thirsty and took a long drink of it anyway.

Her attention back on the business at hand, she asked, "Think we could get a blowup of this?"

"We could, but, judging from the quality of this original, it would no doubt be an indecipherable blur," he told her as he gave her back the photo. Perry could see the problem and nodded in agreement. Changing the subject, he said, "The G-2 people think they may have something more in depth for us by tomorrow. You already saw the preliminary. I talked to them today but I can't repeat what they're planning in front of personnel that lack clearance."

"Yes, you could. You'd just have to shoot them afterward."

"Not funny, Perry," Anzac chastised, his eyes laughing though his demeanor was serious. Her expression was pure imp and he was having difficulty keeping a straight face. He looked away from her to the corpsman and asked, "Can you give me five minutes to apprise the Commander on our current status?"

The corpsman nodded and stepped out. The second he was gone, Perry asked, "Did they tell you anything about that Night Eyes system?"

"A little. They'll be going into it at length tomorrow at the staff meeting. I know you want to be there but you'll just have to make do with getting the news from me. Don't worry, you know I take good notes."

She smiled slightly, liking his bit of humor, and sighed. Perry knew she had agreed to three days of enforced rest but now, almost halfway into her sentence, she was beginning to wish there was some way she could get out of her contract. She swiveled around away from the desk and leaned back slightly. "So, what do you think our chances are of coming up with a way to nail these gomers?"

He shrugged. "Well, I'm no expert but G-2's stealth expert thinks he might have something that could work."

"Oh? Who's the brain with the bright idea?"

He was living in dread of that exact question all afternoon, and he hesitated a long moment before responding. "I'm not sure how to say this in any way that would make it easier for you to take so

I'll just come right out and say it. The stealth technology expert they sent us is Leigh Freneau."

Perry froze for a split second then looked away from him, biting her lower lip. Leigh was a highly regarded expert in that field, having worked on the F-19A, the B-2 Stealth bomber, as well as the current ATF program. She couldn't get him recalled on the basis that he wasn't the best man for the job because he was and she knew it. But, so long as she only had to deal with him on a purely professional level, Perry felt she could manage to get by without losing her temper. It wasn't going to be easy but she was determined to give it her best shot.

When her eyes met Anzac's, he was surprised to read nothing in them except cool determination. "I can handle it," she assured him quietly. "As long as we're only in the same room when the job requires it, everything will be just fine."

She's swallowing the bitter pill a lot more easily than I thought she would, Anzac mused. He approached her desk and dug his hand into the potato chips left in the plate from lunch that she had left sitting between her phone and a can of Coke. Perry's expression brightened and she quipped, "Hey, that's my dinner you're scarfing up there, mister."

"No real food?"

"On this ship?"

He chuckled softly. "Tonight they were serving rollers and beans and they weren't bad. Give me your meal ticket and I'll get you some."

"I would but Wolff has it. He was *supposed* to bring me dinner. I hope, he'll show up soon. I'm starved."

"He's probably off interviewing somebody and lost track of the time. He'll show. Martin's got his faults but he strikes me as a pretty responsible guy," Anzac reassured her. "Look, I'll let you know when the briefing with G-2 is, and Trudy will keep you up to date with the intelligence reports. I'd stick around longer but I've got the enjoyable task of trying to find those lovely black jets in the dead of night."

"Good luck."

"Thanks, but, unless these guys fly with their antismash light on, there's no way anybody's going to find them."

"Maybe they're playing it safe and not risking those birds on night ops," she suggested. "After all, flying at night is the toughest thing we do."

"That's because we have to land on a boat in the middle of the friggin' ocean," he reminded her. "If we had to come in to a land base, night ops would be a piece of cake."

"No shit," she agreed. He smiled at the truth of her statement and she continued, "These guys are coming from a land base. We can assume that the best fliers available are driving these birds, which means they've probably done their share of night touchdowns. But, these aircraft are new, probably exceedingly expensive, and any CO worth his salt would most likely choose not to take the chance on a night hop if he can avoid it. Flying at night *is* more risky, no matter how good a pilot you are. Especially if those guys are doing their zoomin' without antismash lights. I'm sure if these birds are doing test missions they will be going up in daylight but, if these aren't trial runs, then we'll be seeing them after sundown."

"Yeah, but if they were really out to nail us—"

"They would definitely go for it with darkness as their shield because, as far as they know, we can only target them visually. I hope, that situation will be changing real damn quick," she stated. "I know if those birds were mine and I was out for blood that's what I'd do. And since there's a chance their skipper is as wily as I am, the battle group is sailing dark with every ECM we've got available going full tilt. The only exception to the blackout will be the *Excalibur's* flight deck. We're the only target that can be acquired visually from the air and for that reason we've got our gunners up and ready."

"Amazin' what you can get done while flat on your back recuperatin', huh, CAG?" he teased and she cracked a smile.

"Yeah, I guess I proved there's more than one thing a woman can do in that position."

The innuendo wasn't lost on Anzac and he came back saying, "I'm a married man. I wouldn't know about stuff like that."

She laughed waving him out of the room. "Get back to work." He was by the door when she added quickly, "Two things, 'Zac. One, next time you come by, bring me that stack of reading matter I left on top of my file cabinet. Since the Skipper seems bound and determined to have me learn his trade, I'm going to use the time I'm stuck here to get a head start on my education." Anzac chuckled softly. He knew the pile she was referring to; She would need a couple of days to make any headway through it. He saw her expression suddenly change. Perry's eyes were full of concern when she said, "Be careful up there, will you? I can't do this all by myself."

Anzac nodded giving her a broad grin. She smiled back, obviously liking his display of self-confidence. He gave her a jaunty wink before disappearing into the hallway.

Martin Wolff arrived a few minutes after Anzac left, and presented Perry with her dinner of franks and beans, fruit cup, black coffee, and a hunk of blueberry pie. The corpsman greeted him cordially and he smiled back. When he placed the tray before Perry, she dove into the food like she was starving, which was pretty much the case. She had not eaten anything all afternoon except for her leftover chips from lunch and a Coke. Wolff found the gusto with which she consumed her dinner amusing. He left her meal card on her desk and turned to leave when she stopped him with a gesture.

"Are you in the middle of something?" she inquired after swallowing a mouthful.

"No, not really. Why?"

"You've got big ears, Paper Boy. Hear anything of interest that might not have made it into these reports?"

Wolff shook his head. "I couldn't get near the people from G-2. And almost everyone else in the Air Wing is bitching and moaning about flying around in circles and not finding jack. They're all itching for a chance to get a piece of these guys that buzzed us. I guess you can't blame them for that. Also, a lot of people asked if I'd pass along their get well wishes and I'd be here for an hour if I listed everyone that hit me up with that request."

She laid down her fork and smiled up at him saying, "I hope you let it be known that I'd be back by Friday."

"I did. It was obvious from the reactions I got that many people thought you were seriously hurt and were going to be out of commission for a long while. I guess the rumor mill must've started grinding full force when you didn't show up to meet the COD the other night. Especially after Anzac excused your absence by saying you were in sickbay. Folks around here obviously think you only go to a doctor when you're on death's door."

"And not without cause," she said her eyes twinkling.

He liked her impish expression. Then again, he was beginning to like many things about the Commander. This cocky old salt was beginning to grow on him. She was nothing like any other woman he'd ever been with and, although he was usually attracted to the wine and roses type, he found himself oddly drawn to this strong willed aviatrix. As she sat there with that elfish look in her eyes,

Wolff wondered what it would be like to be in Anzac's place. What it would be like to have the pleasures of sharing in-jokes, flying and friendship with Perry McNeil.

"Well, if you do hear anything interesting, let me know, okay?" she said as she resumed eating.

"Sure thing," he replied with a fondness that wasn't lost on her.

She looked up from her plate. Her eyes were pure mischief as she inquired, "You're not getting sweet on me, are you, Paper Boy?"

"Maybe."

She grinned. "I don't think you can handle anything that can move at Mach speeds."

"Try me."

"Well, perhaps I will," she tempted, eyes full of mischief. "That is, if you survive our match. Or did you forget our little gym date?"

He didn't. "You really intend to go through with that?"

"I do, but you're free to back out."

"Yeah, and be called Whiskey Delta behind my back for the rest of the cruise? No, thank you. Your boys rag on me enough as it is. No way I'm adding any fuel to that fire."

She turned back to her food. "Well, when things settle down a bit and I get some free time, I'll let you know when we can go for it."

He rolled his eyes heavenward and sighed. "Whatever you say. I'll see you later." Perry nodded, flashing him a naughty wink that made him smile despite the mixed feelings. He wondered about how much he was willing to do to get Perry's respect and, ultimately, her friendship. Wolff was committed and there was no way he could back out without losing so much face he'd need major surgery just to breath. Of course, had he known she was a black belt in kung fu and very up on Tai Chi, he never would have opened his big mouth but it was too late for regrets now. The only thing he could do to keep himself from getting creamed during the match was easy enough: keep moving and keep ducking!

17 December 0400

God, this feels good, Perry thought as she wrapped the G-suit around her waist, sucked in her gut, and zipped up the side. Thank God it's Friday! Taking a deep breath and holding it, she then bent down to zip the leggings up the inseams of her legs. She remembered, back in flight school, that that little operation used to knock the wind out of some of the guys but it never bothered her much. Either she was born to fly or a woman's body was immune to the effects of self-abuse. Probably the latter, she mused as she stepped into the torso harness, which would act as her parachute harness should the need arise. Women have endured pointy-toed shoes, corsets, and a variety of other things that constricted, pinched or pulled for eons. This outfit was a pleasure compared to the stuff her ancestors had to lace, squeeze and cram themselves into.

She strapped the leg restraints on her calves and these would be snapped onto fittings on her seat in the Tomcat to yank back her legs in case of ejection. While she was bent over doing this, she smiled up at her RIO. Anzac had just entered the locker room. He was already suited up and ready to go. Perry quickly slipped into the survival vest, zipped it and checked for gear: water bottle, flare gun, knife, strobe light, riser cutters, radio, flare and smoke signal combo and, last but not least, her personal 9mm handgun. That wasn't a normal part of the survival gear but, as far as she was concerned, it was something she considered essential for *her* survival. She tucked everything in place and snapped it closed. She carefully put on the padded skullcap, her stitches were still a bit sensitive, and then her helmet. She grabbed her kneeboard off the bench tucking it under her arm, closed and locked her locker, and followed Anzac to the flight deck.

"The Double Nuts was fitted with the experimental IR tracking system your ex described at the meeting the other day," Anzac told her as they crossed the deck to the waiting Tomcat. "It should be able to pick up high intensity heat patterns from objects up to fifty miles away. I know that's not much when you consider that, at full throttle, our bird can cross fifty miles in seconds. But sometimes a few extra seconds can make the difference in a dogfight."

She nodded. "Well, I guess it's the best G-2 could do on short notice."

"They hooked up their system and tied into what we've already got down in the CIC. Supposedly it can pick up and identify incoming aircraft as far away as one hundred miles. I was observing it in action just after they got it going last night and, well, it needs *a lot* of fine tuning. It seemed the farther out they tried to see, the more trouble they had getting that gizmo to work right. The system installed on the E-2s are also designed to go up to a hundred miles. So far, the Hummer's version has checked out perfectly."

"Seems they may be sacrificing accuracy when they shoot for range," Perry observed while making her slow walk around the plane to check it over.

"That discovery they made straight off but, until they can figure a way to fix it, tha-tha-tha-that's all folks," he said winding up the briefing with a Porky Pig sendoff.

She smiled slightly at his summation as she checked the missile placements and fittings. Something scrawled on the side of one of the two Phoenix missiles their Tomcat carried made her chuckle softly to herself. Anzac heard the amused noises and looked for himself. On the side of the missile was written, "If you can read this, you're one dead gomer." During the New Moon War the ordnance people often wrote little notes to the enemy on the bombs and missiles and, although it was against regulations, few people were ever reprimanded for it. The flyers loved it, their CO's tolerated it, and the guys in ordnance got to have a laugh and let off some steam. It had been a long while since she'd carried missiles bearing messages. For a split second, Perry was back aboard the *George Washington* cruising the Med hunting MiG driving camel jockeys.

"Three other Tomcats and two Hornets were also fitted with the same system we've got," Anzac said as he approached the narrow ladder leading up to the rear cockpit. "They're doing it a couple of planes at a time. It takes about six to eight hours to install the trackers and get it integrated into the systems we already have aboard. That's a long time to keep a bird on the ground in an alert situation, so they're taking it slow. Can't risk depleting our air coverage."

She smiled at him. "Spoken like a true CAG," she remarked and he grinned. "Looks like you managed to handle things quite well while left to your lonesome."

"I had a good teacher."

"Come on, let's saddle up. I have to get my fix. Three days on the ground is just three days too many!"

They both climbed up the ladders simultaneously exchanging knowing eyes.

Big Daddy and the CAG flew in a tight perfect formation, streaking like twin comets across the nighttime sky. Their timing and coordination so in tune to each other that they seemed two parts of the same mind. They made a smooth bank to the left, but, with G-suits squeezing at closing up on 3Gs, the movement wrenched the gut a bit. The two seasoned drivers seemed to barely notice the G forces as Big Daddy pulled around to the right following Perry's lead.

The hard banks to the left or right, the tight turns—the Super Tomcat did these maneuvers better than any plane currently flying. Perry loved the feeling of power, the knowledge that this bird would fly any damn way she wanted it to. The F-14D was, in her educated opinion, one helluva great ride. Twin afterburning turbofan engines, swinging wings automatically positioned by the Mach Sweep Programmer, maneuvering flaps that allowed more G to be applied right from the pilot's stick, and leading edge maneuvering slats that could be preprogrammed for automatic deployment. These made the Super Tomcat fly better than the feather-winged creatures it emulated.

The "D" was more than a kickass flier—it was lethal, too. Capable of being loaded with several variations of nice toys like Phoenix, Sidewinder and Sparrow missiles as well as an M61-A1 Vulcan cannon. And utilizing the AWG-9 and a few other weapons systems to get the job done is what made the Super Tomcat the ultimate killing machine.

Only today they were carrying a little something extra—a new IR tracking system code named "Night Eyes." Far more sophisticated than the IR placements already on the aircraft, it should distinguish and identify heat patterns from a maximum range of fifty miles. Supposedly it can tell the difference between us and them, mused Perry as she glanced down at the radar sweep screen, but I'll believe that when I see it.

"How's the new toy workin', CAG?" Big Daddy asked. His Tomcat hadn't gotten the system installed yet but was high on the list.

"Too soon to tell, Beau," she replied. "So far, all I've got on the scope is our guys."

"Well, let's head north, say, about a hundred miles or so and see what turns up."

"Roger, that," Perry said as she made the course change and allowed Big Daddy to take over the lead spot as they headed to their destination.

Sparky, who was patrolling the northern sector, glanced down at his radar sweep as the two green blips moved swiftly across the screen. From the briefing he'd been to the other day, he knew he could ignore the green dots because those were aircraft that showed up on both radar and infrared. What he had to keep an eye out for was for a red blip—something that was being detected by the Night Eyes system alone. Dr. Freneau added the color coding to the design to make sure the jocks using the new equipment would make no errors in reading the scanner.

Windwalker, Sparky's wingman, picked up the two jets crossing their flight path on his radar. His Hornet had not been given the Night Eyes IR package so he had to rely on whatever data Sparky received. If they were to encounter the MiGs, then Sparky would engage while he provided coverage. He silently hoped those MiGs would wait until dawn to make an entrance. Trying to keep his lead's six clear of an enemy flying in a black jet running with no antismash lights on in the dead of night was tough enough. The fact that these gomers didn't show up on radar was going to make Windwalker's job nearly next to impossible.

"I'm going to test the Eyes," Sparky told his wingman as he flipped the switch that tied the system into the HUD and in the right hand corner of his display he saw a three-dimensional line drawing of one of the two planes that just entered his airspace appear. The system identified both planes as being the same and the image that appeared in a matter of seconds was that of an F-14D.

"Well?"

"It works, Windy," he said as he switched off the imager. "Pretty intense graphics. A lot better than what I had expected, considering this was a rush job and all."

"I hope we won't be needing it."

Sparky made no comment even though he agreed with his wingman. Thinking aloud as he watched the two green dots zoom across his screen, he said softly, "Wonder where those guys are off to..."

December 17 0535

Perry checked the radar sweep and the range indicator. They were slightly over a hundred miles from the *Excalibur*, tickling the fringes of Night Eyes maximum usable range from the carrier. Aircraft containing the system patrolled beyond the ship's range as added protection. Perry saw nothing unfriendly on her radar. But, if they did encounter the MiGs, they were ordered to fire only if fired upon. They were to deal with the stealth MiGs as they would handle an encounter with any unidentified aircraft with unknown intentions. When the ship got jumped, they had a case for chasing after the MiGs with cannons blazing. Now if she were to engage then unprovoked, *they* would be the bad guys. She and Big would have to play it real cool. "You know if we trek just a little farther north, you could get yourself some of those Havanas you like to smoke so much direct from the source," she remarked.

"I'll settle for the PX," was Big Daddy's terse reply.

"Big isn't too thrilled about patrolling this close to Cuba's border," Anzac told her over the ICS. "If we get into a situation up here, we'll have to be sure not to drift north. Can't risk an encounter becoming an international incident. Especially since we'll be the ones having to explain what we were doing this close to Castro's sunny beaches in the first place."

"I know," she said. "Humor me, 'Zac. I want to find out if these birds are from Fidel's nest, okay? If not, then we'll look elsewhere."

"I know we tracked them going this way the first time we ran into them but, like I told you before, they could have just flown this way because they knew it would be the best way to lose the pursuit."

"True," she agreed, then added, "But the spooks haven't shown me anything that could prove the cartels are behind this. Not a single island nor isolated jungle field has a landing strip on it that could accommodate a non-STOL fighter."

"But there were a few sites we saw that could handle a Harrier."

"If we *really* wanted to stretch the issue, yes. But I'm not sure these birds are STOL. I don't know what they can do besides hide from us. Maybe when we get back the satellite will have zoomed in on something that will help us piece this puzzle together. Until then, all we can do is keep our eyes peeled."

"Roger," he said. He took a few minutes to check his instruments and assure himself, by a careful look out the cockpit window, that they were not being followed before resuming their conversation. "You remember that picture of what looked like a drop tank? Well, the Admiral thinks you could be right. But, he pointed out that it also looks a lot like a missile. So—"

"So the *Jeopardy* question is still this: have the Cubans gotten their hands on stealth? Or is somebody else responsible and trying to make it *look* like the Cubans are the guilty ones?"

Anzac sighed but made no reply. She had a point. They had nothing concrete to go on that would point the finger at anyone. As far as he was concerned, he was completely clueless and put aside the matter of whether or not the Cubans were responsible for their dilemma. He focused his attention instead on trying to find those mysterious black jets.

The inkiness of night was slowly beginning to give way to the red and orange hues of first light. The sight of sunlight peering over the horizon was a welcome sight to Anzac. Their hop would soon be coming to a close. He was more than ready to log a few Zs after having been awake for the better part of the past four days. He was glad Perry hadn't been completely out of it and was always available for consultation. Even so, he had been running the show and had to keep the sort of crazy hours Perry was famous for. Unlike the lady in the front seat, he could only get so far on adrenaline and caffeine and, right now, the rush from both was finally wearing off. He concentrated on keeping a watchful eye on his instruments, as well as peering over his shoulder to make sure their six was indeed clear. Machines weren't infallible and Anzac wasn't about to take any chances.

On the fringes of their range two red blips appeared on the scope. They were moving in from the northwest and closing fast. It was obvious to Perry that she and Big Daddy had attracted some attention. The Night Eyes system, which was hooked into the onboard computer and weapons targeting system, seemed to be doing what it was supposed to do. In less than a heartbeat she had a bead on them and it looked to her like they were planning to intercept. She punched the switch keying the onboard video camera to begin recording. Any images they could capture during their encounter would be very useful later.

That is, if they survived.

"Beau, we've got company," she told her wingman. "Go tactical."

"Where are they?" Big's RIO Poindexter asked, via the squadron's special frequency, his own instruments showing nothing.

Perry gave him the heading and closure. She commanded, "Let's go see what's on their minds."

"Roger. I'll ID them, you break away and hook 'em."

Perry knew exactly what he had in mind. They had done this sort of thing before and with very positive results. The break away maneuver had a higher than average chance of working in their situation. They were flying in tight and no doubt appeared as a single fighter on the enemy's radar. That was probably why the MiGs were choosing to come in for a look-see. A lone jet was an easy mark. The fact that they were two instead of one wouldn't be apparent until their adversary got within visual range. And, by the time the MiGs got in that tight, Perry would be all over them.

When they were a minute away from visual contact, something that sounded like radar blips hit their headphones. "I've got an eleven o'clock strobe," Poindexter reported. "I think they're locked on us."

"Great, just great," muttered Big Daddy. "We can't do anything unless they decide to pull the trigger."

"Hang in there, boys," was the last thing they heard Perry say before she disappeared from view.

Perry made her break away. She rolled over, pulled hard into a split-S until her Tomcat was pointing vertically downward. The movement pulled high Gs and hurt like hell, but her quick high speed break produced the desired 90° in split seconds and kept the fighter separation to a minimum. On her way into the vertical, Perry dropped chaff to add even more confusion to the picture. If the trick worked, she would not be seen by the enemy's radar until the separation between herself and Beau was wide enough to allow them to be picked up separately. Her deployment of chaff was another trick to fool their foes into thinking there were more aircraft up there. Once she was in the pure vertical, Perry executed a deft 180° roll and wings-level pull-out. She was back on the original collision course with their adversaries and was moving in at 375 knots.

She could see the other F-14, which was way above her and flying slightly ahead of her position. He was cutting back and forth across the sky, trying to break the lock on. The Night Eyes system gave Perry a tight fix on the MiGs. Her weapons system was up and she worked fast to get two heat-seekers targeted on them.

"They're not disengaging!" Poindexter said nervously. "They're coming straight for us!"

Beau gave her the range quickly so Perry could time her pull-up so she would be pointing at them when they and the MiGs made their pass. In the distance ahead Perry could just make out the incoming MiGs. They were coming in head on and looked like they were trying to play chicken with Big Daddy. Big was going into a close pass with them, while Perry would be doing a vertical hook. As the MiGs closed, Big pulled into a climb hoping to lure the Migs into following him and drawing attention away from Perry.

The trick worked. The MiGs followed what they thought was a lone Tomcat and ascended in pursuit of Big. Perry followed. Big's quick ascent momentarily broke the lock the MiGs had on him. He levelled at Angels twenty but didn't stay flying the straight and even for long. The two MiGs got him in their sights again. Big was all over the sky, ducking and dodging in an effort to break the lock-on. The Migs got in dead on his six. The tone in his headset grew insistent.

"They got us. Why aren't they firing?" Poindexter said as much to himself as to Big Daddy. He was genuinely puzzled. Just what the hell was going on?

Perry got a solid lock-on the two MiGs. They so much as blinked wrong and they'd be toast.

Her sudden appearance caught the MiGs looking. They got the message. They disengaged, split and accelerated. The two ebony jets came roaring past Big one on each side of his Tomcat. They were so close that he and Poindexter got a glimpse of them and their lone occupants for a split second. They also got a very quick demonstration of how fast and maneuverable the MiGs were when the pair joined up the second they were clear of the F-14. The duo looked like the Blue Angels as they simultaneously performed a quick pair of rolls before rocketing off up and away right in front of them.

However, the MiGs had been *too* close to the F-14 when they shoved their birds into Zone Five for their quick getaway. The Tomcat passed right through the MiGs turbulence and the blast distorted the airflow to Big's right engine...*boomboomboom boom*—the engine flamed out. With the full thrust on the left, the engine swung the tail around in a yaw. Big yanked hard left on the stick to correct, but it was too late.

The plane was coupling up. Perry watched in horror as Big's Tomcat coupled one yaw to the next, its tail swinging around, going into an ever-increasing flat spin, out of control and heading straight down towards the sea.

The second Anzac saw Big was in trouble, he was on the radio to the ship. A rescue helo would be en route within minutes. He got on the line to Perry saying, "We've been ordered to pursue. You still tracking them?"

Perry saw the blips on her radar. She still had them but they would be out of range in a minute. "Yes," she replied, her voice telling him her attention was elsewhere.

"Let's go."

"But what about—"

"Perry, you can't help them! The helo will be here soon. Let's get moving or we won't be able to catch up to the guys who're responsible for this!"

She knew he was right. She didn't want to abandon her friends but she also was the only one in a position to give chase. She just hoped Big and Poindexter were able to punch out. A flat spin put so much centrifugal force inside the cockpit that Big and 'Dexter could be pinned to their instrument panels unable to move. As she altered her course and kicked in the afterburners to pursue the fleeing MiGs, Perry silently prayed Big and 'Dexter would escape safely from the twirling nightmare . .

"Sir! Eject! Eject!" Poindexter yelled trying to keep the panic out of his voice.

Big Daddy was pinned to the instrument panel by the centrifugal force. Grunting with the effort, Big tried to force his arm to go back and reach for the ejection lever but it fell short of the black and yellow handle by several inches. "I'm trying!" he said as he made a second attempt. It failed. "I'm pinned to the panel!"

"We're low! It's time to—"

The third time was the charmer. Through gritted teeth Big said, "Got it!"

The ejection initiated. Their shoulder harnesses retracted. As the canopy hooks were cut and the Plexiglass bubble was jettisoned, a deafening roar of wind and noise filled the cockpit. Everything happened in the spanse of a heartbeat: the catapult fired, leg restraints were pulled taut, drogue gun and time-release mechanism were tripped. The pilot's seat was set to trigger first, the RIO's would follow four-tenths of a second later. The rocket under BiG Daddy's seat fired him up and out. Poindexter was slammed back into his seat as the ejection seat straps wound up, and then he, too, was shot out of the plane.

'Dexter didn't black out from the shock of the ejection, but he felt drugged, out of it. As he tumbled over and over, head over boots, Poindexter found the silent stillness frightening. When the parachute deployed, the line stretch of the main chute freed him from the seat. As it fell away, his body snapped like a whip when the chute ballooned open over his head. While warm breezes buffeted him as he floated down towards the sea, Poindexter dazedly scanned the skies for any sign of Big Daddy.

The MiGs had a healthy lead on her but they had not flown out of range of the Night Eyes, so Perry was still able to track them. They were in Cuban airspace and, if she kept on course, she would soon be joining them. She knew the longer she tailed them, the bigger the risk she was taking but they had to know exactly where these MiGs came from. And the only way to determine their home base would be to follow them to it....

December 17 0600

The sudden shock of the cold water connecting with his body quickly cleared the post-ejection haziness. Poindexter gasped taking in a lungful of air just before being dragged through the rough waters of the Gulf. His chute had been caught by the wind above the surface and was pulling him at first into the chop and then down deeper and deeper into the salty water that turned steadily darker as he descended into the depths.

He had ejected only one other time in his Navy career. That had been long ago and having done it before didn't make it any less scary. Poindexter tried not to panic but, as he felt himself sinking and his lungs beginning to burn for want of air, he began twisting his body desperately, trying to slip out of the tangled straps. His hands found the lines and, with adrenaline giving him the strength he needed, Poindexter swam up the lines managing not to pull them down. The seawater burned his eyes but he forced himself to keep them open as he followed the lines up, up, up to the surface.

When he made it to the top, Poindexter breached like a whale sucking the air into his lungs the way a man would drink after crossing a desert for days without water. He felt dizzy and weak, but somehow he managed to reach back for the release straps and break himself free from the parachute. It whipped away like a huge white leaf, the strong gale force winds whisking it up and away towards the rising sun.

It was a struggle for him to keep his head above the water. The Gulf was choppy, with waves up to eight feet and this made it hard for him to check out his survival gear. The equipment was waterlogged threatening to drag him down again. He twisted and, finding the inflatable raft attached to his harness, pulled its cord. Poindexter bobbed tasting saltwater with each passing wave as the raft hissed open, two feet wide and six feet long, connected to him by a cord. He dragged his weary body onto it and collapsed.

Lt. Commander Rae "Clouds" Liotta, XO of the Renegades, bit her lower lip anxiously as she watched the pursuit on the radar scope. The CAG was seconds from crossing into Cuban airspace. Gypsy, the CO of the Killer Bees, cast a concerned look at her friend and then glanced quickly back at the Captain and Admiral

Jones. By the hard set to their jaws, she could tell they were not too pleased by the current turn of events. She knew tickling the border, which was a minor violation that occurred now and then, was grudgingly tolerated. That was one thing but what the CAG seemed hell-bent on doing was not something that could be written off as an accident. A Tomcat carrying full ordnance bearing down on Fidel's homeland would only be interpreted one way by the Cuban military observers: it was an act of war.

"CAG, turn back!" Rae warned. "You're about to enter Cuban airspace!"

"I'm not the only one headed for Havana," Perry responded. "These guys look like they're also after some cheap cigars."

"Or they may be headed home!"

"Exactly why I'm tagging along. We've been after their address for over three days. Now, we're going to get it once and for all."

"Perry..." Rae sighed heavily. It was too late. Perry was already over the line and it wouldn't be long before she was feet dry over Cuba.

Oh shit, Anzac muttered inwardly. They were in Cuban airspace and, at their current speed, would be over land within minutes. This was not good. Over the ICS he ordered, "Turn back, CAG! Before it's too late."

"I'm going to get these guys once and for all."

Anzac was getting disgusted and felt free to let her know how he felt via the privacy of their cockpit-to-cockpit hookup. "This is bullshit. Once we're feet dry, we might as well start learnin' fuckin' Spanish! Do you have any idea—"

"I want those MiGs!" she shot back and, as she said it, pulled back hard on the stick pulling them up into a hard vertical climb that kept them hot on the tail of the two stealth planes.

"Son of a bitch!" Anzac swore, not hiding his anger. It usually took quite a lot to get Anzac's temper to rear its ugly head. But Perry had just managed to unleash the monster usually kept neatly tucked away beneath his normally country cool veneer. Going behind enemy lines during a chase was nothing new to him; They'd done it a few times during the New Moon War. They even took out part of an airfield during one of their pursuits. During the war aiming for the heart had been expected from the combat teams and they had their chance to show they were a pair of shit-hot cardiac surgeons. However, things were quite black and white then: they knew who the enemy was and that it was okay to nail them wherever and whenever they could.

This time things weren't so well defined. True, they had been ordered to splash these unknowns if those birds came at them with guns blazing, but they hadn't been authorized to hunt them down and destroy them at their source. Doing that would be overstepping their authority by a very hefty margin and could have very serious repercussions beyond just getting them both hip deep in the kimchi. Perry's gung-ho attitude had gotten them into trouble many times with the brass in the past. But her skills as an aviator had always saved them from being hit with the sort of penalties that could've drowned them both career-wise. But, she'd never dared to step *this* far over the line. There was something going on and, willing or not, he was stuck tagging along for the ride.

Anzac had never been scared to sit in the pit when Perry was at the stick but right now he was terrified. What was she doing? Was she having a flashback and sitting up there thinking she was flying over the Med in hot pursuit of a couple of Syrian birds? He hoped not. This was not the time to drop out of the current time-space continuum and take a Zone Five blast back to the past.

"Perry, we're headed for *Cuba*," he stated pointedly hoping he'd get her head out of whatever cloud it was stuck in. "This is *not good*."

Admiral Jones, who'd been keeping an eye on the COs and caught the words between Rae and the CAG, got on the line to Perry. "Don't be a fool, McNeil" he bellowed. "You're throwing over twenty years of Navy down the head if you follow those birds into the bananas! Get back here and let the experts we got figure out where those birds nest."

"I can do that! Just let me—"

"Absolutely not," Captain Graff broke in sharply, then reminded her, "It isn't just you in that plane, Commander."

A long moment of silence filled the air before they heard Perry state defeatedly, "Roger. Ghost Leader disengaging and will RTB."

Everyone standing around the radar scope saw the green blip on the scope pivot around 180° and break away from its path behind the two red markers. Breaking off the chase and having to return to base was not an easy thing for their let's-go-get-'em CAG to do. But it was her only real option. There was no way she would have been able to follow the MiGs all the way in. Just as Perry made her U-turn, they picked up several aircraft coming into the area. The newcomers looked like they were on an intercept course with

Perry but she had kicked in the afterburners and was moving far faster than the incoming fighters. She would soon be in the safety of international airspace. Rae sighed as she watched Perry easily outrun her pursuers. She could understand Perry's burning desire to end the doubts, to get to the truth once and for all. But it wasn't worth her throwing away her career. Perry had worked so hard to get *this* far...

Dr. Freneau raised an eyebrow at the assembled officers and glanced down at the screen. "Everything all right?" he inquired casually as if he hadn't overheard a single word of the proceedings.

"Fine, just fine," the Captain replied frowning. "Looks like your boys managed to work out most of the bugs." Freneau didn't reply, he only nodded in assent.

Rae tentatively met his icy eyes. The CAG actually was once married to this glacier? She found that hard to believe. Perry was such a passionate person, especially when it came to flying, that Rae wondered how the CAG could ever have been attracted to this cold, yet very handsome, fish. "Any ideas on how we can ID these bogeys?" she asked him.

"They are being tracked even as we speak," he replied. "We should be able to get something usable on them this time."

She nodded. "I hope so. Things are getting a little tense around here."

The voices of Sparky and Windwalker over the radio caught Rae's attention and she shifted her gaze back onto the radar and her focus back on the action. "Say again," she instructed.

Windwalker responded, "The sea is really rough, Clouds. It's going to be really tough to find two guys floating in this chop. Too easy to lose them in the swells."

"A helo is already on its way out there. Pick up anything over the radio?"

"Negative."

"They could've been knocked out or the transmitter might be damaged," suggested Sparky.

"Maybe," Rae agreed hopefully.

"We're going to fly low around the area until that helo gets here," Windwalker told her. "Maybe we might just get lucky."

"Watch your fuel," Gypsy reminded him.

"Roger, Skipper."

Gypsy cast a concerned eye on Rae. "I hate to say this, but there's a chance they didn't make it."

A long pause. "I know."

Gypsy knew what it felt like to lose people in her command. She'd lost four of her best pilots during the New Moon War. This cruise was Rae's first as the Renegade's XO but the shy and soft-spoken woman had demonstrated keen leadership skills as a section leader during her past two cruises, including one during the New Moon War. If Commander Beaumont didn't make it, Rae would be acting skipper for the VF-69. Gypsy knew her younger colleague could do the job if she had to but she also knew Rae was silently praying, with all the fervency of her Italian Catholic blood, for Big Daddy to return home safe.

Rae listened to the chatter of the flyers hoping to hear something to give her a foundation for her hopes. So far, no one had sighted Big Daddy or Poindexter but she brightened somewhat when she heard Sparky announce, "Skipper! I think we got something! Looks like parts of a bird."

"Any sign of Big or 'Dexter?" Gypsy asked.

"Hard to tell. It blew by kinda quick. I'm going to circle and bring her down to a crawl so I can give the Davy Jones's a better idea of where to come lookin'."

"Roger."

A couple of minutes later, Sparky was back on giving coordinates. Then he added, "No sign of Big or 'Dexter yet, but since I've got the gas, I'm going to keep looking. If they punched out, they should be in this area."

"The helo's on its way," Windwalker stated. "They'll be skimming the chop. If they're out there, I'm sure the Davey Jones's will find them."

Rae knew the SH-3 helicopter had a far better chance of locating the two missing flyers than the duo in the Hornets did. She patiently waited for the word from the search and rescue team.

It ain't just you in that plane. Perry sighed. She had come very close to doing something incredibly stupid. Somebody Up There must be watching out for me, she mused, because, if the installation of the Night Eyes system into my Tomcat hadn't been done by 0400, Anzac and I would have done this patrol in the birds Sparky and Windwalker were cruising in. Had she been on her own in a Hornet, Perry knew she would probably have ignored the Captain's warning and gone off half cocked chasing that bird, dodging SAMs, Triple A fire and other MiGs as she pursued her quarry across Cuba.

Anzac hadn't said word one to her since they halted their

pursuit. He had every right to be pissed off at her. Perry came very close to ending both of their Navy careers, not to mention their lives. She had come dangerously close to doing something incredibly stupid and she mentally kicked herself for it. She knew better. This was the sort of thing that, had any other pilot in the air wing been the one in the Tomcat, she would have scalded them down but good. What worried her more than having to deal with Anzac's anger was that he probably was sitting back there contemplating what would have happened had they been in the F-18s.

Both of them kept a keen ear tuned to the radio and were trying to stay optimistic, even though they hadn't seen any evidence that their friends managed to eject in time. Then again, Perry was aware of the small fact that they hadn't been able to stand by long enough to wait to see if there were chutes. Maybe Anzac managed to see something before they left the area. Very little escaped her backseater, even when the fur is flyin' fast and furious. She would willingly admit it was his sharp eyes, not just her shit-hot driving, that had saved their asses more than once.

"Want to make a couple of passes over the area where Big went down and give the Jolly's a hand looking?" she suggested trying to sound casual but failing miserably. She was concerned and it was hard not to have it show in her voice.

"We really don't have the gas for that, Perry," he stated matter-of-factly.

"Oh," she half said as she checked her gauges. They had enough to get back to the carrier safely. She sighed. She wanted to help search for her friends but knew the rescue helo was in a far better position to find them than she was. However, one circle over the area before they flew back home wouldn't hurt...

Perry knew Anzac was still angry with her but he was doing a damn good job of not letting it show. It was always professional when they were in the jet. He'd give her a piece of his mind after they landed. She deserved to be verbally keelhauled for what she did and she was prepared to take whatever hot, salty dish Anzac served her after they trapped.

She hoped her actions weren't so far over the edge as to make Anzac want to bail out as her backseater. There had been one time, a dozen years ago, when they were at the Navy's Fighter Weapons School at Miramar NAS going through the rigorous Top Gun program that 'Zac nearly walked out on her. She'd pulled a few half-assed stunts that had pissed off the brass and almost got them both kicked out. They'd been given a second chance and Anzac had told her, in no uncertain terms, that if she fucked up he'd never get in a Tomcat with her again, ever. *That* made her shape up and fly right far faster than any threats the bigwigs in charge held over her head.

Perry didn't want to lose him but she knew you didn't get into a jet with anyone that didn't make you feel completely comfortable. The person you flew with had your life in their hands, and it wasn't a good idea for the Navy to send up a team in the pricey F-14D that didn't trust each other implicitly. If either one of the pair of fliers on the Tomcat wanted to change partners, then no questions were asked beyond what you were willing to answer and a switch would be made. She prayed she didn't make him lose faith in her. Anzac was a rare combination; He was hell on wheels, when behind the stick of a Hornet, and could out-RIO any other backseater on the *Excalibur*. No one else she knew could match him. If he wanted out because he lost confidence in her judgement, Perry was going to do something that was like handing herself a death sentence: she was going to ground herself.

As she made one long low lazy circle around the area where debris from Big's Tomcat had been spotted, Perry kept a careful eye out for smoke, flares and patches of water colored something other than the natural rich navy blue. Her ear was on the radio listening for the beeps of a homing beacon but, so far, there was no sign either of them had activated their transmitters. There was a possibility they were stunned from the combined effects of the ejection and that horrible spin. They could be floating in the swells unconscious and unable to call attention to themselves. She prayed that was why she could find no trace of them because the alternative was, although an equally likely outcome, too painful to think about. Besides, it was far too soon to give up hope. The search for the missing duo had only just begun....

17 December 0710

A splotch of something white floating on top of all that sapphire blue caught Anzac's eye. It looked like a parachute. He knew he had spotted the landing spot of either Big Daddy or Poindexter. Anzac quickly got on the radio to the rescue helo forwarding them the coordinates of their downed comrade.

"Found one of them," Anzac told Perry. "I'm checking all frequencies to see if he's activated his radio."

"Okay."

She looped back and around keeping the area under surveillance. As she came out of her wide circle she, too, saw the chute. She also noted the swiftly closing SH-3 helicopter that was approaching them from the south. They would be there soon. The MiGs had cost them a plane, but they could replace the F-14. Perry just prayed she would not also have to replace two fliers as well

"Find anything yet?" she inquired.

"Negative," he said sounding both disappointed and worried. "I hope he's okay."

"The helo will be with him up soon," Perry said. She altered course, heading for the carrier, and stated, "I'm taking us in."

"Roger."

Perry bit her lip. The water hadn't been dyed and the radio had not been activated. That was not a good sign. She tried to put the rising fear that something had gone terribly wrong out of her mind and concentrated instead on getting them safely home.

17 December 1147

When he looked up, he saw the sun was almost directly overhead and he could tell by its intensity that it must be almost noontime. Poindexter sat up and was reminded of the pounding he'd taken by an intense throbbing pain in his head. He tried to ignore his headache and took stock of his situation. The dye tube was intact; he stained the water a bright sunny yellow. He had the paddle, but he had no idea where he was in relation to the carrier so he didn't know which way to row. He scanned the surface in all directions for a sign of anything that could help him figure out where the hell he was but all he saw was waves and troughs.

In with his survival gear he found the water bottle. It was warm, but he was very thirsty and took a long swig. He checked his little radio and saw that the homing signal was still going strong. He sighed. He hoped someone out there had their ears on. It felt like he'd been floating there for days, but he knew it had only been a few hours. He hoped someone would get to him before it got dark.

Something floating on the waves caught his eye and Poindexter did a double take. He grabbed the paddle and began to slowly propel himself toward what appeared to be bits of wreckage from his plane. He sighed sadly, as the bits of honeycombed titanium bobbing in the oil covered waves bounced by him, and again surveyed the area hoping to find Big Daddy in amongst the waves.

Nothing. He was alone with only the remains of his Tomcat for company. 'Dexter fought back the tears as he tried to convince himself that Big Daddy was still alive. He was just floating out there somewhere beyond his sight. Big had to have ejected in time! Poindexter knew there was only four-tenths of a second delay between the firing of his seat's rockets and those under his CO. He wasn't going to give up hope.

His eyes still swept the seas surrounding him like living radar as the rescue helicopter, which had picked up his radio signal, swiftly closed in for a pickup.

A knock on her office door momentarily startled Perry, who looked up from the photos and the latest intelligence reports. Her yeoman entered the room holding more data for her to assimilate. Truesdale handed her the folder. He looked like he had just heard some bad news and, fearing the worst, hesitantly asked, "Is he... ?"

Truesdale nodded solemnly. "Commander Beaumont didn't make it. His floatation equipment malfunctioned and, with all that wet, heavy gear on, he...he drowned."

The news hit her like a slap in the face. She let the folder she had been holding fall to the desk. Taking a deep breath to steady herself, she inquired in a controlled voice, "What about 'Dexter?"

"Nothing yet. But they're still looking. Commander Farrell sent up a couple more helos to search. They got hit while they were pretty high up and he thinks the winds could've blown 'Dexter south, into Cuban waters. It's risky sending crews to hunt for him there but we don't have much choice."

"Damn right we don't," she stated firmly. "Keep me posted Trudy."

He nodded. He could see she was working hard to keep her sorrow in check and wasn't sure how to give her the next bit of bad news. In a hushed voice he told her, "Dr. Freneau is here to see you. If you want, I'll tell him your busy and get rid—"

"No," she interrupted firmly yet in such a way as to acknowledge the young man's good intentions. Truesdale knew Big's death would hit her hard but she still had a job to do. And, unfortunately, dealing with Leigh Freneau was a part of that job. Perry sighed heavily. Did everybody on the goddamn boat know Leigh was her ex-husband? It sure as hell was beginning to look that way. "He can come in. By the way, who told you?"

Truesdale suddenly found his shoes real fascinating as he replied reluctantly, "Anzac told me. He wanted me to do my part to keep the peace."

She rolled her eyes. "I know I'm infamous for my Irish temper, but I haven't killed anybody...yet. But if I start noticing too many people going out of their way to keep the good doctor and me from seeing each other, there will be a burial at sea for two members of this air wing. Got that?"

He did. He also didn't want to be number one on that hit list. "I won't say anything. And, when 'Zac checks in, I'll tell him what you said."

Satisfied, she stated, "Good. Now, get Freneau in here. I'd like to hear what he has to say about those black birds."

"Aye, aye, Commander," he replied as he opened the door ushering in G-2's stealth expert.

Perry rose to greet him formally and Yeoman Truesdale marvelled at her cool professionalism. From her behavior it would have appeared to any onlooker that the two of them were complete strangers. The Commander's face was devoid of any readable emotion as she shook Dr. Freneau's hand and offered him a seat.

He realized he'd been lingering in the doorway a little bit longer than he should have been when he heard Perry inquire, "Something you forgot to tell me, mister?"

"Uh...no," he stammered and, quickly recovering, asked, "Can I get you some coffee?"

"Sure," she said. "Would you like some coffee, Doctor?"

Freneau nodded and Truesdale disappeared allowing the door to close behind him with an audible snick.

"If I didn't know better, I would say that boy was looking for an excuse to hang around," Freneau observed.

"He was," she confessed, her eyes betraying the emotions her authoritative tone masked so well.

Perry was angry but behind that glare of held-in-check fury was also a tinge of pain. He had wounded her more deeply than the shrapnel she took over Bekaa but, unlike that injury, the scars Leigh left her with had not even begun to fade. This was the first time they had been alone together since their divorce. Perry had insisted she could handle Leigh's being on the ship. But, until that moment, she had never been in Leigh's company without the reassuring presence of Anzac.

Now she felt like she was flying alone at night strapped into a Hornet that had lost both engines and was refusing to allow her to make that much needed loud exit. That bad feeling was beginning to make her perspire, and her stomach twist into a sailor's knot. She tried to use the relaxation techniques she'd learned, but her Tai Chi training never prepared her for having to deal a situation like this.

Leigh Freneau was perceptive enough to notice that he was having a very bad effect on her composure. Good, he thought, let her sweat it out. Maybe I'll finally get to see Perry instead of Commander McNeil. It's about time she stopped hiding inside that uniform.

A tentative knock on the door made Leigh turn and Perry sigh with relief. "It's open," she stated.

Truesdale entered proffering coffee, which he handed to each of them. He also carried another manila envelope, and a note from Bones, which he gave to Perry. "Two things, Commander. The films the onboard camera took during your encounter with the MiGs were developed. I guess they came out okay. That is, if we can judge their quality by how these stills look."

Perry opened the envelope and began examining the photos one by one. Only a few of them showed the MiGs with any degree of clarity. Of those, only a couple caught the black jet at the right angle to make its unique design visible. "That's it?" she said more than asked, not hiding her disappointment.

"When I picked these up, they told me that these were the best shots. Maybe you might want to review the film itself. I could get it—"

"Later," she interrupted. Changing the subject, she asked, "Got any good news?"

He smiled slightly when he replied, "Sure do. When you get done here, you're wanted in sickbay. Commander Farrell's team just brought in Lieutenant Viel. Doc Melman says as soon as you get the chance, you can stop by and he'll fill you in on how the Lieutenant's doing."

She inclined her head slightly. "Tell the doctor I'll be down to see him as soon as I'm finished here. Also, peek in on 'Dexter for me and let me know if he's up to a visit."

"Yes, Ma'am."

Truesdale left and, again, Perry was alone with *him*.

Freneau broke the silence that hung in the air like a London fog saying, "The results of my research are in this report." He handed the folder to her and she opened it quickly scanning the documents. As she scanned, he continued, "I'll save you having to hunt and peck by telling you this—the substance used to make that jet's hull was invented by an American."

Perry looked up from the papers surprised. "Are you sure?"

"Quite sure. A couple of years ago plans for stealth versions of several aircraft, included your personal favorite, the F-14D, were approved. Test versions were to have been made, provided the defense budget allowed for it. Well, the war soaked up all the money that was to have been earmarked for R&D, so the project was shelved. The metallurgical chemist who developed the radar-proof material for the jet's hull was a part of my group. That substance and the one used on that bird are identical."

"So, what you're saying is your old teammate sold us out," she stated. Eyeing him rather pointedly she added, "Doesn't surprise me one bit."

"I was wondering when you were going to take your best shot," he replied unruffled by her barb. "But *that* was hardly your best."

"My best would hospitalize you."

He rose saying, "If this is going to deteriorate into an airing of old unwashed laundry—"

Perry shot up from her chair to face him. "No, it isn't," she interrupted sharply. "We have *work* to do now. But, we *will meet again.*"

Leigh ignored the implied threat and asked, "Is there anything else you need to know, Commander?"

The report lying open on her desk caught Perry's eye and attention. She picked it up asking, "What's the likelihood that your old chemist buddy had company when he packed up his bags and defected?"

"Look, just because one of the apples went rotten doesn't mean you have to toss out the rest of the barrel," Leigh stated not liking the implication.

"I have justification for my suspicions. None of our people had ever spotted anything like those fighters in this hemisphere before. They were *stealth*, Leigh. The sort of thing that's right up your alley. And you're questioning my accusation that your teammates ditzed you? Gimme a break!" Perry declared as she grabbed a handful of photos taken via satellite and practically shoved them in his face. "Look at these. The one country that *could* have been home to those birds has, so far, been a zero. The Cubans have been busy, that's for sure. There's a hangar here that looks like it's used to maintain their aircraft. But, as you can see, no black jets anywhere."

Leigh perused the photos carefully for a long moment before responding, "*If* the Cubans had anything resembling what we're looking for, then it would have been Russian built. This jet was made, at least in part, by something invented by one of our people. I find it hard to believe anyone I worked with would sell us out to the Soviets."

"The only other people they could hit up with the kind of funds needed would be the cartels. And, much as you like your friends, Leigh, let's face reality. *Everybody* has their price."

"Even *you*?"

"I finally signed those divorce papers, didn't I?"

His expression chilled visibly. His tone of voice didn't reflect what he was feeling as he said, "There *is* a chance we could be up against something my old stealth team created. A *chance*, albeit a slim one."

"Okay, let's go on that hypothesis, then," she said. "It's the best idea I've heard so far. Here, check this out." She grabbed the manila envelope from on top of her desk and opened it handing him the photo-like printouts that had an artist's rendition of the mysterious jet she had described.

The aircraft had the rounded aerodynamic look he expected to see in a stealth fighter but its swoops and curves were no where near as exaggerated as those found on American aircraft, the F-19A being the one plane that came most readily to his mind. The variants on the MiG-29 design were glaringly obvious to Leigh, who had an idea as to where they'd made their modifications to make the most of the unique fabric that made up the vessel's body. He knew that new material had the potential to give the fighter the ability to exceed the ceiling of all its MiG predecessors. It would also allow it to be virtually invisible to all but the most sophisticated IR equipment, of which Leigh knew his patented Night Eyes system topped the list. Also going for the new jet were a pair of high-powered turbofan afterburning engines that he estimated were capable of propelling the bird at 2.5 Mach or better. His figures were based on what he'd read in the reports given during the debriefings of those flyers who had encountered the MiGs. This new MiG was probably faster than anything they had on the *Excalibur*. He also thought it might have the potential to play the same dual role as the Hornet. It could have both fighter and attack capabilities.

Leigh put the sketches back in the envelope saying, "Whoever put this together had to have had some very heavyweight help. A small cadre of scientists, like my team, might have been able to come up with the design. However, they couldn't possibly have built it. Construction requires a large outlay of personnel, equipment and money. This isn't the sort of thing that could be done by a private party."

Perry nodded in agreement. She altered the subject slightly saying, "When I first looked at these drawings, I thought, MiGs. This bird looks like a distant cousin of the MiG-29. Much more aerodynamic, of course, but the lines are still faintly there."

He nodded saying, "Yes. And, although you aren't an expert on aircraft design, you've been flying long enough to know what you're looking at."

"And what I'm looking at is a peck of trouble," she stated as she put the stack of photos and intelligence reports into a basket designated to hold such materials while they were still being used. After she was sure she was finished, the lot would be shredded.

"Not necessarily," he said. "Their buzzing the boat isn't sufficient cause for us to launch an Alpha Strike. But, if it can be proven these birds are Soviet, their action will earn them a reprimand through diplomatic channels. Those same channels might even force them to disclose why they're flying jets with first strike abilities so close to our ships and our border."

"Great. So what are we supposed to do in the meantime? Without firing a shot, they still managed to take out one of my aircraft and get Big Daddy killed!"

"The encounter you had with them was in their airspace, wasn't it?"

"No, but real damn close."

He waved it off saying, "Border skirmish. We played this game of cat and mouse with the Russians for years before they became our allies. Sometimes they would just do-see-do around with our boys. Other times they'd shoot down some of ours, and we'd nail a few of theirs. Then each side would sit back and deny anything happened while the boys in the field, who took part in it, would get their medals, promotions, and their orders to keep their mouths shut."

"Tell me about it."

He grinned. "I don't think I have to, Commander. You're already wearing a few reminders."

She knew which of her ribbons he was referring to and smiled back saying, "Yeah. And I earned 'em while I was *supposedly* on a training mission."

"You always did have a knack for getting yourself into the thick of it."

"Too true," she admitted. Her intercom buzzed and she answered it. "Yes?"

"Commander Edwards is hear to see you," she heard Truesdale say, and she smiled. Usually he wasn't so formal. She never objected to her yeoman referring to her deputy by his call sign when she was alone. Still, she knew he knew he was expected to do it all by the book whenever company was present.

"Tell him I'll be with him shortly," Perry said. "I'm just wrapping things up here."

"Yes, Ma'am."

She snapped off the intercom and turned back to Leigh asking, "What do the boys in Washington have to say about your findings?"

"They were both surprised and incensed when I told them the material used to make the bird's skin was originally ours. I think this situation may wind up being investigated through diplomatic channels, but I'm not sure. Captain Graff and the Admiral will no doubt fill you in on what your place in this puzzle is going to be during the briefing at 1400."

"I hope, we won't be stuck sitting on our hands," she said.

"Perry, the war is over," he stated bluntly. "You can no longer expect to solve problems by going in with your boys at Mach 2 carrying a full payload. That encounter you had today with those MiGs might just be the last time you see those birds."

"And it might not," she countered. "We'll just have to wait 'til 1400 to see what's decided. So, until then..."

He took the hint. "I'll talk to you later. I'm sure you have a lot of work to do."

She nodded yes. Leigh raised a knowing eyebrow at her and departed, leaving the door open for Anzac. Her deputy entered giving the departing scientist a quick once-over before shooting Perry a look that was an odd combination of pleased and perplexed. The moment Freneau was out of earshot Anzac declared in mock surprise, "He's still alive and in one piece. What gives?"

Playing along with him, she replied, "He hasn't outlived his usefulness."

Anzac grinned inwardly pleased his old friend was able to handle a one-on-one meeting with her ex without setting off a major barrage of ground fire. He was also happy to see she had enough of a grip on the situation to know the potential was there for her to lose her infamous Irish temper.

"They developed the films taken by the Double Nuts's camera," Perry told him. "I have some stills here. Unfortunately, they're not what I expected. We'll review the film itself later." She dove into her bottom desk drawer for the official Navy-issued cap that went with her khakis. Ball caps were okay for the day in and day out stuff. But she was off to do something where she would be expected to be by the book in both uniform and behavior. The former she could do in her sleep, but the latter...

"Did he tell you who made the composite used to make the MiG's body?" Anzac said more than asked.

"Yes, he told me," she said sounding concerned. "'Zac, do you still talk to that guy from your old squadron. You know, the one who now works for Naval Intelligence?"

"Yeah, sometimes. Why?"

She picked up the report Leigh had delivered and began rifling through the pages quickly. She said, "See if he can find out what became of that chemist..." Perry's voice trailed off as she paused to scan for the name. "Dr. Schroeck. Peter Schroeck. Got that?"

He nodded. "I'll talk to him. If he finds out anything, I'll let you know."

"Great."

Anzac watched her put on the cap that matched her uniform using the old Two-Finger Rule. He watched as she put the index and middle fingers along the bridge of her nose. The side of her pointer was on her nose and the middle finger on the center of the visor of her cap. Anzac saw that the tried and true method did the job: her cap was on perfect. She noticed him looking and gave him a wry grin. He nodded in return.

"Considering where I had this hat hiding for the past month…" she commented and he chuckled softly.

She started going through her intelligence papers weeding out the outdated information to shred and putting the current data back in her active pile. She was thinking both about 'Dexter as well as their staff meeting at 1400 while she sorted.

Anzac watched her in silence for a few minutes before venturing, "Perry, we have to talk."

"Now?" she queried not looking up from her paperwork.

He sighed. This was going to be hard enough for him to discuss and it seemed she wasn't about to make it any easier. "Yes, now," he commanded, the tone of his voice catching her slightly off-guard. She looked up at him a bit surprised.

"If this is about this morning—"

He cut her off short, not caring to listen to whatever explanation she had prepared to defend herself. "It is, and I'm not interested in hearing any of your excuses. This time, you have gone too far."

"Come on, 'Zac, you know me—"

"That's just it, I *know* you. Only too well. I've seen you get away with stuff that would've gotten anybody else canned for sure. I'll admit there were times when you're doing what you damn well pleased up there was the right thing at the right time. But not today. Today was bad. *Really bad.*"

She couldn't meet his eyes. He was right. She had come very close to doing something that would have been viewed as an act of war. Not to mention the fact she could've gotten both of them killed. Still, she did break off her pursuit in time to keep them out of trouble. "Yeah, I did fly a little too close to the fire this time," she admitted. "But I didn't get us burned. Look, you know as well as I do that coming close only counts in horseshoes. It doesn't mean squat in the game we're playing."

"You don't get it, do you?"

"What?" she said feigning innocence as she met his hard expression.

"That flying with somebody who's going to get me killed is not my idea of a good time," he stated sharply. "Look, balls-to-the-walls is one thing. But when you have the lives and Navy careers of other people depending on you, going off half-cocked is *not* a wise maneuver."

"Look, 'Zac, I know I screwed up big time. But I got a grip on reality in plenty of time to keep us from getting hip deep in it. So I don't see why—"

"Absolutely not," he cut in not about to let her get off the hook. "I'm not going to let this one slide. I've been ignoring all the shit you've been piling up for years. No more. Either you agree to get your act together and behave yourself up there, or you go find yourself another pitman. I've had it."

"Tony, you can't..." she started to say in a hushed voice. During the flight back, Perry had contemplated something like this happening. But, thinking something might come to pass and having it occur are two very different things.

Hearing her call him by his given name told Anzac that he had definitely struck home. "I do," he avowed.

She turned away, stunned. This had obviously been building up for quite some time. It was true he had been letting a lot of things slide over the years. She'd finally piled on that last straw. Perry didn't want to lose him. Having him walk out on her would mean she wasn't fit to wear her wings of gold. She may as well fill out the papers to ground herself right here and now. Perry sighed heavily. She was willing to make concessions to keep him with her as her partner. She would do better. She had to.

Perry took a deep breath to steady herself before turning back to face him. She half-smiled saying, "From now on I promise not to act like a graduate of the Han Solo school of action without thought. Okay?"

"Okay," he agreed. "But you pull *one* stunt, and I'm *out*. Got it?"

She nodded. "Yes."

He closed the distance between them, his expression softening as he embraced his longtime friend. "You drive me crazy, you know that?" he said quietly.

She gave him a quick squeeze saying, "Yeah, but I can be good. You'll see." She gently separated from him and broke the congenial mood by saying, "Come on, 'Zac, we've got a lot of work to do."

17 December 1315

Poindexter awakened with a start. His eyes snapped open and swept around the tiny room like radar trying to lock on to the source of the noise that woke him. He held his breath for a long moment and listened. He hadn't imagined it—he did hear a familiar voice talking just outside the doorway to the sickbay ward. His exhale came out a long, relieved sigh, and he fumbled with the controls to his bed. He found the button that elevated the head of his bed into a sitting position.

Being stuck out on the raft in choppy seas for all those hours had an odd effect on the RIO's equilibrium—he still felt like he was rocking and floating in the water. Though he knew he was lying on a bed that was totally motionless. Dr. Melman and his team had given him a very thorough once-over when he was brought aboard, and said he'd be up and flying in a day or two. His injuries were all of the bumps and bruises variety, and those were all from the ejection. He also had a mild case of exposure and hypothermia from the time he'd spent adrift soaking wet. While the medical team had been checking him out, 'Dexter had tried to find out what had become of Big Daddy. But no one seemed to know anything. They insisted they would tell him when they got the word but 'Dexter had a sneaking suspicion he would only hear about Big if he was found alive.

They don't understand, Poindexter thought, I can take it. Knowledge is far better than ignorance. It would not be the first time he had lost a friend. His thoughts drifted back to the war and the last time he'd been forced to punch out over cold rough water. Their jet had absorbed more anti-aircraft gunfire than it could withstand and Skye had initiated the loud exit the moment they were over the Med. Yet, their escape had not gone unnoticed; A MiG had pursued them and, as the two of them had been floating helplessly by their chutes, had opened fire on them. Poindexter miraculously escaped being shredded but Skye was literally blown apart by the MiG's cannons. Her body had been scattered all over the Med. Though it had been a couple of years since the incident, nightmares of that day still haunted Poindexter from time to time.

When the door opened, Poindexter greeted the somber-faced CAG with a smile. She half-smiled back, but it was obvious she wasn't in a very cheery mood. "How do you feel?" she asked, her voice full of genuine concern.

"Okay, I guess," he told her. "I'd feel a lot better if I knew what happened to Beau. Any news?"

Her expression darkened considerably. "Yes," she responded in a hushed voice. "He didn't make it."

Poindexter looked away from her and he felt his stomach tighten into a knot. After a long moment he dared to ask, "Where'd they find him?"

"His body was recovered about a half a mile north of where you were picked up," she answered. "His floatation equipment failed to deploy. He...he drowned, 'Dex."

Poindexter shook his head sadly and was just barely able to fight back tears. He cried plenty when Skye was torn apart by that MiG, but that was different. He had been all alone then with his grief. No one was around to key up his inhibitions about being demonstrative with his emotions and Poindexter had been able to let his feelings show. Although he knew Perry and Beau were good friends, and his loss hurt her deeply, he didn't feel comfortable enough around the Commander to let her see him mourn.

When he felt her reassuring hand on his shoulder, Poindexter turned back to face her. "I'll come back later," she told him as if she sensed his need to be alone with his sorrow. "We'll talk then."

He nodded and managed a wan smile. Perry gave his shoulder a small squeeze in farewell and departed in silence. He almost called her back but swiftly decided against it. He knew she would be very sympathetic since she, too, was experiencing the same feeling of loss but leaning on her strong shoulder wasn't where he would find solace. Thoughts of cottony soft, lemon-scented hair brushing his cheek as gentle arms held him close brought both a smile to his lips and a tear to his eyes. He wished Alanna was with him. He needed her. But he knew she couldn't visit him until she came off-duty.

Letting out a long sad sigh, Poindexter lowered the bed, rolled over onto his stomach, and silently cried himself to sleep.

Dr. Melman was in the midst of a discussion with a little bulldog of a man who Perry and Anzac recognized as Captain Bellamy, the newest addition to the *Excalibur's* trouble-shooting team. Both flyers had served under him during the War. They knew first hand that Bellamy was tough and very accustomed to having things done his way. As they entered the room, the two Marines that stood silently on guard outside the door to the wounded pilot's room gave them only a cursory glance. Bellamy and the doctor were too involved in their conversation to notice them.

"He's ba-ack," Perry teased low and aside to Anzac indicating Bellamy with a glance in his direction. Anzac's only response was a snort.

Bellamy had been sent by the top Navy brass at the Pentagon to assemble a task force that would be working solely on handling the current crisis. This hand-picked team would be taking orders directly from the Joint Chiefs and the President. He caught Perry and Anzac approaching from out of the corner of his eye and he looked at her like she'd just stepped in something. Seeing her again brought back a combination of good and bad memories.

Of all the squadron Commanders Bellamy had in his Air Wing during the War, Perry McNeil had been the best performance-wise. The Grim Reapers had the highest mission success rate in the Wing, the lowest down-time for their aircraft, and rarely lost a man. The only people who knew more about the F-14, what it could do, and how to fly it than she did were the folks at Grumman. Her flyers worked overtime to match her knowledge of the aircraft and skill behind the stick. They scrambled plenty when on the ground, too. Perry was consistently the first one to get her reports in, her evals and reviews done, and always seemed to still have time to answer a question or handle a problem. Her junior officers thought they had it tough trying to keep up with her in the air. When they were on the ship, they had to make sure the paperwork kept flowing, maintenance schedules were adhered to, and that their subordinates were performing their duties properly. The flyers used to joke that Perry could not only lead the horse to water, but could also make him drink every drop. An uncompromising perfectionist, ruthless efficiency incarnate, and one who expected from others no less than she expected from herself was Commander Perry McNeil.

Still, her squadron's achievements didn't help Perry when it came time for her performance review at the end of the cruise. Bellamy's last duty as CAG was to rank each of his squadron skippers. This rating was put into the personnel files that would travel with them for the rest of their Navy careers. The rankings went from one through eight, one being the best and eight the worst.

Bellamy gave Perry McNeil and her Grim Reapers an eight.

Anzac was thankful Perry was still recuperating when their War cruise ended and he was called into Bellamy's office to be given the bad news. Nit-picky items, like office trash not being emptied daily and fingerprints on the mirrors in the crew's washroom, were examples of the faults he found with how Perry managed her squadron. Had Perry been there to listen to Bellamy's reasons for her poor rating, she would have pounded the Captain to within an inch of his life. Anzac sighed. It had not been easy to stand there and endure all the fertilizer Bellamy heaped on him, but it was better it had been him instead of Perry. She would not have tolerated it.

Anzac caught the look of disdain on his face, and knew that the Captain and his best friend hadn't parted on the best of terms. Not that she had done much during their cruise together to get him to like her. During the War she had lorded over her squadron like Caesar did over the Roman Empire. She did anything and everything necessary to keep her planes in the air, her crews on the ground operating at their peak, and her flyers prepared to meet the challenges of combat. In the name of squadron effectiveness, Perry had gone over Bellamy's head so often he had bootprints on his scalp. Her willingness to bend the rules annoyed Bellamy, who was a stickler for doing things by the book. Her squadron's impressive record had scored her too many points with the brass for Bellamy to do much to her then. The poor review he gave her was his way of letting Perry know what he thought of both her tactics and of her personally.

Anzac cast a quick glance at Perry. He saw she had chosen to ignore the Captain's disparaging glances in her direction. He decided he'd follow her lead on this one. Anzac wasn't about to make waves. He, too, wasn't exactly on the best of terms with Captain Bellamy. Anzac didn't want to do anything that would harm their ability to work together effectively.

Melman cast a tired-eyed gaze onto Perry and Anzac and he smiled thinly at the duo. He had put in a lot of overtime since the MiG attack and it was obviously starting to catch up with him. "Lieutenant Viel will be discharged tomorrow," he said. "He should be able to return to his full duty schedule in a day or two."

"Good," Perry replied.

"Did you tell him about Commander Beaumont?"

She nodded. Noticing the inquiring look Bellamy was giving her, Perry explained, "Commander Beaumont was the pilot of the jet we lost. He is also—"

Bellamy cut her short stating, "I know who Beaumont is, McNeil. He was one of the best flyers I had in my Wing during the

War. He was no slouch on the ground, either. The Renegades were a tight little outfit. Never gave me any grief..." He let the thought trail off for effect.

The ploy worked. Anzac saw Perry's green eyes darken, and knew that it was only Bellamy's rank that was keeping him from getting the tongue lashing of a lifetime. Much as she wanted to, Perry knew she couldn't treat the Captain to a taste of her saltiest verbal medicine. She would just have to ignore his digs and get on with her business. Appearing completely unruffled by his shabby treatment of her, Perry's eyes were on the door being guarded by the two Marines as she replied coolly, "Well, I'll leave you to go and do your job. Since it's obvious you haven't even started yet."

Bellamy was about to respond to her well-placed barb when Anzac broke in asking, "Did intelligence ever get to talk to that guy we picked up?"

"Commander Edwards, I can understand your curiosity about our captive. But any information concerning him that Naval Intelligence feels you should have, you will get *in the briefing*," Bellamy said talking down to Anzac as though the deputy Wing Leader was a child and not his subordinate.

Anzac disliked the way he was being talked to and looked very annoyed. Yet he said nothing.

Perry rolled her eyes. "Any chance you know when we're going to have this briefing?" she inquired in a dubious tone.

He shot her a hard look. "Any chance you could get on with your job before you find yourself in the brig for interfering where you don't belong, Commander?" he retorted, not liking the implied doubts concerning his abilities posed by her question. "It would be a pleasure," she stated, the irony in her voice blatantly apparent.

Anzac knew where this was headed and spoke before Bellamy had a chance to reply. "Perry, our Wing meeting, remember?"

"Right." She quickly gave Bellamy a cordial smile saying, "I'll be in touch. If you'll please excuse us...."

She turned away heading for the door with Anzac following close behind. The two of them had barely taken two steps towards the exit when Bellamy's voice stopped them dead in their tracks.

"Where do you think you're going?" he snapped.

The two of them spun around in unison to face him. "To a Wing meeting, sir," Perry said.

He looked like he was going to take her apart as he closed in on them. "Look lady, I *do not* like your attitude and I don't have to put up with your smart mouth. Do you understand?"

"Yes, sir."

Perry's voice was flat, emotionless. It was obvious to Anzac that she was playing it by the book for one reason and one reason only: Perry knew she could not win in the long run against him because he outranked her. But, Anzac knew that never stopped her from trying to score a few points. Anzac had seen her take this tact before when she had to deal with a superior officer who not only held a conflicting viewpoint but also disliked her.

His eyes narrowed as he looked long and hard at Perry. She was standing at attention, as was Anzac, and if she was feeling anything, it was not apparent in her expression. He gave Anzac only a cursory glance. It was obvious to him that Perry held the bulk of the Captain's attention. And it was also apparent to Anzac that the Captain wasn't going to let them go before he had a chance to give the Commander a piece of his mind.

"I know your record, Commander," he stated just barely able to keep the fact that he found her achievements impressive from coloring his tone of voice. "You're a helluva instinctive pilot. Perhaps *too* good. Maybe that's why you've been allowed to keep your Navy career even though you get off on sassing senior officers and disobeying orders. Your squadron was the best one flying during the War and we both know that's the only reason you were able to get away with all the bullshit you pulled. *But the War is over*! *I* don't care if you can fly rings around everyone on this ship. I also don't care if you have the best fucking Air Wing in the Navy. You'll treat me with respect or you will be *replaced*, is that clear?"

"Yes, sir."

He shot a hard look at Anzac. "That goes for you, too, mister."

"Yes, sir!" Anzac replied quickly.

Satisfied for the moment, he dismissed the two of them with a wave of his hand. The two flyers gave him a by-the-book salute and left.

The second they were out the door, Perry remarked, "I wonder what neolithic rock he crawled out from under."

Anzac cracked a smile. "I thought he retired after the War! But it seems he's heading the task force that's going to be handling our current situation. Like it or not, CAG, we're going to be stuck again with having to report to Captain Butt-pain."

Perry only response to that bit of news was to let out a long, disgusted sigh.

17 December 1400

Martin Wolff was glad he'd run into Yeoman Truesdale. The young man always knew where to find Commander McNeil. Wolff was well aware that, since their run-in with the MiGs, Perry had been much too busy to spend time with him, but he *had* to see her. He overheard something that he sincerely hoped wasn't true but knew could happen quite easily, given what Perry and her team did to earn their Navy paychecks. He was told she and 'Zac would be up in Flag Ops for a meeting at 1400. Hoping to catch her before the talks began, Wolff took the quickest route possible up the carrier's island superstructure: the seemingly endless flight of stairs.

He was out of breath when he reached the correct level and he panted his way down the narrow corridor to the conference room. Perry was already inside, as were the Admiral, Captain Graff, Dr. Freneau, and several other senior officers, some of whom Wolff didn't recognize. She looked preoccupied but Anzac noticed Wolff standing in the doorway and came over to speak to him.

"I can't talk long," Anzac told him in hushed voice. "What's on your mind?"

"Is it true about Commander Beaumont?"

Anzac nodded sadly. "Yes. This is off the record, understand?" Wolff nodded and he continued to explain, "His plane went down earlier today. Poindexter made it out okay, though." He glanced away from Wolff for a second and, seeing they weren't quite ready to begin the proceedings, added quickly, "We have some people here from Washington. I'm afraid I can't tell you anything more until I know what's classified and what isn't."

"I understand," Wolff replied quietly looking past him and into the group that was starting to take their places around the table. His eyes met Perry's and she politely excused herself from the company of Captain Graff and Mr. Piño to join him and Anzac by the door.

"Long time no see," she said to the reporter, who smiled warmly at her. "How have you been?"

"Okay," he said. "I heard about what happened to Big. I'm sorry."

Her expression turned somber and she gave him a half-smile

saying, "Thanks. There will be a memorial service for him tomorrow at oh-eight-hundred. You know you are welcome to come if you wish."

He inclined his head in acknowledgement. "I'll be there."

Captain Graff tapped Perry lightly on the shoulder. "Commander, let's go."

She turned towards the Captain and nodded saying, "I know. Give me thirty more seconds, okay?"

He nodded in assent and would have smiled at Wolff except that the eighteen stitches, which held closed a deep gash that extended from his ear to his finely chiseled right cheekbone, made the gesture painful in the extreme. The Captain had just been released from the hospital that morning. Although he was very good at hiding his discomfort, Wolff had caught a few instances where he had moved wrong, pulled his stitches and winced from the pain.

Perry turned back to face Wolff saying, "Stop by my office around twenty-hundred. Technically, that's when my shift ends but I doubt I'll see any free time until this crisis is over."

"Will you have *any* time for me today?"

She caught the hopeful look in his eyes and the dimple-filled smile and shrugged. Perry was finding his attempts to charm his way into a spot on her tight schedule both amusing and annoying. She sighed. "Yeah, I'll make some time," she heard herself saying. The dimples deepened, as his smile widened, and she stepped back from the doorway concluding, "Twenty-hundred, got that?"

He nodded. "Bye," Perry taunted more than said before closing the door almost in Wolff's face. Graff caught her parting shot and, momentarily forgetting his injuries, chuckled. It was obvious to the *Excalibur's* skipper that Wolff was attracted to Perry but it didn't look to him as though the feeling was mutual.

Perry looked up at Graff remarking, "How much do you want to bet Wolff is still standing out there and has his ear plastered to the door?"

The Captain shook his head. "Not more than I could afford to lose," he replied as he led the way to the conference table. "His presence hasn't been *too* inconvenient, has it?"

"Well, so far he's managed to keep from getting underfoot," she said as she took the seat to the Captain's right. "but, given our current situation, I'm in favor of putting that boy on a leash."

Anzac, who had overheard part of the conversation and quickly figured out to whom she was referring, stifled a laugh. He had been one of many officers who had caught Wolff snooping around places he didn't belong. Although he understood the reporter had a job to do, there were times when Anzac wanted to give that man a boot in the backside. Wolff had been in the CIC when he and Perry almost made their unscheduled visit to Cuba and Beau's plane went down. Beaumont's untimely death was something Anzac wouldn't mind seeing in Wolff's book but what Perry did was another story. If her momentary lapse of good judgement was made public, it could end her career. There was one thing Anzac would definitely do before Wolff and his laptop computer left the ship: he was going to have a serious talk with Wolff and do his best to convince the reporter that he should not put anything harmful to anyone, especially Perry, into his book.

The room fell silent as Captain Bellamy and Admiral Jones stood side by side at the head of the conference table. Behind them the doors covering the almost wall-sized TV screen had been pulled back revealing the blue hued monitor. Perry's eyes darted around the table and observed that she and Anzac were the only senior officers representing the Air Wing present at the table. Master CPO Gabriel sat opposite Anzac and he looked worried. At the foot of the table was Major Vasquez, who was whispering quietly into the ear of the other Marine in the room. This second Marine sat directly opposite Perry and she found it hard to meet the man's steely-eyed gaze without smiling.

Colonel Grimmig had seen his share of fighting during his lengthy career and seemed more than ready to take on their current challenge. She liked his head-on way of dealing with things and his very modern attitudes. Grim was one of a handful of senior officers comprising the *Excalibur's* senior staff who had no problem dealing with the changing times. He was a rare find in that he had a very positive attitude about women in the Corps. When he took command of the *Excalibur's* Marines, Grim had made a point of introducing Perry to the two highest ranking female members of his team. She had been genuinely impressed by the intensity in the eyes and demeanor of the two women. They looked like they could eat nails for dinner and then have the hammer for dessert.

Perry's only temptation to fall off the fidelity wagon had come in the tanned well-built form of Colonel Grimmig. During the War, she and Grim had gotten very close but her loyalty to the husband she'd left behind always stood between them like a bulkhead. She knew he had found her devotion admirable but frustrating. He had found her strong-willed nature attractive and exciting, but quickly discovered it also played a part in keeping her from surrendering to the heat of the moment. She knew he must have been aware of how hard it had been for her to refuse. She had wanted him so bad, at times, it caused her physical pain. But she would not violate a sacred trust, no matter how much it hurt.

Leigh had no idea what she had given up in the name of their love and marriage. Seeing both Grim and Leigh together in the same room both angered and agonized her. She caught Grim's curious gaze in her direction and wondered if the emotions her thoughts were raising showed on her face. She smiled an almost wistful smile at him. He knew she was ready to renew their relationship: she had made that plain when he had visited her while she'd been recovering from her injury. Still, with the crisis they had to deal with, it was going to be really hard to find the time...

The sound of Bellamy's voice cracked through her thoughts like a rifle shot and brought them swiftly back to the present. "Your initial encounter with the MiGs never should have happened," he was saying. Films of the stealth planes taken by the cameras fitted into the birds that had encountered them filled the screen. Some footage Perry recognized as having been taken by the cameras aboard Eggroll Wu's Tomcat and Sparky's Hornet. "At least, that is the word from Washington. I also spoke to the pilot we picked up. He claims he was out on a routine patrol and that *we* jumped *him*."

"That's a lotta crap!" Perry stated. "They're the ones who started it and we've got a deck full of eyewitnesses who'll be more than happy to testify—"

"I'm sure you do, Commander," Bellamy cut in. "But our adversaries have equally strong proof to back their point."

Perry sighed, as she watched the film of the black MiG disappearing into the clouds, and toyed with her pen. That footage wasn't doing wonders for the reputation of Air Wing 21. She felt a little better when the second encounter, her encounter, came up on the screen. But, as she watched, she had to admit that Bellamy did have a point. It was true the MiGs had paid them an unexpected, uninvited call but, although they did damage the ship and injure people, they had done so without firing a shot. The encounter that resulted in Big's death had also been one in which not a shot was fired. It was all so perplexing, thought Perry. Just who were they up against? And what the hell did they want?

"Did the pilot say why they buzzed out ship?" Anzac asked.

"No, but I have my own theories about that. They did that fly by because they were fairly sure we wouldn't see them coming. That run was done as a test to confirm their suspicions."

"Wonderful," Vasquez grumbled under his breath.

"I guess if we had spotted them, they would have taken off the moment any of our planes encountered them," Anzac assumed and Bellamy nodded in agreement.

"What about that encounter where Beau Beaumont was killed? Was that also a part of their "test"?" asked Grimmig.

"What happened to Commander Beaumont was an unfortunate accident. I think those MiG drivers intended to just scare him, not hurt him," Bellamy stated. Changing the subject abruptly, he said, "Look, although we are sailing in international waters, we are spitting distance from Cuba. I don't need to tell you what superpower Castro's in bed with. We have to be very careful about how we handle things down here. The Cuban ambassador has been screaming his head off about our jets violating Cuban airspace. They're also denying responsibility for our problem. But we all know that could be just politics. He could be covering up for a military SNAFU. In any event, gentlemen, the official word from the White House is this: If the MiGs get too close to the task force, our pilots are to *ask them* to leave and escort them out of our airspace. We are not, repeat *not*, to engage them. Is that clear?"

"What if they engage us?" Perry challenged.

"Look, I don't believe they will. But, as it was before, if you are fired upon you may return fire. *But they must clearly fire the first shot!* I don't want one of your trigger-happy hotshots causing an international incident. You read me, McNeil?"

"Yes, sir."

"That pilot that we picked up," Anzac began. "Where is he from?"

Bellamy hesitated for a moment before answering, "He said he came from Cuba."

"So, it *is* the Cubans after all. Even if their ambassador says they aren't up to anything."

Bellamy neither denied nor affirmed Anzac's conclusion. He simply said, "Look, the Cubans and Russians could be up to something. However, until they either admit their guilt or we get some undeniable proof to confirm their responsibility, we can't pin the blame on them."

"What if it isn't the Cubans or the Russians? What if he's just a damn good civilian pilot on the cartel's payroll?" Perry suggested. "I saw some pretty fancy flyin' when I was up there."

"I don't doubt that you did, Commander. But did you happen to notice anything other than that? Something that might back up that idea of yours, perhaps?"

Bellamy was sticking it to her and she knew it. She ignored his jab and his questions completely. "Look, there's no hard evidence to say it's the Russians or the Cubans. What makes you think it's them?"

"What makes you think it's the cartels?" he shot back. She didn't reply immediately and he added in a less strident tone, "If you know for certain where those MiGs came from, then tell me. I would like to hear it."

"Well...no, not exactly," she began pausing for a moment to organize her thoughts. All eyes in the room shifted on to her she said pensively, "There is a chance that whoever is behind these attacks might be trying to scare us off. To get us out of this area. Our whole purpose for being down here is drug interdiction. I think there's a good possibility the cartels could be the one's responsible. After all, we *have* been putting a major damper on their operations."

A few heads nodded in agreement, including Captain Graff's, but Bellamy wasn't convinced. "Stealth of this caliber isn't available on the black market. I know you and your boys ran into some rogue Phantoms a while back, but that was the sort of thing we expected you to find. We knew the Medellin were getting a lot of firepower through underground sources. That's why there's a carrier task force assigned to this region. The DEA can't handle this on their own."

"Maybe they didn't buy it. Maybe they hired people to build it for them."

At this point Dr. Leigh Freneau put up his hand to stop the discussion. "Commander, your point has merit. But, although the Medellin have the financial resources to back such a project, they lack the essential support structures required to scratch build a jet. True, they have what's needed to keep their F-4s flying, but maintenance and construction are two different things. And building stealth is far and away more arduous than knocking together a Phantom or a Corsair."

"Are you saying it's impossible for them to be behind this?"

"No," he said daring to meet her eyes. "Just damned difficult."

"So, we aren't going to rule out the cartels after all."

"Until we have a definitive answer, we are keeping *all* options open," Bellamy told her.

Perry made no further comment. The images on the screen changed from films to slides taken by the satellite. The shots were of known and suspected Cuban airbases. There were several good close ups of MiGs in operation, but nothing looked new to Perry. As Bellamy went on about the strengths and weaknesses of Cuba's air force, Perry was only half-listening. She found the latest reconnaissance photos far more telling than anything being said. A photo of a harbor and of something that looked like the forward section of a missile lying in a frame box lay on one of the piers. It was either being loaded or offloaded from a ship. When Perry and Anzac saw it, they both straightened up in the seats. It was obvious from Anzac's expression that he had seen something of interest.

The slide changed. The next shot was of another harbor but, as far as the two Wing members were concerned, there wasn't anything of interest to see. Anzac interrupted Bellamy asking, "Could you please go back to the previous slide, sir? There was something on it that I need to take a second look at."

Bellamy shrugged, not sure what was on Anzac's mind, but complied with his wishes. "This what you wanted to see, Commander?" he asked.

"Yes, sir."

The slide that had caught the eye of the deputy Wing Leader was again before them. Anzac asked, "Can you zoom in on that?" He pointed at the object being taken on or off the ship.

The Captain looked past Perry and eyed Anzac quizzically. "See something?"

"Think so," he replied quietly.

Soon the screen was filled with a very grainy image of what looked like the fuselage of an aircraft disassembled for transport. It was hard to see because it was black for starters and the intense magnification brought out every imperfection in the photo.

"See that?" Anzac asked indicating the sparkle to everyone. "That's a cockpit."

Everyone scrutinized the photo, Bellamy included. It was hard to tell but, under very close inspection, the upper portion of the pilot's seat was just visible.

Jones looked at Anzac. "You saw that from all the way over there?" he queried.

"Not exactly," Anzac admitted. "It was the shape and that dark spot that looked like an opening that clued me in."

"It's just the fuselage, sir," Perry said. "But, I think if we were to compare it to photos of those jets we saw earlier today, there would be a definite resemblance."

"That picture doesn't really tell the whole story, though," Anzac said more to her than to the assembly. "You can't tell if that part is coming or going."

She nodded in agreement. "I know. But, if the satellite managed to snag this one, there's a chance there's others..."

The Admiral broke in saying, "Look into it, Captain." Bellamy nodded and Jones continued, "One thing that made us shoot down every likely suspect in this hemisphere was their lack of ability to do construction. If that is the fuselage from one of those MiGs, which it does look like, then we know one thing. These jets were shipped broken down and were put together like a model at their final destination. Which means they could belong to *anyone* and could be from *anywhere*. Any competent team of aircraft mechanics could assemble a knocked down jet."

"So, it seems we have managed to narrow the field down to almost every nation bordering the Gulf of Mexico," commented Grimmig.

"We'll be narrowing it down a lot tighter than that, Colonel. Before this day is out, we should have only a handful of places to check," Bellamy assured the Marine.

Grimmig raised an eyebrow skeptically but offered no further remarks. Admiral Jones's dark eyes scanned the group for a long hard moment. When his gaze came to rest on the two flyers, he said, "After this briefing, the two of you are going to assist Captain Bellamy and his team with their investigation. And you will adjust your flying schedules accordingly."

"Yes, sir," Anzac and Perry replied in unison.

He shifted his eyes on to the group at large before concluding, "After Captain Bellamy finishes bringing us all up to speed on this, the floor will be open for questions. Captain?"

Bellamy gave the Admiral a polite smile before resuming his dissertation. The slide show also continued and Perry's attention was focused entirely on the screen. She was hoping to spot another piece of the puzzle to add to the one Anzac had found. However, the rest of the photos were of airfields, airports, and airplanes, both civilian and military. And there wasn't so much as a hint of a black jet in any of them.

Perry noticed Anzac had been taking notes during Bellamy's talk. Good. She usually took notes, too, during senior staff meeting but, this time, her pad was blank. She had been more intent on finding clues in the photographs than in taking down key points to remember. Anzac caught her peering at his scribbling and gave her a slight smile.

She leaned over and whispered in his ear, "See anything else, Eagle Eyes?"

He grinned. "No," he replied softly so as not to be overheard. "Spotting that was luck."

"You knew it wasn't a missile."

"*Suspected*, not knew. It looked funny."

Perry raised an eyebrow thoughtfully. She returned her attention to the meeting in time to hear Bellamy say, "That is all the information we have now. Alert status will be maintained until the order comes through to stand down. You will be apprised of any changes. I am sure we will soon have a better idea as to who is responsible for harassing us, so we can take care of them once and for all. So, until then, that is all. Any questions?"

There were a few, mostly to clarify a few technical items, but nothing that caught Perry's sharp ears as being useful to her. She borrowed Anzac's pad and gave the pages a quick scan. She glanced up and quietly inquired, "Hear anything from your Intelligence buddy?"

"Not yet. He said he'd buzz me as soon as he found out anything. It may take a little while. He's going to be doing this unofficially. It's not like the brass seems interested in what became of Dr. Schroeck."

Perry nodded, her eyes back on the notes. Before departing to join Captain Graff and the Admiral, Anzac leaned over and teased, "Study hard. We're getting a test on this at twenty-two hundred."

She cracked a smile but offered no comment. Glancing up from the pad to scan the room, she noticed the meeting had officially ended. The group was breaking up into small clusters to discuss the proceedings. When she saw both Leigh and Colonel Grimmig headed her way, Perry sighed. She hoped she had enough diplomacy to handle a discussion with both an ex-husband and an almost lover.

"Sorry to hear about Beau," Grimmig offered meaning it. "It's going to be tough to explain this to his family."

Perry nodded sadly. "I know. And I don't want to send Lorraine some impersonal pile of crap. She deserves the truth. It's just that right now we don't *know* the truth. Until we know who's responsible for his accident, I can't put together a letter."

"Even when you do know, there is a chance what we're doing here could all be termed classified. Which means you won't be able to tell Beaumont's next of kin anything," Leigh pointed out. "So far, none of this has hit the papers. And, should it turn out we are dealing with a sovereign nation and not a bunch of drug traffickers, this matter could be shifted into diplomatic channels and handled *quietly*."

"But, if it is the cartels, this'll be front page news," Perry stated. "The drug pushers have stealth technology! This will push the President to have the military get even more involved in interdiction. We'll become cops in warplanes!"

Leigh caught the intensity behind her declaration and knew she believed in her theory that the drug war may have escalated into something of consequence. When their eyes met, for a fleeting instant he regretting losing what they once had together. The cocky jock, whose motto was "if it's got wings, I can fly it," had caught his eye quite by chance. She stood out from the usual crowd at Manhattan's hip *Stringfellows* club. Perry and her small group of Naval officer companions had dropped by the night spot after a formal function. She looked striking, glittering from rows of medals pinned to her Naval formal dress uniform, and carried herself with the air of a *grande dame*. She acquired a small coterie of admirers, who had latched themselves onto her almost from the moment she arrived. Perry was the only women in the place who wasn't wearing as little as they could legally get away with, but she wasn't keeping what she had a complete mystery either. Her form fitting uniform had been specially tailored to make the most of her well-honed body.

The first slow song the band played had been his cue to ask her to dance and she had accepted. The song, *Georgia* by the Righteous Brothers, was a few weeks later the first song they danced to as husband and wife at their wedding. A quick courtship was all they had time for: Perry and her squadron had about a month before they had to join up with the rest of Carrier Air Wing 18 aboard the USS *Abraham Lincoln* for a seven month cruise. Leigh knew he had to move quickly if he wanted to have Perry as a permanent part of his life.

It had been an intense month. When she flew off to meet the ship with the rest of the Grim Reapers, he almost didn't mind the upcoming period of separation. It would give his body a chance to recuperate. She had a lot more energy than he did and he knew it wasn't just because she was ten years his junior. He'd been with women far younger than Perry and none of them came close to matching her endurance and skill.

Perhaps if he had he gotten to know Perry in more than just the Biblical sense he might have thought twice about marrying her. Once she returned from her cruise and they settled into something of a routine, he quickly discovered where her priorities lay. Not that she didn't love him, she did, but her first love was for flying and the Navy and it seemed there was little he could do to alter that fact. She never told him outright he came in second to her F-14. But he could see her devotion to her first love in her eyes whenever the subject of flying found its way into their conversations. As time passed, Leigh realized he could not handle the separations, the long hours, and the dangers inherent in his wife's chosen profession. Had he felt he was first in her heart, Leigh probably would have tried to handle the tough side of being a Navy husband. It was because he knew he was number two that he didn't try to work out his problems with her. Instead of trying to hang on to what he had with Perry, he spent the long months of the war looking for greener pastures.

Perry must've seen the wistful look in his eye for he noticed she was eyeing him curiously. It seemed to him like she must have been reading his mind when he heard her inquire, "Thinking about how you screwed up a good thing?"

"Maybe," he allowed.

Major Grimmig's eyes darted back and forth from him to her and back again like the tennis ball during Wimbledon. He regarded the duo thoughtfully and stood silently in the shadows like an IFF/APX Data Link, taking in all the signals and swiftly processing the information.

The closeness of him was beginning to make Perry uncomfortable. She quickly scanned the room for a long moment before her gaze locked with Anzac's. He was engaged in a conversation with the Admiral and Captain Bellamy and, seeing her escape route, refocused her attention back onto her ex-husband. Out of the corner of her eye she caught a knowing look on Grim's face. She wondered for a fleeting instant if he had gleaned from her brief bit of private conversation with Leigh the reason why they split. Early on in the cruise she had told Grim that she was divorced, and that Leigh had dragged her though the mud in court, but she had not gone into detail. Grim had always been keenly perceptive, and she knew it would be better if she told him what happened rather than having him get the word via the Air Wing grapevine. She owed him the truth. Turning her eyes completely on Leigh she said politely, "I'll see you later. Anzac and I have to help Captain Bellamy play detective."

He nodded. Her job on the carrier kept her flying in more ways than one. Freneau was certain he would run into Perry again, and not necessarily at a staff meeting. She rose and gave Colonel Grimmig a quick smile before joining her deputy, Captain Bellamy and Admiral Jones.

Anzac gave her a knowing wink and she just grinned back. "You still on the status board for a hop at 1800?" he asked.

She nodded. "Have to keep up my hours on the Intruder," she told him. "Haven't done any night flights in the A-6F in a while. The bird I'm taking up tonight has had the Night Eyes installed, so I'll be prepared to do some MiG hunting."

He smiled saying, "I'm also going out for a little drive around the neighborhood tonight."

"Just make sure you stick to the main street, 'Zac," Perry admonished. "You are not expendable."

"Neither are you."

"Both of you had better be spending some time on the ground this evening," Bellamy cut in obviously not finding any amusement in the two flyers congenial exchange. "You're *supposed* to be helping me, remember?"

"Our flights are hours apart, Captain," Perry reassured him. "We'll both be available to assist you and your team for the bulk of our shift."

Bellamy gave her a hard look and grunted in acknowledgement. Perry did her best to ignore the fact Bellamy disliked her. It was annoying, though, since she knew his antipathy dated back to the time she had served in his Air Wing during the war. Bellamy caught on too late that she was willing to go to great lengths to get the job done. Which often meant that, if she couldn't find a JO or a crew chief to do the work, she did it herself. He found it only mildly annoying when he caught her doing routine inspections or other duties normally performed by her subordinates. But, Bellamy nearly blew a gasket the first time he saw her helping one of her crew chiefs repair a damaged plane. His complaints about her behavior fell on deaf ears because of her achievements. Her squadron had the highest mission success record in the Fleet. They also managed to keep their planes flying despite the horrendous shortages of parts and maintenance materials. The fact that she had to be a jack-of-all-trades to accomplish this bothered no one but Bellamy. Not even the ship's Captain seemed to care that he had a squadron skipper who played grease monkey whenever the VF-13 maintenance crew got shorthanded.

It didn't matter to him that her record would show how hard she had worked to earn this command. Bellamy despised her whatever-it-takes-to-get-the-job-done way of handling things. He thought that she had no business running an Air Wing with that kind of attitude.

But, Perry was determined not to let him get to her. She politely excused herself and left to wrap up some unfinished paperwork. Perry would need time to get prepared for her upcoming flight in the Intruder.

17 December 1925

The pall of low clouds hung over them like a shroud. Tiring of the empty blackness both above and below, Perry pulled the stick thrusting the bomber up through the clouds to the starriness of the night above. She turned away from the instrument panel to contemplate the midnight velvet of the sky and the stars, that glittered like a multitude of tiny diamonds. The little sliver of moon illuminated the quilt-like layer of clouds that looked as soft and inviting as a feather bed. Its small light also reflected off the silver shell of the A-6F.

"Beautiful, isn't it, Tyger?" Perry said softly.

Lieutenant Kelson "Tyger" Llewellyn, the bombardier-navigator, sat on Perry's right with her face pressed against the black hood that shielded the radar screen from extraneous light. Integrated into the jet's normal detection equipment was Dr. Freneau's "Night Eyes" system. Although it had seemed to the BN that the new IR device had been more or less tacked on, she was impressed by how well the new merged with and enhanced, what the bird already had. She turned away from the screen and glanced up at the sea of stars above and sighed.

"Yeah," she agreed and began humming *When You Wish Upon A Star* as she resumed her ceaseless task of optimizing the radar presentation.

Perry recognized the tune and chuckled. "Is that the best you can do?" she teased the BN, who, with her driver, was renown throughout the Air Wing for her musical talents.

The hood hid Tyger's thoughtful expression and, her eyes never leaving the screen, she began singing one of her compositions, a moody piece about an Intruder team shot down behind enemy lines after a bombing raid. Tyger was a New Moon War veteran. The fear, pain and hopefulness the words her song conveyed were evident in the tenor of her voice as she brought tune and lyric together as one. Kelson was yet another enigma: what was someone with such a gift doing sitting in a BNs chair?

That was the sort of question Wolff would think of, Perry mused as she turned the aircraft a few degrees to keep them on course. The bird had drifted a minute amount while her attention had been momentarily diverted. She looked left at her Dash Two. Filk was at the stick and had corrected in tandem with her. The two Intruders were flying a loop that always kept them within five miles of the carrier and were acting as yet another pair of eyes on lookout for potential trouble.

It was destined to be a quiet night, Perry mused. Her attention was equally divided between the radio chatter and Tyger's ballad. When the song ended, an eerie silence filled the plane and for a long time they flew their circular route without speaking. The somber piece had made each of them remember a time they both would rather have forgotten. The two women spent the rest of their shift devoting their attentions to their respective jobs and trying to keep the memories of the war from clouding their thoughts and judgement.

Anzac scrunched up his nose in distaste at the cup of lukewarm coffee he had just finished. The red glow of lights from the CIC cast their sunset hues on his face and illuminated the faces of the Admiral, and Captains Bellamy and Graff. Jones looked like a bulldog straining at the leash as he read the latest intelligence. He had always gotten on Perry's case about being so gung-ho all the time, but it was obvious to 'Zac that the Admiral was getting just a bit antsy. Not that he wanted a fight, Anzac knew that was the last thing Jones desired. What he did want was a quick and, hopefully, peaceful resolution to the crisis. Nothing had changed since 1400 and it was that small bit of bad news that had the Old Gentleman gnawing at the bit.

Another item Anzac observed was that Bellamy stopped treating him like a piece of gum stuck on the bottom of his boot the moment Perry wasn't around. The Captain was actually *nice* to him. The first time it happened, had caught 'Zac so much by surprise he had nearly choked on the cup of joe he had been drinking at the time. He had asked Anzac's opinion on a bit of strategy and then, later, cracked a rather off-color joke, which was what made 'Zac almost lose the coffee. If he knew he could get away with the gag, Anzac would have had the fact that Bellamy possessed something resembling a sense of humor given as a special report via the ship's TV station during its 2300 news broadcast.

The skipper stood staring contemplatively at the radar screen and mused aloud, "We could be stuck out here waiting for them to make a move for quite some time."

"What makes you say that, sir?" Anzac asked.

"Think about it," Graff said looking away from the screen and at Anzac. "They must know every ship, plane and man is out there looking for them. The longer they lay low and wait, the more likely the searchers are to lose their vigilance due to fatigue. We saw this when Operation Desert Storm was Desert Shield and our troops were waiting around for something to break. All the casualties that happened during that waiting time were due to accidents. In many cases, these mishaps could be linked to errors made by people tired of the seemingly endless drills and desperate for something, *anything*, to happen."

"So you think they're going to leave us hanging?" Bellamy said more than asked.

"I know I would if I were in their shoes."

Anzac smiled and inquired, "Sir, with all due respect, it doesn't sound as though this estimation of the situation was an idea that just suddenly occurred to you."

The *Excalibur's* Captain smiled with his eyes as he responded, "No, I've been discussing the enemy's possible tactics with Perry and she came up with this idea."

Anzac grinned. He thought he had detected a familiar note in what the Captain had said. Graff's admission he had been talking tactics with Perry brought a scowl to Bellamy's face but he kept his opinions to himself. He wasn't about to tell Graff what he thought of Commander McNeil and her bright ideas. Especially when, he hated to admit it, she had latched onto something that he hadn't even thought about. If their opponents were going to be clever and play a waiting game, then they all could be in for a long, long haul.

18 December 0837

Martin Wolff entered the blue and silver forecastle in the forwardmost part of the ship and stood silently just to the right of the doorway. The harsh look from the anchor chain and windlasses in the forecastle was softened by the table holding a cross and candles. There were upholstered chairs set up in front of it for the senior officers on the *Excalibur*. Metal bridge chairs, for the officers of the VF-69 and the Ghostriders, formed a separate rectangle in front of the makeshift altar.

The aviators, most of whom were clad in their flight suits, were sitting or standing together. The landbound officers that came to pay their respects also kept pretty much to themselves. The only group that was interspersed between the two were the sailors who worked the flight deck. Wolff could easily pick them out because of their sweatshirts colored to designate their jobs: brown for the plane captains, green for maintenance, purple for fuel, etc. Wolff also spotted Filk, who had his guitar, and Tyger, who was seated behind the organ, at the side of the altar. They were playing a mournful song Wolff had never heard before. He assumed it must have been something they had composed for the occasion.

The memorial service for Commander Beaumont was drawing to a close. After the musical interlude, he saw Perry rise and take her place behind the podium. As she stood there speaking to the group, she looked like a student council president under a lot of stress. She had worked hard on the eulogy. She was determined to keep it from being flowery but wanted very much to capture the spirit of Big Daddy. He could hear her perfectly, her voice carrying well due to both the acoustic nature of the room and her skills at public speaking. He knew, by the absence of emotion in her voice, that Perry McNeil had done this sort of thing before.

As he listened to Perry detail the highlights of her friend's long and distinguished Navy career, Martin Wolff quietly walked over to where the Ghostriders were seated. They were too intent on Perry's speech to acknowledge his presence. He quickly scanned the room and noticed the Commander had captured everyone's full attention. When his eyes met those of the Wing Leader for a fleeting instant, Wolff thought he saw the beginning of tears which added to the somberness of her expression.

"...family are left with nothing but lasting memories. Lorraine Beaumont and her children, Beau Junior, Jean Paul and Evaine, can be proud of their husband and father. He died serving his country. His legacy will go on. The people he touched in life are better for having known him."

Perry paused for a moment and rubbed her eyes. She had not delivered a eulogy since the war. She knew full well there were a myriad of ways to buy it in a jet. But Perry had not expected to lose one of the wiliest flyers she had ever known during a peacetime cruise. What made it worse was that he hadn't died flying but in the water. He had drowned. Dying that way was every Navy pilot's worst nightmare. Perry had been up for most of the night working on the speech she had brought to the podium with her. It had not been easy to find the words, especially when her mind kept replaying that last flight over and over again...

She sighed deeply before resuming in the same steady tone, "Beau would always try and find little things to say or do that would inspire his squadron to keep on their toes. He kept this little notebook full of quotes he found in newspapers, off TV, from all over and the better ones always seemed to find their way onto the VF-69 bulletin board. One in particular, first said by Bill Musselman, was one Beau always used to quote to his team. "Defeat is worse than death, because you have to live with defeat." That became the motto for the Renegades during the War and, today, it is proudly emblazoned on their ready room wall. Beau was a fighter, who lost his life doing the one thing he loved above all others: flying for his country. Beau Beaumont, Big Daddy to those of us who served with him, will be sorely missed. We salute you. May God bless you soul and hold you dear to Him."

Wolff noticed a few of the flyers had tears in their eyes, but no one was openly displaying their grief. Lt. Commander Liotta, who was now the acting CO for the Renegades, looked like she was calling on every ounce of self control she had to keep from breaking down. As she passed by him, Liotta's dark eyes met Wolff's. She gave him a sad nod in greeting before turning away quickly to respond to a query from one of her men. Then she headed towards the door talking quietly to one of her section leaders. It was Crunchy, who got his tag from an eagle-eyed wingman that caught him snacking on a Nestle's bar while he was inverted at Angel's eighteen. He was too involved in the conversation to even acknowledge Wolff as he walked past.

The senior officers, officers of the VF-69, and the sailors filed out of the forecastle. The only people who lingered were the Ghostriders and their leader. Wolff wasn't sure if he should leave or stay. Some of the more interesting passages in his book have been about the exploits of the Ghosts. Still, he wasn't sure if they would want the public to know how they acknowledged the passing of a teammate.

He felt a hand tugging at his sleeve. It was Jugs. She looked wonderful even though her expression was very subdued. She was wearing a loose fitting flight suit that camouflaged her curvaceous figure. "You going to devote some space in your book to Big Daddy?" she asked.

"Yes, of course. I didn't know Big Daddy very well, but, he was a good pilot and a good person and..." Wolff shrugged, not sure of how to complete the thought. Funerals in general made him uncomfortable. This one even more so because he was the only one there who wasn't one of Big Daddy's friends or subordinates.

"Perry told me to tell you we'll be saying our goodbyes in about a half hour at the fantail," she said. He nodded and, as though suddenly remembering something important, added in a firm voice, "What we do is *not* for public consumption, understand?"

What he saw was not to be put into his book was what she meant. He got that loud and clear. "Okay," he replied.

She gave him a nod and rejoined her fellow Ghosts. Tyger and Filk stood with their backs to the huge chains that stretched across the length of the room. Wolff noticed Filk's twelve string guitar had attachments on it for hookup to an amplifier but today he had disdained using the volume enhancer. Tyger was beside him hugging the black leather binder full of their original scores tightly to her chest. The ship's bards were recent additions to the Ghosts. Although they were competent flyers, it was their musical gifts that earned them their place in the company. Wolff enjoyed listening to them, especially when they performed tunes that they sang together. The two of them harmonized as well in song as they did in flight.

"I think we should play Big's favorite," Filk said quietly to her. "Give him something to laugh at while he's waiting for Saint Peter to answer the door."

"Well, Pete better not keep Big waitin' too long," she replied. "Or else he's liable to climb over the gate!"

The two of them chuckled at their irreverent humor and Wolff smiled. He knew from his interviews with the aviators that they would rather honor their dead by going to a bar and drinking and laughing as they recalled all the crazy things their friend did while he was alive. Somber memorial services were right out as far as they were concerned. Most of the flyers he talked to had a section in their wills that set aside money for their spouses to take down to the O-Club bar and blow on a round of drinks for everyone. He found out from Anzac that even Perry's will read like that.

Anzac motioned to Wolff to follow him and the reporter complied with the unspoken request. The fantail was at the opposite end of the ship. Even with Anzac to lead the way down the quickest route, it was still a walk. He was glad the Ghosts were allowing a half hour for everyone to make it to the ship's stern. They would have to go down long narrow companionways, often pausing to allow others to pass, and up and down a few flights of narrow stairs to get to the fantail. He sighed with relief when he arrived at their destination.

As he glanced down at the wake churned up by the four screws that propelled the huge carrier, the froth churned up looked St. Patrick's day green. Wind whipped the salty air all around them. The sky was clear and, in the distance, he could see one of the jets coming in for a landing. Perry leaned against the railing. She was wearing her Class As, her colorful ribbons prominent against the dark fabric of her jacket. Wolff finally got the chance to see what a Medal of Honor looked like up close. This was the first time he had seen her wearing the award itself. She usually wore its signifying ribbon mixed in with the others on her top rack. It almost looked to him like she was trying to hide it.

She noticed him looking at her and asked, "Something wrong?"

"No, I was just wondering what you and the Ghosts were planning to do out here."

She gave him a wan smile. "You'll see."

The two of them stood together in silence. Wolff watched her as she watched the plane that thundered over them, its successful landing felt as well as heard by everyone standing in the fantail. The reporter had a feeling they had no place in this part of the ship during flight ops. They would all be Spam if a ramp strike occurred. But, thoughts of their safety quickly departed when Wolff's gaze returned to Perry. As she stood there with the wind rustling through her hair and her attention fixed on the horizon, Wolff thought he saw tears brimming in her eyes.

A man who looked like he would have to fold himself up to fit into the cockpit approached Perry. He was clad in full flight gear and was slightly out of breath. It looked to Wolff like he must have run all the way from the flight deck to get to them. He towered over the Commander, who was only four inches shy of six feet, and smiled, his white teeth in sharp contrast to the coal color of his skin.

"Got the stuff," he told Perry. He unzipped his speed jeans and withdrew a bottle of Jack Daniel's Old Number Seven from its hiding place. "Sorry I missed the service, 'Stormer. Skipper had me on the board for a hop at oh-seven-hundred."

"It's okay, Too Tall," she said taking the bottle from him. "Beau would rather have you here to honor him *our* way, anyway."

The big man gave Wolff a cursory glance before turning his attention back fully on Perry. "I saw you're taking a hop with Gypsy's bunch this mornin'." She nodded in assent as she opened the bottle. Too Tall raised his voice slightly as he continued, "Gonna give 'Zac his landin' lesson, huh, CAG?"

Perry looked up and could tell by the expression on Anzac's face that he heard the query. She grinned. Anzac was going to have to endure a lot ribbing from the Ghosts for the rest of his Navy career because of his screw up. The Ghosts were a bunch of elephants, they never forgot anything. She turned to face Too Tall saying, "Yes, but first I'm going to make sure I have a little of Big's favorite refreshment to steady my nerves."

She took a healthy swig from the bottle before passing it to Too Tall, who did likewise. He passed it on to Sparky, who took his pull, and soon everyone, including Wolff, had had their shot at the bottle. When it was empty, it was given back to Perry. She took it and tossed it by the neck into the sea. Everyone was by the railing to see if they could locate where the bottle hit. Wolff, too, tried to spot where it came to rest but couldn't see where, in the spanse of choppy or churned seas, it landed.

His attention was then captured by something he hadn't expected. One by one each of the Ghostriders removed the black armbands they had been wearing and they ignited them with a match or a lighter. They held the flimsy pieces of burning cloth until the flames lapped dangerously close to their hands before releasing them. The smoldering ashes and bits of fabric looked like ebony confetti as it trailed behind the ship like a somber snowfall. The Ghosts slowly dispersed the moment the last fragment was swallowed by the sea.

18 December 1840

Perry entered the dirty shirt wardroom followed closely by Anzac. He was clutching a stack of paperwork under his arm and, it was obvious to anyone viewing the pair, they intended to make this a working supper. On the cafeteria line just ahead of her was Commander Jules "Barbarian" Barbari, the CO of the Grim Reapers. He gave the former skipper a wide grin which Perry returned. Anzac smiled, too. He liked the little bulldog of a man who was almost as much a workaholic as Perry. And like Perry he was a two-sided coin: he could be brash, demanding, impossible and dangerous but also could be warm, brilliant, inspiring and futuristic. If he had to go to war again, the Barbarian and Perry were the two people he would chose to take with him to the front.

"Finally ran out of gas, huh, 'Stormer?" Barbari teased Perry as she motioned to the sailor dishing up the pasta to toss an extra spoonful onto her plate.

"Well, gotta let the purple shirts do their job," she quipped back. "Can't keep those afterburners goin' without lots of good ol' Number One."

"Figure out how to put down in a Hornet, 'Zac?"

Anzac rolled his eyes and Perry chuckled. When he didn't get an immediate answer, the Barbarian went on saying, "Hell, you don't have to torture yourself this way. You're the best pitman on the boat, you don't *need* to learn to drive. Anybody here'd be more than happy to cart your butt around."

"Gee, thanks," Anzac muttered. Perry had to work hard to keep from laughing out loud. It seemed everyone had chosen this day to get on his case and she knew it was beginning to get to him.

As she led the way to an unoccupied corner at one of the long tables, Perry nibbled on a hunk of garlic bread. She was followed by Anzac and Barbari. The three of them sat together eating and tossing japes at one another. Barbari's wire brush wit was mostly reserved for Anzac, although he did toss a few bristles Perry's way now and again. She didn't mind being the brunt of his humor. It had been a while since she and the Barbarian sat down and just chewed the fat.

Anzac looked at the stack of paperwork parked beside his tray and sighed. He wasn't looking forward to slogging through that mountain of reports and reccy photos but it had to get done. He and Perry had been dividing the load between them: due to their current situation, the volume of information they had to review was beyond the capacity of one person to handle while retaining a grip on their sanity.

Perry noticed him glancing at the pile and said, "I know. Give me some of that."

He handed her a bunch remarking, "You know how many trees the Navy must kill every year to keep all *this* churning out?"

"Not as many as you'd think," she stated. Indicating a symbol on the bottom of a page, she explained, "See? Recycled paper!"

"When they figure out how to recycle eyes and brains, let me know. Okay?"

She snickered. Perry looked somewhat amusing as she sat forking spaghetti into her mouth with one hand while the other held a report she read while she ate. Anzac was doing pretty much the same thing. Barbari, after observing their behavior for a few minutes, commented, "And people call *me* job obsessed!"

Perry smiled at him, her eyes not leaving her reading.

Barbari returned the smile and sighed. He didn't drive anymore: he failed the vision test last year and now was only able to backseat. He still loved to fly and felt Perry was fortunate to still be driving at her age. She was only a couple of years his junior and he knew it was only a matter of time before she lost her privilege to farsightedness. It was a good thing she could RIO or BN because it would be a rough adjustment to be suddenly landbound after all those years of being an eagle soaring in the skies.

After a few minutes, Anzac caught Perry eye. She put down the report she had been perusing and queried, "Well?"

"I found out about Dr. Schroeck. Seems after Leigh's group lost their funding and had to break up, he disappeared. As in gone, poof, vanished off the face of Mother Earth."

Perry's eyes widened slightly in surprise. "Where'd he go?"

Anzac shrugged. "Beats the hell out of me. What's ever stranger is that Neil, my buddy at Intelligence, he said Schroeck isn't the only one they've lost track of. There's a couple of other Einsteins that have also gone poof."

"What do they think happened to them?"

"Neil's had his ear to the wall and he thinks they've gone over the wall. That they're on the Soviet payroll. But, when I mentioned the drug angle to him, he agreed that could also explain why no one's heard from them."

Perry sighed. "So that still leaves us with two suspects, the cartels and the Cubans."

Anzac nodded in assent. He was about to add a thought of his own when he heard a familiar voice coming from behind him. He peered over his shoulder and saw Dr. Freneau and a couple of the other G-2 reps on the cafe line. He looked away quickly and buried his face back in his work. A few seconds later he lifted his eyes to surreptitiously see if Perry had spotted her ex. Her eyes were focused on the report in front of her and Anzac breathed a quiet sigh of relief.

"Commander McNeil?" a voice with a slight Parisian accent inquired from two steps to the left of Perry. She turned away from her reading and glanced up at Dr. Freneau. He handed her a sealed envelope saying, "Our latest data. There are also some reconnaissance photos enclosed."

"Thank you," she said politely.

"May we join you?"

"If you insist," Anzac stated icily making it clear that he was *not* welcome.

Perry made no comment and managed to keep her cool even though Freneau took the seat beside her. Anzac glowered at him for a long moment before refocusing his attention back on the work at hand. Perry opened the envelope and pulled out the photos. She gave them a quick scan and then returned them to the envelope. Her attention then went back to both her dinner and her reading.

Barbari watched the temperature drop fifty degrees and he could feel the tension. He knew what was going down. He wasn't sure if he should stay to make sure Perry didn't do anything that would get her tossed into the brig, or go and avoid being around when the shit hit. Perry seemed to be in control for the moment, but Barbari knew her well. He realized she was exerting a great deal of self-control to maintain her outward calm. Anzac wasn't doing such a good job of keeping his feelings to himself. He wasn't saying or doing anything improper: he was just glaring at Leigh anytime the scientist dared to look in his direction.

When Perry finished reading the ORE report, she pulled the photos out of the envelope and began to scan each one carefully. Some looked current, others did not and, when she checked the dates stamped onto the back of each, she noticed that a few of them were a couple of months old. She looked at Leigh and asked, "What gives?"

"Commander Edwards had spotted what turned out to be a

fuselage in a reconnaissance photo. These are shots of that same pier taken at various times that had other things being shipped in or out that we thought looked like jet parts."

Perry looked again. One of the objects looked like the empennage from those Black Birds but she couldn't be certain. She had only seen them up close for seconds at best. Even with reviewing the films they had on them it was hard for her to look at these bits and pieces and say with certainty that, yes, this is what we're after.

She handed the photos to Anzac saying, "Look at these and tell me if you see anything promising."

He nodded stiffly and began to carefully scan each picture.

She turned her gaze back on Leigh asking, "Are those birds coming or going?"

"My guess is coming, but it's hard to tell. In every shot the suspected parts have been on the dock beside a cargo ship. We have not had any photos come through of those planes being assembled or even of the parts being transported overland. Admiral Jones thinks the Cubans are testing something for the Soviets, you suspect the cartels and, as far as I'm concerned, you both could be wrong."

"Oh? And what's your hypothesis, Doctor?"

"I'm reserving my opinion until I have more information. I like to stick a foot in to see if the water's cold or not before leaping in head first."

"Oh? That's a switch. You sure leaped into *this* lake fast enough."

He knew she was referring to their rather swift courtship and marriage and remarked, "Maybe I should've paid attention to the "no swimming" sign."

Perry rose and made a rude gesture saying, "Swim *this*!" She had had enough. She grabbed her paperwork and her tray and was halfway to the door when a smart remark coming from one of the G-2 people made her turn with a start. She wasn't sure who had made the crack but that didn't matter. To Leigh's supporters she snapped, "Mind your own damn business!"

"Perry, let's leave the skeletons *in* the closet, okay?" Leigh said as he rose. He was trying to appeal to her sense of military decorum.

She passed her tray to a junior officer, who was about to bus his own, and strode back towards the table. Leigh intercepted her before she could rejoin the group and drew her aside. He really didn't want to have it out in front of everyone in the wardroom. But, it seemed he wasn't going to be able to keep the dike from bursting this time. He could see it in her eyes that she was out for blood.

"Did you really expect to come aboard this ship knowing full well I was her CAG and *not* have to own up to the hell you put me through?" she demanded in a low menacing tone letting go the reigns on her Gaelic temper.

"You brought it on yourself, *Commander*," he retorted using her rank instead of her name purposely. "If you hadn't turned our divorce into a landbound dogfight, things would have turned out a whole lot differently."

"For you, maybe. You'd have a beach house for shacking up with Miss Teenage America."

"Amanda isn't *that* young," he stated in a manner that made it clear he was tired of treading down that well-worn path. "And, unlike you, she doesn't spend nine months of the year away from home."

"Don't make your lack of fidelity *my* fault, mister," she countered sharply. "I went without for just as long as you did. And I had no problems keeping *my* pants on."

"You didn't need to take them off to mount your favorite ride."

Perry's retaliatory strike was as swift as it was unexpected. As he leaned with his back against the bulkhead, Leigh felt as though he had been hit by lightning. When he and Perry were married, they had quarreled but she never laid a hand on him. And obviously for a very good reason. Now he knew what it felt like to have jaw almost shattered by one well-placed punch. His ex-wife didn't need a pistol to deliver a killing blow.

Her eyes were narrowed as though she were peering through a gunsight as she said in a voice full of controlled fury, "You have *no idea* how lucky you are to be alive. If Anzac hadn't been with me, you wouldn't be breathing."

"That's bullshit and you know it!" he declared hotly. "Maybe you would have shot me to prove a point, but that's all. You never loved me *that* much. There's no way you would have thrown all of this—" he did a sweeping motion with his hand "—away over me."

"You don't know that!" she stated defensively. "You haven't a clue how I felt about you!"

"Oh? Well I know how you felt about the Navy. And flying," he told her. Daring to get within striking distance, he added, "And those two always were ahead of me on your list of loves."

"And that was something you knew *up front*! I was always a Navy jock first and your wife second. And you never said that it bothered you," she affirmed. "Then, I come home after two months in the hospital to find you banging your research assistant!"

"While you were a little nun for the entire War?" he said mockingly. "Yeah, right."

She was about to put his rump on the deck when Anzac caught her arm commanding coldly, "Knock it off."

Perry flashed her deputy a fiery look but said nothing. Leigh glanced at Anzac commenting, "Good to see she still obeys you."

"Don't start with *me*," Anzac said in a low threatening tone. "I don't have to take any shit from you."

"Then go back and sit down and you won't be given any."

Perry broke in saying, "'Zac, let me handle this."

"I would, but the whole goddamn room saw you slug him," Anzac stated. He drew her close and added *sotto voce*, "For Chrissakes Perry, half the flight is in here!"

"They all know about Leigh and me by now! It's no mystery I used to be hitched to this cheatin' turd."

Anzac was standing protectively close to Perry and Leigh viewed this as the perfect opening for a well-timed round. "And it's no mystery the two of you have been flying united in more ways then one for years," he stated.

This time it was Anzac who lost control and was aiming for the jugular. Perry physically blocked his path to Leigh ordering, "Stop! It's not worth it!"

"But he said—"

"I know," she interrupted in a steady tone locking eyes with Anzac. "*I know*. Let's get out of here. We've done enough damage for one day."

Anzac silently grabbed the paperwork off the table, joined up with her, and headed for the door. He could feel everyone's eyes on his back. This was intolerable. He turned back towards the table and shot at Leigh, "For someone who's supposed to such be a fuckin' genius, you sure are goddamn *stupid*!"

He and Perry were out the door before anyone, Leigh included, could respond.

23 December 0845

Anzac entered the CATCC, his eyes half on where he was headed and half on the reccy photos and reports he was clutching in his right hand. Captain Lucarelli caught him entering the compartment and remarked, "Who's this guy? Does he belong on this ship?"

Anzac grinned. It had been a long time since he spent some time up in Pri-Fly and he kidded back, "No, so send me home. My wife misses me."

The Air Boss snorted and motioned to Anzac to take the empty chair next to him. The early morning sun streamed in through the angled windows casting its warm glow throughout the room. The chance to read by Nature's light was a welcome change for Anzac. He was getting a little tired of seeing everything through the courtesy of fluorescent bulbs. He glanced up from his paperwork to look at the status board on the opposite wall. Listed on it was every sortie the *Excalibur* had airborne plus all those waiting on deck to be launched. Four enlisted men in telephone headsets stood behind the plexiglass board and kept its information current by writing backwards on the board with yellow grease pencils.

Anzac scanned down the list of names until his eyes rested on McNeil. For once they had her down by her name instead of listing her as CAG or, the usual favorite, Double Nuts. Maybe because Admiral Jones had been spending a lot of time in air ops had something to do with it. Lucarelli let his boys have a little fun now and again, and would turn a blind eye to their using the flyer's call signs instead of their surnames on the status board. But, with the brass paying constant unexpected calls, everything was being done by the book until their current situation was resolved.

He could tell by the fuel amount that Perry could easily stay airborne for another hour or so before having to hit the Texaco. This was assuming she didn't run into any trouble. They were going into the fifth day of seeing nothing and the waiting was making everyone antsy. It was because of all the tension in the CIC that Anzac came up top to take a breather. Bellamy was a real Type A personality and Anzac was not used to working with a guy who spent so much time stressed out. He could deal with people like Perry, who were very driven. But there was a difference between being highly motivated towards accomplishing goals, which described the CAG, and getting so fired up about the job that you give yourself and everyone else working for you ulcers.

The day had barely started and he was already tired. He wasn't sure if it was the lack of sleep catching up with him or that the latest pile of reports he had to plough through were as stimulating as Muzak. He sighed deeply, rubbing his eyes with the fingertips of his left hand, and started examining the photos. More of the same, he sighed to himself. Still can't seem to get our hands on anything to piece together this puzzle...

23 December 2210

Perry ran a quick hand through her hair and sighed. The briefing was going into overtime and she was getting antsy. The three patrols she flew turned up nothing. After the last one she and Too Tall, who was flying her wing, played a little Intruder tag. The A-6F is a very nimble little flyer, far more so than one would think by looking at its ungainly body. She had fun chasing him all the way back to the carrier. It was the first time she cut loose and just enjoyed flying since the MiG encounter. That ten minutes was all the vacation she needed. She had come back to the ship feeling a whole lot better than she did when she left.

The screen behind Captain Bellamy went blank. The brightness of the white bulb of the slide projector shining against the equally white screen lit up the room making Perry squint. After an hour of staring at slide after side, her eyes had gotten used to the dimness. Anzac, who was sitting across from her, slipped on his shades and grinned at her. She smiled back, liking his little joke.

Bellamy noticed what Anzac did and gave him a sharp disapproving look. Anzac quickly removed the sunglasses. Perry deftly stifled her laugh into a cough. Bellamy didn't pay any attention to her as he put a new photo up on the screen. It was of an airfield and the camera had caught it in use. A MiG 29 was caught doing its takeoff run. "As you can see, we have yet to catch images of those new MiGs in action. Yes, they're out there but they're not in Cuba. So, we're not going to waste any more time and the taxpayers money on this wild goose chase. Admiral?"

Bellamy stepped aside to let Admiral Jones take over the session. "The Night Eyes system will allow us to see them. But, since we've gotten everybody on line with Dr. Freneau's invention, we haven't seen the MiGs. The President has been in contact with the Cuban government. They insist nothing is going on and the Soviets are also claiming they are not responsible. Commander McNeil's suspicions that the Medellin or another drug cartel could be behind this was suggested. The go-ahead to pursue the drug angle was approved because the DEA pushed for it. They happen to think the cartels are capable of anything, including getting their hands on stealth. We're going to be cruising in the Caribbean for a while longer while we try to see if we can determine if indeed we are up against the cartels. Those MiGs do represent a threat, no matter whose they are, and we must defend this battle group."

All seated concurred in their own way with the Admiral's last statement. Perry caught the Admiral's eye and inquired, "Have our orders changed as to how we are to deal with those MiGs should we encounter them again?"

"You are still not to fire unless fired upon," Jones told her. "However, the Jamaican government is allowing us to use one of their airfields. We are going to try and impound these MiGs in much the same way as we have impounded other aircraft being flown by traffickers. You'll be given all the details after this session."

Perry nodded. Jones concluded, "I'm not convinced we're up against the cartels but, we have our orders, so let's get to it. Perhaps the next time we spot the MiGs, we'll be given the chance to make a positive identification..."

24 December 1910

Today had been one of *those* days for Perry. First one of her Hornet's engines cuts out on her and didn't relight after a stall, forcing her to cut short her flight. Next she accidentally shredded some key reccy photos that got mixed in with her out of date memos. Then during the meeting Jones tells her the supply ship with the needed ordnance will be arriving early Christmas morning. They just had to hope that the MiGs waiting until then to show their faces. And, to top off what had been a real *dinka dao* day, she lost the bottom rack of ribbons off her work khakis. She had no idea where or when it happened and was clueless as to where to even to begin to look. She had been almost *everywhere* on the ship during the afternoon.

She was too stressed out to eat so, instead, she took her dinner break in the gym. After her bitch of a day, she needed to burn off a lot of frustration-laden energy. She hit the Universal and the Nautilus machines with a passion, spending a good hour working up a healthy sweat. When she completed her sets, she snagged one of her former squadron mates and he sparred with her for a while. He wasn't at her level in the art of kung fu but still provided enough of a challenge for Perry. While she was taking a break from trading kicks and strikes, she noticed Martin Wolff doing reps on the Nautilus circuit. She politely excused herself and headed over to speak to him.

Wolff was lying on his stomach and using the leg machine to work out the muscles in the back of his legs. He happened to glance up in time to see the glistening body of the Commander standing over him. She was drying her face and neck off with a small towel and looked like she had just completed a very thorough workout.

He paused in his reps and asked, "Just finished?"

She gave him a smile that was full of the devil. "Yes and no. I wore out my last sparring partner. Interested in taking his place?"

He remembered she had never officially called off their challenge. Not sure of her intentions, he inquired, "Is this for fun or what?"

"That's a dumb question," she told him. "I'd fuckin' *kill* you if we went at it for real."

Which he knew was true enough, given her level of expertise in hand to hand combat. But she didn't have to be so arrogant about it. "Maybe I should rephrase the question. What I meant to ask was, am I just going to be your practice partner or are we going to be the entertainment for all the wing nuts present?"

Perry chuckled softly. "Both."

He rolled his eyes heavenward. "You want to do it *now*?"

She draped the towel around her neck and stood over him looking like she could take on the world. "I can wait until you finish your circuit. Just come over to the ring when you're done. I'll be warming up in the meantime."

Perry still had that impish glint in her eyes when she left to rejoin her fellow Tomcatter for another round. He watched her go at it for a few minutes. This is going to be a humiliating experience, he thought. I can't fight like *that*. He sighed. He knew he couldn't back out. A lot of flyers were in the gym and more than a couple overhead Perry inviting him to spar with her. He knew that they'll razz him if he loses, but there would be no living with the boys in the Air Wing if he declined. He completed his workout like a man eating his last meal and then headed over to the ring where everyone was starting to gather.

He stepped into the ring decked out in his Queens College sweats and tried not to look uncomfortable about being there. His attire drew chuckles from the more scantily clad men and women. They had taken a break from their workouts to watch the match. Wolff was motioned over to a corner by a few Marines, who began giving him pointers and trying their best to be helpful. Diagonally opposite him was Perry. She handed her weight belt to one of her fellow flyers and started stretching and limbering up like a ballerina about to enter a *pas de deux*.

Wolff noticed the graceful movements and liked the way her well-defined muscles moved beneath the skin tight fabric. Perry was barefoot and wearing one of her usual unitards with the deep cut arm openings and severe scoop neck and back. Her colorful tattoo of a leaping Chinese tiger, which covered her entire left breast, was only partially obscured by her top. He had a feeling her choice of attire was going to give her an advantage. They had not even begun and already Martin found his gaze transfixed on the big cat's glowering golden eyes.

Colonel Grimmig and a couple of his junior officers were in her corner making rude suggestions as to how she could end the contest right quick. Their sentiments were echoed by the flyers, who had found their way to her corner. The Wing members knew she was a black belt in tiger style kung fu and could easily take Paper Boy down legitimately but they were having too much fun coming up with lewd ways for her to win. Wolff may have been distracted by her clothing but Perry was equally distracted by all the crude talk coming from her supporters. They were making her laugh and it is very hard to laugh and fight at the same time.

One of the flyers, a lanky A-6F driver known as Beanpole, climbed into the ring. Playing the part of referee he waved everyone to silence before reciting in his best imitation of a heavyweight title fight announcer, "In this corner, at five-feet-eight and weighing in at one hundred and forty pounds and able to take a seven-G bat turn without blinking an eye, our CAG. The one and only Commander Perry "Barnstormer" McNeil!" Perry swiftly got into the fun of it and took several campy bows and turns around the ring while her shipmates cheered, hooted and whistled. She went back to her corner grinning and feeling somewhat foolish. But it was obvious from the reaction of the spectators that this little match was giving everyone what they needed: a momentary diversion from the job.

Beanpole continued the introductions with equal gusto as Martin Wolff made his way around the ring. "And our challenger, at six feet and one hundred and seventy pounds hailing from the mean streets of New York, Martin "Paper Boy" Wolff!" Some people booed but it was obvious from the tone that it was meant in jest while the rest applauded and shouted words of encouragement.

Perry and Martin met in the center with Beanpole towering over them as he said, "Okay, this is simple. Best two out of three falls wins." The two contestants nodded and before they parted Beanpole said almost as an afterthought, "CAG, take it easy, will you? Civilians break easy."

Chuckles came from those who were close enough to hear the warning and Perry's only response was a wicked grin. This was going to be more enjoyable than she had anticipated. She had no intention of hurting Wolff: she had enough experience in her style of hand to hand combat to be able to take him down without injury. Still, she *was* going to play with him like a cat on a mouse. She had to. If she didn't, everyone would go away very disappointed. The contest would be over in all of five minutes.

Wolff had to grin when he locked eyes with Perry. She was staying just out of his reach and taunted him with lascivious gestures and occasional glimpses at what little her top kept hidden. He knew she was trying to get him to lose his composure so he would attempt to jump her. Still, Martin managed to do a good job of keeping his cool. The audience, on the other hand, was not so in control. They were making so much noise it was a wonder the Captain wasn't calling down from the bridge demanding an explanation for all the hoopla.

She was turning him on but he knew he would have to do a whole lot more than just win the match to get more than just a peek at her obvious charms. But, he was also well aware of the fact that his chances of winning were slim, considering she was a black belt and all. But it would be fun to get her down just once though, he thought, if only because it would show everyone that I can do more than just type and look good.

Perry sighed and, realizing she was going to have to make the first move, caught Martin off-guard with a quick foot strike to the chest that sent him sprawling. The crowd cheered. He sat up with a surprised look on his face. When Perry saw he wasn't hurt but was just startled, she said, "Fun and games are over, sailor. Let's go for it!"

Martin clamored to his feet studying her intently. He didn't even *see* how she hit him. One second he was standing, the next he had the air knocked out of his chest and he was flat on his back. God, she was good! And it only hurt when he was struck, but when he was on his feet he hardly felt a thing. She was obviously taking to heart what Beanpole had said about civilians being breakable. Not that he had come into this match looking to hurt her but he was expecting to dish out as well as receive a few bumps and bruises. To have anything less as the outcome would be nothing short of remarkable.

He attempted to grab her but she deftly moved aside avoiding him. It was hard for Wolff, who boxed a bit in high school and wrestled in college, to think of ways to down an opponent who came at him from such a completely different school of combat. He made a few more tries but wasn't even able to come close to catching the agile flyer. Hard to believe this one's a middle-aged mama, Wolff thought after failing yet again to make a successful grab and pin down. Allowing myself to get talked into this was definitely a huge mistake….

Perry did a sweep clipping Wolff's legs out from under him and he fell backwards head first onto the mat. He swiftly discovered what people meant when they talked about seeing stars. Dots of colored lights danced across his field of vision partially obscuring his view of Perry and the spectators surrounding their combat square. He had taken fall number two and, knowing the contest was over, decided he would stay where he was and see what happened.

When he didn't get right up again, Perry quickly knelt by his side. Through his dotted vision he caught the concerned look in her eyes. Before she could speak, he took advantage of the situation. He pounced on her like a cat on a cornered rat and pinned the startled Wing commander into the mat face down. Perry wasn't well-versed in wrestling breakout maneuvers. Even so, it took her just seconds before she came up with the right set of movements to free herself from Wolff's grasp.

The instant she was free, the momentarily caged lion turned on her captor with a vengeance and had *him* on his back for the third time. She was holding him by the throat with one hand pressing painfully on some nerves he never knew he had, her green eyes two smoldering embers of green fire. "That was a really cheap trick, Paper Boy," she told him, not sounding as angry with him as she looked.

"Yeah, well, there was nothing in the rules about foolin' your opponent," he replied giving her a devilish grin. "And I *did* fool you, CAG."

She let him go and he sat up still smiling. "Your bag of New York tricks didn't help. You still lost three to one."

"Yeah, but at least I didn't lose three to zip!" She gave him a shove that sent him sprawling backwards and got up. He noticed she looked more amused than annoyed and he asked, "Can the loser buy the winner dinner?"

"Only if it isn't boat food," she replied.

He chuckled. He, too, was getting a little tired of the fare served aboard the carrier. It wasn't bad, just routine. "You got it."

She reached down to offer him a hand up but, just before he could take her outstretched hand, she pulled it out of his reach commanding, "No funny stuff, right?"

He nodded, his eyes dancing mischievously, and she easily helped him to his feet. The strength in that grip told him quickly she had, indeed, been pulling her punches. He liked her impish smile and the way the fluorescent light danced in her eyes. Wolff got close enough to her so no one else but the Commander could hear him before querying, "When does your shift end?"

"Why?" she asked, wary of his further requests on her time.

"I was thinking maybe we could wrap up that interview we started the last day you were stuck in bed," he said.

His hopeful expression wasn't lost on Perry. She shrugged saying, "Not tonight. When I get off, I'm going to hit my rack. Maybe some other time, okay?"

Perry quickly made her escape before Wolff could respond. She joined Colonel Grimmig and his companions, who were waiting ringside for her. Wolff sighed. Even though he noticed she wasn't always on her guard around him anymore, she was still reluctant to talk about herself. Perry would answer questions about anyone in the Wing and give him every minute detail. But, if he wanted to know anything personal about her, she would deftly switch the topic to something else. Learning the back seat in the Tomcat had been tough, but Wolff felt getting the Commander to open up about herself was destined to be the biggest challenge of the cruise.

The Colonel excused himself and Perry from the group and the two of them found a corner where they could speak privately. He hadn't had an opportunity until after the funeral to spend time alone with her. Because of the crisis, her job was keeping her going almost round the clock. During the War the business of running her squadron had kept her almost equally busy and, he, too, had been up to his ears in work. He used to joke that they were the only ones that truly knew the meaning of the expression "quality time."

Perry smiled as she gazed deep into Grim's craggy dark eyes. She had been too wrapped up in managing the Air Wing to spend much time with him. Even so, what little time they had to give one another was savored as though it was champagne and caviar. The night after the funeral was the first time they were able to give each other a full evening. They had passed the night catching up with postwar life and settling back into the comfortable chair of old friendship renewed.

He had overhead Wolff's query to her about wrapping up their interview and he remarked, "You got out of that one like a real pro, 'Stormy."

She grinned, her eyes sparkling with mischief. "Thanks."

He liked her full-of-the-devil expression. But he knew her well enough to see she was hiding the long day she had put in behind that lighthearted look. "You feeling okay?" he asked.

"I'm fine. I just need to shower," she replied and, whispering low into his ear, teased, "Want to help me scrub my back?"

He chuckled softly. "If only we could snag a private stall...."

Her eyes glinted devilishly and, in a very naughty tone, said,

"We can't. But I have a private room."

He leaned over and kissed her upturned nose. It pleased him to see their long separation had had no effect on her feelings for him. She looked like she wanted him then and there, and it was a big switch for Serric to see her this way. During the War, she had been married and bound by a contract she viewed as sacred. The physical expression of their mutual attraction had been right out. She had been as immovable as a mountain on that point, even though he knew she cared for him deeply.

Things were different now. Perry was single and free to share herself with whoever pleased her. As he put his arm around her damp shoulder, Serric was glad to see he was still the one who kept her engines humming....

24 December 2230

Perry was checking herself in the mirror, when she heard a light tapping on her cabin door. She opened the door slightly and poked her head out. It was Grim. He smiled at the sight of her standing there in a skimpy black silk teddy clutching a long-stemmed rose. As he leaned over to kiss her waiting lips, he drank in the heavenly scent of her perfume. She let him in and he saw the glaring light from her desk lamp had been muted by a red gauze scarf thrown loosely over it. *Unchained Melody* by the Righteous Brothers was intoning softly from her cassette player. It was glaringly obvious that Perry McNeil had something very nice and naughty in mind.

It took him no time to remove his clothing and get into the spirit of the evening. When Grim took her into his arms, he chuckled softly as the rose she was holding tickled his naked back. The silk teddy she was wearing was a gift she had received for Christmas during the War. The boys in her squadron had all kicked in to buy her the costly present. It looked delectable on her. Too bad no one responsible for her having this scanty outfit would ever see her in it, Grim mused as he drank in the view.

"Didn't it fit?" he queried.

"What?"

"What I gave you."

She gave him an impish look saying, "Your little get well gift would definitely improve the health of a lot of the guys on this ship."

"Too bad none of them are going to see it."

She grinned. "I was saving that as your Christmas present. You want to have *something* to look forward to, considering we'll be stuck on the boat instead of someplace infinitely more pleasant."

Seeing her decked out in the vampish costume would do much to lessen the disappointment, Grim mused. Perry disengaged from their embrace and walked over to her sink. He watched as Perry took a cup and filled it with water. The bad news that they would be spending Christmas at sea had dampened the spirits of even the most cheerful members of the crew. Grim and the other officers in his command were determined to do what they could to keep up morale. Christmas this year was going to be a working holiday, since they were not only on Alert status but also readying the flight for a possible ground strike. They were going to try to adjust schedules to allow everyone a chance to get some time off but no promises were made. Parties were being planned, and ready room and dining halls were decorated to reflect the season. No one knew if they would have the time to enjoy the holiday but, from what he had observed, all concerned were trying hard to make the best of a sad situation.

The Colonel slipped around behind her and began kneading her shoulders. She leaned back against his fuzzy chest and purred throatily like a contented cat while he massaged her tired muscles. Her hard body had the softest skin he ever felt. He lingered over her back, since he knew the only thing that got her more turned on than flying was a good back rub, and she trilled with pleasure.

"He likes you, you know."

"Who?"

"Wolff."

She rolled her eyes. "I know." The reporter had caught her just before she reached her cabin. He said he wanted to conclude their interview but she sensed he also wanted the chance to spend some time with her. She managed to put off the interview until tomorrow. But, she doubted she would ever be able to get Wolff to put aside any desire to get involved with her.

Serric stopped in mid stroke. "Oh?"

She turned to face him. "Look, I have eyes. I know he hasn't been following me around all week just to get my story. But, get real! I wouldn't boff him if he was the last man on earth." Serric appeared unconvinced. Perry fumed. Looking him straight in the eye she challenged, "Grim, would I be in here with you if I wanted him?"

He raised an eyebrow as though pondering an answer to the question and she growled. It was obvious she intensely disliked the idea of him doubting her. Well, that was one thing he always liked about Perry McNeil. It was always hot or cold, there was no lukewarm on her emotional thermostat. And he knew exactly where the needle flipped whenever they were together.

Grim cracked a smile. Perry quickly realized he had been giving her leg a royal pull. Annoyed, she moved to give him a healthy swat but he caught her arm and drew her close. As their bodies intertwined, the nearness of her aroused him. "You'd rather be with this old warhorse than a young buck like Wolff?" he queried half-seriously.

"You aren't the only old warhorse," she reminded him.

"True," he admitted.

Her arms held him firmly yet with a gentleness that seemed a little out of character for the tough-as-nails Wing leader. He was seeing a side of Perry he knew no one on the boat, with the exception of her ex-husband Leigh, ever saw and he was determined to savor the moment for as long as possible. He had been so involved with enjoying the closeness of her and the sensation of her skillful tongue playing with his own that he barely noticed she had turned out the lights. He stood naked tingling from the touch of her silk teddy as it lightly brushed against his bare flesh. The craving for the feeling of skin to skin contact intensified and he slid the thin straps off her shoulders baring her chest. The tiger's eyes seemed to glow with the heat of an entirely different emotion as he eased her back toward the bunk.

No fantasies could ever be as warm and wonderful as reality, Serric thought as he lay naked beneath her. He gasped as Perry's well-schooled muscles grabbed, held and caressed him to the point of ecstacy. He had no idea it was possible for *those* muscles to get developed. As he lay there glistening with perspiration from their early morning workout, he stared up at the metal ceiling and sighed. Although Serric had a wealth of experience in this area he felt that, if he had to compare her to his past lovers, she was vastly superior to any who had come before.

Perry saw his starry-eyed look and smiled. Apparently he felt the wait had been worth it. And he had waited a *very* long time for this moment. Although there had been ample opportunity for them to get together early on in the cruise, he had not taken advantage of it. Serric had heard from friends that her divorce had been a real slice and dice affair, and knew she would need some time alone to lick her wounds. But, when he heard she had been injured in the attack, he knew he could wait no longer. He came to see her, secretly hoping her heart had healed enough to be given again. He was pleasantly surprised to find her ready and willing to rekindle what they once had together.

As Perry sat there looking down at him, Serric gently caressed her naked back. It felt like touching a wall covered by a layer of velvety-smooth perfume scented skin. Her cheek, on the other hand, was far more yielding beneath his fingertips. He smiled as she nibbled playfully on the hand that stroked her. She leaned over and took his mouth with hers, the lips gentle, the tongue hungry for more. Perry was ready for a second go-round and he, too, found himself wanting more. As he proceeded to comply with her demands, Grim realized that the monkish existence he was forced into by the carrier assignment had one positive aspect: the energy of suppressed desire was indeed strong enough to insure his ability to keep up and running for as long as Perry wanted him.

Which turned out to be often throughout the night. She, too, was running off the same fuel that kept him fired. During one of their intervals of sleep, Perry awoke with a start. She sat bolt upright on the bunk, drenched with sweat, and trembling as though her body was wracked with fever. He embraced her, trying to comfort her, but she rebuffed his attempts. For a long while she sat staring blankly straight ahead, her body stiff and unyielding to his touch. Perry didn't speak, and Serric didn't pressure her into talking about the nightmare. She was glad he knew better than to ask. As much as she cared for him, there were still some things she couldn't tell him.

Perry didn't lie down back on the bunk beside him until nearly an hour later.

When he awakened just before dawn to find no sign of her, he quickly assumed duty had called. A skillfully folded foil-paper version of an F-14 resting on the nightstand inches from his head caught his eye. Serric reached over for it. He idly examined the plane from all sides before taking it apart to read the note hidden within. Its salty message made him smile. He knew she had gone up on deck to take part in the FOD walkdown and, without further ado, he arose, washed and dressed and headed up top to join her.

25 December 0637

The rising sun's red hues colored the clouds hanging low on the horizon an odd purplish grey. The early morning haze was swiftly burning off under the growing intensity of the tropical sun. Although the stars had all but vanished from the sky, the moon still shone its dimming light upon the strangely silent flight deck. Round the clock flight operations were suspended after 0400 so the deck could be washed down. The lack of air traffic and its accompanying quiet made Perry McNeil feel strangely uneasy.

Perry glanced at her watch. Flights Ops would be resuming at 0700 and she knew by the gathering crowd on deck that it was getting close to the time for the FOD walkdown. She stood clutching the rail for a long moment as breezes damp with sea spray rustled her hair and whipped at her flight suit. The past few days had moved as if snail propelled. Keeping the heebie-jeebies from setting in had been difficult. Perry managed to keep from getting antsy by logging more airtime during those seven days than she had in any week since the war.

The War. Last night she had awakened drenched in sweat because her overloaded brain had chosen to give her an instant replay of her nearly fatal flight over Bekaa. She never told anyone, not even Serric or Anzac, how much time she spent being scared to death during her ninth cruise. As she stood staring at the sea she hugged herself, her fingertips lightly stroking the patch on her left arm. She could feel the stitched pattern of the blood colored moon setting over a sea of silver blue. She didn't need to see it to know what it looked like. All the New Moon War veterans wore these patches to signify their service in the conflict.

A hand giving her shoulder a gentle squeeze pulled Perry momentarily out of her reverie. She smiled slightly when her eyes met those of Martin Wolff He smiled back. Since she got hurt, he had been stepping and fetching and following her all around like a hound dog. At first, his constant presence was a bit of a nuisance but, as she got to know him better, she had to admit he was beginning to grow on her. She knew he wanted more from her than just some juicy tidbits for his book but Perry was not interested. She was just as parsimonious when it came to the giving of her friendship. Some of her friends she's had longer than either of her two husbands. The reporter had scored a few points to earn him the title of "acquaintance" but he had a way to go before she would be interested in having him as a friend.

Wolff had managed to work his way on to her list of people she didn't mind running into from time to time. Perry had stopped by his cabin the other night to check up on him. Her surprise visit had pleased Martin beyond words and he gave her bits and pieces of his manuscript to read. They had passed an hour talking about flying, his book and, of course, more flying before duty called and she had to leave. He enjoyed Perry's company and, as he stood beside her on the flight deck, he could tell by her eyes that she was sincerely happy to see him.

"You going to get in on the FOD walkdown?" he asked.

She nodded. "Yes. You go on ahead. I'll catch up."

Concern tinged his voice as he inquired, "Are you feeling okay?"

"I'm just tired. I didn't sleep too well last night." She caught a knowing look in his eye and added quickly, "*That's* not why I didn't get much rest. I had too much on my mind to sleep."

He made no comment and she looked away returning her gaze to the sea. She was glad he accepted her explanation. She wasn't about to tell him the real reason she was half-awake.

Perry had been snuggled up against Serric on her narrow bunk when that nightmare had jerked her into wakefulness. He held her trembling, sweat soaked body close and tried to do what he could to make her feel better. She couldn't tell him about the dream. Though she knew he would understand and sympathize, it was hard for her to talk about that almost fatal day. Serric was aware of what went on aboard the *George Washington* and had his share of dark times. He had been there with her during the War but, for her, it was still too recent, too agonizing a memory. Perry had seen too much pain, too much blood, and too many young people pay for the failure of diplomacy with their lives. This was not a topic she would ever volunteer to discuss, even with another veteran.

"Please go, okay?" she said softly.

Wolff nodded, seeming to understand her need to be alone, and went to join the rest of the deck crew and flyers for the FOD walkdown.

After a few minutes she turned away from the sea and began scanning through the thicket of people congregating at the carrier's bow for familiar faces. Gypsy and a few members of the Killer Bees were swapping japes with their shipboard rivals from the other

Hornet squadron, the Freebooters. Towheaded Sparky, who was wearing mirrored shades and trying desperately to look cool, stood by his skipper's side and smiled his usual perky smile. Perry also spotted Boomer and his backseater Radar talking to two yellow-shirted ladies. The girls looked like they were barely out of high school and by the way they stood there hanging onto every word the men spoke, it was obvious to Perry that the boys had struck pay dirt. She didn't approve of the much older flyboys taking advantage of the wide-eyed kids, who made up the majority of the flight deck crew, and wasn't above telling them so on occasion.

Perry sighed. Telling Boomer to behave himself would be a colossal waste of time. Fighter pilots will be fighter pilots, there was no escaping it. She had been no better when she was his age. And Perry knew that no one was more aware of that than Anzac, who, during their early years together, had found her freewheeling lifestyle a bit of a bear to handle. She remembered how happy he was when she and Crazy Kyle tied the knot. He would no longer have to put her on a leash the minute they made a liberty stop. The day Perry married was the day she put her party-hearty days behind her. The much older Lt. Commander McLoughlin taught her responsibility and that helped get her career started on its upward track. She owed much of her success to Kyle. Though they had been divorced for almost eleven years, a day didn't go by when Perry didn't think about him.

She smiled wistfully when her gaze came to rest on Martin Wolff, who was fumbling with a trash bag. The reporter was getting some encouraging words from the deck crew, and they seemed to be enjoying his company. It was true that he had a tendency to try too hard to be liked and fit in. Even though that small fact had bothered her at first, she never gave it a second thought now that she had the chance to know him better.

She remembered joking with Anzac at the very start of the cruise that the reporter was the only male on the ship she could have without worrying about the consequences. They had both laughed at the truth of it and after that Perry never gave the idea a second thought. His personality hadn't scored any points the day she took him up for a ride in the Super Tomcat. But, she did like the view she got when he stood on deck with his flight suit unzipped. He had a hot body, that she would willingly admit, but it took more than good looks to win over Perry McNeil.

But during the past week Wolff had managed to worm his way both into the Ghostriders and into her heart. He had a barnacle's way of growing on a person: he stuck to you until you either gave up and let him stay or scraped him off. Considering how quickly her little ship moved, it was a wonder the barnacle could hang on at all. He was persistent, which was one trait they both had in common. But he was also learning, in their time together, when it was okay to hang on and when he should go latch on to someone else's keel for a while.

Two strong hands gently massaging her shoulders made Perry smile. She gazed up into Grim's craggy dark eyes. She had been too wrapped up in her thoughts to notice his approach but his presence was a welcome interruption. She leaned back against his wall hard chest and he wrapped his arms around her waist holding her close. He nibbled on her ear. Tickled, she laughed quietly to herself.
"Want to get in on the FOD walkdown?" Serric queried softly in her ear.
"I'd rather go back to bed and have you fuck my brains out," she countered and he chuckled squeezing her tighter.
"I'd love to, but we've got to get to work," he said simply. When she tipped her head back to look up into his face, he bent down and kissed her waiting lips.
Perry sighed. As they stood together by the railing, it was as though time had stood still. They were so close, closer now than they had ever been during the War. Being with Serric again was like enveloping herself in a down quilt, all warm, soothing and calm. She knew she could give him her heart and her trust. He had not betrayed either in all the time they had known one another and she knew why. He, too, had had his heart ripped apart by a faithless spouse and, because of this, was always very guarded about getting deeply involved with anyone. Perry knew how hard it had been for him to allow himself to lift the gates around his heart and let her in. When she gazed up into his eyes, she could tell he was glad he had let himself fall in love again.
He released her and began walking towards the ship's bow with Perry at his side. Well over two hundred people were gathered in a straight line across the bow from port to starboard. They were just starting to slowly make their way aft when Perry and Serric joined them. The eyes of all in the line were cast down at their feet as they searched for loose bits of non-skid, wires, anything that could get sucked into a jet's intake and damage the engine. Though the deck had been hosed down quite thoroughly, the

walkdown was being performed as a precaution. Perry had been the one to order this double check because she knew how essential this task was. On the cruise she had taken just prior to the War, Perry's squadron had lost one of its plane's engines to a two-inch-long bolt.

The two officers got a lot of smiles and hellos from the youngsters that comprised the deck crew. Their eyes were on Perry moreso than Colonel Grimmig but that didn't surprise the Marine. Perry had been well-liked by the enlisted men aboard the *George Washington* when she'd commanded the Grim Reapers during the War. Most of the *Excalibur's* flight deck personnel were college-age kids, young enough to be the sons and daughters of Perry and the Marine commander. These youngsters were responsible for getting up and back the multimillion dollar aircraft in Perry's charge. Working the flight deck was a dangerous business and Perry had seen some very nasty, fatal accidents happen during her years at sea.

Grim smiled and put his arm around her shoulder and she nuzzled his chest. He easily got her turbines cranking into full military power. The war and the passion created by the intensity of such a situation was a blaze that still burned strong in both of them. She knew she was so lucky he hadn't forgotten about her. During the War she had thrown so much CO_2 on his fire that she thought he didn't even have a spark left. But she found out last night just how wrong she had been. They were still close, the memories of the war, its hardships and good times, binding them together in a special kind of love that was destined to last a long, long time.

A grin crossed her face the moment she noticed a couple of drivers and RIOs from the Renegades, who were also doing the walkdown, smiling and giving her the thumbs-up sign. A stray piece of non-skid caught her eye and, when she bent over at the waist to retrieve it, someone gave her bottom a friendly spank. She jumped and was coiled and ready to pounce on the bold Navy boy who had had the audacity to flirt with her so openly. She was about to give Martin Wolff a taste of her razor sharp tongue but he spoke to her first.

"Slam dunk that baby right here," he quipped proffering a waste bag for her to deposit the fragment into. "Whenever you are ready, I'm ready to finish that interview we started."

"Fine," she said. "We'll wrap it up after the walkdown." Perry remembered she had agreed to finish their interview at the FOD walkdown. She hated having to deal with the press. She had had her fill of them, and their incessant questions, after Bekaa. The sooner I do it, the sooner it will be over with....

"Think you might be able to work me into the flight schedule?" Wolff asked. "It's been almost a week and—"

"You need your fix," she interrupted.

Wolff had been itching to get it up again in the Tomcat and she couldn't say she blamed him. Flying an F-14 wasn't just a job: it was an adventure. But, they were still on alert and that meant the reporter would just have to keep finding airborne satisfaction as a passenger aboard the E-2C Hawkeye. There was no way he could ride in the fighters until the likelihood of a MiG encounter was ended.

He gave her his most charming smile querying expectantly, "Well?"

"I'll have the Warriors make room for you," she said as she resumed eyeing the deck for debris. The Warriors, the name by which the VAW-110 was known on the carrier, were the E-2C squadron.

Wolff rolled his eyes heavenward. "Aw, come on!" he griped sounding like a high school football jock who had just been sent to the bench by his coach. "Not the Hummer again!"

"Sorry, but that's all you can get. Take it or leave it."

"There isn't *anything* I can do to rate another hop in the Tomcat?" he asked in a way that left no doubt as to the lengths he would be willing to go for another shot at the F-14D.

She broke up. "You *are* getting desperate!"

"Maybe," he agreed and, dropping to his knees in a very theatrical manner, begged, "Please?"

She looked down her nose at him. "Absolutely not."

He sighed, defeated. "You have no heart."

"I have orders," she told him flatly. "When this situation we're in resolves itself, *then* you can go up for a ride. But not now."

He rose saying, "No one has seen those MiGs for days."

"I know. But that doesn't mean they're gone for good. Only gone for *now*."

Wolff held the bag open for a couple of crewmen to put the bits of junk they found into it. He watched Perry rejoin the forward portion of the line and resume scouring the deck for whatever didn't belong. Colonel Grimmig was with her. Judging from the way the Marine was looking at Perry, Martin sensed the scuttlebutt going around about the CAG and the Colonel being "an item" probably had more than just a grain of truth in it. He heard from

Anzac that the Colonel and Perry had been tight during the War but she had been married back then. So nothing happened. As he slowly walked the deck, Wolff sighed sadly. There was no way he could win Perry over. He could not compete and win against the handsome battle-hardened Marine commander who looked as though he had already stolen Perry's heart.

Serric glanced back in Wolff's direction remarking, "Taking that boy up with you was a big mistake, Stormy. You know what they say about keeping 'em on the farm after they've seen Paris."

Perry smiled. "Too true. Maybe he wouldn't have gotten so hooked if I'd had somebody else do the drivin' instead of me."

"You didn't?"

"What? Give him a taste of the sort of flying I'm famous for?" Perry caught the knowing eye and admitted, "Well...I did cut loose a little bit during our hop together. Nothing to write home about, though."

"But good enough to merit a few pages in Wolff's book, I'm sure," the Marine stated and she chuckled. The elfish glint in her eyes told her old friend more than any words could.

"Yeah, after that hop, I had him ready to enlist," she confessed to Grimmig and he laughed.

"Yeah, that's all you need. One more moony-eyed kid in love with the Tomcat and tearing up the skies at Mach 2."

She sighed remembering a time when that statement would have described her perfectly. Perry glanced back at Wolff and, when their eyes met, he gave her a wistful smile. She had been on the planet long enough to see it wasn't just the flying that got Paper Boy's engines revving. She could understand why Wolff was drawn to her. She was a fighter pilot, a war hero and someone who had cheated death on more than one occasion. Martin Wolff wasn't the first man she had even met that was attracted to her because he thought she would be exciting. During the interview she was going to set him straight.

She bent artfully over at the waist and picked up a pull tab from a soda can. As she rose, Perry's mouth curved into a wry grin at the thought of hitting yet another patch of turbulence in her flight of life.

25 December 0726

Anzac entered the CAG office and was surprised by the amount of foliage surrounding Yeoman Truesdale. "Some gardener die and name you in his will?" cracked Anzac as he made his way around a rather plush fern.

"You think this is bad? You should see Commander McNeil's office!" Truesdale declared sounding more amused than annoyed.

"What gives?"

"It's Christmas and the Commander's birthday today," the Yeoman explained as he opened the door to Perry's office, which looked more like a florist's display window than the hub of air wing activity. "I guess with all the stuff going on it slipped your mind."

Anzac smiled mischievously at his best friend's aide, who caught the look. Not too sure he knew or wanted to know what schemes the Perry's deputy was up to, Truesdale hesitantly inquired, "This wasn't all your doing, was it, sir?"

Anzac shook his head. "No, not guilty this time. Is this the way you found the place?"

"What you see is what was here at oh-six-hundred this morning."

Anzac picked up a small potted violet plant in full bloom from the corner of the desk and glanced at the card tucked in among the leaves. It was from Rae Liotta, the acting skipper of the VF-69, and, as he glanced at the other gifts, both green and floral, he found most of them were from the officers and crew of Air Wing 21. Not all the gifts were living: a tape of original "flying-inspired" songs by Filk and Tyger had been left by her Walkman. There were other boxes wrapped with colorful paper tucked about the room. Perry was going to have an interesting time sorting through all of this, mused Anzac. He glanced down at the rectangular bulge in the leg of his flight suit thinking he would have less competition if he were to give Perry his gift in person.

He glanced back at Truesdale remarking, "Nice having a boss who's so popular."

The young man grinned saying, "It would be nicer if she were allergic to plant life. *I'm* the one who's going to be stuck having to water, feed and groom all this!"

Anzac laughed. It was too true. He knew if it was left to Perry, all of these plants would have bought it and be on their way to a burial at sea by Twelfth Night. He looked at the long white box that barred access to the seat of her swivel chair and was surprised when he recognized the handwriting on the outside of the envelope taped to the box's center. This gift was from Leigh Freneau and Anzac sighed, shaking his head. During the War when she was forced to celebrate a birthday on the other side of the world, Perry would have appreciated receiving the dozen long-stemmed roses and the sentiment the gift intended. Then the present from Leigh would have meant something. Now it just looked like he was begging for her forgiveness for being such a Grade A asshole. 'Zac would have loved to track down Freneau and tell him exactly where he could stick his roses. However, he had left the ship a couple of days ago. Even if he had been aboard the *Excalibur*, Anzac would not have gone after him because he knew Perry would be furious with him for minding her business.

Truesdale noticed Anzac studying the white box and said, "They're from Dr. Freneau."

"I know," Anzac stated as he picked up the box, put it on top of the desk, and collapsed with a sigh into the chair. Somewhat sarcastically, he remarked, "Nice that the guy remembered."

Not certain if it was his place or not to butt in with his observations, Truesdale said quietly, "Doc Freneau and the CAG haven't been fighting, sir. They've been getting on okay from what I've seen."

Anzac studied the young man, who swiftly grew uncomfortable under the intense scrutiny. Perry's yeoman sometimes was too perceptive for his own good. Since the blow up in the wardroom, a truce had been declared between Perry and her ex-husband. After that, they managed to work together cooperatively. His invention had proven invaluable to the Air Wing: after a full week of hard work by the combined forces of the G-2 engineers and the Wing's own maintenance teams, all the fighter-interceptors, radar planes and attack birds had been fitted with the Night Eyes IR system and had demonstrated the machine's combat effectiveness. The minute his work aboard the *Excalibur* was completed, he and the members of his design team departed. Although on a personal level Anzac thought the man was slime, he would be the first to agree with Perry that Leigh Freneau had a long way to go before he outlived his usefulness.

"What the hell...?" a familiar voice cried from the outer office and Anzac tried not to laugh as he rose to meet Major Grimmig and Perry. She looked both amused and moderately peeved as she led the way into the CAG office.

"Happy Birthday, 'Stormy," Anzac greeted his face breaking into a rather dopey grin as the two of them approached the desk.

"Is this your idea of a joke, sailor?" she accused eyeing him sharply.

"Not guilty," he stated flatly, then added, "But this would be something I would think of doing, given the time and the bucks."

Her eyes glinted devilishly as she replied, "Thank God you've had neither!"

"Want me to clear out some of this stuff?" offered Truesdale.

"No, it's okay. Just scrounge up a machete so I can clear myself a pathway and I'll be fine," Perry said. Truesdale smiled up at her as she made her way past him and took her place behind the desk. She picked up the long white box and stared at it thoughtfully for a long moment before untying the ribbon holding it closed. Inside was a dozen long-stemmed red roses and she half-smiled as she placed the opened box back on top of her desk and read the note. Glancing up at Truesdale she said, "Could you please find something to put these in so they'll live for longer than a day? Also, find out if I'm still listed on the status board for a hop this morning."

Truesdale nodded and hurried off to do her bidding.

"You're going to spend your birthday flying without me?" Anzac asked feigning disappointment.

"You know perfectly well why we're not flying together," she responded sounding more like a mother than a CO. Her tone changed when she added, "Anyway, this is the first time I will have Tomcatted since…you know. Since we lost Beau."

Anzac knew she'd been logging all of her airtime these past few days behind the stick of either a Hornet or an Intruder. And it wasn't solely because she needed to keep up her hours. "Who's pitting for you?"

"Poindexter."

Anzac sighed. He knew why she had requested Beau's RIO. Both of them needed to get back in the saddle again. "After your patrol, what's on your agenda?"

"Same shit, different day," she replied indicating the pile of paperwork on top of her "In" basket. As he sat on the corner of her desk facing her, she eyed him suspiciously and asked, "Just what are you up to, mister?"

He never could keep a secret from her so he wasn't even going to try. "Well, some of us got together and—"

"A party?" she broke in and he nodded. "I should have known. When?"

"Eighteen-hundred. In the Renegade ready room," he said looking a little sheepish. She gave his belly a teasing poke and he laughed a little adding, "Try to look surprised, okay?"

"No problem. You know I wouldn't miss your party, Zac, unless the fertilizer hits the fan while I'm up there and the game runs into serious overtime," she assured him. He smiled pleased to see she was actually looking forward to the upcoming festivities.

Grimmig gave her a wry grin remarking, "I knew you were popular, Stormy, but are *all* your friends nature buffs?"

She chuckled softly. "Closet nature buffs," she explained. He shoved aside a plant to join her behind the desk. He kneaded her shoulders slightly and she glanced up at him adding, "You get me something for my birthday? Or, are you going to be like my old man always was and give me my present on Christmas?"

"Rough being born the day before Santa time, huh, Perry?" the Marine teased.

"Tell me about it," she groaned. He could tell by her expression and tone of voice that she wasn't really upset, just pretending.

He leaned over and whispered in her ear, "You'll get your birthday gift tonight."

She caught the naughty inference glinting in his dark eyes and she teasingly grabbed the lobe of his ear in her teeth giving it a nip. Anzac tried to act as though he hadn't caught the exchange but it was hard to miss. He cleared his throat loudly and asked, "While you're waiting for Trudy, want to open one of your presents?"

She turned at the sound of his voice looking a combination of startled and embarrassed. Perry had momentarily forgotten he was still in her office. He was giving her a knowing eye and she stated, "Go ahead and say it, 'Zac."

In his most fatherly tone he replied, "I approve. Just confine it to your quarters, okay? The bulkheads have ears and mouths."

Perry grinned and nodded. "We'll be discreet," she assured him and he chuckled softly.

When their eyes met, Anzac smiled slightly and he looked pleased to see she was back with Grimmig. During the War, he had seen her and Grim spending a lot of time together. But, because she was married back then, they were just each other's best friend, sharing the kind of closeness she had only experienced with

Anzac. Now that she was free of Leigh, Perry no longer had any reason to keep Grim at arm's length. As he watched them whispering conspiratorially to each other, Anzac got the feeling Grimmig might be the one to get Perry to take another swing at marriage.

Anzac's mind leaped back to the present when he heard one sharp knock on the door. It was Truesdale, who stepped into the office saying, "You're on the board, CAG. You've got Lieutenant Viel as your RIO."

"Good," she said and, her eyes on Anzac, she continued, "I'd rather have you with me but, since Bellamy has more or less chosen you to coordinate things from here on the ship, that sort of makes it impossible for us to be a team again until this crisis is over. I don't know why we got stuck with a landlocked type as a mission leader! He wasn't so bad when he still had his wings, but now?" Perry rolled her eyes. "Oh, well, can't do anything but bitch and moan and hope that this situation gets resolved real quick. I'm more than ready to have everything get back to normal."

"Me too," Anzac agreed. Eyes twinkling he added, "Enjoy your holiday hop."

"Merry Christmas to you, too, 'Zac," she remarked sarcastically.

He grinned. Anzac unzipped the leg pocket on his flight suit and pulled out a long black velvet box. He passed it over to Perry saying, "A little something for you from the Edwards clan."

Perry caught the devilish glint in his eye and asked, "Can I open this in polite company?"

Anzac nodded and she opened the box. Inside was a gold chain bracelet that had at its center her call sign written out in gold script. Grimmig helped her put it on her wrist. She quickly discovered it was crafted so that the script side would tend to remain on the back of her hand where it could be seen by everyone.

"It's beautiful, 'Zac. Thank you."

Still full of the devil he quipped, "At least I got you something maintenance-free."

Perry chuckled. "Wish everyone else did."

Truesdale interrupted the camaraderie saying, "Commander, you're supposed to be on deck and in the bird by oh-eight-hundred." She nodded at the young man, who looked worried with good reason: it was less than ten minutes to eight.

Perry's eyes widened when she noted the time. "Got to fly—literally! Catch you later."

She was gone before either of the three men could say a word.

25 December 0816

Boomer leaned over into the cockpit where his friend O'Reilly sat strapped in and ready to go and stated, "Told you those Deck Dolls would say yes to joining us for the Commander's party."

"Well...I don't think asking them was such a great idea," O'Reilly responded looking up into his friend's expectant face. "There are rules—"

"Screw the rules," Boomer interrupted. Radar was about to set him straight but Boomer went on saying, "Look, if anyone says anything, we'll go back to our quarters and have our own little party."

O'Reilly caught the mischievous look in Boomer's dark eyes and was glad his helmet hid enough of his face to keep his driver from seeing that he was starting to blush. The pursuit of the opposite sex had never been one of the shy RIO's strong suits. In his own odd way, the bold as brass Boomer was a good influence on his friend. Boomer tried his best to play matchmaker for his backseater and, if nothing else came of it, at least Radar would get some chances to work on improving his social skills. The two girls they had met while doing the FOD walkdown seemed receptive to the idea of spending their free evening with them so maybe the four of them might just have some fun at the party. That is, if the rest of the guests don't toss them out on their ears for daring to bring dates to a party that *they* barely managed to get invited to themselves.

Boomer glanced at the empty front seat saying, "I hope the Commander won't get peeved that 'Dexter roped me into doing her preflights for the Double Nuts. You know how particular she is."

"She's also running way behind schedule," Radar noted. "I hope nothing happened."

"Look, if she couldn't make it, she'd send somebody to replace her. And, since no one has shown up, she's probably on her way."

Radar nodded saying, "I hope she likes the Dead. I loaned 'Dexter my Best of the Grateful Dead discs to play to make the patrol a little less routine."

"Yeah, well, I don't know if she is going to let him plug in his head. The TISS system is *not* regulation."

Radar grinned. The TISS system, an acronym for Tomcat Integrated Stereophonic Sound, was nothing more than a Sony walkman hooked into the pilot's or RIO's helmet. The practice was not limited to the F-14 teams, the other flyers in the Wing sometimes sneaked music up with them too. The Tomcatters were just the first to give the illegal hookup a nice military sounding name.

"Maybe she'll let it slide," Radar said. "I heard she is into Golden Oldies. Mostly stuff from the Sixties and early Seventies, you know, like the Supremes, Righteous Brothers, that sort of thing."

Boomer's eyes glinted mischievously as he cracked, "That's because she *is* a Golden Oldie!"

"Don't you have someplace you're supposed to be?" a stentorian voice commanded from the deck beneath Boomer. He turned, looked down, and cringed slightly when he saw the Commander standing there glaring up at him.

"Oops," he heard Radar tease softly. He quickly climbed down the ladder trying to hide his embarrassment at being caught. Boomer had finished helping Radar preflight their bird half an hour ago and was on standby until the CAG arrived. He was *supposed* to be strapped in and ready to go, not perched on the ladder hanging out like he had nothing better to do.

Perry had heard Boomer's smart comment to his buddy. She had grounds to bring his disrespectful rump up on charges. But the thought of the paperwork involved with charging him made her cringe inwardly. She knew all the JOs made cracks about her but this one bothered her because it was true to some extent. Surrounded by these flyboys, some of whom were half her age, it was hard *not* to feel over the hill. Boomer stood before her looking like a kid who got caught sneaking out past curfew. She could tell by his guilty expression that he knew exactly what he had been doing wrong.

"Two things, Lieutenant. One, keep your opinions to yourself, or you'll find you'll be expounding your thoughts to the bulkheads in the brig." Boomer paled slightly. "Two," she continued, her eyes locking onto his and holding them transfixed as though bound by steel chains. "Tell me what were you doing up there?"

"Well...when it looked like you were going to be late, Poindexter asked me to help him preflight the Double Nuts. So, I did and I was just about to go and get myself strapped in when you got here," Boomer explained quickly after an initial moment of hesitancy. He didn't like to admit it but the Commander scared him sometimes. It wasn't just the uniform, it was *her*. Perry McNeil could be real tough, he made that discovery early on, but never unfair. Anytime she'd ever laced it into him, he had always deserved it.

"I see..." she replied allowing the thought to trail off because she knew it would unnerve the young lieutenant a bit. Let him squirm, Perry thought, he needs to be kept on his toes. After a few seconds that felt like hours to Boomer, Perry continued, "Everything checked out?"

"Yes, Ma'am."

"Good. Now get your butt where it's supposed to be."

"Yes, Ma'am."

"Move!"

He was up the ladder and in the cockpit before she had a chance to take a breath.

Perry walked quickly over to the Double Nuts and vaulted up the ladder. She took a quick glance back at Poindexter, who gave her a slight smile. "Sorry I'm late," she said. "Something came up."

"I know. Happy birthday, Commander."

She rolled her eyes smiling slightly as she climbed into the cockpit and strapped in. Even though Boomer had done the preflight checks, she ran through them again. Not that she didn't think Boomer was capable of doing the checks, she did. But Perry could have God Almighty preflight her bird and she would still double check to make sure He didn't miss anything. Once she was satisfied that all was in order, she put on her helmet and waited for the plane captain's start signal.

Within minutes Perry taxied towards the number-four waist cat and waited for her turn to launch. Planes shot off the waist cats went off the angled deck instead of the bow. While she was standing by awaiting her turn, she watched the energetic warrant officer in charge of launching on the waist cats. The bosun prowled the flight deck like a lioness. One eye always on Pr-Fly and light signals mounted there and the other on the aircraft and the Shirts tending them. Once a plane was cleared for launch, the bosun really got moving. She checked the wind speed and set the steam pressure for each aircraft while monitoring the hookup of the Tomcat on the other waist cat. Each plane was launched individually. First, she would signal the pilot to crank the bird up to full power while she checked it. Then she took the salute and gave the launch signal, a fencer's lunge into the wind that whipped wildly at her clothing. She held that musketeer pose as the wing of the accelerating fighter swept over her head. She averted her face in time to avoid taking on the chin the wind and hot exhaust blast that swirled around her like a squall against a statue.

The minute the JBD on cat four was lowered, Perry was signalled to take her place on the cat. The jet blast deflector was a hinged flap located behind each cat and it directed the exhaust gases of the launching aircraft up and away from the flight deck. While she had been waiting behind the JBD for her turn, a group of maintenance people had been all over the Double Nuts performing final safety checks. She was armed for bear and ordnancemen checked all her stations to make sure was ready for combat. Everyone was intent on their jobs, yet always vigilant to keep from being sucked up into an intake, run over, or blown down to the deck by the blast furnace exhausts.

Perry felt the engines winding up and saw the catapult officer whirling her fingers in the "full power" signal. Crewmen scurried from under her plane and ahead of her the bow of the ship rose and fell in time to the rhythm of the Gulf. Everything had checked out fine. They were a go for launch. Perry positioned herself so that her eyes would always be on her instruments and steeled herself for the shot.

Two and a half seconds later the Tomcat was airborne. Perry made a slight turn to the left to clear the bow, then slowly brought the laden fighter up to 500 feet and retracted the flaps and slats. When the TACAN indicated five miles from the carrier, Perry began her ascent. The VFR, Visual Flight Rules, specified a slightly farther distance but a check with the CATCC and her instruments told her that, for now at least, it was okay to bend the rules.

When she broke Angel's fifteen, Perry spotted a KA-6D tanker and a couple of Hornets roughly four miles ahead of her. As she motored past them, she got a quick call over the radio from one of the Hornet drivers waiting to tank up.

It was Rebel, who was with the VFA-40, the Freebooters. "CAG, we ran into a whole lotta nuttin'," he told her sounding disgusted. "I think those guys packed up their toys and went home."

"Rebel, you always were a lousy poker player," Perry stated. "Always too quick to fold." He made no reply and, under her oxygen mask, she smiled to herself. The CAG wheeled the bird into position to meet her wingman and brought the bird up slowly until she broke Angel's twenty. Boomer had been shot first and had plenty of time to get to the rendezvous point.

She was scanning the skies when she heard Poindexter say over the ICS, "Boomer is coming up hard and fast on our five o'clock."

"Cowboy," she muttered under her breath as the other Tomcat artfully zoomed up and then dropped into perfect formation off her right wing. She glanced out the window and Boomer gave her the clenched fist salute of the Ghostriders. Perry rolled her eyes and turned away muttering with a bit more acid in her voice, "Fuckin' cowboy!"

She heard Poindexter snort over the ICS and remarked, "Glad *one* of us is having a good time."

"Sorry, CAG, Boomer cracks me up. He...he stopped by to see me when I was in sickbay. Gave me a balloon toy that looked like an airplane. Guy's a little strange, but his heart's in the right place."

"I know," she agreed. "That's one of the reasons why I put up with his bullshit."

Poindexter had to stifle another laugh. He knew deep down Perry really liked Boomer and a lot of her antipathy was just for show. The brash nugget had been on and off the CAG's shit list from the first time he trapped aboard the *Excalibur*. That fact was always one of the top items for ready room gossip. Bets were on as to how long Boomer would last. With the cruise a third of the way gone, a lot of people lost because they didn't think he would make it *this* far. 'Dexter's money was on the longshot: the whole nine months. Not only couldn't he beat those great odds, but, if he won, he would be collecting enough bucks at the end of the cruise to host the outchop party of the decade.

He checked his instruments. The battle group was currently sailing roughly fifty miles south of Santiago de Cuba. So far, they hadn't seen those MiGs or any other suspicious aircraft. After the last of their birds got hooked up with Night Eyes, Dr. Freneau and his team left the *Excalibur*. He thought he heard someone say they were headed for the Pensacola base, but he wasn't sure. In any case, he did notice Perry was a lot more relaxed since he ex-husband split.

They were flying on a patrol along the very fringes of Cuban airspace. Their job was to give the carrier some more coverage with the Night Eyes. The sky was crystal clear and the lush green mountains of the Sierra Maestra were visible off their port side. He scanned the scope for any sign of trouble. No one there who wasn't expected. He wasn't one to toss in his cards early but 'Dexter was not looking forward to another run in with those MiGs. After what happened the last time he was airborne, he was praying Rebel was right, and these gomers did pack up their gear and go home. He didn't like to admit it, but those MiGs scared him. They were faster, meaner, and harder to hit than anything he had ever been up against. Big couldn't nail them, and he was one of the Navy's finest. The CAG, too, had a reputation for being unstoppable in the air. But would she be able to do what Big Daddy couldn't?

Poindexter tried not to worry about their chances as he kept his eyes peeled.

25 December 1011

"Commander, we've got company!" Sparky announced as the Night Eyes system picked up a quintet of aircraft. He and Jugs were flying their F-18s along the Windward Passage, just off the southeastern tip of Cuba. He looked at the scope. The five jets were in tight formation and, judging from their current course, they looked like they intended to intercept. "Five of them. And they're headed our way!"

"Booter Three-Oh-Five to Arthur, we've got five bogeys incoming!" Jugs announced. Arthur was the *Excalibur's* radio call sign.

"Roger, Three-Oh-Five," Anzac acknowledged her. "We're tracking them. Time to "play dumb," team."

"Gotcha," Jugs acknowledged.

Sparky's grim expression was hidden by his oxygen mask and the intensity behind his blue eyes was obscured by his helmet's visor. He made a lazy bank that his wingman followed and headed back towards the carrier. To anyone observing them, it would look as though they had just wrapped up their patrol and were headed for home. Still, this was all in keeping with the instructions Commander McNeil had outlined in a briefing given to all the flyers. If they encountered the MiGs, they were told to pretend they didn't see them. They were to "play dumb," and track the MiGs. Their job was not to fight them but to find out where they came from. If they were fired upon, that was another story. They were allowed to engage the MiGs if they made the first aggressive move. The CAG had been very clear about one thing; She didn't want to lose any more of her people. *Not* engaging the unknown enemy was a sure way to insure everyone stayed alive.

"They're accelerating, Sparky," Jugs informed him. "Looks like they're trying to catch up to us."

"We can't speed up because they'll know we are onto them!" Sparky bitched. "Shit!"

"Arthur, I think we could use a little backup over here," Jugs stated.

"Give me ten minutes," Anzac responded.

"These guys will be on us in less than two minutes! Get on it!"

The *Excalibur* had turned into the wind. The flight deck was a swirl of motion, like the eye of a hurricane. The Alert Fives were launched to intercept the approaching MiGs. Two Hornets, standing by on Alert Fifteen duty, were shot skyward after the Fives. They, too, were destined to intercept the MiGs. Other fighters were being readied in case the quartet shot skyward needed assistance. The crews of the airborne fighters knew it would take them roughly ten minutes to reach their target. They prayed their comrades could hold out that long...

The quintet of MiGs were closing the distance rapidly. Sparky tried to keep his cool but with five MiGs bearing down on him, he was beginning to sweat. "They're almost on us!" Sparky said in a voice of forced calm.
"Hang on, Sparky. Help's on the way!" Jugs reassured him.

Perry and her wingman heard Jugs and Sparky's call for help. She knew where they were patrolling. Of all the teams flying, hers was the closest. Perry got on the line to Boomer. She gave them an intercept course and said, "Time to show these party crashers the door!"
"Roger!" both Boomer and Radar said in unison.
She swept the stick right and did an about face. As they turned, the force of seven Gs smacking into her made Perry feel like she'd been sat on by an elephant. Instinctively grunting in response to the pressure, she kept her eyes glued to her instruments knowing she would need to rely solely on them to home in on the MiGs. Her wingman also executed a hard 180∞ turn. The maneuver loaded on so many Gs that for a few seconds Boomer felt like he was seeing everything through a telescope. Shoving the twin turbines into Zone Five, both Tomcats headed off after the MiGs.
"Arthur, this is Ghost Leader. Going supersonic. Will intercept in less than two minutes."
"Roger," Anzac acknowledged. "Be careful."
"Will do."

"If those MiGs came here to pick a fight, we could have us a real clusterfuck," muttered Anzac shaking his head. His eyes were on the radar screen and he worried his lower lip as he watched Perry leading the way towards engaging the MiGs. He got on the radio to Gypsy and Wildflyte, the leaders of the Hornet and Tomcat squadrons that were flying CAP. They and their air crews were warned about the incoming flight of MiGs. They had to be prepared in case the intentions of the MiGs turned out to be hostile and Perry and the others flying with her got in over their heads. To the Alert Fives and the backup team of Hornets he gave the intercept coordinates and commanded, "Maximum warp! Double Nuts will be engaging in less than thirty seconds."

Jones sighed heavily as he watched the screen. The Admiral had found the entire situation a puzzlement from the get-go. Almost every scrap of intelligence that crossed his desk said the Cubans were innocent. They had one photo of what appeared to be the fuselage from one of the MiGs being offloaded from a ship. It was identified as having been taken in the port of Havana but he had seen other photos taken at the same port and they looked somehow different. He couldn't put his finger on it but something wasn't quite right. Perry's idea about drug traffickers being the guilty party was, in the Admiral's opinion, very far-fetched. Still, the brass in Washington seemed more than willing to let her run with it. Checking out the drug angle kept them in the Caribbean and in the general area of where those MiGs were believed to be hiding.

Jones got on line to Perry saying, "Backup is en route to give you a hand, just in case. It shouldn't take them more than a few minutes to intercept. If they give you any trouble—"

Perry clicked her mike twice, interrupting him yet letting him know she not only received his message but was aware of what she had to do. Jones's brow furrowed slightly and Anzac let his breath out as a silent whistle as they saw the gap between the two Hornets and the five MiGs closing very, very quickly...

The MiGs made their intentions apparent the moment they got into rage. One of them got a lock on the lead F-18.

"I'm locked up!" Sparky announced. "Shit!"

Alarms screamed through the cockpit. Sparky pulled up hard into the vertical. The MiG followed. He put the Hornet through it's paces, burning up the sky at 400 knots, turning tight corners and bucking through six and seven Gs. When he came out of the buck-and-wing and looked around, the MiG was not only still there but the tones blaring through the cockpit told Sparky he was still locked-up.

"I can't shake him," Sparky said beginning to sound worried. Suddenly the tone went nuts. The on-board warning system was telling him to eject, that a missile was incoming. Acting on survival instinct alone, Sparky bat-turned sharply to the right dropping flares and saying prayers that the heat-seeker would miss.

It worked! He guessed he beat the missile because his jet was intact and the lock-on was broken. He didn't see the contrail of the rouge heat-seeker but that didn't matter to Sparky. The adrenaline rush from cheating death was still firing his blood as Sparky hooked around to get a bead on his opponent.

Jugs had lost visual contact with Sparky but had him on her instruments. She saw him looping around to get behind the MiGs. He was going to get *them* locked up and, hopefully, scare them enough so they would leave. Good. So far, the MiGs were only following her. They had not made any aggressive moves. Yet.

Sparky came out of his loop and was coming in on the MiG flying off Jug's eight o'clock. He was above and to the left of his intended target. This wasn't the guy who had shot at him but that didn't matter. They had been fired upon, so Sparky was more than ready to return the favor. His attention was keyed to tracking the dancing jet in his HUD. It bobbed and weaved, avoiding the target zone. Sparky gritted his teeth as he maneuvered in, trying for a better position.

He heard the growl of a Sidewinder in his headset. Good tone. Sparky fired.

An explosion erupting behind Jugs made her turn with a start. One of the MiGs just got blown out of the sky. She saw Sparky's Hornet faintly in the distance behind her. "What the hell are you doing?!" she screamed.

"Returning fire!"

"But they didn't—"

She stopped short as her cockpit was lit up by warning lights. They had her. She made a fast break and roll trying to dodge the incoming volley of cannon fire coming from the two MiGs on her tail. The shot ripped through the Hornet cutting into its port wing at the root and midsection. The hit connected with the fuel tank, which erupted in a ball of fiery hues.

"I'm hit! I'm hit!" she announced in a voice barely under control. "She's breaking up! She's breaking up..."

"Jugs...!"Sparky gasped as he saw the wing explode. The jet began falling apart before his eyes. Pieces of it rained down out of the sky towards the sea. The starboard wing also exploded when the fire hit its fuel tank. He didn't know if she punched out in time. He couldn't see any trace of a chute.

As she closed, Perry had been listening to the radio exchange between the two Hornets. Sparky had gotten locked up but managed to escape, that much seemed clear. But did they shoot? Jugs didn't think so, but the point was moot now. The MiGs just shot down one of her people. Perry had no choice but to get in there and do her best to either splash them or send them running for home.

Perry was too intent upon the MiG she was zeroing in on to take time out to tell Sparky she had arrived. Since it seems these guys want a fight, Perry thought, I'll give them one they'll never forget! She coaxed her Tomcat to give her every ounce of performance it could as she closed the distance between herself and her opponent. She angled in on the MiG that had initially been pursuing Sparky and allowed the Vertical scan lock on to acquire her target. Got him!

"Fox Two!" she announced as she launched the Sidewinder. This one's for you Beau, she thought. And you, too, Jugs.

The MiG broke hard right and dropped flares to dodge the incoming missile but hadn't been quick enough. The missile struck home, snapping off the Mig's tail. The plane rolled over and began tumbling down towards the sea. The fuselage erupted, the canopy spinning away like a Frisbee gone mad, and the pilot ejected. He cleared the rapidly descending plane and his chute opened, just as his midnight black jet erupted into thousands of pieces. The debris that had been the MiG drifted downward like confetti thrown from a tall building. The pilot hung in his straps floating on the wind heading towards a meeting with the cold blueness of the Caribbean.

"Splash one, splash one bogey!" Perry reported. "Double Nuts engaging. Three bogeys still incoming."

Poindexter checked the DDD and saw the three remaining MiGs had broken formation. She had succeeded in getting their attention. They were turning to engage. As they made their move, Perry had made one of her own. She went after one of the two MiGs flying to her left.

Perry pulled back hard on the stick and Poindexter grunted through gritted teeth as the G forces slammed into his body. Transonic vapor hovered above the wing roots as the Tomcat reefed effortlessly into the pure vertical in pursuit of the MiG.

Boomer came into visual range of the three remaining MiGs just as they broke formation. All the MiGs knew the two F-14s had joined the fight. Boomer had had Mig Three locked up and was just about to fire his missiles when the MiG broke right swiftly. He tracked him and saw they were trying to angle around him to line up for an attack. Migs One and Two, neither of which were in good position for him to engage, went in two separate directions. MiG One went vertical and was already being chased by the CAG. MiG Two was hanging back and looked like he might be going after Sparky.

With a MiG attempting to nail him, Boomer knew exactly what he had to do.

Sparky eased back on the throttles dropping out of Zone Five. The agile Hornet responded instantaneously to his touch on the HOTAS. His radar showed one MiG was in the distance behind him, a second flying high with a Tomcat on its tail, and the last one was angling in on the other F-14. The Tomcat giving high speed chase Sparky knew was Perry. The one being chased was Boomer. Sparky knew he had a good lead on the MiG that was trailing him and was sure he elude his pursuer. He wanted to get back into the fight. He had a comrade in need of assistance. Sparky headed off to give the man a hand.

Boomer was running on pure adrenaline, as he hit 7.5 Gs in a hard vertical afterburner climb. He was trying to get that MiG off his tail. Radar was doing his best to advise his driver but his tactical know-how was all textbook. He could only guess at what their adversaries might do and pray that his guesses were right.

He pulled back hard on the stick and the F-14 went up and over the top in an inverted loop. He saw he was being followed. But, because of his position, he thought there was a good chance he could get around and on to the tail of the MiG who wasn't engaged. As he came back down and around, he levelled off and checked his six.

"Shit!" Boomer muttered under his breath. The sky around him was clear. He couldn't see anything anywhere. His eyes were scanning his instruments when he heard Radar's voice.

"Boomer, Hard left! *Hard left!*" Radar ordered, his eyes on the Detail Data Display in front of him. The DDD was one of the systems integrated into Night Eyes. It showed the RIO a red blip moving in on them at high speed from behind. "MiGs coming in at five o'clock high and closing at warp speed!"

Boomer pulled the stick left, and the F-14 took an impossible right-angle turn. The infamous bat-turn, the flyer's nickname for this maneuver, was one move few aircraft in the world could perform with the Tomcat's dexterity. The MiG tried to emulate but roared past them into a wide arc.

"Radical, Boomer!" Radar exclaimed.

"What about the other guy?" Boomer asked. He rolled into a turn on a direct intercept with the MiG that had just flown by. His attention was completely focused on trying to get that evading MiG into the diamond. He had to depend upon his partner to keep him apprised of where their second adversary was and what he was up to. Lose sight, lose the fight was what he had been told in flight school. When Radar didn't respond immediately, he demanded, "Well?"

"Eight o'clock," Radar told him. He looked up and back and was able to make out the MiG through the light spray of clouds. "And closing!"

Boomer broke off from his pursuit and went evasive. The MiG was flying just above him. He dropped altitude and increased speed as he maneuver in for a shot on the dodging Tomcat. The MiG Boomer had been chasing altered his course of action. He, too, was angling in for a shot in case his wingman failed to score a hit.

Sparky no longer needed to rely solely on her instruments to see the two MiGs zeroing in on Boomer. For the moment all three of them were in visual range. He silently prayed he would get the few seconds he would need to get the MiG flying off Boomer's starboard side into the diamond...

The MiG was off on Perry's port side. Perry rolled under him like a hawk on a pigeon. Another twenty degrees more and I'll have this guy, she estimated. The MiG saw her coming and ducked, making a hard left dive that got him away from Perry's oncoming roll. The MiG led her into a descending Lufbery, a tight circle looping downward towards the sea. Perry struggled against nearly six Gs as she tried to bring the Tomcat's nose to bear. She saw she had the advantage. She was closer to the MiG's tail than he was to hers, but she still couldn't close, couldn't line up for a clean shot.

"Shit!" she swore fighting Gs and her own frustration.

"Hang in there," Poindexter encouraged his voice strained.

Perry kept turning in a hard circle, going round and round without gaining on the MiG. But she knew her opponent was also pulling severe Gs and was having his own problems. She was having about as much success as a dog chasing its own tail. Perry pulled the circle in tighter, keeping her eyes on her opponent rather than on the HUD, and angled in for a guns kill.

For a split second she had him lined up. That was all the time she needed. As if by instinct, Perry's thumb hit the switch. The MiG was assaulted by a volley of fire from the Tomcat's cannons that raked its port side and clipped the wing. Wounded, but still flying, the MiG swiftly disengaged. He broke out of the pattern, kicked in the afterburners, and went up on a hard vertical climb.

Perry was with him all the way.

Boomer cut trails in the sky, but the two MiGs were stuck on his tail as if held there by cement. He pushed the throttle forward to Zone Five, full afterburner. He remembered hearing in the briefing that the MiG's top speeds were in excess of those of the F-14, but that didn't matter now. Boomer was going to pull every trick he could with the Tomcat: bat-turns to the left and then right, loading on Gs by pulling up hard into the vertical and the going over the top, unloading Gs as he dove towards the sea. The MiGs stayed with him.

So far, he had managed to keep them from getting a shot. That was the good news. The bad news was, the duo worked as a tight unit, never giving him the opportunity to get out of his defensive position. As he pull up out of his dive, he heard Radar state, "Climb another Angel's ten. Friendly standing by."

Thank God! He kept on climbing. The MiGs trailed. When he broke Angels eighteen, for a split second he saw the incoming Hornet.

The F-14 hotly pursued by the MiGs flashed before Sparky's eyes like the pop from a camera's bulb. He followed, gunning the Hornet, trying to coax Mach 2 out of her. He soon eased into position behind the MiG flying off Boomer's port side. He heard the growl of a Sidewinder in his headset. Good tone.

Yes!

His hand was on the button ready to fire. The Mig showed up in the diamond—he had him in his sights. The tone went wild.

Sparky took the shot.

Suddenly, the two MiGs were coming at him from five and seven o'clock. Warning alarms blared. They had him locked up!

Boomer was stuck in a cross fire. He gasped and realized instantly he had no place to go but *out*. He grabbed the loud handle and pulled. The canopy blasted off.

The MiGs closed in tight on the fleeing Tomcat wounding it with a barrage of cannon fire.

Boomer instinctively pulled the black face cover down as the seat rocks fired. Four tenths of a second later, Radar was shot from the plane.

The MiGs split. A Sidewinder rocketed harmlessly through the space they had just occupied.

Wounded and crewless, the F-14 fell over on its back and dropped down towards the sea. The fire from its exhaust attracted the rogue Sidewinder. The missile struck the out of control aircraft, which detonated like a bomb. Flying wreckage barely missed Boomer and Radar, whose chutes deployed moments after their jet was shattered.

Perry made a hard right turn pulling six Gs as she tried to loop around and get behind her opponent. No luck. He easily evaded her. She tried another tight turn hoping to get on his ass. Again, he evaded. Perry hung in there trying to bring her weapons to bear on the fleeing jinking MiG. Outmaneuvering the agile MiG was going to be tough; Out thinking him was another story…

"What's his range?" she asked.

"Three-quarter mile but we're closing," Poindexter told her.

The MiG kept dodging the pursuing F-14 but she was steadily getting closer and closer to him. She wanted to get him into guns range. He would have to be in that tight in order for her plan to work.

She was almost dead on his six when the MiG pulled a balls-to-the-walls maneuver. Perry was hot on his heels as he took them on a wild rollercoaster ride. Trying to evade the Tomcat's attack, the MiG broke fast heading downward towards the sea. Then he led the way upwards to the sky, the Tomcat still nipping at his heels. The Gs of that last hard climb pinned Poindexter to his seat. He felt that steep uphill climb in every bone in his body. He groaned in pain.

Perry finally managed to get them in a position to do some damage. She was in tight, in guns range, and ready to let him have it the moment he was dead in her sights. Perry eyes were transfixed on the target as it danced around the kill zone on the HUD. Almost…. Almost….

Now! Yes!

Sparky was having difficulty keeping up with the much faster moving MiG. When the two that had attacked Boomer split, he had chosen the one who'd flown off towards his starboard. His missile had missed and now he had to make up for lost time. The second of the two Migs had bugged out. He guessed he was probably headed for home but was too busy to track him. The MiG he was after was all over the sky, leading him on a merry chase. Although the MiG could have easily outrun him if he had chosen to kick in the afterburners and blast off, the MiG instead tried to out maneuver the pursuing Hornet. He was trying to get behind Sparky and get him in his sights. He was doing everything in his power to keep him from achieving his goal.

The two planes wove in and out, each trying to gain the advantage, but neither one was able to get a clean shot. He pulled up hard into the vertical with Sparky close behind. He easily pulled ahead of the slower Hornet but that didn't really save him. Sparky was still tracking him via Night Eyes. He was almost in line for him to take a shot. The growl of the heat-seeking missile in his headset made him smile slightly.

Almost...

Alarms blared in the cockpit and Sparky broke hard right and rolled out evading the incoming volley of cannon fire. His action saved him from taking the hit directly across his aircraft's belly. Instead, the shot connected with his right vertical stabilizer snapping it off neatly at the root. It also took a chunk out of his right horizontal stabilizer as well but most of it was left fairly intact. Sparky was now defensive. The MiG, who Sparky thought had headed for home, closed in on the injured Hornet. The loss of the stabilizer meant a loss of maneuverability. Sparky altered course and headed for the carrier. The MiG he had been after was now above him. He could come after Sparky at any time. He had to get out of there if he wanted to escape with his skin intact.

"I'm hit!" Sparky declared. "I'm hit!"

Anzac was expecting the sound of a canopy being jettisoned and ejection rockets firing to fill his ears but instead heard the Hornet pilot say, "Lost a vertical stabilizer!"

Many tense eyes studied the screen. The Admiral could see the Alert Fives and Fifteens closing fast but it might not be fast enough. One blip headed towards the strike force was being closely followed by two red blips. That must be the Hornet. He could tell by their positions that only one of the two MiGs was actively pursuing. The other was probably acting as cover.

"Hang on! I'm coming!" Perry's voice filled the ears of everyone wearing a headset.

Anzac bit his lip. Things weren't going quite as planned. They had lost two aircraft but, fortunately, the three occupants had apparently escaped. Their radio signals had been picked up. One of the helos flying plane guard were already en route to their position. His eyes were on the scope again. Anzac could tell by the rate at which the lone blip moved that Perry had kicked in the afterburners. She would be with Sparky very soon.

Now would be a good time for the calvary to come, Sparky thought. He was getting nervous with that MiG hovering so close to his tail. So far, he had managed to keep him from getting a lock on. It was tough doing evasive combat maneuvers at high speed in a wounded bird. He kept his movements crisp, hard and simple. No fancy stuff and no heavy loading and unloading of Gs. Too much stress could snap off his damaged stabilizer. He tried to finesse all the speed and dexterity he could from his Hornet in his attempt to keep himself from getting fried.

Perry's instruments picked up Sparky and his pursuer long before the duo were in visual range. The last of the MiGs was flying above them. Perry also saw her reinforcements were closing fast. She banked neatly angling in on the pursuing MiG.

The MiG saw Perry coming and abruptly disengaged. His wingman, too, also made an about face. They were bugging out. Perry followed. She wasn't going to lose out on this opportunity. Their job was to get a firm ID on these gomers so the brass would know whether to call in the DEA or contact an embassy. This time Perry was going to follow them all the way in, even if they led her to Castro's doorstep.

"CAG, you're on your own. I'm headed back," Sparky announced. "I've lost a vertical stabilizer and my starboard engine's acting up."

"Roger."

Sparky altered course and started to ease her crippled bird towards the carrier.

The Alert Fives were tracking the retreating MiGs and their lone pursuer. The lead F-14 was driven by fellow Ghostrider Lt. Commander George "Pug" Mahon, the XO of the Grim Reapers. His wingman was Lieutenant Wu. Pug got on the line to Perry and informed her they would be providing backup. As things stood, they were roughly a minute or so behind Perry. Pug knew that fact would present a problem if the MiGs decided to stop running and start fighting. Fearing the worst Pug and Eggroll kicked in the afterburners and sped off to join up with the CAG.

Perry saw land coming up hard and fast ahead of her. Soon she could see they were flying over a bay with beachhead, boats, lush green land, and the products of civilization on all sides of the waterfront. The MiGs had led her to Cuba. This time Perry was not going to turn back. She was well aware of what she was doing and the risks she was taking. Sparky must have been fired on. He would not have engaged the MiGs otherwise. Well, she knew if there was to be an international incident, it would not be because of anything the Americans did. *We didn't start this*, she said to herself through gritted teeth. *But, by God, we are going to finish it!*

During their run for home, the MiGs had been slowly descending. Perry matched their movements and, as she soared at a little over five thousand feet, she noticed they were slowing. She decelerated but first allowed herself to get within guns range of the two jets before cutting her speed. They were lowering their landing gear heading in. Their home base was close at hand.

"'Dexter, let me know the second you see a reception committee coming to meet us," she said.

"Roger."

There was noting showing up on radar. Yet. However, he was sure they must be scrambling their Alert Birds. And whatever patrols they had in the area were also probably en route to intercept them. There was no way the Cubans would allow them to fly in and poke around unchallenged. At that moment, they were flying over Guantanamo Bay. Poindexter scanned all the radio frequencies hoping to pick up the one the MiGs were using to talk to the control tower. So far, he hadn't been able to find it. As he checked, he remembered the US used to have a Marine base in Guantanamo but it they were forced to abandon it at the turn of the century. They had to go because Castro refused to let them renew their lease. So the Americans had to deal with losing their outpost in the Caribbean. With all the interdiction work the Navy had been involved in during the past decade, the loss was a major one. He remembered reading many stories about the closing of the base in the papers....

He got on the ICS to Perry saying, "CAG, no company yet. Those MiGs look like they're heading to our Marine base."

"You mean *ex*-base," she corrected. "That bit of prime real estate is Castro's now."

"Think his air force are there now?"

"Looks like it," she surmised. To herself she added, "It figures they'd take over *our* base and use it against us...!"

Anzac rubbed his eyes and sighed. It was too late. Perry was in Cuba and, if they shot her down, then no doubt he probably would never see her again. Though they now had the evidence they needed to show they were not the aggressors but the victims, that wouldn't help much if Perry was to go down and find herself in a Cuban military prison.

"I knew it. I *knew it*," Jones muttered.

Anzac got on the line to Perry. "Ghost Leader, this is Arthur. Finish playing Japanese tourist and come home. There is an intercept team en route that could make you become a permanent resident."

"Roger. Will RTB as soon as I get a good shot of home plate."

"Make it quick. They'll be all over you in less than two minutes!"

She knew she didn't have much time. But she still needed those incriminating photos to insure that they would have an airtight case when this matter came up before the UN Security Council. Perry was well aware of the huge risk she was taking but she always was willing to put her life on the line when the cause merited. Anzac hoped the reception committee Castro had sent to greet her wouldn't get there until either she had a chance to bug out or the backup teams arrived.

The MiGs were definitely in a landing pattern now. Perry could see the concrete runway in the distance ahead. The MiGs had their wheels down and locked and were headed straight for it. Her Tomcat's cameras captured the entire landing for posterity. She overflew the runway and several hangars before she banked, turned, and headed back for a lower pass. She was flying as slowly as she could and remain airborne when she made her second and final sweep of the area. She spotted soldiers, a few jeeps and other evidence that proved the base was in use. The camera was going, taking all this in, including an image of the large flag that flapped in the warm tropical breezes.

Perry, too, saw the flag flying high on a pole before one of the buildings in the complex. As she recognized it, she felt the color drain from her face and her body went numb.

It was the Stars and Stripes.

Her voice quavering with emotion, Perry said, "They're ours! Oh my God, 'Zac! We've been fighting *our own people!*"

25 December 1301

Wolff sat with his laptop computer perched on his knee and was typing at a fevered pitch. Everything had happened so quickly he hoped he had managed to assimilate it all. Although his energy was keyed to the work at hand, one ear was kept open for the sound of the door to Perry's room opening. The CAG was in sickbay. The shock of seeing that she had fought against and possibly killed fellow American flyers had struck her like a bludgeon to the back of the head. Pug, the lead on the Alert Five team, told Wolff it was a wonder Perry managed to hold herself together long enough to evade the Cubans and make it back to the ship intact. She had been *that* shook up by what she had seen.

The second Perry told them the MiGs were American, Jones was on the line to Washington demanding an explanation. He was so incensed he looked ready to have an apoplectic fit. Wolff had been very careful to stay out of sight otherwise he might not have been allowed to hear what the *Excalibur* battle group had been up against.

They had been guinea pigs in an experiment gone wrong. Very wrong. What was supposed to have been a test of a new chemical compound designed to make the next generation of Navy fighters virtually invisible to currently used detection equipment had not come off as planned. NAVAIR wanted to see how well the new substance could elude what was currently in place aboard its ships of the line. At the same time, they cooperated with a special team under the Secretary of the Navy. This group wanted to use the fighters to test the ingenuity of their task force leaders and see how they would handle dealing with an unseeable unknown enemy. The had the planes built using the MiG body design purposely to keep the *Excalibur* people wondering and convinced they were up against an actual threat. To also maintain the illusion, the flyers of the stealth jets were instructed in the use of the same types of psychological games Soviet fighter pilots used on Americans. The mock engagements, the cat and mouse games full of implied threats, all were performed as part of the test.

The results the Navy Department got were not exactly what they expected. True, they did find out their commanders could think well on their feet and adapt. But they also discovered that, although the bulk of the flyers of Air Wing 21 were nuggets and new to the combat game, they were not as overmatched by the top guns at the stick of the MiGs as NAVAIR thought they would be. But they did tend to rely more on their instruments than on their eyes, a fault that resulted in a combat, which never should have happened, and the loss of one test pilot.

The door to Perry's sickbay room opened and Wolff looked up in time to see Dr. Melman and Colonel Grimmig step out. Melman's face was expressionless but the Colonel appeared concerned yet relieved. Grimmig saw Wolff eyeing him expectantly and he approached the reporter.

"She'll be okay," he said quietly.

"Does she know the whole story?"

"Not everything. 'Zac will be—"

He stopped abruptly when he saw Anzac enter the space. Anzac greeted them both and, noticing Wolff's laptop computer was up and running, stated, "I hope you realize that none of this—"

"I know," Wolff interrupted. "The information officer already got to me." Changing the subject, he asked, "What going to happen to Lieutenant Sparkman?"

Anzac shrugged. "I don't know. He insists they fired a missile at him. His flight recorder bears him out, even though the films we recovered don't. It had to be a computer glitch, that's the only explanation. Sparky's too experienced..."

"Some glitch," Wolff muttered.

Anzac rolled his eyes. "Sparky's grounded until the results of the investigation are in." He sighed, not really up to getting into the dire fate that could befall the Lieutenant if things went against him in the hearing. Sparky had made a serious error that resulted in him killing a fellow American pilot. That fact was going to haunt the him for the rest of his life. Anzac hoped the young man also wouldn't have to endure the pain of losing his Navy career.

Wolff quickly saved what he had on his machine, logged off, and closed it. It looked like a small white briefcase when snapped together. On the floor beneath his seat were some letters and an envelope containing photos. The mail was Perry's, but the photos were ones he had taken of the crew and officers of Air Wing 21. Wolff was hoping to get a minute or two with Perry so he could give the bundle to her. Considering what she had been through, she would probably find some comfort in the notes from her family and seeing images of her friends. Changing the subject, he asked, "Can I have a minute or two with the Commander. You see I have some mail—"

"Yes, you may come in with me," Anzac told him. "She's groggy from the sedation, so we can't stay long. I have to tell her what you already know. So, keep your visit short, okay?"

Wolff nodded. He picked up his computer and quietly followed Anzac. Perry was awake but her eyes were heavy-lidded from the medication. She was neatly tucked into the stark white bed. Perry smiled slightly at Anzac before shifting her gaze to Wolff.

"What can I do for you, Paper Boy?" Perry inquired her words coming slowly and with effort.

"Nothing. I just stopped by to see how you were feeling and to give you this." He handed her the mail and the envelope and her smiled widened a bit when she recognized the postmarks on the envelopes.

"Thanks," she said motioning to him to take the seat beside her bed. He complied with her unspoken request. Anzac dropped the rail on Perry's bed and sat beside her, taking her hand in his. As their eyes met, her expression brightened visibly but her voice was still weak as she joked, "Helluva way to spend Christmas."

"And a birthday," Anzac added with a wry grin.

Perry closed her eyes and sighed. Fighting the sleepiness, she forced her eyes open and tried her best to look alert when she told her deputy, "Let's hear it."

Anzac took a long deep breath to prepare for the recitation he was about to give. In a quiet gentle tone he said, "Well, 'Stormy, you found out the hard way that those MiGs were ours. What you don't know is what they were doing there and why. So, it's like this…"

THE END

About the Publisher

QUEST PRESS (aka Quest Productions) was founded in 1994 as a multimedia publishing company, originally focusing on developing games of intrigue and imagination for play on the PC or in the living room. The company's interests shifted away from gaming and into pursuing high-tech avenues when the current Developer/Publisher, Ronni Katz, took over running the company full time in 1995. Ronni has a very eclectic background. She was awarded a BA in English from Monmouth College and, while still a student, sold two technical books to a local publisher. While pursuing an MBA in Economics and Finance at Fairleigh Dickinson University, Ronni had several articles on the making of the film Annie published and did freelance work as a staff writer/editor for a local newspaper. She also is an avid gamer, who will show you (if plied with the right amount of Fosters Lager) her original boxed set of AD&D manuals. It was that love of gaming that got her involved with Quest and inspired her to write several short stories that were published in a local SF-oriented journal and she was a contributing author for the IST Super Teams book published by Steve Jackson Games, as well as a researcher/ consultant on other Steve Jackson game books that dealt with historical subjects (King Arthur, Robin Hood).

The book, *Wing Commander,* marks Quest's entrance into the "big leagues" as far as publishing goes. Our other commercially available product is through our video division Quest Productions. The video is entitled "Robot Warriors" and is a documentary about Robot Wars, an annual robotics competition held in San Francisco. It is a non-profit educational and entertaining look at robots and the engineers and designers who build them. It is available through *Robot Science & Technology Magazine* or can be ordered via Email by writing to us at Questinc@aol.com or by sending a letter to our offices. Our mailing address is P.O. Box 84, Franklin Park, NJ 08823-0084.

We hope that all of you enjoy *Wing Commander.* Email us at QUESTINC@aol.com or send us a "snail mail" note with your opinions and we do respond to all who write to us. PROMISE!